BOOKS BY FRANK CONROY

✦

STOP-TIME

MIDAIR

BODY & SOUL

Frank Conroy

BODY & SOUL

Delta
Trade Paperbacks

A Delta Book
Published by
Dell Publishing
a division of
Random House, Inc.
1540 Broadway
New York, New York 10036

A portion of this book previously appeared in *Gentlemen's Quarterly.*

The trademark Delta® is registered in the U.S. Patent and Trademark
Office and in other countries.

ISBN: 0-385-31986-X

Reprinted by arrangement with Houghton Mifflin Company

Manufactured in the United States of America
Published simultaneously in Canada

July 1998

10 9 8 7 6

BVG

for TIM

That which thy fathers have bequeathed to thee,
earn it anew if thou wouldst possess it.

— Goethe, *Faust*

PART ONE

1

HIS FIRST VIEW of the outside was through the small, fan-shaped window of the basement apartment. He would climb up on the table and spend hours peering through the bars at the legs and feet of people passing by on the sidewalk, his child's mind falling still in contemplation of the ever-changing rhythms and tempos of legs and feet moving across his field of vision. An old woman with thin calves, a kid in sneakers, men in wingtips, women in high heels, the shiny brown shoes of soldiers. If anyone paused he could see detail — straps, eyelets, a worn heel, or cracked leather with the sock showing through — but it was the movement that he liked, the passing parade of color and motion. No thoughts in his head as he stood or knelt at the window, but rather, from the images of motion, a pure impression of purposefulness. Something was going on outside. People were going places. Often, as he turned away from the window, he would muse on dimly sensed concepts of direction, volition, change, and the existence of the unseen. He was six years old, and much of his thinking, especially when he was alone, went on without words, went on beneath the level of language.

The apartment was small and dark, and he was locked inside until that terrific moment each day when his mother came home with her taxicab. He understood about the cab. There were passengers. She picked them up in the street and took them from one place to another (as the people walking outside were going from one place to another), but she herself had no destination. She went where the passengers told her to go, and remained, in a sense, a witness, like himself. The cab started out in front of the apartment in the morning and returned at night. It appeared to him to be going around in circles.

Usually he would hear her coming down the iron stairs to the door. She was big, and moved slowly, the entire iron structure clanging with each step. Then a moment's silence, the sound of the key opening the locks, and the door would swing open. In the dimness he could see her shift her six-foot-tall, three-hundred-pound body to come through. He could hear the sound of her breathing, a steady, laborious sighing, as she entered the room.

"Claude!" Her voice was clear and musical.

He stepped into her field of vision.

"There you are," she said. "Get me some beer."

He went to the kitchenette, took a quart of Pabst Blue Ribbon out of the refrigerator, pried off the cap, got a glass, and returned to the front room. He placed the beer on the low table in front of the couch and backed off a step. She sat down and put her change maker and a roll of bills next to the beer, along with a folded copy of the newspaper *PM* from her hip pocket.

"I don't care if the Nazis win," she said. "It couldn't be worse than this." She poured a glass of beer, drank it in one go, and refilled. "He gives me a two dollar ticket! What for? Too far from the curb, he says, the dumb mick. Too far from the curb! Are you kidding? You don't have anything else to do but persecute the working class?" She poured again.

Claude sat down on the floor. He was attentive to her mood, to its direction, in case escape was necessary. Sometimes when he ran around the couch or slipped under her arm she would lose interest. He knew that almost always when she hit him, she held back. He'd seen her open the door once to find a drunk pissing in the small area at the foot of the iron stairs. She'd felled the man with one blow to his chest, methodically kicking his ass and then his head until he lost consciousness, and then pulled him slowly up the stairs by his collar, step by step, to the street. There had been blood on the stairs, red spots on the black.

Now she worked the levers and emptied the change maker, stacking the coins neatly, counting them, and making notes on a scrap of paper. She counted the bills — mostly ones, but with an occasional five — her wide lips moving soundlessly as she tallied up. Finally she would separate the money into two piles, one to take out in the morning and the other to go into the steel box she kept in the top drawer of the bureau in her bedroom.

In the kitchenette she opened another quart of beer, selected a couple of cans, and began preparing his supper. She made noise in the cramped space, banging pots and pans abstractedly, tossing various utensils in the sink without looking. Claude could smell the coils of the hot plate when she turned it on. He sat on a tall stool at the counter and ate what she put before him. (She herself had eaten outside.) She would drink until her eyelids grew heavy, and then go into her bedroom and close the door, not to emerge until morning.

He slept on an army-surplus cot in the back room, which was filled with boxes of old trip cards (to be retained for two years by order of the taxi commissioner), stacks of newspapers, old suitcases, a set of spare tires, boxes of motor oil, a steamer trunk, bookcases, racks of her old clothes, and up against the back wall, half buried under piles of books and sheet music, a small, white console piano with sixty-six keys and a mirror over the keyboard. In this room Claude had found a radio, a small one with a fuzzy green cardboard case about half the size of a loaf of bread, which he had placed on a folding chair beside the head of his cot. He would lie with his ear near the speaker, listening to music, or to the voices. When the voices spoke, he often spoke with them, repeating the words and phrases a split second after they came out of the speaker. He could do this well, with speed and accuracy, even when he did not understand what the words meant.

In the morning she let him out, with twenty-five cents, to go to the corner for a quart of milk and two hard rolls. He paused at the top of the stairs. Already, windows were open on the upper floors of the tenements, women with their elbows on the sills, staring at the street, occasionally shouting to each other. Sunlight angled in over the elevated train tracks on Third Avenue to flare off the windshields of parked cars. It was hot, and the sidewalk smelled of city dust.

In the store, Claude waited his turn, watching to see if the storekeeper would use the long pole. Sure enough, someone wanted a box of cornflakes and the old man took the pole, reached up to a shelf near the ceiling, squeezed the grip, and with astonishing gentleness enclosed the box in pincers and extracted it. When he released the grip the box fell directly into his other hand. There was a deftness, a precision, to this almost automatic act that Claude found fascinating. He put the quarter on the counter, received the milk and rolls in a brown paper bag, and began to turn away.

"Tell your mother I'd like to talk to her," the old man said.

Claude nodded and held the bag to his chest. He waited to see if the old man was going to say anything else, but a customer moved between them.

Back in the apartment, he ate and drank and watched his mother clip the change maker to her belt. She wore work pants and a gray short-sleeved shirt. With a sigh, she bent her big body and tied her open-toed sandals. "I'll talk to him when I get a chance," she said. "I know what he wants, anyway."

"What does he want?"

"Money." She paused, staring at the floor. Wide-set blue eyes, straight nose, a big chin and mouth. A Slavic face, although her people had been Irish. "It's always money." She got up and left, double locking the door behind her.

Most of the day he spent in the back room at the piano, making sounds and listening to them. He had learned to pick out little melodies — sometimes phrases from the radio, sometimes bits of his own invention — and play them over and over until his fingers got tired. He might play the same four or five notes in sequence for half an hour or longer, as if afraid to stop. The sounds were reassuring to him, their reality strangely soothing, and the repetition enhanced this effect. Occasionally he would simply crash and pound with his hands, forearms, and elbows, sometimes shouting at the top of his lungs into the cacophony, but he would always return to the more interesting business of repeated phrases. He had discovered octaves. He had discovered the key of C, which he played hour after hour, entranced by its symmetry.

In the afternoon he sat on the floor near the radio, hearing the voices but not listening to them, and built castles with a deck of cards. He built a simple maze, trapped a cockroach in a sheet of newspaper, and spilled the insect into the maze. It moved back and forth for an instant, antennae waving, and then scurried up and over one of the cards and disappeared under the cot. Claude gathered up the cards and built another castle.

At dusk he climbed up on the table in the front room and stared out the fan-shaped window, watching the people go by. When his mother came home she told him that, pretty soon, he'd be going to school.

"Is it outside?" he asked, gesturing to the window.

"It's three blocks away," she said. "What do you mean is it outside?"

"Which way?"

"That way. Uptown."

He felt a flush of warm excitement, something like what he felt for a moment or two when listening to music on the radio — a sense of things in the offing.

He was to walk Third Avenue for many years, until it became so much a part of him he didn't see it anymore. But at first it was a feast. People moving on the sidewalks, automobiles threading through the columns of the el, trucks rumbling in the striated shadows — he drank it in, his eyes leaping from image to image. He would forget to watch where he was going and stumble into a carton of tomatoes outside a fruit and vegetable shop, or bump into the newspaper rack of a candy store as he raised his eyes to watch a train rush by overhead. If he fell down and scraped an elbow, it shocked him into remembrance that he was indeed there, that he was physically real. But soon after regaining his feet, when he began to see the hubbub around him once more, the power of the world seemed to render him bodiless.

He stopped at the cigar store, stood close to the window, and watched the Negro in his stained apron making cigars. A brown world — the tobacco leaves hanging or laid on the work surface, in hues of tan, cinnamon, coffee, and dark leather. The tin sinks with brown water into which the Negro would deftly dip a cut leaf. His brown hands and pink palms rolling the wet leaf over a stone slab. The polished wooden handles of his knives and clippers. The pate of the Negro's head as he worked, never looking up — a warm, milk-chocolate glow. Dark brown cigars laid out in brown wooden boxes.

He stopped at Weisfeld's Music Store to look at the gleaming trumpets, guitars, and banjos, the dense and mysterious accordions, harmonicas of all sizes, and the slender flutes. Brass, silver, ebony, and mother-of-pearl shone at him through the glass. The door to the shop had a little bell, so that when someone went in or out, Claude could hear it ring — an intimate, icy sound that raised goose bumps on his arms.

P.S. 31 was set far back from the street, behind the tall iron fence and gates, behind the flat concrete expanse of playground. Children of all sizes flowed through the gates to mingle in the schoolyard, their sharp cries bouncing off the brick walls of the neighboring tenements. Games of hopscotch (girls), off-the-point with a pink rubber ball (boys), jump rope (girls), and running bases (boys) overlapped one another in a sea of constant motion. Claude stayed close to the wall and made his way to a spot near the main door. He sat with his arms wrapped around his knees and watched the games, the boys pushing one another, the girls clustered in little groups talking intently, looking over their shoulders every now and then. When the bell rang he went directly inside, before the others, and was the first one in his classroom. He sat very still in a back seat, so still that when the teacher entered and went to her desk, she didn't notice him. After a few moments the other children came in, and Claude was relieved. Instinctively, he felt it was safer not to call attention to himself.

He was in third grade before he ever raised his hand. Miss Costigan's class in room 202 was the first in which children had to stay seated, remain quiet, and follow orders. A thin, gray-haired woman who stared at the class through pince-nez, Miss Costigan had, on the first day, smacked one rambunctious boy on the back of the head with a wooden ruler. The boy, well known to Claude as a schoolyard bully, had been shocked into silence and subsequent obedience. The rest of the thirty-odd children in the room followed suit, and she never used the ruler again, except to bring it down on the surface of her desk with a loud crack. Claude admired her, and was afraid of her, and somehow sensed that was what she wanted him, and all the others, to feel. She was distant and seldom looked at anyone directly, preferring instead to aim her remarks at the rear wall.

"What do you wash first, your hands or your face?" she asked one morning.

Claude had been staring out the window, watching a pigeon strut back and forth across the sill, but the novelty of Miss Costigan's question caught his attention. This was not from a workbook, or part of one of the slow and incredibly dull lessons that took up so much class time. Claude recognized the question as being a kind of trick, something like a riddle, and he was surprised at the silence with which it was greeted. After several moments he raised his hand.

"Yes?" Miss Costigan tilted back her head.

"Your hands."

"Why?"

"Because then your hands are clean, so you can wash your face with them." This was pure mentation, since Claude seldom washed at all, was, in fact, slovenly and far beyond such niceties of personal hygiene. He hated the dark, fusty-smelling shower stall in the back of the apartment.

"Correct." For a split second through her pince-nez, Miss Costigan held him in her gaze. Claude flushed and looked down. He was pleased with himself and hoped she would go on asking trick questions, but she did not. She began the lesson, which he heard with half an ear while returning his attention to the pigeon.

In the schoolyard at recess and lunchtime the boys played war games. Nazis and GIs. Capture the spy. Sergeants and privates. They marched in columns, saluted each other, and carried toy guns in their pockets or the belts of their pants. The girls carried books of Victory Stamps and showed them to one another, or brought in balls of tinfoil for the war effort.

"Are you Italian?" an older boy asked him as they waited to play off-the-point.

"I'm American." Claude had black curly hair, brown eyes, and slightly olive skin. He was small for his age, and thin.

"You look Italian. What do you think of Mussolini?"

"Mussolini stinks."

"Well, okay then," the older boy said. "Let's play."

When it became clear to Claude — from reading the papers and listening to the radio — that the war was almost over, he realized with a start that this great historic event might have some bearing on his life. He timed his question. It was always better and safer to talk to her in the early evening when she came in from work, between the first and the second quart. She sometimes paid attention then. In the morning she ignored him or, if he was insistent, had a tendency to snap, or slap.

"You said my father was a soldier," he said.

She continued stacking coins.

"So what's going to happen? Will he come back?"

"He shipped out a long time ago, before you were born," she said. "He could be dead for all I know."

"But I thought —"

"Forget about it. When you were a baby I told you baby stories. If anybody asks, tell them he died in the war."

Claude stood silently for a moment, then moved a step closer. "But if he died, wouldn't they have told you?"

She looked up. "They? Who is they? *They* don't know anything about me. Or you, for that matter. Now shut up with this stuff."

He went into the back room and played scales over and over again, until dinner.

On V-E Day, late in the afternoon, he went to Lexington Avenue and Eighty-sixth Street — the center of the neighborhood, with a newsstand at every corner to service the crowds pouring in and out of the IRT subway. Five movie theaters, restaurants (Nedicks for hot dogs, Prexy's for hamburgers), coffee shops, cigar stores, Florsheim shoes, beer halls, clothing stores, drugstores, were all brightly lit in the gathering twilight. VICTORY was spelled out on the marquee of the RKO theater in oversized letters. Thousands of people gathered on the sidewalks, spilled out onto the streets where the cabs and trucks moved slowly. A sign outside McCabe's Bar said, "Free Beer for Anyone in Uniform," and a dozen young soldiers stood outside, some of them dancing with girls while others sang accompaniment.

"We're going to Times Square," a soldier said, slipping his arm around the waist of a woman trying to weave her way through with a bag of groceries. "Want to come?"

"No thanks," Claude heard her answer. "But here's a kiss for you." She leaned forward, kissed him full on the mouth to the cheers of the crowd, and broke away. The sailor threw up his arms and turned in place to acknowledge the applause.

Down the street, in the bright light spilling from Loew's Orpheum, a small Salvation Army band played "America the Beautiful" and people threw coins onto a blanket in front of them — a continuous rain of coins glinting in the air. Everywhere people smiled, laughed, slapped each other on the back. Claude noticed an old man sitting on a car fender, tears shining on his cheeks. Somebody's dog had broken loose and ran through the crowd, leash trailing, jumping on its hind legs every now and then.

Dizzied by the excitement, Claude wrapped his arms around a lamppost and moved his head from one side to the other watching the action. An American flag was unfurled from the second-story window of a pool hall. A man with a gray beard halfway down his chest stood on a box in front of a candy store, shouting words Claude could not make out, his arms jerking as if pulled by strings. Horns blared on the street. The subway rumbled underneath.

Claude realized that all these strangers were caught up in something together, that an unseen force had wiped out all differences between them and made them one. They were joined, and as he clung tighter to the lamppost he felt his own tears starting because he felt entirely alone, entirely apart, and knew that nothing could happen to change it.

2

WITH A NICKEL he'd stolen from his mother's change maker the night before — deftly pressing the lever, his heart racing, while she stared into the refrigerator — he walked into the Optimo store at the corner of Lexington and Eighty-sixth and bought a pack of Beeman's pepsin chewing gum. He tore off half a stick, put it in his mouth, and stepped out into the bright sunshine. It was necessary to chew for a long time, long past the point when the flavor had gone, in order to get the right consistency. He sat on a brass standpipe and watched the street. Thus far there were no other kids working the subway grates, which was good, since the other kids were invariably big, and usually tough. Getting chased off was humiliating. He would burn with shame for hours, hating his thin arms, his weakness.

When the gum felt sufficiently tacky he moved to the edge of the sidewalk and lay down on the subway grate, cupping his hands over his brow to gaze down into the dimness. Soot, small bits of paper, candy wrappers, cigarette butts, anonymous trash. He inched forward on his belly, concentrating, looking for the gleam of coins. Pedestrians walked around him. He was barely aware of the enormous tire of a bus as it pulled up a few inches from his head, or the hiss of the pneumatic doors. When a train approached underground, causing an updraft, he would simply close his eyes, wait it out, and then resume crawling. He spotted a dime lying in the gloom and raised himself to his knees. From his pocket he took a length of string and a piece of wood roughly the size and shape of a small cigar. He tied the string on one end, removed the gum from his mouth, and pressed it carefully to the other end. After a moment of study he picked a square through which to lower the block of wood. Then he lay down again, payed out the string very slowly, keeping the wood as stable as he could during its descent. He was lucky, having picked the right square on his first attempt. The wood was directly and precisely over the dime. Sensing the tension of the string with the tips of his fingers, he allowed most of the weight of the wood to press down on the coin. Holding his breath, he gradually pulled up string, wood, tacky gum, and dime. Exquisite care was necessary at the end, slipping the block back up through the square as smoothly as possible. He raised himself to his knees once more and removed the dime.

It took him a couple of hours — sometimes swinging the wood, gumless, back and forth through the trash to uncover hidden coins — to make thirty-two cents. By then a big kid was on the grate across the street, glancing up now and then, and Claude decided to quit and avoid a confrontation.

Once a well-dressed man had stopped to watch. This was unusual, since adults paid no attention to him, seemed not to see him even as they stepped over him, their heavy bodies hurrying along with mysterious urgency.

"What are you doing?"

"Dipping for coins."

The man stepped closer and peered down. "Dipping?"

He took out a quarter and flipped it with the back of his thumb. It clanked through the grate and fell. "Can you get that?"

The coin had landed on a ledge halfway down and was easy to retrieve. The man hunkered beside Claude — who caught the faint spicy odor of his body — and watched every move. Claude took the quarter off the gum and held it out.

"It's yours," the man said, standing up. "Keep it." He tapped his lips with his forefinger for a moment as if considering something, turned abruptly, and walked away.

Claude looked at the quarter. It lacked the magic quality of the coins he truly found, coins that seemed to have sprung into existence out of nothing under his eye, orphan coins, but it was a lot of money. He went into Nedicks for a hot dog and a small orange drink. He got ten cents in change, which he decided to save. He liked always to have one or two coins in his pocket. It was reassuring.

. . .

The piano was a puzzle. Why were there black keys, and why were they laid out like that, in groups of twos and threes? How come if you played the white notes from C to C (although he did not know the names of the notes, or even the fact that they had names) it sounded right, but if you played the white notes from E to E it sounded wrong? He sat at the bench and played the C scale over and over again — one octave, two octaves, up and down, in the bass, in the treble — experiencing a curious sense of satisfaction. The sound itself seemed to wrap him in a kind of protective cloak, to encase him in a bubble of invisible energy.

There were times, for instance, lying on his cot with the radio off or sitting on the floor motionless, staring into space, when he would become sharply aware of his own existence and the fact that he was alone. Either the basement apartment was empty, his mother out to work or her discussion meeting, or she was holed up in her room. The sense of being alone would come over him, causing not so much fear as uneasiness. He would go to the piano, make noise, and slip into the protective bubble. He would forget about himself. Many months passed this way.

One day as he sat fooling with a single note — playing it loud, then as soft as he could, then somewhere in the middle — he suddenly wondered what was inside the piano. He got up and examined the instrument. He cleared the stacks of old newspapers, trip cards, and magazines from the top of the case, opened the hinged lid, and looked down. An impression of density, and of order. The strings angled down toward darkness. He reached in and turned first one wooden latch and then another, barely catching the mirrored front of the case as it surprised him by falling away. Now he could see the felt hammers, the pins, levers, and tiny leather strips of the action.

He returned to the bench and played the single note again, watching the hammer fly forward to strike the string. Moving up until his nose was almost touching the mechanism, he pressed the key again and again, trying to understand the forces at work between the key and the hammer. Slots. Little brass pins. Felt pads. Small rods. It was a discontinuous mechanism and extremely complicated, with tiny springs and screws whose function he could not guess at, but after a while, playing now soft and now loud, he came to a rough understanding of how it worked. He tried one key after another, mesmerized. He touched the strings and felt them vibrate.

In the bench he found some sheet music. There was a neatness to the lines and mysterious symbols that reminded him of the inside of the piano. There was a connection, surely, and he knew where to go to find out exactly what it was.

The icy tinkle of the bell as he entered. The shop was empty of customers but filled with musical instruments hanging on the walls, displayed in showcases, lined up in rows — guitars, trombones, clarinets, trumpets, accordions, oboes, violins, ukuleles, saxophones, all meticulously arranged. Mr. Weisfeld, a small, rotund man with sharp black eyes and a thin mustache, sat behind a counter.

"So, finally you come in," he said. "I've seen you out there with your nose on the window." He closed his newspaper and set it aside. "What can I do for you?"

Claude put the sheet music on the counter. "What is this? I found it in the piano."

"You have a piano? You must be rich." Weisfeld opened the music. "You don't look rich."

"A white piano. With a mirror. It's in my room."

"Well, that's good. A piano is a nice thing to have in your room." He tapped with his finger. "This is the sheet music to 'Honeysuckle Rose,' written by Fats Waller."

Claude reached up to point. "But what are those, those things?"

"Those things? They're notes. Those are the notes." He looked at Claude, who suddenly turned the music around and studied it with a slight frown. Weisfeld got up and came around a tall glass case filled with harmonicas. He picked up the music. "Here. I'll show you." He led the way to the back of the room and the upright piano.

"That's big," Claude said. "That's much bigger than the one in my room."

"It's a Steinway. Old, but good." He sat down on the bench and spread out the sheet music. "You see this note printed here? The one with the line through it? That's middle C. A good name for it because it's in the middle, between the treble clef up here and the bass clef down here. You can come down the treble and that's middle C, or you can come up the bass and that's middle C. Are you listening? This is important. They're both the same note — middle C — even though one is printed a little bit lower than the other. Both the same." He glanced at Claude. "You understand?"

"Yes. But why do they put that one there and that one there if they're the same thing?"

"An excellent question. It goes back to the old days. They didn't have clefs in the old days, they just had ten lines, or twelve, or sixteen. But then they found out it was easier to read if they split it apart, so they split it apart, five lines up here and five lines down here, and they print it this way, in clefs." He held his forefinger in the air and then played a single note on the piano. "This is middle C on the piano. This key. This note. See how it's in the middle of the keyboard?" He played it again. "So this" — with his free hand he pointed at his forefinger on the key — "is what that" — he pointed at the printed note on the music — "means. All these notes are about all these keys. They are, in fact, symbols."

Claude looked at the sheet music, down at the keys, and back up at the sheet music.

"Okay," Mr. Weisfeld said. "I'll start at the beginning. See? Here is the first bar, which is four beats in this case. I'll just play the keys the printed notes refer to." He began playing the tune with both hands at a moderate tempo, his fingers moving with apparent ease. "When I'm taking sips," he sang in a scratchy voice, "from your tasty lips, I'm in heaven goodness knows. Honeysuckle Rose." The sound of the piano filled the shop. He let the last chord die in the air and shifted slightly in his seat.

"So it tells you," Claude whispered. Their heads were on exactly the same level, only a few inches apart.

"Yes." Weisfeld stared curiously into the boy's enormous brown eyes. "It tells you."

Claude pressed down a note and held it until the sound disappeared. An odd sensation came over him, as if he had lived through this before, as if he had somehow slipped out of time, as if he were simultaneously in his body and out of it, floating around somewhere looking down on himself. The scene began to darken and he felt his knees begin to give way. Suddenly he was aware of Weisfeld's hands on his shoulders, holding him firmly, supporting him.

"What's the matter?" Weisfeld asked. "What's wrong?"

"Nothing." Claude stepped back. It seemed of no importance. His mind was racing now with the significance of Weisfeld's demonstration.

"Are you sure? Does that happen to you often?"

"How can I learn that?" Claude asked, nodding at the piano. "To do that, the way you did."

Weisfeld watched the boy for a moment to reassure himself that he had indeed returned to normal. "How come you're so thin? Do you get enough to eat? When did you eat last?"

"I have to learn how to do that, with the music."

"You have to?" Weisfeld looked away. "He has to?" His tone was not mocking but ruminative, as if trying to sense the implications of the boy's seriousness.

"Please."

Weisfeld listened to the word fade into silence, as Claude had listened to the note. He stood up and looked down at the boy. "Of course," he said.

Back behind the counter, Weisfeld pulled a thin paper-covered book from the shelf. "I happen to have a used copy of *The Blue Book for Beginners*. Marked down to thirty cents."

"I only have a dime," Claude said. "But I can get more."

Weisfeld considered the matter, his plump hands holding the primer. Claude's eyes were locked on the book. "Considering you live in the neighborhood," Weisfeld said, "maybe we can work something out. Let's say you give me a dime today, a dime in a week, and another dime in two weeks."

"Okay. Good." Claude got out his dime and reached for the book. "What day is it?"

"It's Monday." Weisfeld's eyebrows went up. "The first day of the school week. Don't you go to school?"

"Sometimes."

"Can you read? Words, I mean. This isn't going to do you any good if you can't read."

"I can read. I read all the time."

"All the time," Weisfeld repeated. "That's good. So, tell me, what do you read?"

"The newspaper. Sometimes she brings *Life* magazine or the *Reader's Digest*. I read books, too."

"Books! Excellent." Weisfeld handed him *The Blue Book for Beginners*. "If you get stuck someplace, let me know. Otherwise I'll see you Monday." He reached over the counter to shake hands.

"I could read when I was four," Claude said.

·   ·   ·

He kept his eyes open for bottles. You got two cents deposit for the small ones, and five cents for the large. He ranged through the neighborhood, up and down Third Avenue and the side streets, checking garbage cans, alleyways, and gutters. If he saw someone on a step drinking a Coke, he might loiter inconspicuously on the opposite side of the street. He was almost always disappointed. It was a tenement neighborhood, and people were careful with money.

Eventually he left his familiar environs and explored to the west, across Lexington to Park and Madison avenues. Here the streets were clean, the buildings were tall and guarded by uniformed doormen, and the comparatively few pedestrians were well dressed. People got out of big yellow De Soto taxicabs, crossed the sidewalk under canopies, and disappeared inside. There were no subway grates, no visible clutter, and initially it seemed hopeless. But one day he noticed a delivery boy from a grocery store pulling up his three-wheeled bike near a small side entrance to one of the fanciest buildings on that particular block. The boy opened the big wooden box between the front wheels, removed a bag of groceries, closed and locked the box, and went into the building. As Claude approached, he saw a discreet sign that read SERVICE ENTRANCE. Stairs led down to a doorway. Claude retreated and waited ten minutes, until the delivery boy reappeared and rode away. Then he descended the stairs, paused a moment, and pushed through the door.

A maze of pipes — great thick tubes hanging from the ceiling, running in all directions, vertical stands studded with valves, elbow joints, and connectors. He moved cautiously through the gloom, following the occasional bare light bulb, each one casting a weak nimbus of light over a boiler, a bank of fuse boxes, a set of pressure gauges, an open doorway. The sudden clanking and groaning of machinery startled him as he passed the closed doors of the service elevator. Nervously, he started down a corridor that seemed to lead back in the direction from which he had come. After several turns to the left and then to the right he realized he was lost. He stepped through a doorway and immediately bumped into a large ashcan. He was surrounded by ashcans. The faint glow of light from yet another doorway beckoned him. He threaded his way through the cans and peered into the room.

Claude saw a tall black man in an undershirt working the ropes of a dumbwaiter, sweat glistening on the back of his neck. He pulled hand over hand until there was a dull thump. Then he reached into the darkness and lifted out cans of garbage, which he emptied into larger cans. When he heard the clink of bottles he would retrieve them and place them on the floor against the wall. There were more than a dozen, and as Claude watched, the black man added two large Canada Drys.

Claude moved behind a stack of wooden crates, stepped on an ashcan lid in the darkness, and froze. The black man turned around and stood for a moment, his head cocked, listening. He reached into his back pocket and drew out a small, shiny revolver. He held it loosely before him, aimed at the floor, and moved forward slowly. Claude felt warmth flooding his body. The black man approached the crates, and then suddenly stepped around and stared down at the boy.

"Stand up," the man said. "Come out here."

Claude obeyed, moving into the light, his eyes shifting back and forth from the man's narrow fox-like face to the revolver at his side.

"I know every kid in this building," the man said, returning the gun to his pocket, "and you ain't one of them."

"I just came down the, I saw the grocery boy and I thought I'd see if I could, then I couldn't find the —"

"Hold on a minute, now. Just slow down." The man hunkered down, reached forward, and slipped two fingers behind Claude's belt buckle and pulled the boy forward until their faces were only inches apart. "What you doing here?"

"Bottles. Looking for bottles. For the store."

After a moment the man released him, but neither of them moved. Claude felt his legs shaking.

"You telling me you in here looking for deposit bottles? In *my* building, looking for *my* bottles?"

"I'm sorry. I didn't know."

"Didn't know what?" His brown eyes were steady.

"I mean your bottles. I just thought . . ." Claude found himself giving a great shuddering yawn.

"You caught, little man. Couldn't find your way out and now you caught. Ain't that right?"

Claude nodded.

The man seemed to be studying Claude's face. After several moments he sighed and stood up. "All right. We'll talk."

"Which way is out?"

"I say we going to talk." He moved away, back through the doorway to the dumbwaiter. Claude followed. The tall man pointed to his collection. "My bottles," he said. "Sixty-four cents' worth."

"Can I go?"

"Can you go?" The man's voice ascended in an arc of incredulity. "Can you *go*?" He left it hanging there for a moment, then looked down at the floor and shook his head. "What about trespass," he said sadly. "What about unlawful entry."

"I don't know," Claude said. "I don't know about those things."

"I expect you don't." The man nodded. "So maybe I'll give you a break. Give you a chance, even."

"Which way is out?"

The tall man shifted his head and stared into the darkness at the bottom of the dumbwaiter shaft. He raised a finger to his lips in a sign for silence and at the same time pulled out the revolver. He raised it in front of his face, barrel pointed up, and then very slowly unfolded his naked arm to full extension, aiming at the dark shaft. He stood there like a bronze statue for several seconds, and then fired.

Claude felt the explosion in his ears and on the skin of his face. He jumped back involuntarily, and at the same time a rat flew out of the shaft, as if ejected by a spring, and fell twitching on the cement floor. The man stepped forward, examined the animal, picked it up by the tail, and threw it in the garbage. He pocketed the gun and turned to Claude.

"You got to be close," he said. "Ain't like that bullshit in the movies." He scratched his head and went over to the bottles. "Look here. I got a business proposition. I'm a busy man. This is a big building and I got a lot to do. I ain't got time for every little thing. So you take these bottles down to the A & P and get the sixty-four cents. You hear?"

"Yes," Claude said.

"Then right away you bring the money back. You hear?"

"Yes."

"Now once you got the sixty-four cents there's going to be a little voice inside your head telling you to keep the money." Claude started to speak but the man cut him off. "No, no. I know what I'm talking about. Just for a moment you going to think, I don't have to go back to that crazy nigger with the gun. But you are going to come back. You know why? Because when you come back I'm going to give you twenty-four cents." He smiled, his thin face seeming to grow broader. "And what's better than that is we can keep on doing it. Every week or so I'll give you more bottles for the A & P and you make more money. See what I mean? It's a business proposition."

Claude looked at the bottles and nodded.

The tall man disappeared into the darkness and came back pushing a large perambulator. He snapped the chrome braces and folded down the hood. "Put the bottles in here and I'll show you the back way out."

Claude laid the bottles carefully in the baby carriage. Then he followed the black man along a complicated route to a set of large sliding doors. The sunlight was almost blinding as they opened.

"You know where the A & P is at?"

"Yes."

"Go to the back and ask for George. Tell him Al sent you, he give you the money."

Claude pushed the perambulator into the light and up a long ramp to the sidewalk. He felt a certain excitement, a certain pride, even. The vehicle was heavy, with dark purple sides and spoked rubber wheels, and he imagined people thinking there was a baby inside.

When he returned with the carriage and the money, Al was rolling ashcans into the alley.

"Next time," he said, counting out Claude's share, "come this way and push the bell if the doors are closed. Want to avoid the doormen. They drink down in the front sometimes, and they mean. Come this way it'll be me, you'll be all right."

"George talks funny," Claude said.

"Yeah," Al said, wrestling a can. "He got the sleeping sickness down south. He slow, but he ain't dumb."

Claude considered the exotic idea of sleeping sickness. "I hate to sleep," he said.

Al wiped his brow with the back of his hand and looked at the boy. "Is that a fact?"

"She sleeps all the time," Claude said. "I hate it."

The Blue Book for Beginners was organized along logical principles that Claude recognized immediately — a series of lessons numbered one through twenty, starting easy and getting harder as you went along. The first night he read it over and over again in his cot, skipping the words he didn't understand as he tried to grasp the overall shape. Sometimes the text went into capital letters, which impressed him. DO NOT SKIP LESSONS. DO THEM IN SEQUENCE. YOU HAVE NOT

FINISHED A LESSON UNTIL YOU HAVE MASTERED ALL OF THE EXER-
CISES LISTED AT THE END OF THE LESSON. DO NOT SUBSTITUTE
YOUR OWN FINGERING FOR THAT INDICATED. The severe, no-non-
sense tone of these admonishments thrilled him. They suggested that
the author of the book was aware of Claude, able to predict where he
might, in his eagerness, go too fast and get sloppy. He trusted the voice
and believed that it sprang from a wisdom that he might someday
share. There was a kind of intimacy he had not experienced with
anything else he'd read. He slept with the book under his pillow.

Now when he went to the back room after dinner and closed the
door, he went with a purpose. Each time he began on page one, playing
everything over again, recapitulating the exercises and the scales, faster
each time until he reached the place where he had left off. But he never
rushed. Even though he knew the early lessons backwards and for-
wards, could play them without consulting the book, he took pleasure
in doing them at a measured pace, concentrating, listening to the
sound. When a lesson was completed to his satisfaction, sometimes
after many hours, he would not go on immediately to the next, but
would create little variations of one kind or another on the lesson he
had learned, playing it fast, then slow, loud then soft, or adding notes
or phrases that sounded good.

His hands gave him relatively little trouble, although the indicated
fingering sometimes seemed to make things more difficult than they
had to be. He followed it religiously nonetheless. Meter was another
matter, and halfway through the book he knew he was doing something wrong.

One night his mother surprised him by coming into the room. "No,
no, no," she said. "It's supposed to go dada-dada dum dum." She
loomed over his shoulder and raised her thick arm. "Frère Jacques,
Frère Jacques," she sang in a clear, beautiful voice, "dormez-vous,
dormez-vous." She pointed at the notes. "Dada-dada dum dum. Dada-
dada dum dum." Claude was so stunned by the unexpected loveliness
of her voice it took him a moment to understand what she was saying.
"Dada-dada dum dum," she repeated. "You've got to count. Do you
count?"

"Yes, but sometimes I —"

"When you count," she interrupted, "go one *and* two *and* three *and*
four." She tapped the music with the accents. "One *and* two *and* three.
Like that." She turned and left the room.

When he'd recovered from his surprise he turned to the music and began to count in the way she had suggested. It did make things easier, and he spent the next couple of hours going over old material that he had been playing, correctly, but without really knowing what he was doing. There was always the temptation to follow his ear, but now he was proving what his ear had told him, and he found it exhilarating.

Later, lying on his cot with the lights out, the music danced in his head. It was almost like listening to the radio, except better, because he could control the sounds — add strings or horns, or take them away. He could listen to two lines at once, put them in harmony, hear things backwards or upside down. He could create simple canons out of phrases from the *Blue Book* and hear them as clearly as if someone were in the room playing them. His mind was hot with music, and he did not think at all until it began to cool down.

Sliding into sleep, he pondered the mysterious beauty of her voice. It seemed to come from somewhere else and simply go through her, like the Mozart he heard through his cardboard radio. And how did she know about counting? It had been a useful tip, but it worried him. The music was his. He touched the *Blue Book* under his head. He didn't want her somehow taking it away from him. Under the covers his knees gradually worked their way up to his chest, and he fell asleep.

At Weisfeld's Music Store he put a dime on the counter and held up the *Blue Book*. "I'm finished," he said.

"It takes patience," Weisfeld said, looking up from some paperwork. "You should have told me. Show me where you got stuck."

"I didn't get stuck. I learned it all."

Weisfeld gently put down his pen. He took the dime and dropped it into the open drawer of the cash register. "I hope you will not take umbrage if I say that's a little hard to believe."

"What's 'umbrage'?"

"Offense. I hope you don't take offense. I hope you don't get mad."

"Can I show you?"

Weisfeld got off his stool, came around the display case, and led the way to the piano. "Be my guest," he said with a wave.

Claude put the *Blue Book* up, opened to the first lesson, and laid his fingers on the keys. "I'm not completely sure, but I think I did everything right." He began to play, moving quickly through the early lessons and exercises, turning the pages with his left hand. When he began to play with both hands Weisfeld stepped forward and turned pages for him. He watched Claude's fingers intently, occasionally taking a quick glance at the music. His face was expressionless. Somewhere in the middle of the book Claude asked, "Is it right? Am I doing it right?"

"Yes," Weisfeld said. "Keep going."

The last piece in the book was counterpoint, twenty-five bars from Bach's Two Part Inventions. Claude paused for a moment. The music had been hard to read. Tricky in terms of meter, and he'd played it wrong for a couple of days, feeling uneasy. Eventually he had forced himself to count everything out without touching the piano. One *and* two *and* three *and* four, until everything seemed to fall into place. Only then did he allow himself to play it, over and over again, and he hoped now that his counting had been correct. He set the beat in his head and began to play.

"Hold it, hold it," Weisfeld interrupted. "That's much too fast. Play it slower."

Again Claude silently counted, at a slower tempo, and began to play. It was harder, somehow, to keep track of everything at the slow beat, and about halfway through he made a mistake. He took his hands off the keys.

"I'll start again."

"No, no, keep going," Weisfeld said quickly. "When you're playing a piece straight through and know you've made a mistake, keep on going. Don't start all over again. You can correct it the next time." He tapped the page with a finger. "Start here and keep going no matter what happens."

Claude did as he was told and played through to the end without any errors that he was aware of. Claude closed the book and stared at it in the silence.

"Was it right?" he asked, turning.

Weisfeld seemed to be absorbed in thought, his round face tilted upward, staring at the wall.

"Was it right?" Claude asked again.

"Yes," Weisfeld answered.

The icy bell announced the arrival of a customer. Weisfeld muttered a foreign word under his breath, rubbed his cheeks with his hands, and turned.

"One minute," he said to Claude as he moved away.

Claude took the *Blue Book* from the piano and went back to the counter. In the front of the shop Weisfeld conferred with a large woman who pointed at something in the window display. After a few moments the woman left and Weisfeld returned. He stepped behind the counter and arranged the papers on which he had been working into a neat pile, papers covered with handwritten music.

"What's that?" Claude asked, peering.

"Parts to a string quartet I'm copying out for a customer."

"The notes are awfully small." Claude put the *Blue Book* on the counter.

"I owe you an apology," Weisfeld said, and stroked his mustache with thumb and middle finger. "I'm very surprised you could do that by yourself, and even more surprised you could do it so quickly. You must have worked hard."

"Oh, it was fun. I like it." Claude opened the *Blue Book* and flipped to the end of the first lesson. "You said I did it right."

"That's correct. You did."

"You see here at the end of every lesson there's a place where the teacher is supposed to sign it."

"Yes."

"I don't have a teacher, but you could sign, maybe."

"I'd be delighted." Weisfeld reached for his fountain pen.

"And there's a place for a star. It says you can get a blue star, a silver star, or a gold star. Have you got those? Then everything would be filled in, I mean it would all be finished and filled in." He looked up, and once again Weisfeld felt a slight frisson at the intensity of the brown eyes. "I know I made a mistake on the last one," Claude said.

Weisfeld paused for a moment. He pulled out a couple of drawers until he found the little boxes of paste-on stars, which he placed on the counter. A box each of blue, silver, and gold. "All right," he said, taking the book and signing the first lesson. He carefully pasted in a gold star where indicated. While Claude watched, he turned the pages and signed, reaching for a gold star each time. At the last lesson he signed and looked at the box. "You mentioned the mistake."

"It was hard to do it that slow."

"I understand." Weisfeld's hand hovered over the boxes. "Ordinarily it would be a silver star, but I'm making an exception because you did it without a teacher. You definitely deserve a gold star." He removed one from the box and pasted it in. He closed the book and handed it over. "Good work."

"Thank you," Claude said.

From his side of the counter Weisfeld reached down for a wooden stool, passed it high in the air to the boy, and motioned for him to be seated. Late afternoon light streamed through the front windows, amber shafts over the gleaming instruments. The entire shop trembled infinitesimally from the el train rushing past overhead. Weisfeld folded his hands on the counter.

"Tell me all about yourself," he said, his voice calm and even. "Take your time and tell me all about yourself."

And Claude did.

3

I T WAS WINTER and Claude was halfway through the John Thompson piano method. He emerged from the back room one morning and was surprised to find his mother sitting in the big chair, drinking a cup of coffee.

"What are you doing here?" He rubbed his eyes. There was something wrong with the light — a weak paleness in the room, an underwater feeling — and he glanced at the front window. A translucent, pearly gray effect, as if someone had painted it during the night.

"Two feet of snow, that's what I'm doing here," she said. "Have to dig out the cab. Eat something and let's get going."

He fixed a bowl of cornflakes, moving slowly. In general he slept very deeply, and was slow to wake up. The mild sense of unreality he felt this morning was no more than a variation on what he usually felt anyway. Midway through the cornflakes he spoke up.

"Why not just leave it?"

"That's what everybody else is doing. I put the chains on yesterday. Make money today."

He heard the low murmur of voices from the cathedral radio on the table beside her. He could tell from the position of the dial that it was tuned to WEAF.

"The rich are usually stingy," she said. "I don't know why, since they live off other people's labor." She sniffed and wiped her nose with the back of her hand. The chair creaked as she put down her coffee cup. "But when cabs are scarce they'll wave dollar bills in the air. Ha!"

"We don't have a shovel," he said.

"I got a couple from the boiler room." She put her hands on the arm-rests and pushed herself up. She wore high-top army-surplus boots, work pants, a sweater, and an Eisenhower jacket. Claude finished eating and went back into his room. He got dressed and then put on a second pair of pants, and a second shirt. He had two pairs of sneakers and chose the older pair. He buttoned his coat all the way to his neck.

He followed his mother through the front door, grabbed the short coal shovel leaning against the wall, and climbed the iron stairs in her footsteps. The air was hazy but very bright. He was struck by the almost perfect silence and the impossible whiteness of the snow where it lay unbroken against the buildings, or drifted up in smooth curves over the parked cars. When they got to the cab he stood for a moment, turning his head, taking it all in.

"This is wonderful," he said.

She fell to immediately with the long-handled shovel, working with a steady rhythm, throwing the snow in large chunks onto the plowed street. Claude stood on the sidewalk, uncertain where to begin.

"The front wheel, there. Right in front of you," she said, her breath visible in the air.

It was quite easy at first. The snow was light and powdery, and it was fun to get great piles of it on the blade of the shovel and toss them aside. But very quickly the shovel grew heavy, and he began to sweat. He kept on, aware that his mother was going three times faster. He would slip when he lost his stance and adjusted to another, his feet already so cold and wet he could barely feel them. As he paused to catch his breath, he watched her. Bend, dig, up, and toss. Bend, dig, up, and toss. Her big body was planted firmly, arms swinging evenly while behind her more and more snow spread out fan-like over the plowed part of the street. She moved from the front of the cab to the rear, steady, inexorable, as if she could continue forever. She did not look up until her side was clear. Her round cheeks were aglow and her eyes sparkled.

"Now the front," she said.

They were working directly across from each other in the space between the front of the cab and the next car. The contrast between her strength and his weakness was particularly obvious now, and as cold, wet, and miserable as he was, he began to get mad — furious at his puny body, at his helplessness, at the whole situation. Disregarding his dry mouth and his pounding heart he worked furiously, hissing through his clenched teeth, trying to match her rhythm even though the shaft of the shovel turned in his hands. She seemed to notice nothing. At the end, their blades clanking together, his feet went out from under him and he fell into the snow. He scrambled up quickly, numb with shame.

"That ought to do it." She swept the hood with the handle of the shovel and cleared the windshield with her forearm. She opened the door, got behind the wheel, and after a couple of tries, started the engine.

"C'mere!" she shouted.

He came around to the driver's side.

"Just keep your foot on the accelerator while it warms up." She got out and he got in, the engine almost dying in the process. He revved it way up. "Not so hard," she said. "Not so hard!" He let up on the gas and she went back to the stairs and down to the apartment with the shovels.

He sat on the edge of the seat, his toe on the accelerator and his hands on the wheel. The cab smelled musty, something like the odor from the subway grate. Behind him, the back of the seat was bowed, pushed back as if from some enormous blow. The cumulative effect of the weight of her body had molded it thus.

She reappeared with her clipboard and change maker, and they switched places once again. As he stepped away, she put the cab into gear, rocked it a couple of times, lurched out into the street, and kept on going. She rode off in a cloud of exhaust.

He got sick that afternoon. First nausea and a feeling of weakness. He was too dizzy to sit at the piano, his arms and hands like a rag doll's — a sensation so novel it might have been interesting if he hadn't been preoccupied with vomiting into the toilet bowl — and he finally took to his bed. For several hours he fluttered between sleep and wakefulness, his mind drifting in and out of self-awareness, until the fever struck with the suddenness of a thunderclap. Alternating chills and sweats took him over as he turned and twisted in the cot, now throwing the covers off, now pulling them up. The light bulb hanging from the center of the ceiling seemed too bright, and the whole room with its familiar objects was both innocuous and weirdly threatening. The chair with the radio was clearly the chair with the radio, but as he stared at it he felt the sensation of someone looking at a fantastic prehistoric bird about to strike. The piano was the piano, but it was also the three-dimensional projection of an unseen four-dimensional torture machine of unimaginable complexity and depth, capable of sucking him right out of the cot into its maw. Everywhere he looked something was wrong. A water glass seemed enormous, much too big, or then too small, or paradoxically too big and too small at the same time. Everything was split somehow, everything doubled into its opposite. He passed out, his body rigid as a board.

When she came home that night she made him soup and put a large pitcher of water on the floor by his cot.

"Drink as much as you can," she said. "Just keep drinking."

He lost track of time. Sometimes when he woke up it would be day, sometimes night. Sometimes he could hear her in front of the apartment, sometimes not. Trips to the bathroom were long, tiring, and seemed to occur in slow motion. If he heard something from outside — a car horn, children yelling, the rattle of coal sliding down a chute — it would shock him into a momentary awareness that the world, which felt very distant, was going on as usual. In those moments he knew time was passing. He knew he was sick, but he did not think of it as an adult might think of it, as an anomalous period to be endured until health returned. He'd forgotten all about normalcy, and lived moment to moment entirely defined by the swirling sensations of his illness. He floated.

A loud buzzing sound woke him up. The instant he opened his eyes he knew he was well again. He sat up, yawned, and stretched, enjoying a feeling of spaciousness, like someone emerging from a cave. As he moved there was a sense of well-being, a mild euphoria. The buzzing sound began again, louder and more focused, and after a moment he realized there was someone at the door. He could not remember when he'd last heard the sound — no one ever came to the door. He dressed quickly and went to answer it.

Mr. Weisfeld stood at the threshold, wearing a black overcoat, a scarf wrapped around his neck, and a black beret flat on his head. "Claude," he said. "May I come in?"

Surprised, the boy stood motionless, reluctant to open the door all the way, instinctively averse to letting the man see the apartment.

Gently insistent, Weisfeld entered. He removed his beret. "I've been worried. I haven't seen you in a week." He kept his eyes on the boy.

"I was sick."

Now Weisfeld glanced around the dim room. Beer bottles. Dirty dishes. Newspapers strewn on the chair and the floor around the chair. A spare wheel for the cab leaning against the wall. Stacks of trip cards piled here and there. Cockroaches. His face revealed nothing. "May I sit down?"

Claude went and removed the newspapers. Weisfeld unbuttoned his coat but did not take it off. Claude glanced out the fan-shaped window.

"What time is it?"

Weisfeld sat. "Around five-thirty."

"I just woke up."

"I see."

"I was sick. What day is it?"

Weisfeld paused only a moment. "Saturday."

The euphoria was passing now and Claude sat down, clear-headed but a bit wobbly. "How did you find, how did you know where . . . ," he began.

"I asked," Weisfeld said.

"Oh."

"I'm glad to see you're feeling better."

"It was the day of the snow. First I was throwing up and then I got sick and went to bed."

"Very sensible, under the circumstances." Weisfeld looked around. "Where's the piano?"

"In back."

Claude led the way, past the kitchenette and through the door. "It's kind of messy, I mean, I just got up and I didn't have time to . . ."

"Of course. I understand."

They went to the white piano. Claude stood at the bass end while Weisfeld, standing, played a scale and some chords with his right hand. "This is what they call a nightclub piano," he said. "Sixty-six keys. It doesn't sound all that bad, actually." He struck a fifth. "Out of tune, as I'm sure you know." He noticed that the white keys were darkened with grime except for an ovoid white space on each key, where the pads of the boy's fingers, as he played, had kept them bright. "Looks like you've put in some time on this instrument."

"I like playing."

"Well, you would have to, to do what you've been doing." He glanced at the music. "Is this where you are?"

Claude nodded. "I was almost through the lesson."

"Wait a day or two. Until you get your strength back."

"Oh, I can play now," the boy said quickly.

"I'm sure you can. But it's a matter of concentration. Give it a day or two. Practice doesn't mean anything, as I've told you many times, unless you concentrate on what you're doing."

"Okay."

"Are you hungry?"

"Yes."

"Put on some shoes and get your coat. We'll go around the corner to Prexy's for a hamburger. You like hamburgers?"

Claude was surprised to find the streets empty of snow. On the avenue, light from the shops spilled out onto the sidewalks still wet from rain. It was getting dark. Clouds of steam billowed out from manhole covers.

They took seats at the long counter, toward the back where it was less crowded, and Weisfeld ordered. Claude was so hungry he felt, at the smell of food, a tremor of anticipation. When the hamburger came he grabbed it from the plate and took a bite.

"Eat slowly," Weisfeld said. "Chew." He raised his own hamburger delicately. "Believe me, I know about these things. I didn't eat for three days once."

"Why not?"

"Why not? I didn't have any food, that's why not. It was the war."

"I know about the war."

"Yes, well, it was somewhat different over there."

Claude ate for a while. "My father was in the war."

"So you told me. I'm sorry."

"Do you think he died because he didn't have any food?"

Weisfeld glanced at the boy. "Very unlikely," he said. "The soldiers were always well fed. Most probably he died in battle, fighting the Nazis."

Outside, in the dark, they walked to the corner, where Claude stopped abruptly.

"What?" asked Weisfeld.

"She's parking the cab." He stared up the street.

"Your mother? Good, I want to meet her." He started forward, and then looked back. "Come on."

Reluctantly Claude followed.

They met at the head of the iron stairs.

"So you're up," she said. "Who's this?"

Weisfeld took off his beret and gave a slight bow. "Aaron Weisfeld. Maybe Claude has mentioned me. The music store?"

"The lessons," Claude said.

"Sure," she said.

"I wonder if you could spare a moment."

"Spare a moment?" she said, drawing out the words. "You mean like Mrs. Roosevelt? Or Gloria Vanderbilt, who spares a moment now and then? Like that?"

Weisfeld, momentarily nonplused, squeezed his beret and glanced at Claude, who was staring at the sidewalk.

"Sure," she said. "Come on in. Have a beer." She led the way.

Inside, she fell heavily into the big chair and motioned for Claude to go to the refrigerator. "A long day." She unlaced her boots.

"Yes," Weisfeld said. "Well, I'm glad to finally meet you, Mrs. Rawlings. Claude is a remarkable boy."

"He took to it fast, didn't he?"

"Very fast. Faster than anyone I've seen."

She accepted a quart of Pabst Blue Ribbon from Claude and watched as he put another in front of Weisfeld. "Get the mugs," she said. Claude went into the kitchenette and returned with two World's Fair beer mugs. She downed hers and refilled it immediately. Claude went and sat on the stool at the counter, his face averted.

"It's a gift," she said. "Like a flair for chess, or mathematics."

"Absolutely," Weisfeld said. "A God-given gift." He poured himself a short beer.

"God has nothing to do with it," she said.

"My apologies. A figure of speech, then." He sipped carefully.

"Claude. There's a pint of whiskey under the sink."

The boy got the whiskey for her and returned to his stool. She opened the cap, took a swallow, and offered the bottle to Weisfeld.

"No, thank you."

She smiled. "You sure?"

"Thank you, no."

She chased the whiskey with a long pull on the Pabst Blue Ribbon. "I used to sing."

"Really."

"Before the war. I still have my card."

"Well, there you are," Weisfeld said. "Music often runs in families."

"They sent somebody once. A truant officer, he called himself. Some little pansy. I settled his hash for him." Her hand was so big the quart bottle seemed to shrink to ordinary size as she emptied it into the mug. "You're not a pansy, are you Mr. Weisberg?"

"Weis*feld*, Mrs. Rawlings. No, I'm not. I had a family of my own once."

Her eyes were beginning to shine from the alcohol. "Not that I've got anything against them, you understand. It's just he's a beautiful boy." Weisfeld saw Claude's back stiffen at the description, almost as if he'd been struck. She leaned forward and raised herself out of the chair. "Zat dat de dah," she whispered, singing, and broke into a soft shuffle in her stocking feet, the floor creaking beneath her. "Zat dat da-da de dah . . ." She stopped and went into the kitchenette. "Vaudeville. I was fourteen, I think. On the Loew's circuit. But then I got fat." She bent over to get another bottle from the refrigerator.

Claude turned his head and Weisfeld looked directly at him. The boy appeared on the verge of tears, and Weisfeld made a small patting motion in the air, a reassuring gesture. He continued to look at the boy while speaking to the woman, still out of sight, bent over behind the counter. "I've been giving Claude some lessons, as you know." The clink of bottles. Claude's large eyes were steady now. "I believe he has talent. A special talent. A rare talent. I may be wrong, of course, but I don't think so." She was up now, with the beer on the counter, prying off the cap. "I want to press until we get somewhere close to his limits. The time is right and I think he can do it."

"Unh-huh," she said warily.

"It will involve a great deal of work. A lot of time."

"Well then, forget it. I can't afford it. I've got payments on the medallion, and the black-market prices for repairs are high. I work fourteen hours to stay even. Go teach the capitalists on Park Avenue. Teach the little debutantes." She gave a short, barking laugh. "Music lessons! You've got to be kidding."

"You misunderstand me, Mrs. Rawlings. Claude and I have worked out the financial arrangements. He pays for his lessons himself."

She glanced at the boy and then back at Weisfeld. "He does? How much?"

"Twenty-five cents."

"Twenty-five cents a lesson?" Incredulous.

"Twenty-five cents a week. The fee will remain the same even though he'll be doing more. That is, if you agree."

She came out from the kitchenette, sat down, drank, and stared at Weisfeld for several moments. "So what are you talking to me for?"

He felt a flash of anger, an acceleration of forces flaring in his head, begging for release. He took a deep breath and stroked his mustache while gaining control of himself. "It will affect his life," he said finally. "He'll be playing three or four hours a day. Quite soon arrangements will have to be made for him to work on a full-sized instrument, and that means a good deal of time away from home. He'll be under pressure. A lot of pressure for a child. There'll be periods of frustration, and anger. Times of doubt, ups and downs. Joy, perhaps, sometimes." He paused, holding his beret between his knees, running the rim through his fingers, around and around. "That's why I'm talking to you."

"My, my," she said. "Goodness gracious."

"I can do it," Claude said as if talking to himself.

"I take it you have no objections?" Even through his anger Weisfeld sensed that this preposterous giant of a woman was not as simple as she apparently wanted him to believe. There was something slightly theatrical in her vulgarity, some hint of role playing in the exaggerated carelessness with which she drank her beer and her whiskey.

She shrugged. "Hey, it's okay with me. He's more or less on his own anyway."

"Good. That's settled, then." From the corner of his eye he saw the boy smile and duck his head quickly. "I'll also be giving him some books to read. That will be going on continuously." He said this for Claude's benefit, hoping for a tacit commitment. "Playing is one thing, music is another. We'll be working on both."

"I've been reading a lot myself since I joined my group."

"Ah," Weisfeld said. "A book club?"

"No, no," she waved an arm. "Economics. Politics. It's a real education. An eye opener."

Weisfeld stood up and reached over to shake her hand. "A pleasure to meet you, Mrs. Rawlings."

She burped quietly. "Call me Emma." She did not get up.

"Fine, then. I'll be on my way."

Claude stepped forward, opened the door for him, and together they climbed the stairs to the sidewalk.

"Go back in now," Weisfeld said. "It's cold. Don't work until you've got your strength back. I'll see you at the store."

"Yes sir."

"Go on, now."

The boy climbed down the stairs, and Weisfeld heard the door fall shut.

The oblong door to the furnace was wide open and Al stoked coal, giving an extra push and a quick turn of the wrist at the end of the toss to spread the black chunks evenly over the bright bed of yellow and red fire. Claude stared at the trembling air within the chamber, blinking rapidly at the effect of the radiant heat. It was a special world in there, endlessly fascinating. Al paused in his work and lighted a cigarette. He gave Claude the empty book of matches.

"Throw it in," Al said. "Don't get too close."

As Claude approached he felt the pressure of the heat against his face. He threw quickly and missed. Al retrieved the cardboard with the blade of the shovel, crumpled it in his hand, and gave it back to Claude.

"Try again."

A perfect throw this time. The cardboard sailed in over the brightness and exploded into flame. A flare, and then nothing. Claude was delighted. Al swung the door shut with the shovel, pressed it home, and knocked over the heavy cast-iron latch. It was profoundly satisfying to see the power contained that way, the awesome energy locked away, sealed with a few deft gestures. Al put up the shovel.

"All right. Let's get to it." He began to move away. "What's the matter, boy?"

"Nothing."

"Hey. You don't have to do it. Did I ever tell you any of those times that you have to do it?"

"No."

"Hell, I'd go myself if I could." He tapped a pressure gauge and led the way out of the boiler room. Claude followed as they wound their way through dark corridors to the south garbage room. They sat down at an old card table and Al took out a piece of paper.

"I was up there last winter to fix a radiator. There's a door here" — he pointed at his rough map — "right next to the icebox. That's it. That's the cupboard."

"What if —" Claude began.

"I done told you. They gone for a week. I heard the doormen talking. Anyway, you listen like I told you. If you hear anything, don't go in. That's simple, ain't it?"

Claude stared at the paper.

"Be a lot of stuff in there — a lot of stuff. Don't mess with anything big. Don't mess with anything comes in a set, you hear? You looking for ashtrays, like if there's a whole lot of different little silver ashtrays like I think there is, then you take one or two. Take two if there's a lot of them, otherwise one, and if it ain't small enough to fit in your pocket, leave it. You hear?"

"Yes."

"Good. Here's the screwdriver."

They got up and went over to the dumbwaiter. Al brushed it out with his hand and then held the ropes.

Claude bent down and climbed into the small enclosure, pulling his knees to his chest and covering his nose and mouth with his hand against the smell. His head bumped the top of the wooden box.

"You ready?"

Claude nodded.

Al pulled gently on the ropes and the boy ascended, looking down at Al's hands and arms until the wall of the shaft and darkness intervened. He could hear the faint creaking of wood and the whisper of the ropes sliding along the outside of the box. In the darkness he was very aware of his body, hearing his own breathing and the dull thump of his heart. The ascent was slow, almost silent, and magically smooth. He touched the rough plaster wall with his fingertip, feeling it slide by. Hairlines of light outlined the door of the first floor as it passed. At the second floor he could hear the murmur of voices. Although he knew his speed was constant, it seemed to take longer and longer to get from one floor to the next. Thin light again at four, creeping up to five, and an eternity until he stopped at last at six.

He held his breath, put his ear against the crack, and listened. Nothing. Breathing softly through his mouth, he listened for a long time before carefully inserting the tip of the screwdriver into the simple latch. The door fell open a quarter of an inch and Claude remained motionless in the dim light, listening. Finally satisfied, he slowly and carefully pushed the door open and stared into the kitchen, the white, still room suddenly right there. After another moment he climbed out and stood on the tiled floor.

Silence. Now he could feel the faint touch of air on the back of his neck, flowing from the dumbwaiter shaft behind him. He knew immediately that the apartment was indeed empty. The kitchen was enormous — larger than the whole apartment in which he lived with his mother — and very clean. He went to the cupboard, opened the door, and turned on the light inside, arrested by the blazing crystal that seemed to float in a haze of prismatic colors, by the high glaze of china teapots and platters, by the hard brightness of silver. Goblets, bowls, bottles, tureens, trays, cocktail shakers, dishes, cups, candlesticks, gravy boats, ice buckets, salt cellars, butter dishes, ladles, spoons, and there, in a back corner, stacks of various-sized silver ashtrays. He moved into the brightness, took two ashtrays, stepped back, turned off the light, and closed the door. They fit in his pockets.

Crossing back to the dumbwaiter, he noticed a large jar, in the shape of a fat man, standing on a counter next to the stove. Raised letters on the bottom of the fat man's apron spelled COOKIES. Claude opened the jar and put in his hand. To his surprise, he felt paper. He pulled out a wad of money — dollar bills, a few fives, a ten. He stared at it for a moment, put it back, closed the jar, and turned away.

As he climbed into the dumbwaiter, he looked down through the two-inch crack between the sill and the box itself. Way down, far away, he could see the glow of light at the bottom of the shaft, an impossibly small patch in the dimensionless blackness. He folded himself into the box, pulled the door shut behind him, tested it, and reaching around the corner of the box with his slim hand, found the two ropes and gave them a sharp pull. Almost immediately he began his slow descent, Al working carefully down below.

Two things happened simultaneously. First, the bell — loud, piercing — startling him so that he banged his head. He knew what it was: the signal people used to summon the dumbwaiter in the event they had missed the morning pickup. Second, there was light below him. He could see his knees and his hands and the wall slipping past. The light grew brighter and suddenly he was descending faster, almost as if in a free fall.

For a split second, as he passed the open door of the third floor, he was bathed in light. He saw a kitchen, similar to the one above. The refrigerator was different, but it was in the same place. The door to the cupboard was there too, except it was green instead of white. A black woman stood at the stove reaching for a pot of coffee. Her face began to turn toward Claude, and then all he could see was the blur of the shaft wall.

He landed with a bump. Gesturing rapidly with one hand and reaching in with the other, Al pulled him out.

"Al!" came a voice from above. "Is that you?"

Al tilted his head to call up the shaft. Claude sat down on the floor and rubbed the back of his head.

"Right here," Al yelled.

"She might have seen me," Claude said.

Al's eyes snapped down. "What?"

"She might —"

"Well did she or didn't she?" Al said. "Quick!"

"I don't know. It was too fast."

The woman called from above. "What's going on down there?"

Al stared upward and didn't say anything for a moment. Then he shouted, "What you mean, what's going on?"

"You hear me ring?"

Claude could see the relief on Al's face. "Sure I did."

"Well, didn't that thing just fly by here like a subway train?"

"It was the ropes. The ropes got messed up. Just hold on a minute, I'm coming." He began to pull, hand over hand. To Claude, he said softly, "That's Madge. She didn't see nothing."

"I don't want to do it anymore."

Al began to laugh. "Well," he said, giving a little gasp, "I can see that."

He came home one day to find that a telephone had been installed. It stood next to the radio, and he felt both curiosity and excitement. The gleaming black instrument was provocatively modern in the dingy apartment, suggesting, in this dark room where everything for as long as he could remember had remained more or less the same, the possibility of change. A telephone! He examined it closely. The number printed on the round insert in the center of the dial was ATwater 9–6058. He picked up the receiver, listened to the dial tone, and replaced it in the cradle.

"Don't play with it," his mother said, coming in from her room. "Just leave it alone."

"But what's it for?" He noticed a thick telephone book on the floor. "I mean, who are you going to call?"

She paused, staring at him. He began to worry that he had inadvertently said something wrong, but then she turned away. "Just don't worry about it," she said.

For days it simply sat there. It never rang, and in the evenings she never used it. Browsing in the yellow pages, Claude stumbled upon the Music Store section, his eye caught by the illustrations of various instruments. It was thrilling to find a listing for Weisfeld's, and after a few false tries, he got through.

"Hello."

"This is Claude."

"Claude!" Mr. Weisfeld said. "What a pleasant surprise."

"We got a telephone." He looked down and touched the base with his fingers. "It's right here next to the radio."

"Good. I'm glad to hear it."

A long pause. "I like boogie-woogie."

"I thought you would. No more than half an hour at a time, though. It can be bad for your left hand."

"Okay." Claude listened to the hum of the line. He didn't know what to say, and it felt odd. "Goodbye."

"Goodbye, Claude. I'll see you tomorrow."

And then one night, in the middle of the night, it rang. He sat up on the cot and heard his mother come out of her room to answer it. She said a few words and put the phone down as Claude peeked through his door. She got pencil and paper and returned to the phone. "Okay, ready," he heard her say quietly, and then she wrote. When she hung up he ran back to the cot and pulled up the covers.

Suddenly the lights went on. She stood at his door, naked, her great white body startling him into full wakefulness.

"Get dressed," she said. "We're going out."

"Now?"

"Quick." She turned away. "And bring a blanket."

He obeyed, and found himself following her up the iron stairs into the dark and silent night. As they approached the parked cab he asked, "What's going on?"

She opened the rear door. "Just get in. You can go back to sleep. I can't drive around with the flag up at this hour of the night, that's all." He stepped up into the cab, and she went around and got behind the wheel.

As they pulled away from the curb and moved toward Third Avenue he stared out at the scene — familiar and yet transformed by the dark stillness, oddly ominous. She drove downtown, and after a while he lost track of where they were. He dozed off, his head resting lightly on the back of the seat.

He woke up as she parked, on a crosstown street at the corner of an avenue. She turned off the headlights and the engine, but left the meter running.

"Where are we?"

"Downtown," she said. "I've got a couple of special pickups. We'll wait. We're early. When he comes I want you to get up front here with me." He could sense a subtle tension in her voice, a controlled excitement.

Every few minutes the meter would click as the cylinder rolled up, five cents at a time. A dollar ten. A dollar fifteen. His mind wandered. A dollar sixty-five. A dollar seventy. They sat in silence.

"Oh, shit," she said, and he sat up straight.

From the avenue, three people were approaching the cab. Two young men in tuxedos and open black topcoats, and a woman in a long dress and fur stole. The taller of the young men waved in an exaggerated manner, his coat flapping.

"Just sit tight and keep quiet," his mother said, rolling down her window. "The cab's taken," she said as the young man reached for the rear door.

"I don't see . . ." Claude saw the flushed face, the sandy hair falling over the forehead, as the man bent over to look inside. "Oh. Yes."

"Sorry," she said, and began to roll up the window.

"It's taken," the man said, turning back to his companions while at the same time putting his hand on the rising window, stopping it. "A woman driver! How extraordinary. Perhaps you could just take us along to Sixty-ninth Street. Plenty of room back there. Ten dollars?"

The woman in the stole was laughing at something with the shorter man, who stumbled against the front fender.

"Sorry," Claude's mother said, her right hand clenching and unclenching on the steering wheel. "The Hack Bureau. Rules."

The tall man still held the window. "I offered ten dollars," he said to his friends, his tone aggrieved.

The short man lurched forward, putting his face in the window. "Twenty! Twenty bucks and let's go." His wet lips shone in the dim streetlight. The tall man had removed his hand and now she rolled the window shut with a violent motion of her arm.

The tall man and the woman drifted back toward the avenue, but the shorter man remained, standing now by the front fender, staring through the windshield. Claude's mother kept both hands on the wheel. The man took one step backward, opened his fly, and began to piss on the front tire.

Claude heard a kind of *oof* sound from somewhere deep in his mother's throat, as if she'd been punched. "Stop him," he said, "stop him."

"I can't get into anything," she whispered.

The man finished, shook his penis — all the while staring into the cab — and smiled as he zipped up and turned away.

There was a sharp snapping sound, like the crack of a whip.

"What? What was that?" Claude asked.

"Jesus," she said. "I broke the wheel." She bent over and examined it, running her fingers over the hairline fracture. "It's okay. I can still drive."

"Why did he do that?"

"Ah, Christ." She slumped back in her seat, the whole cab jolting slightly.

Fifteen minutes later the meter read two dollars and thirty cents. A small, stocky figure in a navy pea jacket came around the corner, and Claude felt his mother's sudden alertness. He came directly to the cab and she rolled down the window.

"The cab's taken," she said.

"May first?" he said. He wore odd-looking glasses, perfectly round with steel rims.

"Get in, please. Claude, come up front."

Claude took his blanket and got in the front seat. The man sat in back. She pulled away from the curb and turned uptown on the avenue. Claude noticed the man twisting his body to look out the back window.

"It's okay, sir," she said. "I'll know." She glanced at her side mirror and then the rearview. "I'll know."

"Of course," the man said.

Claude was surprised to hear her call him sir. He could not remember hearing her call anybody sir.

"It's ridiculous," the man said with a foreign accent. "Melodramatic. But we have to be careful."

"Yes."

"We are very grateful. We know you work hard and long hours."

"It's an honor, sir."

They drove through the dark city, the streets almost empty, going uptown two blocks, west one block, uptown two blocks, west one block, again and again in such a way as to catch all the lights.

"A good trick," the man said, and Claude recognized his accent as German, the kind he heard often in Yorkville. "I did not know this trick."

She pulled to the curb at the corner of Madison and Ninety-second. "We're on schedule," she said.

They waited in silence, the meter ticking near Claude's head. After some time a man in a light brown coat emerged from an apartment building and approached the cab.

"It's him," the German said, and opened his door for the newcomer, who slipped into the cab.

"Gerhardt."

"This is foolishness," the German said.

"Well, they were meeting anyway. I thought they should see you."

She made a U-turn on Madison and proceeded downtown.

"You know where to go?" the newcomer asked. He was an American.

"Yes." She glanced into the rearview.

"I don't see what you hope to accomplish," said the German.

"Money, for one thing," the American answered. "It's expensive to be on the run. The more you have, the better. And there are other reasons we don't have to go into."

The German sighed heavily.

"Just let me handle it," the American said. "These people are submarines, mostly. Completely undisciplined. They'll blather on all night about Browder, white chauvinism, and God knows what else if you let them. They're like children."

"I can imagine. I don't know how you put up with it."

"I have very little choice, obviously."

She parked near the East River. Claude watched the electric signs go on and off on the other side, floating in the darkness.

"The house should be two blocks down," she said.

The men got out and crossed the street.

She looked down at Claude. "Pull that blanket up and go to sleep. This will be a while."

He lay on his side, his hands folded under his head, and drifted off.

·   ·   ·

A bright, windy afternoon. Weisfeld had closed the shop early and now, after hot tea and donuts at the luncheonette on the corner of Third and Eighty-fourth, they walked to Park Avenue.

"It's a concert grand," Weisfeld said. "Nine feet. A Bechstein. Maestro Kimmel brought it with him on the boat years ago. A fabulous instrument. But he can't play anymore."

"Why not?" Claude asked.

"He's an old man, and he's got some kind of muscle disease. But he still writes." He tapped the manuscripts under his arm. "He writes incredible music."

"But how can he do that if he never comes out of his room? If he can't play it, how does he know what it'll sound like?"

Weisfeld laughed. "In his head, my boy. He hears it in his head. Strings, brass, tympani, everything. He doesn't write for piano anyway."

"And they play it on the radio?"

"Oh, yes. Yes, they do. The older stuff."

They turned south on Park Avenue. The wind whipped the stiff hedges in the islands running down the center of the street. In the distance, clouds sped behind Grand Central Station, creating the illusion that the building itself was in motion.

"Here we are."

Claude stopped in his tracks. It was Al's building.

"What's the matter?"

"Nothing," Claude said.

"There's no need to be nervous. You won't even see the man."

For a moment it seemed to Claude that it was simply too great a coincidence, that Weisfeld had somehow found out about Al and the trips in the dumbwaiter, and that a reckoning was at hand. But a glance at Weisfeld's earnest, open face reassured him. The very idea that Weisfeld might find out made him feel slippery inside, as if a stone had rolled over in his chest.

The doorman touched his cap as they went inside. The gleam of marble, dark wood, the smell of wax. The elevator car was mirrored and had a small padded bench. They entered and the attendant came after them, closing the doors and the safety gate. Claude watched the numbers through the small window as they ascended to the tenth floor. He felt relieved — he had never gone up that high for Al.

At the door to the apartment Weisfeld removed his beret and rang the bell. "You will wait for me at the piano. I won't be long."

After a moment the heavy, ornately carved door swung open. A thin elderly man with a pronounced stoop stared out at them from over his glasses. His Adam's apple was so large it looked like a bone stuck in his throat. Weisfeld urged Claude forward with a hand on his back.

"Franz," he said.

"Herr Weisfeld. So this is the wunderkind?"

"Just so. Shake hands with Franz, Claude. He will be looking after you."

Claude obeyed.

"How is the maestro?"

"Good. He worked all morning, so a little tired, but good."

"Wait in there, Claude." Weisfeld indicated the living room, behind a set of half-open sliding doors. "We won't be a minute."

Claude slipped into a large room. A thick oriental rug, heavy drapes, an entire wall of books, couches, a wing chair by the fireplace, footstools, hundreds of framed pictures and photographs everywhere on the walls and tables, and there, at the far end of the room, standing free in a large open space, an enormous black piano. As Claude approached silently he could see his reflection in its side. He sat at the bench, opened the lid, and stared at the keys. He didn't move until Franz entered and walked, stooping and with a slight limp, across the room to open a side door.

"A small bathroom here," he said, closed the door, and approached the boy. "Should you ever need to call me or Helga from the back, just pull this." He tugged a ribbon of heavy cloth hanging over the drapes. "Gently. Don't jerk it."

"Who is Helga?"

"Helga is my wife. She is the cook." He glanced back at the other end of the room. "The big doors will be kept shut while you practice."

As he said this, Mr. Weisfeld came in. He was rubbing his hands together as he walked. "Now, Claude. Do you have any questions? Has Franz explained everything? Good."

"What about the man at the door downstairs?" Claude asked.

"They will be given their instructions," Franz said.

"Don't worry," Weisfeld said. "You come after school at three-thirty and you leave at six. Monday, Wednesday, and Friday. They will know all about it. So."

The two men looked down at the boy.

"Why don't you try it before we leave?" Weisfeld said.

Claude flushed. "What should I play, I don't have, I didn't bring any —"

"Try the little Schubert piece. You don't need music for that. The little one you were playing in the store."

Claude raised his arms, opened his hands, and began to play, instantly adjusting to the fact that the keys seemed to go down without resistance, or just enough resistance so that he could feel them, every key the same. He had the sensation of playing almost without effort — as if the piano itself were playing, and he was simply moving his fingers along with it. When he finished he looked up.

"It's different. It's very different."

Franz was nodding, a faint smile on his face.

"Of course," Weisfeld said. "I told you."

"I like it," Claude said.

"Well, maybe if it likes you, it will teach you," Weisfeld said. "We will see."

Sometimes the phone rang two or three times in a week, and then there were long periods — a month or more — when he almost forgot it was there. The shrill sound would pull him out of sleep, and he would get up and get dressed like an automaton, follow her up the stairs, into the cab, and fall back asleep almost instantaneously.

It was always the small stocky man with the round glasses, sometimes by himself, sometimes with others, and the pickups and drop-offs were always at corners. People appeared out of the night and disappeared into the night, as if in an extended, interrupted dream. The German spoke very little but was invariably courteous to Claude's mother, and sometimes he gave the boy a gift of candy (licorice pastilles, strong and bitter tasting). Occasionally, while dozing, or shifting in his sleep, his feet bumping his mother's huge, hard thigh, he would catch an exchange from the back.

"Don't they have instructions for us? Don't they know what's happening?"

Gerhardt: "No instructions. Perhaps eventually."

"Eventually will be too late. I can't believe this!"

Mostly the other voices were anxious, or fast (which might have been why Claude would tune in momentarily), but Gerhardt was always calm, and he often sighed.

.   .   .

It was many months before Claude looked up from the piano, as it were, and allowed himself to wonder about the maestro. The boy was so in love with the Bechstein, so protective of the conditions that allowed him to play it, that he had instinctively made himself small, almost invisible, putting everything else out of his mind when he would ring the bell and be ushered in by Franz, saying next to nothing as he slipped into the big room, head down, and walked a straight line to the instrument. The silence, dimness, and peaceful stasis of the place worked on him in a strange way — he was not afraid to play, but he was almost afraid to breathe, as if the vulgar fact of his being alive might somehow disturb things. (Although he continued to pick up the bottles in the basement once a week, going in by the back service entrance, he had not told Al about the events upstairs, about how the doormen knew him now, or about how Franz and Helga set out a glass of milk and two almond cookies on the coffee table near the piano as a silent greeting every Monday, Wednesday, and Friday, nor did he think he ever would tell Al. He was not aware of having made the decision, it somehow just happened.) But one afternoon, after almost half a year, he found himself gazing at the framed photographs and identifying the maestro simply because he was in more pictures than anyone else. He felt a small shock and a vague sense of guilt, as if he weren't supposed to be looking.

There were cities, some of which he recognized from pictures he had seen in *Life* magazine. Two men and a woman standing in front of a café, and far off in the distance, the top of the Eiffel Tower. A shot of Piccadilly Circus, double-decker buses jammed in a circle, bowler hats, servicemen, signs and advertisements. But most of the pictures revealed an exotic city of old buildings with rococo embellishments, spidery wrought-iron arches over narrow streets, a river, a cliff, and a castle atop the cliff. A strange city with very few signs in a strange alphabet made up of odd letters. Everyone wore dark clothing, and there, towering over everyone else, a bear of a man, often in a fur hat, often carrying a cane, was the maestro, or the man Claude took to be the maestro, since Claude had never seen him. His size, his full beard, his unnaturally penetrating eyes, all contributed to a near-palpable feeling of power. He dominated every photograph in which he appeared. Once, he seemed — a trick of the eye — to move ever so slightly within the frame. Claude jumped back, as if rebuked, and returned to the piano.

Weisfeld continuously monitored Claude's feelings about scales. Every few months he would check — is it getting too boring, too tedious? Can you maintain concentration, or do you get dreamy? Claude reassured him. Scales were something he liked to do. It felt good. There was a sense of progress. In addition to traditional drills, Weisfeld would give him new exercises of his own design. Contrary motion, three octaves both ways, ascend in half steps. Ascend in thirds, fourths, fifths. Delayed scales — the left hand entering first, the right hand entering three notes later, descend in whole tones. Then reverse the process. Claude particularly liked the sensations attendant to playing different scales simultaneously — F major in the right hand against D-flat major in the left, for example — not so much for the sound, although it was fun to split his mind in half and listen to both of them, or to hear them converging and diverging harmonically, but for the physical feeling in his hands, the slow-wave feeling that emerged from the various patterns, different kinds of waves with different pairs of juxtaposed scales.

The perception of the waves, and the nodes of the waves which gave his hands, while they were in motion, a series of home bases, quite different from the root notes themselves — this perception led him to realize that there were thousands of interesting scale exercises, perhaps tens of thousands, waiting to be played. Thus the finite eighty-eight-key reality of the Bechstein contained a possibly infinite number of different wave forms concealed within its configuration. Claude enjoyed catching the waves and riding them. It just felt good.

He noticed that Franz would occasionally leave the big sliding doors partly open. Was it an oversight, or was someone listening? Eventually they were left partially open almost all of the time.

And then one day as Claude went through the doors into the foyer on his way out, Franz appeared out of a dark corridor. "If you could just wait a moment," he said. "If you could just stand here, please." He indicated a particular spot on the parquet and retreated into the corridor.

After a few moments the boy discerned movement in the distant darkness — shapes, a low dark shape gliding from one of the rooms into the hall. A wheelchair? Low voices. Franz re-emerged. "The maestro wants to get a look at you. Please hold your hands up like this." Claude held his hands up, palms forward. "Yes, that's it," Franz said. "Now stretch them wide. Excellent."

Was that a head? A shoulder? Claude strained to see.

"How much do you weigh?" Franz asked.

"I don't know."

"You can put your hands down now. Thank you." Franz gently led him to the door. "Until next Monday, then."

One afternoon, in his room, Claude sat at the white piano working on "The Choo-Choo Boogie," one of a number of blues and boogie tunes he'd found in the bench. His left hand pounded out repeated fifths and a little figure with his middle finger while his right hand ran up and down doing some complicated but entirely symmetrical variations on the simple melody. The beat was as powerful and relentless as the locomotive on the front of the sheet music. He'd used up the half hour when his mother came in.

"Claude!" she shouted. He stopped immediately. "I need you."

He got up and followed her through the apartment and up the iron stairs to the cab. "I almost had it," he said, getting in the back.

"Had what?"

"That tricky part where it sort of curls around."

"What are you talking about?"

"When it goes back to F. That part."

"We're picking him up and going to the docks," she said, pulling away from the curb.

He was waiting on the corner of Twelfth Street, dressed in a suit and tie and wearing a topcoat that looked brand new. He carried a small leather suitcase, which he placed on the floor as he got in beside Claude.

"Mr. Eisler, is that all you're taking?" she asked.

"It is more than I arrived with."

"So this is it."

"I have no choice."

They drove across town in silence. When she got to the pier a cop waved her through the gates to the embarkation area. She pulled up behind another cab.

The boat was enormous, a gray wall with portholes looming high over everything. Claude pressed his face against the window and looked up to see the banked railings, the bridge, the huge smokestacks, the boom crane pulling up great rope nets filled with cargo. The pier was crowded with stevedores, sailors, cops, ship's officers, workers manhandling crates, forklifts scooting, people shouting orders or waving up to others already on board. A sense of excitement, of purpose. Here was the idea of destination compressed into a single huge, busy image as passengers flowed up the long steep gangways onto the ship, the SS *Batory*. Claude stared up at the bright superstructure shining in the sun, seagulls wheeling, and felt a longing so deep it was like a sickness, the same feeling he'd had clinging to the lamppost on V-E Day years ago.

"Take this." Eisler leaned forward to hand her a hundred dollar bill.

"I can't," she said.

He shook the money impatiently. "Take it, take it."

She did.

"Now listen to me, woman. If you are wise, you will break off all connection with your group. Completely. Do not go to any more meetings. Do not respond if anyone attempts to communicate with you. Forget that you had anything to do with any of them. Wipe it out."

If he had struck her, he could not have shocked her more. She stared, her mouth open.

"They are amateurs. Dreamers. They can't protect themselves, and they can't protect you. Do you understand me?"

"Yes, but —"

"It is a house of cards. It will collapse."

Claude was astonished to see tears in her eyes. "But they're my friends."

"They are false friends. They have no discipline, and they will, how do you say it, they will roll over." He got out of the cab. "Goodbye, comrade, and thank you for your help." He walked to the nearest gangway without looking back and boarded the ship.

Claude was mystified, but as he stared at the back of his mother's head he sensed it was not the time to ask questions.

They sat silently for a long time, looking up at the great ship, until she finally started the engine, pulled at the wheel, and drove away.

"The maestro would like to see you put on some weight," Franz said. "A little more strength in the upper body, hmmmm?"

Claude pointed to one of the photographs. "Is that him?"

"Taken many years ago."

"He's big."

"Push-ups are good for a pianist. Do you know how to do push-ups?"

Claude shook his head. Franz lowered himself to the Persian rug and demonstrated. "Nothing should touch but your toes, your hands, and your nose. Ach. I can't do it anymore. But keep straight, keep your tush in the air. Now you try it."

Claude managed to do three. They lay together on the floor, side by side, breathing hard.

"He suggests that you do them after practice. It will come quickly because you are young. You'll be surprised."

"I'll try." It was odd lying next to him. Claude sneaked a close-up look at the Adam's apple, which bobbed as Franz swallowed and caught his breath. The old man got up slowly, first to his knees and then, bracing himself on the piano bench, to his feet. He ran his fingers through the long white hair on the sides of his head.

"He also suggests that you eat here after practice. At six-thirty in the dining room. Will that be agreeable?"

Claude got up. "Yes. Thank you."

"Good. Come in back now and we'll talk to Helga."

They moved across the room, through the big doors, the foyer, the dining room, and the swinging door into the kitchen. Smells of cinnamon, coffee, and lemon. Helga wore an apron and a small white cap on her graying head.

"So," she said, shaking hands. "We make you fat, *ja?*"

Claude looked at the floor and she touched his head lightly and quickly. He felt uncomfortable talking about his body because he hated his body. He resented the earaches, recurrent in his left ear — the sharp pain, the cracking sounds, the crusty yellow stuff he would dig out with his finger. He resented the chilblains he got in cold weather, the way his scalp itched in warm weather, the scabs he got on his knees and elbows. Something was always wrong. Recently he had discovered, quite by accident, that his foreskin had adhered to one side of the head of his penis, and every night, grimacing with pain, he would pull it back, every night a bit more, ignoring the spots of blood, hoping it would eventually break free. He was thin and weak, and in his heart of hearts he did not believe anything could be done about it. But he would go along with push-ups, he would go along with eating, and pretend whatever they wanted him to pretend. He was ashamed, but he recognized their good intentions, and that made it a bit easier. They would not use his shame against him, the way his mother sometimes did.

"What do you like to eat?" Helga asked.

The question stopped him. He'd never really thought about it. Most things came from cans. Is that what she meant? "I guess . . . I don't know. Everything, I guess."

"Everything. That is good."

"I like hot dogs," he said. "I like Prexy's."

She turned to Franz. "What is this Prexy's?"

"Hamburgers," Franz said.

"I like milk."

"*Ja.* Milk is good." She rubbed her hands and smiled at Franz. "I make something special for Friday."

And so it began. At the end of the next practice session Claude tugged the bell pull and Franz came in to watch him do his push-ups. After washing his hands, the boy followed him into the dining room. A full service had been set up at the head of the table. Claude paused, intimidated by the elaborate setup, the gleaming plates and silver.

"Sit," Franz said.

"What is all this, how do I, which —"

"Relax, please. He wants you to learn this. There are different courses. It's very simple. Take the napkin from the ring and spread it over your lap. That's right. Now I will serve the soup."

Franz ladled out a pale green liquid. Claude sat perfectly still, watching the deft moves of the old man at his shoulder. The soup smelled good.

"Cream of asparagus. Use the outside spoon. And here is bread and butter. This is the butter knife. It stays on this little plate. Go ahead now." Franz surprised him by going off into the kitchen through the swinging door. After a moment Claude heard the soft murmur of their voices. The clink of plates, a chair scraping.

He picked up the indicated spoon and took a sip of the soup. Claude had never tasted asparagus, never eaten a soup made from scratch, and was entirely unprepared for the warm, slow-motion explosions of pleasure that now filled his head. (Asparagus soup was to become a lifelong favorite, although he would never find the equal to Helga's inspired ambrosial mixture of stock, tips, herbs, and cream. Nor would he know he was the beneficiary of her training in the lost royal kitchens of the Austro-Hungarian Empire.) He ate as if in a dream.

Franz appeared, to remove the shallow bowl and replace it with a plate bearing Wiener schnitzel adorned with a thin slice of lemon, potato dumplings in butter, and a glistening mélange of string beans and sliced red peppers. "At a formal dinner," he explained, "each of these might be brought around the table, and of course you would not begin to eat until the host or hostess began."

"Okay."

Franz returned and Claude picked up his knife and fork. The dream continued — he barely heard the soft laughter from the kitchen, the chiming of the grandfather clock in the foyer, or the creak of the upholstered chair on which he sat. He was immersed in swirls of texture, color, and taste. He ate slowly, sometimes closing his eyes.

Franz regarded the empty plate. Even the lemon slice was gone. "Dessert," he said, removing the plate and setting down a bowl of bananas and cream dusted with brown sugar. "Two desserts." A saucer of apple strudel, still warm from the oven. "She is a good cook, Helga. Don't you think?"

He was speechless. He could only nod.

His mother, who had more or less stopped drinking during the time of the night driving, began again, mixing beer and whiskey with abandon. She talked to herself, roaming from her room to the front room muttering imprecations, asking questions, sometimes waving her arms. Claude stayed out of the way, sensing a dangerous mixture of confusion and anger.

He was secretly grateful when he came home to find her passed out in the armchair, snoring lightly, her head tilted, surrounded by a surprising number of newspapers. He carefully lifted one from her lap and was astounded to see a photograph of the round-faced man with steel-rimmed glasses.

EISLER REPORTED STOWAWAY; SEIZURE IN BRITAIN ASKED

A man who has identified himself as Gerhardt Eisler, native of Germany, is fleeing from the United States aboard the Gdynia-American liner Batory, it became known yesterday. The fugitive is believed to be the former Comintern agent named by the House Un-American Activities Committee as America's No. 1 Communist, jumping $23,500 bail to escape serving a year in jail and other penalties.

The fugitive is bound for Gdynia, but the ship, which sailed last
Saturday, will put into Southampton Saturday. To make sure that
Polish Communists aboard the ship do not balk a return, the State
Dept., at the request of the Dept. of Justice, notified Scotland Yard
of the incident and asked that top investigators meet the ship on her
arrival in the English port. Scotland Yard was asked to hold the
suspect.

If Eisler, the convicted Communist agent, has fled the jurisdiction of the Federal District Court, his bail would be forfeited even
though the English authorities returned him, it was said at the
Federal Building.

The forfeiture of the $23,500 bail would be a blow to the Civil
Rights Congress and the American Committee for the Protection of
the Foreign Born. For a good part of the funds to assure that Eisler
would remain within the jurisdiction of the courts was put up by
Communist workers and sympathizers, who made sacrifices to do
so. The two agencies have fought one of his cases up to the Supreme
Court.

Claude glanced up to find his mother watching him.

"He went first class," she said, reaching for the Pabst Blue Ribbon.
"I don't feel bad about taking his money."

"What did he do? Was he a spy?"

She shrugged. "Who knows." She leaned forward and angrily
pointed at the paper. "They say he filled out forms wrong. They say
he didn't report eighteen hundred dollars on his income tax, so he
owes them eleven hundred ninety-one dollars. What kind of bullshit is
that?"

"A spy for the Nazis?"

"He's a Communist, for God's sake. The Communists fought the
Nazis. They fought them harder than anyone else."

Claude sensed that he was not going to understand, and that if his
mother understood, she wasn't going to tell him. He read the newspapers thoroughly, learning that Eisler was married and had left his wife
behind, that he had a sister who had denounced him. But Claude could
not find anything in clear language describing what the man had done.
This was a disappointment, since it would have been thrilling were he
a bank robber, or better yet a murderer — someone like the villains in
radio programs. The Green Hornet or Jack Armstrong. But even if the
evil in question remained tantalizingly vague, Claude followed the
reports in a state of tremendous excitement. This was something real,

something that he was connected to, something that all those people who kept going back and forth outside the fan-shaped window knew nothing about. He could loiter by the newsstand on Lexington Avenue and feel, however temporarily, the importance of his own existence.

He was thrilled to see a photograph of the British authorities carrying Eisler from the *Batory,* holding him by his arms and legs. He followed the descriptions of the subsequent legal proceedings as well as he could, and felt a certain ambivalence at the front-page headlines that announced that the British were not going to send him back to the United States. Claude was happy for Eisler, who had, after all, treated him kindly and given him licorice, but sad too, because the story was over, and Claude could no longer enjoy his secret sense of superiority at the newsstand.

The maestro died in the late spring. One morning, according to Franz, he did not wake up. Claude had done well with scales, with Bach above all, and also with Chopin, Schubert, Mozart, Bartók, and Gershwin. The push-ups seemed very gradually to add strength to his upper body. Franz had said that when Claude reached puberty progress would be faster. Weisfeld had given him two small black rubber balls to squeeze to help build his hands, and said, when Claude complained that his reach was small, that time would take care of it. In the meantime Weisfeld showed him how to roll large intervals. The effect was different from unisons, but it at least allowed him to play through the music without losing notes.

He had eaten well, and although he was still slight he had more than kept up with a spurt of upward growth. Paprika beef stew with noodles. Chicken with tarragon cream sauce. Ham with beans and hot potato salad. Leg of lamb. Lentils with sausages. Chocolate cake. Crème fraîche. Ice cream with hot fudge. Strudel. Eclairs. Franz had extended Claude's education from table manners to the rudiments of social intercourse. "Avoid the extremes," he had said in an expansive mood one day. "Neither the Germanic stiffness, the Swedish formality, nor the regrettable American tendency toward overfamiliarity. The model is the mid-European gentleman — courteous, attentive to the needs of others, and yet entirely relaxed, entirely flexible. Don't be so good that you embarrass people." Claude hadn't the faintest idea what he was talking about, but filed it away. He had come to admire Franz, not just because of the bond of affection he sensed between him and

Weisfeld, but because of an innate gentleness, a quiet dignity despite the absurd Adam's apple.

"Claude," Weisfeld said at the end of a lesson, "the maestro died last night."

"Oh." He glanced around the store and then looked at Weisfeld, hoping for some hint as to how he was expected to react. "That's too bad."

"He was an old friend, but we knew it was coming and he went quietly in his sleep. Franz couldn't wake him this morning."

"So it didn't hurt."

"No. I don't think so."

They sat silently for a moment.

"Franz and Helga are upset, of course," Weisfeld said. "They've been with him a long time. They're moving to Florida as soon as things get sorted out, so I'm afraid it's the end of our arrangement."

Claude gave a start. "You mean no more lessons?"

"No, no. I mean no more Bechstein. No more sauerbraten."

"But we keep on? You and me?"

Weisfeld got up abruptly and stood with his back to the boy. "Of course," he said, giving a little wave in the air. "Of course we do." Claude's keen ear caught the slightest thickness in his voice.

4

CLAUDE, his mother, and Weisfeld sat in the waiting room of the law firm of Larkin, Larkin & Swift. Brass lamps, hunting prints, and oak bookshelves, ten stories above Madison Avenue.

"You never even met him," she said.

"I almost saw him, but it was too dark."

"Old people can be funny. Like children sometimes," she said. "It's your good luck."

Weisfeld stroked his mustache and looked out the window.

Mr. Larkin was a distinguished-looking man with a straight nose, a strong chin, and pale blue eyes. He moved quickly and smoothly as he showed them into his office, indicated chairs, and sat down behind his desk. On the polished surface was a single file folder, which he opened and read for a moment. When he raised his head he looked directly at the boy. "May I call you Claude?"

"Yes. Sure."

"Very good, then. I understand Mr. Weisfeld has informed you that you were named in the will."

"The piano, yes," Claude said.

"Good." His eyes moved to Emma Rawlings. "I thought it would be appropriate for us to have this brief meeting so that I could explain the terms set out in the will and answer any questions you might have. Thank you for coming."

"I'm parked in a hack stand," she said.

"This won't take long. Claude, you are a minor. As usual in such situations, and pursuant to my advice, a trust has been set up with you as beneficiary. Mr. Weisfeld has agreed to serve as trustee. When you reach the age of twenty-one the trust will dissolve and title to the piano will pass to you fully and completely, without restrictions. Do you understand?"

"Do I get to use it in the meantime?"

"Most certainly." Larkin smiled and tilted his head toward Weisfeld.

"The piano is yours, Claude," Weisfeld said. "You'll have it right away. This is just legal, the way it has to be done."

"How much is it worth?" she asked.

Larkin consulted the file. "The estimated value is five thousand dollars."

"That's three medallions."

"I beg your pardon?"

"You can get three taxi medallions with that kind of money."

"Really?" Larkin said. "Well, I'm not surprised. It's a valuable instrument, Mrs. Rawlings."

"It surprises me," she said, pursing her lips.

"Any questions about this?" Larkin paused a moment and then continued. "It would be helpful, Mrs. Rawlings, if we could have a copy of Claude's birth certificate. Perhaps you would be so kind as to mail it to us?"

For a long time they all just sat there. Claude looked at his mother, who tilted back her big head and stared at the ceiling. "I don't have it," she said finally.

"Perfectly all right," Larkin said. "It happens all the time. If you can just give me the hospital and the date, I'm sure we —"

"He wasn't born in a hospital."

Claude could not take his eyes off her, and he could tell she was aware of him listening. All of this had been forbidden territory.

"I see. At home. Well, perhaps the doctor could —"

"There wasn't any doctor," she interrupted again, her head coming down as she looked at Larkin.

"A midwife?" Larkin essayed.

She shook her head. Again a long silence.

Weisfeld twisted in his chair. "Is the certificate absolutely necessary? Isn't there some other way to proceed?"

Larkin thought it over. "Well, any record will do, I suppose. A baptismal certificate," he kept on despite her audible snort, "doctor's records, vaccinations, that sort of thing."

"There aren't any records," she said. "There's just him. There he is right in front of you."

Larkin sat back and folded his hands. He glanced quickly at Weisfeld, who gave the faintest shrug. Larkin reached into his desk and withdrew a pad of paper and a pencil which he pushed across the desk. "Mrs. Rawlings, if you would write down the date and year of Claude's birth, we will prepare an affidavit for you to sign. It should suffice."

She leaned forward and scribbled on the pad.

"Thank you," Larkin said, taking it back without a glance. He tore off the sheet and put it in the file. "There is a second codicil in the will," he said, speaking more rapidly now, "which provides funds for reasonable expenses incurred in the training of Claude Rawlings as a pianist. These funds are limited to payment for piano lessons up to the age of eighteen. The administrator and trustee is Mr. Weisfeld, or in the event of his death, myself. I believe that covers everything." Mr. Larkin got up, came around the desk, and shook hands with everyone. To Claude, he said, "Best of luck in your studies. You've been given an opportunity, and I'm sure you'll make the most of it."

"I'll try," said the boy.

Downstairs, on the sidewalk, she gave him a nickel. "Take the bus uptown. I've got to get to work." She nodded goodbye to Weisfeld and went to the cab. Claude ran after her and caught her as she was opening the door.

"Well then, where was I born?" he said. "I had to be born someplace."

"What difference does it make?" she said, getting in.

He stood by the window, staring at her until she sighed. "You were born in the back of a church uptown. I used to have a job up there singing."

"A church?"

"Yes. A Baptist church. And I took you home the same night. So now you know, and what difference does it make?"

"I don't know," he said.

"I wasn't about to tell that snooty lawyer. It's no business of his. It's no business of anybody." She started the engine and pulled away.

At the bus stop with Weisfeld he said, "I was born in a church, she says. In the back of a church."

"Such things happen," he said. "You probably came fast. Eager to get out and join the comedy."

"But why didn't she just tell him? I don't understand. She could have told him. And how come she never told me?"

"I don't know." He put his hand on the boy's shoulder. "Your mother is a complicated woman."

As the bus pulled up Claude said, "I don't want to go home. I don't want to go there right now."

"Come to the store with me. You can help me put up the sheet music. It just came in."

Claude sat on the stoop in front of his house, waiting for the truck. Munching on a dill pickle, he watched the street, the passers-by, the women at the windows of the tenements. A bottle of Pepsi stood beside him, and every now and then he'd take a sip. Three girls were playing jump rope on the opposite sidewalk. They were sisters, Italian, and they never spoke to him, instantly averting their eyes if they met accidentally in the candy store or the grocery. The eldest was about his own age and he thought she was pretty — dark eyes and hair in long black ringlets. Her name was Rosa, but he knew she didn't know what his name was.

He watched the street in an abstracted state, warmed by the sun and by a sense of anticipation about the arrival of the piano. Somewhere in his mind, almost a separate, fenced-off area of his consciousness, he was playing a game to the beat of the skipping rope as it snapped on the cement.

> Pepsi-Cola hits the spot,
> Twelve full ounces that's a lot,
> Twice as much for a nickel too,
> Pepsi-Cola is the drink for you.

He heard a variation, an embellishment in eighth notes, and then a bass line going with it. It continued to run in his head after the girls stopped jumping, the music simply there without thought or concentration, his awareness of it fading in and out, as it might had he been monitoring his own breathing. It did not feel as if he was making the music, but as if the music existed independently of him, flowing along in a corner of his brain. The sensation was one of tuning in, the way a person is capable of somehow tuning in on one conversation, perhaps at a distance, in a noisy room. He often found himself playing this sort of game. While walking, for instance, when he might give a little skip, to syncopate the melody. Or while riding in the subway, to the clacking of the wheels, when in the general roar he could hear the shadowy presence of massed orchestras playing like fury.

The truck was bright red. It came slowly down the block and stopped in front of him. PINSKY PIANO MOVERS read the side. Three large men got out of the cab, and when the back of the truck was opened a fourth jumped lightly to the asphalt. He wore a clean gray uniform and walked over to the stoop.

"Rawlings in this building?" He glanced up at the façade, moving back a step.

"Yes," Claude said. "We're in the basement."

Meanwhile, the three big men were lowering the piano, wrapped in brown quilted tarps, out of the truck onto a large flat dolly.

"You got the key?" asked the first mover. "Let's take a look."

They went to the iron stairs.

"Uh-oh," said the mover, looking down.

They descended and Claude unlocked the door. The mover did not enter, but stood studying the frame of the doorway. "This don't look so good."

"What do you mean?"

"No room to play with down here. Is there another way in?"

Claude closed the door and they went back up. The piano was now on the sidewalk, standing on its side, attended by the three big men. It looked longer than it had in the maestro's apartment. The first mover ran up the stoop and disappeared inside the building. A few people began to stop, and more old ladies appeared at the windows of the neighboring buildings. A small brown dog sniffed the tarp until one of the men shooed it away. The first mover came down the stoop.

"Any windows?"

With a sinking heart, Claude pointed at the fan-shaped window.

"In back?"

"Two. But they're just like that one."

"Well, it ain't gonna go," he said. "Even if we took out the stairs it ain't gonna go."

Claude said, "Can you wait a minute? I'll get Mr. Weisfeld. I'll be right back."

"Who's he? The super?"

Claude ran down the street and turned the corner. He dodged through pedestrians and arrived at the music store out of breath.

Mr. Weisfeld was in front, rolling up the awning with a long iron rod.

"It's too big," Claude cried. "They can't get it inside. It won't fit."

"I should have thought of that." Weisfeld tucked the rod into its fixture and locked it in place. "I'll put the sign up."

When they returned to Claude's building the crowd had grown — perhaps a dozen people were standing around watching. The moving men were drinking sodas.

"I'm Aaron Weisfeld. I signed the delivery order."

The first mover nodded. "It won't go." He glanced at the building. "Up there, we could use a block and tackle from the roof, get it through a window. We've done that lots of times. But the basement, that's another story. You'd have to knock out the wall."

"Let's knock out the wall," Claude said.

"We can't do that, Claude," Weisfeld said. "But don't worry. We'll arrange something."

"So?" asked the mover.

"Take it back," said Weisfeld.

In the basement of the Park Avenue apartment building Al switched on the hanging light bulb in storage room B. The Bechstein, still wrapped, had been partially reassembled and stood on its legs.

"Why didn't you tell me?" Al asked.

"I didn't know it would go on so long."

"Hey. I heard about it last year. A kid going up there for lessons."

"It wasn't lessons, just practice," Claude said.

"And it was you?" Al shook his head. "If that don't beat all."

"The pedals aren't on."

Al pulled out the bench, got down on the floor, and studied the underside of the piano. The pedal cage, an elongated structure of wood and metal rods, lay beside him. He picked it up and slid it easily into position, knocking in the wooden holding latches with the heel of his hand. "Go ahead," he said.

Claude pulled up the bench and sat down. He pressed the pedals and they felt fine. Then he folded back the tarp and opened the keyboard. When he played a chord the sound was muffled, but clear.

"The movers told me it's worth a lot of money," Al said. "A lot more than just any old piano. You gonna sell it?"

"No. It's a trust."

"A what?"

"A trust. I can't sell it till I'm twenty-one, but I won't do that anyway, even when I am. He trusted me." He ran some quick scales with both hands and then played some Bach, watching his hands fly the way they could not on the piano at home.

"Holy shit," Al said when he'd finished.

"It's a really good piano." Claude played some boogie-woogie, throwing himself into it, showing off.

"Where'd you learn that, child? That's Meade Lux Lewis you playing."

"I've got the music at home."

"You mean you read it off the paper? How'd you learn to do that?"

"Mr. Weisfeld taught me. He's my teacher."

Al sat down on an old trunk, rested his forearms on his thighs, and slowly shook his head.

"So is it okay if I come and play? Mr. Weisfeld says he's going to find a place to move it but it might take a while and I want to keep on doing scales and I could play right here."

"Yeah, it's okay," Al said. "You do what you want. This is my territory down here. Nobody gonna say nothing. You need to play, you just go ahead and play."

A week later, in the basement of Weisfeld's Music Store, Claude held the end of a tape measure as Weisfeld walked behind stacks of boxes, crates, furniture, books, file cabinets, and old trunks.

"Hold it up," Weisfeld shouted. "Hold it high."

Claude obeyed while his teacher rummaged around, and then returned winding the reel of the tape measure.

"There is room," he said. "We can make room."

"Can they get it down here?" Claude asked.

"The freight elevator under those plates in the sidewalk. I measured it. Just barely." He sat down on an old display case and looked around. "Most of this is junk anyway. Amazing how it piles up. I'll take the files upstairs to my rooms. Mrs. Keller next door says she can give me some space in her basement for the other things. It will work."

"I can practice here."

"The acoustics might be strange, but the piano will be safe. Good storage, actually. Steady humidity, gradual temperature changes. And no neighbors to complain about noise. We better get upstairs. There might be a customer."

The day before the piano was to be moved, Claude went over to Park Avenue to practice for the last time in storage room B. He went through the back entrance and was surprised to find Al sitting at the old card table with another man, a stocky, well-dressed Negro smoking a cigar.

"Claude, this is Mr. Oliver. He's an old friend of mine."

Claude nodded, and Mr. Oliver made a saluting gesture, the cigar trailing smoke in the air. "Al and me came up from Georgia together many years ago," he said, "in a first-class boxcar."

"That's right," Al said. "And look at you now."

Mr. Oliver hunched up his shoulders in a silent laugh.

"I want to show him the piano," Al said.

"Sure."

They went into the storage room. "It's all wrapped up," Claude said, opening the keyboard. "It sounds better when it's open." He played some chords in the bass, a little fugue he had memorized, and a tune called "Sugar" he'd found in the racks at Weisfeld's.

"That sounds good," Mr. Oliver said. "Looks like you've got a jump on things."

"Mr. Oliver plays," Al said. "He got records."

Claude got up immediately.

Mr. Oliver looked around for someplace to put his cigar. Al took it and said, "You through?" When Mr. Oliver nodded, Al dropped the cigar and stepped on it.

Mr. Oliver sat down, stared at the keys for a moment, shot his cuffs, and began to play, making a low grumbling noise deep in his throat and chewing his lower lip, like a man in pain. He played uninterrupted stride and boogie for more than half an hour, his hands darting, arms pumping, but his head and torso remained motionless. After a while a faint sheen of perspiration glowed on his brow. It was a blizzard of notes, and Claude watched with fascination as the man's arms crossed, uncrossed, moved together and apart, his fingers working with unbelievable speed, plucking out clear themes from the almost overwhelming swell of music.

"It sounds like a whole orchestra," Claude said when he'd stopped.

"You think so?" Oliver smiled.

"Like on the radio."

"Well, look here. Al says you play the blues. Why don't you sit down here" — he patted the treble side of the bench — "and I'll show you a few things."

They would not sit. The older man stood under the fan-shaped window with his hands behind his back. The two younger men, neatly turned out in dark suits and somber ties, flanked her at a respectful distance from the armchair. She hadn't even had time to get a beer.

"This isn't a good time," she said. "I don't want to leave the boy alone in the house."

Claude wondered if they knew what a howler that was.

The older man said, "Agent Burdick will remain here until we bring you back from the interview."

"That's right," said Agent Burdick. Crew cut, vaguely military, he gave Claude a quick wink.

"If you have questions," she said, "why don't you just go ahead and ask them?"

"I'm afraid we can't do that, Mrs. Rawlings," the older man said. "Interviews are conducted at headquarters. That's the policy."

"Are you arresting me?"

"Certainly not. Why would we arrest you?" The man spoke in an almost perfect monotone. "It's just that we feel you can help us. There's a gentleman from Washington back at the office and he thinks you can help us. We'd be very grateful."

Claude could tell she was frightened. He didn't know how or why, but he could tell. He took a step forward. "Is this about the piano?" he asked.

The older man shifted his head slightly to look at him. "No, son," he said after a moment. Then he looked back at Emma. "Shall we go?"

Eventually she rose. "Might as well get it over with."

"That's the ticket," he said, moving away from the window. "The car is right outside."

5

CLAUDE WANTED TO KNOW what was going on, but she wouldn't tell him. That first night he had tried to pump Agent Burdick for a while.

"What does that mean, 'Agent'? He called you Agent Burdick."

"That's right. That's my title. I work for the FBI."

"What do they want to talk to her about?"

"I wouldn't know, son. They don't tell me things like that."

"He said questions. What kind of questions?"

Burdick smiled and shrugged his shoulders. It was more than two hours before his mother came back. She went directly to her room. The next day she would not respond to Claude's questions, snapped at him, and went to work.

During the next few weeks she seemed to close down, coming and going without a word, jumpy and abstracted. She stopped drinking entirely. There was beer and whiskey in the house, but she didn't touch it. The telephone was removed, and then, after a few days, mysteriously reinstalled.

Late one afternoon, after a long lesson on the Bechstein in Weisfeld's basement, he came home to find the apartment completely changed, the few pieces of furniture rearranged, the kitchenette cleaned up, floor swept, windows washed. Bewildered, he found her in the bathroom, on her hands and knees, washing the floor. He was too stunned to frame a question. As she turned her head to look at him, he realized he was afraid. She shifted onto her rump and leaned against the shower stall.

"They came and searched the place," she said. "A whole bunch of them. Hours. They took all my trip cards. A lot of books. They kept looking for letters, but I don't have any letters. They took boxes of stuff. Stuff from your room, too. Old papers. I don't know."

"Why? Why would they do that?"

She stared at the toilet. "So I thought, what the hell, I'll clean the place up." Her big round face began to undergo a spooky metamorphosis, a kind of wrinkling, while her features seemed to move toward the center, nose, eyes, and mouth gathering together. He realized she was about to cry and he didn't know what to do. "They've got me," she said. "They can take the hack license anytime they want to." Her face returned to normal. A spasm, it had lasted only an instant. "Butter wouldn't melt in their mouths, those guys."

"What do you mean they've got you? What do they . . . ?"

"Forget it." She waved her arm. "It's too complicated."

"All you did was drive him around," Claude said.

She raised her huge body from the floor, threw the rag into the sink, and left the room.

Now when the phone rang at night it was them, telling her to come to headquarters immediately (only a short distance away on Sixty-ninth Street) or at a specific time the next day. Over the months it became a pattern. More calls, but a routine similar to the old one. She said nothing about it to Claude, her words in the bathroom having been her last words on the matter.

He became aware that she was changing, and with a rapidity that made him nervous, as if she were becoming an unknown person. The drinking stopped, and she never seemed to eat breakfast anymore. She began to lose weight, gradually, though she still carried a lot of hard fat. She spoke very little, stopped reading and listening to the radio. She seemed drained of emotion, and moved through the days like an automaton. She put in long hours driving the cab, and Claude would often not see her for days at a time.

He'd been working the warm summer evenings at the southeast corner of Lexington and Eighty-sixth for five or six weeks. Al had scrounged up a padded folding chair from the basement and Claude had bought the box, with its brass footrest, from another kid. His spot was near the newsstand, and most of his customers would sit down with a late edition while he worked on their shoes. He didn't need to hawk. They would drift over, flipping pages, barely glancing at him, and go to the chair.

First the liquid cleaner, brushed in and wiped down. Then two applications of wax — either black, brown, or neutral — a brisk brushing, a final touch with a pop rag, and they would give him a quarter and tell him to keep the change. They always said it that way. "Keep the change." And he could hear a certain mild satisfaction in their voices. Most evenings he made three or four dollars and then went to the cafeteria with a newspaper of his own. The dinner special was usually eighty or ninety cents, with dessert. Then he'd go home and practice, or read.

As the summer deepened a great heat wave struck the city, and the newspapers made much of it. Week after week the sun beat down and the nights were utterly still, breathless. Claude could feel radiant heat against his cheeks from the sides of buildings when he walked near them. The asphalt in the streets softened, and a peculiar stillness overcame the neighborhood.

In the general torpor specific noises stood out in high relief — the wheezing of a bus, the clacking, rattling rush of the el, angry voices from inside a tenement, the crash of a storefront grate — thick sounds rising with an eerie clarity against the unnatural silence. On an empty street he might watch his own feet, as if to reassure himself that he was not dreaming. He might wipe the sweat from his face with the back of his hand and then look at the back of his hand. He was often dizzy.

When he passed under the marquee of the RKO Eighty-sixth Street, he sometimes felt a waft of cool air as someone pulled open a door from the lobby. AIR CONDITIONED said a sign over the box office, the letters dripping with painted icicles. One particularly hot day he joined a line of kids, bought a ticket for twenty cents, and went inside. He followed them through the marble-floored lobby, released into the light comfortable air, past the bright candy stand dense with color, and into the darkness of the auditorium. There was a matron dressed in white shining a small flashlight down the side aisle toward the children's section. He took a seat and stared at the theater curtains looming in the darkness right in front of him.

The boys and girls around him were fidgeting, talking, moving around, exchanging seats, giggling, sending somebody back for candy, whistling in their impatience for the show to begin. The matron would flash her light over the section when things got too noisy and the kids would immediately quiet down. Claude watched them with a certain detachment. He was no longer afraid of them, as he had been when he'd started school. They were, he realized, just kids, but there was something about them — their easy spontaneity, their recklessness, their almost manic self-absorption, the way in which they seemed completely taken up in the present moment — that made him uneasy. He did not for an instant think of himself as one of them. He sat with them only because the rules forced him to. In an odd way he felt like an impostor.

There was a tremendous burst of music as light streamed from the distant projection box. On the theater curtains a highly distorted image of the American flag appeared — pulled, rolled, squashed, smeared, ballooned, and edgeless in the thick folds. As the curtains parted the image grew from the center out, crisp, bright, and perfectly focused. Old Glory against the sky. Everyone stood and sang the national anthem, following the bouncing ball at the foot of the screen. Claude found a peculiar fascination in the bouncing ball. It seemed a persona, jumping deftly from syllable to syllable. The music was loud and satisfying.

Cartoons! Followed by a newsreel, the narrator's voice both urgent and important, sounding over the flash of images. And then the first feature, about a tough sailor who marries a librarian but doesn't take life seriously until they have a baby. The second feature described the adventures of a boy who could talk to horses. Claude watched them all with total attention, so captivated that it was a shock when the movies ended, as if his soul had been flying around in the dark and had now slammed back into his body. Outside, the unnaturally still street and the implacable heat seemed to claim him, to smother the quicksilver emotions of the films and flatten him in his contemplation of the meaningless, eternal, disinterested reality of the street, of its enduring drabness and familiarity. To come out of the RKO was to come down, and he rushed home to the safety and company of the piano.

But on that hot day he had discovered, by accident, staring up at the ethereal brightness of the screen, a force that would gently press its weightless light upon him through the years of his growth, becoming finally a part of him, as if he carried the memories of a thousand lives he had never led, of lives, indeed, no one had ever led, but which seemed nonetheless real.

Weisfeld sat on a tall stool behind Claude's right shoulder, so that he could see both the music and the boy's hands. Most sessions followed a loose structure. A review of old stuff. A review of the last lesson. New stuff, and finally nonstop sight-reading (or as close to nonstop as the boy could manage) through different manuscripts, selected by Weisfeld, that Claude had never seen before. This last was the most fun — the payoff, as it were, for getting through the slower work. Sometimes the unseen Weisfeld voice — which for all its nearness and intimacy became more and more disembodied as the lesson progressed — would abruptly pose a series of questions. Claude would take his hands off the keys and answer, staring straight ahead.

"Relative minor of G?"

"E."

"Relative minor of E?"

"C-sharp."

"Relative major of C?"

"E-flat." Claude smiled when he knew Weisfeld was being easy.

"Subdominant of D?"

"G."

"Dominant of A?"

"E."

"Of A major or A minor?"

"Both."

"Four flats is . . . ?"

"A-flat major or F minor."

"Five sharps is . . . ?"

"B major or G-sharp minor."

"Good," said Weisfeld, his arm appearing over Claude's shoulder, his finger tapping the page. "Play this again for me please, and watch the fingering in the fifth bar."

"Was it wrong?"

"Indeed it was. Like everybody else, you want to avoid your fourth finger."

"I hate that finger. It feels like a hot dog."

Weisfeld laughed. "That's good! Splendid. You know, Schumann built this cockamamie machine with strings and pulleys to strengthen his fourth finger. He'd play like that, his finger pulling the weight, making it harder to hit the notes. Poor soul."

"What happened?"

"He wound up worse than when he started. He wound up with a hot dog bun. Well, there are no shortcuts, my friend." Weisfeld got up and put a pile of manuscripts on the piano. Claude took the first one, opened it, and set it on the stand, quickly checking the key signature, the time signature, flipping the pages looking for any changes, clef displacements, or special kinds of notation. Only then would he go back to the beginning and start to play.

Unbeknownst to Claude, Weisfeld put a good deal of thought into the music he selected for this part of the lesson. He considered degrees of difficulty of execution, varieties of style, mood, and period. He drew from the sixteenth century to Tin Pan Alley and jazz. He included, but rarely, atonal music (of which Claude was not fond), in order to train the boy to sight-read music that was idiomatically unfamiliar to him and to develop his ability to hear the music written on the page. He wrote out little pieces of his own containing jokes, musical barbarisms, satires of famous composers, and takeoffs of popular music, and was inevitably delighted at Claude's relish in playing these. The boy was spookily sophisticated in this regard and would sometimes laugh so hard, so explosively, he would have to stop playing. He begged Weisfeld for more of these, and copied them out in his laborious child's hand to take home. (It was a quiet, slightly guilty pleasure for Weisfeld to see the boy's notation evolve away from the attempt to imitate printed music toward an echo of Weisfeld's own handwriting.)

As Claude struggled through a not particularly difficult piece of Beethoven, Weisfeld pondered once again the surprising fact that sight-reading was hard for the boy, and progress slower than average. His own dead daughter had moved twice as fast at a younger age. It was puzzling.

"That's a dotted half note," he broke in. "Why are you holding it so long?"

"I'm sorry."

"You do that a lot, you know. Hold on, or interrupt the flow."

The boy looked down at his lap.

"Are you aware of it?"

"I guess so." He paused. "But usually it's after. I mean it's after, so it's too late."

Weisfeld stroked his mustache. "After what?"

"After . . ." He stared out over the piano. "After I hear the sound."

Weisfeld nodded and remained silent.

"I can't hear the chords that fast," Claude said. "If it's just notes one after another like the melody or something it's okay, but the chords, they're all so different, they sound so different it's like, it's like . . ."

Again Weisfeld nodded. "Interesting. Go on, please. Try to tell me." He felt the boy's anxiety clearly, like a scent in the air, but something told him to press a bit. Weisfeld had no illusions about what he considered to be his limits as a teacher. He was simply prepping the child, getting him ready for others who would deal with higher matters — interpretation, technique, inner voices, dynamics, and all the rest — and sight-reading was a major part of that prepping. The important teachers would never take him on without it. As well, Weisfeld was truly curious.

The boy puffed his cheeks, blew out the air, and suddenly struck a chord from the Beethoven. He let it ring for a second and then talked over it.

"See? It's moving." His hands immobile on the keys, he twisted to look at Weisfeld. "Hear it moving?"

"Yes."

Claude played another, more complicated chord. "And this one." He let it ring. "It moves more. It's moving a lot. You know what I mean? Inside and outside all moving around."

"I understand."

"So I guess I want to hear that before I let it go."

"This is a great help," Weisfeld said. "There are ways we can approach this."

"What is that?" the boy asked. "Why does it do that?"

Weisfeld got off the stool and began to pace back and forth. He looked around the crowded basement. "Well, we'll have to get a blackboard down here." He moved to the piano, cleared off the sheet music, and raised the lid. As he fixed the wooden rod to hold it up he asked, "How are you with numbers? Have you done much arithmetic at school?"

"Sure," Claude said quickly, eager to return to the question of the chords. "I hear the sound, and then I hear stuff inside, like different notes coming and going."

"Come over here and stand by the strings."

The boy obeyed and Weisfeld went to the keyboard.

"I'm going to play a chord," he said. "Stick your head in there and listen."

The chord was played. Weisfeld kept the sustain pedal depressed. As the sound echoed Weisfeld said, "Now the soft sounds you hear, is this one of them?" Very gently he pressed a note higher on the keyboard.

"Yes, yes!"

"Now come over here." When the boy could see the keyboard Weisfeld replayed the chord, and then the high note.

"It isn't in the chord," the boy said with wonder. "The high note isn't in the chord."

"Exactly."

"So what do I, how come it, what is it —"

"Harmonics," Weisfeld said. "Overtones. It's quite logical, nothing weird. But we have a great deal of work to do for you to understand how it works. It may take some time."

"You can't tell me now?" Claude played the magic high note several times, as if the tip of his finger could somehow give him the information.

"We have to start from the ground up. You must be patient," Weisfeld said.

She was sitting in the chair staring up at the fan-shaped window when he came home from shining shoes and eating corned beef hash at the cafeteria. The faucet in the kitchenette dripped at long, regular intervals.

"They're taking me to Washington," she said in a flat voice.

"Why?"

"I'm not sure. I'm not supposed to worry. I'll be in a nice hotel. They'll give me twenty dollars a day."

"That's good."

She sighed and shifted her weight. "Some meetings or hearings or something. They don't tell me much. They say all I have to do is watch."

"Watch what?"

"I don't know. They're probably lying."

Claude didn't know what to make of this remark. In the movies — and he went now whenever he could — the G-men were clearly good and never lied. The authorities were a benevolent force. Maybe she was drinking again, but he couldn't smell it and there weren't any bottles. He had seen Agent Burdick now several times, and he didn't think the man was a liar. He liked Burdick.

"I'll be gone a few days," she said.

"Okay." He went to his room.

He lay down on the cot and stared at the ceiling. She was in some kind of trouble. For the first time he began to put things together in a vague sort of way. The newspapers talked about Communism, the Red Menace, Russia, Stalin, spies, and something called "fellow travelers" (the precise meaning of which was unknown to him, but he knew it wasn't good). There was a whole lexicon — dupes, pinkos, radicals, agitators, intellectuals, subversives, cell members, bolsheviks, and so on — used in what he understood to be a description of a great contest going on between the forces of good and the forces of evil. (He had first learned to scan for some of these words when he'd read about Eisler.) But it was the very enormity and grandeur of this struggle, like battles in some mythical context, that kept him from ever connecting it with his mother. The idea seemed ludicrous on its face. Nevertheless, he began to entertain the notion that somehow a mistake had been made. He sat up and was about to go in and talk to her, but he stopped himself, realizing that he didn't really know what to ask or how to begin. Knowing, as well, she would volunteer nothing.

Some instinct kept him from saying anything to Mr. Weisfeld. It was the same impulse he'd felt when Weisfeld had shown up at the door — not to let him in, not to let him see — although on that occasion things had turned out well.

She was away for a week, longer than expected, but Claude barely noticed. He could almost believe he had forgotten about her as he kept to his routines. At night he contemplated the implications of harmonics at the kitchenette counter, making diagrams and fiddling with numbers.

It had been, at first, a distinct shock to learn that the beautiful and reassuring orderliness of the keyboard and of the harmony he had thus far learned was impure, a compromise with nature. Tempering seemed like tampering. If A was 440 vibrations per second, and an octave above was 880, wasn't that a clear sign? Weisfeld had gone to the blackboard to explicate, checking back to see if Claude had understood each model before he erased it and went on to draw another.

Over a number of sessions Claude paid full but edgy attention, unconsciously resisting the whole idea.

"So you mean even though a half tone is called a half tone, it isn't necessarily half of the whole tone?"

"Exactly," Weisfeld said. "Not in natural tuning. The whole tones can be different too, compared to tempered."

"So instead of letting the mistake happen all at once, you sort of spread it out over everything?" Slightly grudging acceptance.

"Yes. That's a good way to put it." He stroked his mustache, getting chalk on it. "I don't know if I'd use the word 'mistake,' but I know what you mean."

But then one afternoon it all came together. Weisfeld had drawn two diagrams, a circle and a spiral, corresponding to tempered and natural tuning. He filled in the sharps and flats, double sharps and double flats, checked the letters, and stepped back. For several moments there was silence as they stared at the board.

"You see?" Weisfeld indicated the circle. "This really does make it a circle. Everything comes back. Go up the sharps in the cycle of fifths and you get back. Go the other way with the flats in the cycle of fourths and you get back. You can go around and around."

"That's wonderful," Claude said, relishing the neat, closed beauty of it. "I get it. They *had* to do it."

"Hmmm." Weisfeld was absorbed in the board. After a moment he tapped the spiral. "And this is worth thinking about, worth remembering. As you go around the sharps, the note is sharper than the starting point. Or go twelve times with the flats, and the note would sound too low to us. So in a sense the actual nature of the scales changes as you move." He stepped back from the board. "Worth remembering, philosophically speaking." He spread his arms. "An infinite number of scales in nature." He brought his hands in, palms facing each other as if he were holding an invisible loaf of bread. "And we work in this little area. This part of the spectrum."

When she came home she started drinking again, flushed and angry in her chair, rambling on until all hours. She was incapable of staying on a single subject for more than a few minutes, veering off into the past or into a discourse on some public figure, or on the working class, but eventually he put together what had happened in Washington, D.C.

At first they had put her in the waiting room of a small office. She had only to sit on the couch and read magazines. Day after day, people were brought through the door, past the couch, and into the interior office. She could hear voices droning. Some of the people looked at her when they emerged. She recognized only a few, but gave no sign to them or anyone else.

Then she was moved to a large public room where hearings were going on. Microphones, photographers, spectators, seated and lining the walls. She was placed in the front row of a special side section in such a way as to be visible to anyone at the witness table. Once again, all she was asked to do was to sit and remain silent. Then one night she'd had a few beers, and without telling anyone, went to the station and caught the train to New York.

"They can all go fuck themselves," she said from the chair, raising bourbon in an ironic toast. "The feds, the finks, and the noble assholes with their precious honor — they can all go fuck themselves."

The next day she received a letter by certified mail telling her that her hack license had been suspended for sixty days, effective immediately. She made Claude come with her to the Hack Bureau. They took the subway downtown, rocking on the straw seats in the silent roar. Claude watched the strap loops swinging back and forth and counted the stations flashing by.

The Hack Bureau was set in the corner of a huge municipal building. Under tall, narrow, grimy windows, people moved along the perimeter, stopping or lining up at grilled windows and doors leading to the interior and a maze of offices and cubicles. The high, angling light in the smoky air created a sepulchral mood. Claude's mother approached the appropriate grill and handed over the certified letter.

"Who do I see about this?"

The clerk, an elderly bird-like woman with pronounced wattles and thick glasses, examined the paper.

"It's a suspension." She looked up. "This is you? You're a driver?"

"Yes, it's me. Now who do I see?"

"Goodness." She looked at Claude and then back at Emma. "Well, you better wait. Over there." She turned and summoned another clerk, handed her the paper, and muttered something.

Claude and his mother found places on a long wooden bench. A constant flow of people moving in both directions passed before them, many of them clutching papers or forms of one kind or another. Some stopped to read with puzzled faces before they turned around to retrace their steps. Every now and then a cop would go by. Two old women sat beside them on the bench. After an hour Emma went up to the window again, and then returned. One of the old women ate an apple. Claude was both fascinated and repulsed by the stray white hairs on her chin.

It was another hour before the clerk beckoned them forward from behind the grill with an index finger. She disappeared for a moment and then opened a door and beckoned them again. Claude and his mother entered the enormous interior in which it seemed a hundred telephones were ringing at once in a continuous unsynchronized sheet of sound punctuated by typewriters clacking, voices shouting, and doors slamming. The bird-like woman led them this way and that, past a low gate to a cubicle and a pudgy, red-cheeked young man in a white shirt and checked necktie.

"Mr. Simpson," said the clerk, and withdrew.

Simpson shuffled through the papers on his desk and found the certified letter. Emma sat down in front of him while Claude stayed to the rear by the low gate. Simpson studied the document on both sides, reached for a file which he perused for several minutes, and finally looked up.

"I can't go sixty days," Emma said. "I've got a kid to feed." She swept an arm to indicate the boy.

Once again Claude felt a stir of admiration at the brazenness of her lies. He had been feeding himself for quite some time. He had bought the sneakers on his feet at Thom McAn with his own money.

"A hardship," said Simpson. "I can certainly appreciate that." He spoke in a precise, fluty voice.

"I never heard of anybody getting sixty days," she said.

He took a small pamphlet from his drawer and slipped it forward across the surface of the desk with two fingers. She looked down at it but didn't pick it up.

"It's quite within the powers of the —"

"I didn't do anything," she said.

Simpson's face betrayed a hint of irritation — a minuscule tightening at the corners of his mouth. He turned the letter over and tapped the back. "Code G is checked. Transporting a passenger with the flag up."

"I never do that. Not ever. Not once in all these years."

He consulted the file, holding it in such a way that she could not see what he was reading. He flipped several pages. "It *is* surprising. You have a spotless record heretofore. Not even a moving violation. Remarkable." He sighed. "Nevertheless, an inspector saw you on the Seventy-ninth Street transverse with the flag up and a passenger in the rear on the second of July at four-fifteen in the afternoon."

She leaned forward. "Let me see that. What inspector? It's a flat lie, goddamn it."

He tilted the file to his chest. "The identity of the inspector is privileged information."

"I want him to say that to my face!"

"My hands are tied, Mrs. Rawlings, I'm sorry. And as you may have noticed, there are additional boxes checked. Box A, for shortchanging in an amount in excess of five dollars. Box K, inappropriate attire. Box M, disrespectful attitude towards the customer with the use of foul language. These are from members of the general public."

"This is horseshit," she whispered. "This is all made up, cooked up."

"There are procedures for appeal," he offered, raising his head and holding her eye.

"How? What?"

"Fill out form 1219-ws, submit it to the bureau, and a hearing will be held. You are entitled to counsel, and you may present witnesses on your behalf."

"And how long will that take?"

He adjusted his tie. "Well, of course, I don't know how long it will take you to prepare your —"

"No, no," she interrupted. "I mean, how long before the Hack Bureau holds the hearing?"

He reached into his desk again, withdrew a small book, leafed through it, ran his finger down a page, and said, "Ninety days." Was that an infinitesimal smile on his bland face? "They have up to ninety days. Of course, it might actually take less."

"Ninety days to act on a sixty-day suspension?"

"Yes, I know. The rules sometimes seem —"

"You call that fair?" she cried, her voice rising.

"I don't call it anything, Mrs. Rawlings."

"Anonymous accusers? You call that fair? How am I supposed to defend myself?" She slapped her thick hand on the desk.

He looked at her hand and then went back to the file, slowly leafing through.

"Why?" she asked. "Why would I leave the flag up? It's my cab. I own the medallion. Am I supposed to be stealing from myself?"

"Perhaps you simply forgot. But the rules are the rules."

She made a little hissing sound through her teeth. Claude edged a bit closer to the gate. After several moments of silence she got up. She was approaching Claude when Mr. Simpson spoke.

"There is something here in your file . . ."

She froze, looking directly at Claude.

"A memo," he went on. "In the event of trouble you are to call a Mr. Burdick?"

And now she seemed to be looking through Claude. He watched a red flush climb up her neck to her face. Her upper lip pulled away from her teeth. She whirled.

Simpson was momentarily paralyzed as she rushed forward. By the time he raised his hands it was too late. She had bent over the desk to grab the top of his trousers with one hand and the knot of his checked necktie with the other. She lifted him in the air and, with his head firmly grasped in her armpit, swept the desk with the lower part of his body, sending files, papers, pencils, paper clips, trays, telephone, and a coffee cup scattering in all directions.

Simpson began to scream, his arms first flopping around her big body, then trying to hang on.

One after another, two policemen came through the gate, just in time to see her throw Simpson through the air against the wall of the cubicle. There was a snapping sound and the wall, as Simpson slid downward, began to fall back to a forty-five-degree angle. The startled faces of two women in the next cubicle were revealed as they backed away.

The cops came at her from two sides, one tackling her and the other trying for a headlock. She tottered but managed to grab the second cop by the shoulder and twist him around so that he landed on the desk. He stood up and jumped down on her, his full weight on her shoulders. They fell to the floor with a heavy thump. A third cop appeared, pulling out a set of handcuffs as the cop who had jumped pressed his knees into Emma's neck. Simpson began to crawl toward the gate. Except for grunting and thumping, the scene was played out in silence.

When Claude saw the first handcuff snapped into place he edged sideways, backed through the gate as the observers gathered there, and ran away, zipping through the maze until he found a door to the outside corridor and, eventually, the street.

·   ·   ·

Mr. Burdick brought her home a couple of days later. It was mid-morning and he passed Claude a donut from a paper bag. He gave Emma a container of coffee. "Well, I'm glad this all worked out," he said. "Sorry you had to spend two nights in there."

"In where?" Claude asked.

His mother looked at him. "In jail is where he means."

"The thing is, Mrs. Rawlings, the clerk had a separated shoulder." Burdick sipped his coffee. Suddenly he laughed. "He was unprepared for the perils of civil service, I would say. Definitely caught by surprise. But he finally listened to reason. Charges dropped."

"Did you talk to him?" she asked.

"No. The people from Washington."

"The FBI?"

Burdick shook his head. He put his container of coffee on the table, sat down, rested his elbows on his knees, and folded his hands. "I know you haven't asked my advice, Mrs. Rawlings, and even though I'm just a messenger boy in all this, I hope you'll give it some thought." He spoke in firm, quiet tones, looking straight at her. "Don't fool with these people. They are powerful. They have their own investigators, their own files, their own sources, and you just can't take the risk of second guessing them. Between you, me, and the lamppost, I don't care for their methods, but they are a fact of life. They can crush people. They do it every day."

"What are you saying?" She was surprised.

"I'm saying they're dangerous."

"So you're not with them?" Claude broke in.

"They do stuff like this and they just get away with it?" She shook her head slowly.

"This is nothing." Burdick got up and went to the door. "At least they lifted the suspension. You can go to work. Next time they won't do that." He opened the door, ducked his head, and was gone.

"Sight-reading," Weisfeld had said, "is not a big deal. Mechanical. Eye-hand coordination. It requires no thought, no emotion, no sensitivity. It is like typing. Like typing on a typewriter. A monkey practically could do it. A chimpanzee." He had shaken his head. "So here's what we're going to do. We're going to separate things. Don't listen, just play. Listening you can do later. We can put it back together later, you see what I mean?"

"I think so," Claude had said.

"Don't get involved is what I'm saying. Just play whatever it is and don't think about it."

"Even if it's —"

"Yes! Yes!" Weisfeld interrupted. "Particularly if it's. Especially if it's, because that's when you'll start to get involved. Play like a machine. Don't stop, don't think, and don't feel. Just play. Play the notes."

"Really?"

Weisfeld had nodded.

"It doesn't sound like fun."

"Fun will only take you so far." He paused, stroking his mustache. "There are deeper pleasures than fun. Fun is good, it helps things, helps to forget things. But it isn't everything."

Claude had gone to work, and for the first few months his inability to make his hands the slaves of his eyes — exclusively of his eyes — made for slow going and flares of temper. At the white piano in his room he would explode in frustration, sweep the music aside, and play boogie-woogie until his hands ached. He would stand at the keyboard and pound away, lost in sound and the beat. Then he'd go out, walk around the block, and come back to try again.

One day, on a whim, he'd turned on the radio, tuned to a news program, left the volume up, and sat down to sight-read an early section from Bach's *Art of Fugue*. Almost immediately he realized he'd made a valuable discovery. He was able to divert much of his ear to the radio, with enough left over to monitor the piano. With his attention thus fragmented, it was much easier to follow Weisfeld's instructions. His progress in sight-reading accelerated rapidly, and after another six months he only rarely used the radio.

The critical age, as far as the movie theater people were concerned, was twelve. At twelve you were supposed to pay full price for your ticket, but you no longer had to sit in the children's section. This policy was common to the theaters clustered on Eighty-sixth Street: the RKO, Loew's Orpheum, Loew's Eighty-sixth Street, and the Grande (which showed foreign films and didn't really have a children's section). Claude exploited his small size and baby face at the box office, but once inside he sat wherever he wanted. The constant chatter and restlessness of the children's section was no longer tolerable, since the whole point was to find some quiet seat in the dark and sink completely and utterly into the dream.

He forgot himself as he watched the other worlds, entering them not as a character but as elements of those worlds — the scrublands through which the wagons moved, the ocean bearing up the pirate ships, the sunlight on the side of a white house. He became the air, the sky, the light in which the dramas occurred. He was himself without boundaries as he watched the people in the films. Bodiless in the dark cathedral, he absorbed the parables of good and evil that linked the movies together — a kind of grand arc through cowboys, gangsters, cops, moms and dads, factories, armies, lovers, thieves, angels, cities and towns, animals, kings and queens, cab drivers, gamblers, priests, detectives, the devil (Claude Rains: "What in my domain is that?" The boy the only person in the theater to laugh), beauties, beasts, comics, and ghosts. It was nothing less than the infinite story of life, and he attended.

If he was nothing, or almost nothing, with no idea of where he had come from or where he was going, why he was living or what he was supposed to be doing (the piano only an elusive hint), and if, further, he was buffeted by forces he could not name but which were loneliness, sadness, longing, anger, fear, and spiritual nausea, would he not deeply attend the infinite story of life? Would he not pay the fucking twenty-five cents to get into the cathedral and see the light?

6

HIS FINGERS no longer carried the stain of shoe polish. He no longer collected bottles, although he sometimes went over to the building on Park Avenue for a game of gin with Al. Now he wore a white shirt and tie, black Florsheim shoes, and worked in the music store. Weisfeld paid him by the hour, and it was enough for food, the movies, and incidental expenses.

They sat side by side on stools behind the main counter. Weisfeld read a German newspaper, folding it neatly in thirds as people did in the subway. Claude, having swept up, was polishing a Cohn trumpet from the front window with a soft cloth.

"Take out the valves," Weisfeld said.

Claude, handling the instrument gingerly, stared down at it.

"Under the keys," Weisfeld said. "Unscrew the rings and lift them out."

Claude did so, placing each piece on the glass. The valves were about three inches long, gleaming with a faint sheen of fine oil. Three steel tubes with holes at irregular intervals. Each tube made a little click so he'd know which went where when he'd put them back.

"Brass instruments are really all the same." Weisfeld put down the paper. "From the mouthpiece, a flow of vibrating air. It goes through the tube" — he traced the curved lines with his finger — "and comes out the horn. Two factors influence the pitch. How hard you blow, which allows you to climb the overtone series, and how long the tube is, which allows you to break it down into tones and half tones. Every brass instrument works that way." While Claude looked at the trumpet, Weisfeld got off the stool and took an old, somewhat battered trombone off the wall. He extended the slide fully, blew a low note, and then without moving the slide blew a note an octave higher, and then a fourth higher than that. "You see? That's by blowing. How am I going to get the notes in between?"

"The length?"

"Correct. If I pull up the slide, what am I doing to the length?"

"Shorter. It makes the tube shorter."

"Thus higher." He began with the slide fully extended, blew, pulled the slide in bit by bit and played a major scale. Then he pushed the slide out without stopping and smeared down to the original note. Claude laughed. Weisfeld put the trombone back. "So," he said over his shoulder, "how does the trumpet work? Look at it carefully."

Claude placed the instrument on the glass, just below the valves. He traced the tubing with his eyes. He turned the valves and looked at the holes. After half a minute or so he said, "It must be . . . I think . . ."

"Yes? What?"

"When you press the key, then the air can go through different holes, and then through a different tube. It looks like three different tubes. This little one here, then this one, and this one. It's those holes. They must line up like that inside."

"Stick your finger inside and see if they do."

The boy did so. "That's it!" he said. "That's nifty."

"It's good to know these things," Weisfeld said. "All instruments are similar. A long string on the piano, a long column of air on a wind instrument. Vibrations. Overtones. Stops. Keys. Fingerboards. All alike." He swept his arm to indicate the whole store. "All the instruments in this room are variations on a single idea. Now use a little oil wherever you touched the metal."

Claude reassembled the trumpet and laid it in the felt depressions of its case. He carried it back to the front window and placed it, lid open, for display. As he straightened up he saw a black limousine pull up in front of the shop. The rear door opened and a girl stepped out, her black patent-leather shoes catching the sun, the buttons of her blue coat gleaming like coins. As she raised her head he felt a shock. (Not as strong as, but curiously similar to, the sensation he'd felt once on the Madison Avenue bus when he'd looked up from his book to see a

soldier with a badly scarred face sitting across from him.) Black hair,
fair skin with a hint of pink over the cheekbones, large eyes, the nose
and mouth exquisite, as if carved from marble.

Now he could see what surely must be her mother trailing on behind, both of them making for the shop, and he began to back up. By
the time the bell tinkled he had ducked behind a bookcase to retreat to
the back of the room. He fussed with some sheet music without knowing what he was doing.

"Mrs. Fisk," he heard Weisfeld say. "A pleasure to see you again.
How can I help you?"

He heard the soft murmur of voices, and then Weisfeld called out.
"Claude? Could you bring a chair for Mrs. Fisk, please?"

Weisfeld had moved from behind the counter and stood in the aisle
beside the woman. The girl was out of sight, somewhere in the front of
the store. Claude unfolded the wooden chair. Weisfeld took out a
handkerchief and flicked the seat twice. She sat down, Weisfeld's hand
under her elbow, and the boy suddenly realized something was wrong
with her. A faint, continuous tremor affected the upper half of her
body — her hands, arms, and head were vibrating slowly. She was
extremely thin, her face handsome but pallid, the lips compressed and
slightly twisted. Her eyes, which rested on him briefly, burned with
such intensity he felt himself start as if she had touched him.

"I'll see the flute," she said, and Weisfeld gave a little bow.

Claude retreated to the back and sat down at the Steinway, his hands
clasped between his knees. When he heard a faint rustle behind him he
leaned forward and began going through sheet music as if looking for
something. In a flash of blue, the girl was standing next to him,
casually turning the display carousel of show tunes and popular music.
No more than two feet away, she did not even glance at him. He
remained motionless, staring at the lid of the piano, aware now of a
faint scent, a mysterious, warm perfume like nothing he could name.
His hands rested on the music stand. The carousel creaked every now
and then.

She lifted some music and held it out, still without looking at him.
"Play this." He saw her neck, the smooth, curved black wing of hair
just below her jaw, her lips, the sharper curve of her eyelashes. He took
the music, put it on the piano, and began to play. E-flat minor. A ballad
called "Tenderly." As he approached the second ending, she had already chosen something else.

"An insipid piece of music," she said when he'd finished. Her voice was light, not yet fully mature, with diction clear as crystal. "This one."

As he closed his hand on the music she looked at him briefly, without expression. She had given him a piece called "Cow Cow Boogie." He tore through it happily, and played it a second time, adding some decorative figures of his own.

"Barbaric," she said.

The third tune was "Love for Sale," by Cole Porter, in a fairly complicated arrangement. He almost stopped playing at the shock of her nearness when she bent over his left shoulder and extended her arm to turn the page.

"I'll take that," she said when he'd finished. He felt a ridiculous thrill of pleasure that he had finally pleased her. She walked away as abruptly as she had arrived. He folded the music and followed her to the counter. Mrs. Fisk was writing a check on her lap. Claude handed the music to Weisfeld.

"Can he sight-read Mozart?" Mrs. Fisk asked.

"Yes," Weisfeld said.

"Catherine," she said, "take the flute, please."

The girl received the thin black case from Weisfeld. At a sign from him, Claude moved forward to assist Mrs. Fisk as she rose from the chair, but she did not give him her arm, so he simply hovered there. Weisfeld escorted them to the front of the shop, the bell tinkled, and they were gone.

"Who are they?"

"Old customers. Good customers," Weisfeld said. "Rich customers. She wants Catherine to try the flute, so what does she get her? A Cohn, a Selmer? No. She gets her a hundred-year-old solid-silver Zabretti for sixteen hundred dollars."

"What?" Claude was astonished.

Weisfeld waved the check. "She just bought the most expensive instrument in our inventory." He rang open the cash register and slipped the check under the front drawer. "In fact, she got a good price."

"Can she play? Catherine?"

Weisfeld shrugged. "She started on recorders years ago. Mrs. Fisk and the son play violins. I don't know how many instruments I've sold that family."

"Where do they live?"

Weisfeld looked at him quickly. "She's very pretty, isn't she, that girl," he said, as if thinking aloud. "They live on Fifth Avenue. A mansion. Mrs. Fisk is the daughter of Senator Barnes."

"What's wrong with her? The way she shakes like that?"

"It's a shame. She and her sister were famous beauties. They were in the social columns all the time back when I first came over. A very important family."

Claude detected the slightest touch of irony in his tone, but didn't know what to make of it.

"When we close up," Weisfeld said, "I'll take you to dinner at the Rathskeller. A little celebration."

"Can I have a Wiener schnitzel?"

"Absolutely."

Ever since the gold stars in *The Blue Book for Beginners*, Claude had considered Mr. Weisfeld his teacher, his real teacher, the teacher behind all the other teachers with whom, one after another, he had studied. Weisfeld, with the approval of Mr. Larkin, the lawyer, had sent him to various people, and while Weisfeld did not discuss matters of pedagogy with the boy, seemed in fact almost laconic about what the teachers were asking Claude to do, he nevertheless monitored the boy's progress, coming down to the basement once or twice a week to sit on a folding chair and listen. And it was Weisfeld who decided, with only the minimum of discussion with Claude, when it was time to leave one teacher and get another. The effect of this was to create a certain distance between the boy and those instructing him. In varying degrees, he was not so much interested in pleasing them as he was in pleasing Weisfeld through them.

The first, when Claude had been quite young, was Professor Menti, a slender man with a large nose, heavy lips, and a high, prematurely balding forehead. Claude took the Eighty-sixth Street crosstown bus to Riverside Drive and then walked downtown to Menti's sparsely furnished apartment on the ground floor of an old subdivided townhouse. The man always opened the door in a daze of absent-mindedness, taking a moment or two to recognize his pupil, finally ushering him into the dim interior and the Steinway. There he would place a special raised seat on the piano bench, forcing Claude to play from a much higher position than he was used to.

They had started with a C major scale in the right hand.

"So," Menti had said. "Everything is wrong." He spoke softly, with an Italian accent and a twinge of sadness. "Get ready to do it again. I will show you."

Claude placed his hand on the keys, and Menti reached into the pocket of his tattered dressing gown and withdrew a penny, which he placed on the back of the boy's hand. He nodded, and Claude began the scale. Middle C with the thumb, D with the index finger, E with the third finger, and then, as he passed his thumb under his palm toward F, the coin fell off his hand.

"*Eccolà,*" whispered Menti.

Claude had expected the coin to fall, although he'd tried to keep it there. He had no idea why it mattered one way or the other, but he didn't ask, feeling that it might be impertinent. Throughout his time with Professor Menti he simply did what he was told.

"Hold your hand like so." The wrist up, the hand arched, the last joint of the fingers pointing straight down. "Play the keys like so." Lift the finger high, the rest of the hand motionless, and strike straight down, pressing into the key.

It felt odd to the boy. It was as if each finger existed independently, each finger isolated, like wooden soldiers hopping up and down one after the other. For the first few weeks he could not play this way for more than five minutes without a break. His hands and wrists would grow increasingly tight and stiff, subordinated as they were to the fingers. As he grew tired, he would unconsciously move his wrists, and even his arms.

One day Menti brought out an odd-looking contraption — two long metal bars with springs, screws, and plates at each end. He fastened it to the Steinway so that the rods hung horizontally above and in front of the keyboard.

"Put your wrists on the lower bar," Menti said.

The boy obeyed.

Menti knelt down, glanced at the boy's hands, gauged distances, and made a few adjustments to the rods.

"Play the C major scale. Both hands. Contrary motion."

Claude did so, sliding his wrists across the rod without losing contact, his fingers going up and down like pistons.

"Now the B-flat major scale."

This time his wrists lost contact with the rod. Menti, still kneeling, noticed it immediately.

"Aha!" he said, lowering the second bar over the top of the boy's wrists. It was now impossible for Claude to raise, lower, or twist his wrists. He could only slide them sideways.

"This," Menti said, "is how you will practice scales. Two hours a day. Take it with you and put it on your piano. All keys."

Claude had fitted the device, which was adjustable, to the small white piano in his room, and practiced scales as directed, playing through pain. Menti also gave him various short exercises — trills, mordants, arpeggios, turns, and phrases — to play over and over again, fifty times, a hundred times. Menti acknowledged that exercises became boring quite rapidly, and advised him to place a book or a magazine on the piano and read while his fingers worked. Claude preferred to listen, or to daydream.

Once, while Claude was doing an exercise on the Bechstein in the basement of the music store, Weisfeld had come down on some errand and stopped. "What is that?"

"You have to hold five notes down," Claude explained, "and keep them down while you play one after the other without moving your hand." He demonstrated, playing C D E F G, C# D# E# F# G#, and then D E F# G A. "It's hard."

"Particularly the fourth finger, hmm?" Weisfeld had gone back upstairs without further comment.

It was quite a while before Claude was allowed to spend much time on any actual music. Professor Menti was aware that the boy was able to play more advanced pieces than he was assigned, and the boy was aware that Menti kept the music simple so that he shouldn't slip back into using his wrists and his arms. Menti said little about interpretation, and it was understood that technique was paramount. In a sense, it was as if the music were only an opportunity to test the skills developed through hundreds of hours of scales and exercises.

Claude played easy pieces by Bach, Couperin, and Mozart. Toward the end he committed to memory Clementi's Sonata, op. 2, and Mozart's Sonata in D Major, no. 8. Playing for Menti, he learned to mask any emotion in his face, to sit still, and to concentrate on clean execution. But in the basement of the music store he would play another way, closing his eyes the better to feel the wash of colors, forgetting his hands, himself, listening to the structures and interweaving lines. He played right through mistakes, eager to feel the kind of exaltation that could rise in him when he sensed the music taking over — an emotion so intense he would sometimes feel tears in his eyes.

He was relieved when Weisfeld decided it was time for him to leave

Menti. The incessant drills, the dark apartment which had seemed to grow darker with the passage of time, the bitter-almond scent of Menti in his dressing gown — all this he was glad to leave behind.

"I think it's time for *The Well-Tempered Clavier*," Weisfeld had said. "For that, you'll see Herr Sturm. He lives in the neighborhood."

Herr Sturm was a short man with a large, square head, a fierce expression Claude found unsettling (as if the man were forever threatening to break into a rage), and the habit of pacing as he talked, making violent gestures with his arms, bobbing and weaving.

"Do you know what this is?" he asked, pressing Book One of *The Well-Tempered* to the boy's chest.

"Well, I've played a, I've looked at some of the . . ." Claude covered the score with his hands.

"Preludes and fugues in all keys!" Herr Sturm cried. "All keys! Can you play in all keys?"

"I guess, well maybe I don't know, but I —"

"Sit! Sit! Play me something. Play anything."

Claude, aged ten at the time, had been more than a little nervous in the presence of this electric man, although Weisfeld had warned him ("He shouts, he tears his hair, he jumps up and down, but it doesn't mean anything, he can't help it"), but Claude instantly decided to play Bach's Invention VII to show off the various trills and mordants he loved to execute.

Herr Sturm wandered around the room, grasping his hands in front of his belly, throwing them up on the beat, bending his knees, cocking his head, turning back and forth in constant motion.

"Good, good," he said when it was over. He shuffled through a mass of music stuffed into a bookshelf and pulled out a folio. He turned the pages so violently Claude thought they would surely rip. "Maybe dry a little bit, yes? Not cold, but maybe chilly a little bit, yes?" He came to Claude's shoulder and pointed his thick, hairy finger at the music. "Here. At bar eleven and twelve, where this business starts — da-da da-da da-da da-da da-dum, dah — you didn't sound confident. You just played it to get through it."

Even though the notes had been played correctly, Herr Sturm had somehow heard that Claude hadn't really felt the figure, and the boy was thrilled at this magic. Menti could never have done it. "It's the sixteenth note before the bar line, I think," the boy said.

"No. It's the trill before that. Don't think about the trill. Make the sixteenth note fit the one in your left hand. Think about that. Now try it."

Claude did.

"Good. Practice that at home. And then here — this B pedal point down here, tied through these measures. Press it hard. I don't mean play it loud, I mean press it hard after you've played it. Make it sustain. Squeeze it. Keep your fingers on the keys and use your *wrists* for the phrasing. Supple wrists!" He swung his arm and gave the side of the piano a tremendous slap, a cracking, open-handed blow. "This is a piano, not a harpsichord! Dig into it! Make it sing!"

Over the next few months Claude felt his memories of Menti fade away as he dealt with Sturm, who was sometimes scary but a great deal more fun. Walking into a lesson was sometimes like walking into a hurricane, but the boy began to realize he was being encouraged to play the way he most enjoyed it — with feeling. Scale work continued, and C. P. E. Bach and Cramer exercises, but no more than an hour a day. Sturm wanted him to spend most of his time on substantial pieces of great music.

"Work, work on this part here," he would say, and then turn the pages, "this section here, and the development here," turning more pages, "and then all of this which sounds like mud the way you play it. By Thursday, you hear?"

He would grab the J. S. Bach folio and hold it aloft. "Work, work! It's all in here. Everything is in here." He brought his big head down into the boy's face. "It's how I learned to play, and you must work even harder than I did."

"How come?"

"Well, for one reason, you're not as strong. I was strong. It helped."

Sometimes, at the end of a lesson, Herr Sturm would come up with a surprise. "Play these five notes in the bass," he said, leaning over to play a simple figure with his thick hand, "and improvise with your right hand."

"Improvise?"

"Yes. This is an instrument. Play the instrument. Make something up."

"But what's the theme?"

"There isn't any theme."

"But then how do I, where should the —"

"All right, all right," Sturm said impatiently. "The notes in the bass suggest perhaps a scale. More than one scale. Pick any of the scales. The theme, if you must cling to that idea, the theme is the notes of that scale in any order."

Claude stared down at the keyboard. "You're kidding." The idea felt exhilarating. He caught on rapidly, laughing at the surprising patterns his fingers seemed to find on their own.

"Fifteen or twenty minutes a day," Sturm instructed. "Real players know how to improvise."

But mostly Claude worked on *The Well-Tempered Clavier.* It took more than a year to get through Book One. He was two thirds of the way through Book Two when Herr Sturm went away to South America for an extensive tour.

"Finish" was all he said at the last lesson. "You can finish by yourself."

By this time the stiff wrists, motionless hands, and rigid forearms as dictated by Menti were completely out the window. All he retained from the Italian was finger strength, and what he had learned from Herr Sturm was how to use it to get inside Bach.

It had taken them six months to get everything they wanted from Emma Rawlings. She had signed affidavits, submitted to long and often mysterious interviews, revealed the names of every person she had ever met (that she could remember) at political gatherings and reading clubs, repeated every scrap of conversation she had overheard in the presence of Gerhardt Eisler, and consistently denied that she had ever been a member of the Communist Party. During this period she received one hundred dollars a week, in the mail, from the Committee for American Values — no member of which to her knowledge she had ever met — and was constantly threatened, by all her interrogators, with the possibility of being forced to testify in public proceedings. As it turned out, she was never used as a witness in a court of law or in congressional hearings. The money stopped coming, the requests for her presence ceased, and the whole matter appeared to be closed. The last person she saw was Burdick, who said, "It's over. Forget about it. You were lucky."

Claude, who was practicing five hours a day at the time, thought of little other than music and stayed in his room when he was home. Eventually he realized she was back to her old schedule, driving the cab, drinking at night, and littering the main room with newspapers and magazines. He also realized that she had reached a level of continuous, generalized anger deeper than anything he'd seen in her before.

"Look at this man," she said, holding a newspaper under his nose. "This creep. This corrupt, money-grubbing mackerel snapper."

Claude saw a man on a platform, head thrown back, one hand in the air, apparently giving a speech. "Who is he?"

"The mayor! The mayor! He gets his money from the gangsters, and the man is the mayor of New York City."

"La Guardia?" He snatched the name from memory.

"No, no," she said. "He was good, but he's long gone. Now we've got this piece of garbage." She threw down the paper. "La Guardia was honest, but he didn't leave anything. No party, no organization. Nothing but that Park Avenue fathead Newbold Morris. So the sharks took over again."

Claude watched her, her big face redder than usual as she stared up at the fan-shaped window, her eyes popping slightly, her mouth set in a hard line. As if sensing something, she turned. "What?"

"Nothing," he said.

But in fact strange thoughts had been going through his mind. Perhaps because he had paid so little attention for quite some time, it was a shock to look at her now, not as part of the general background of life in the basement apartment, but as a large, angry woman caught up in an ongoing harangue that seemed to feed on itself. What did all those names from the newspapers have to do with her? It occurred to him that she would always find things to be angry about, so what difference did it make what she said? He felt sorry for her, and it scared him.

At night she would sit on the floor with a large, bright pair of scissors and clip articles, scribble notes on loose-leaf paper, and slip it all into any one of half a dozen cardboard file boxes spread around her. She worked very fast, muttering to herself or sometimes speaking to an invisible companion. "See that? What did I tell you?" she would say, clipping furiously. In the morning there would be paper everywhere.

She bought a used typewriter at a pawn shop. "Everything has to be typed or they won't read it," she said. "Handwritten, they think you're just a nut."

"Who?"

"Everybody," she said. "All of them."

In a matter of weeks she had learned to type. At night, he would play the white piano in his room, and between pieces he could hear the staccato rattle of her machine through the closed door, the syncopated pings of the warning bell, the crash of the returning carriage.

Shortly after his thirteenth birthday, Claude had begun study with Mr. Fredericks. Awakened at five-thirty in the morning by the new Big Ben alarm clock Weisfeld had given him, the boy ate breakfast in the kitchenette, walked the still-dark streets to the subway, and took the downtown express to Grand Central. There he boarded a northbound train at six forty-five, read stories from the latest issue of *Astounding Tales,* "A Magazine of Science Fiction," and disembarked at the small station called Frank's Landing at seven-twenty.

Following a map drawn on the back of an envelope by Weisfeld, he walked through the village toward the Hudson River, feeling uneasy in the exotic surroundings. Hedges. Trees. Lawns. Wooden houses set back from the deserted streets. Nobody about but the milkman and a paperboy on a bicycle. In the unnatural hush he could hear the wind moving in the trees. It was like something from the movies.

Mr. Fredericks lived in a castle, an enormous turreted, crenelated edifice of stone looming over gatehouses, garage, and a semicircular driveway. The gravel crunched under Claude's feet as he approached the main entrance. He rang the bell and stood before the great oak doors.

After some time they opened, and an elderly black man looked out at him. "Master Rawlings?"

Confused by the honorific, which he had never heard before, he nevertheless nodded.

"Very good," the old man said. "Please follow me."

White marble floor. Twin curved stairways on either side. High above, a crystal chandelier. They walked forward through a padded door into a hallway, turned right along a wider, carpeted hallway, and stopped at another leather-padded door. The old man opened it and stepped aside. "If you would wait here in the library, Mr. Fredericks will be with you shortly."

Claude entered and the door was closed behind him. A pair of tall windows let in thick shafts of sunlight. Bookshelves rose to the ceiling on either side of a large fireplace, before which clustered a black leather couch, a wing chair, a loveseat, and a low table holding neat piles of books and music manuscripts. Claude sat on the edge of the loveseat.

The library was completely silent except for the infinitesimal ticking of the large porcelain clock on the mantel. The time was five minutes to eight. Half a dozen dark portraits of different men, all posed similarly and dressed in the fashions of earlier times, covered the far walls.

At precisely eight, when the tiny chimes from the clock began to sound, a pair of double doors at the end of the room swung open and a man entered. He was small — not a great deal taller than Claude — and slender, with a narrow head, curly hair, and a long chin. "Good morning," he said with a slight bow as Claude sprang to his feet. "Thank you for your punctuality. With me, things go by the clock." He went to the wing chair, sat down, crossed his legs, and looked at the boy for several moments in silence. "Sit down, please," he said at last. "May I call you Claude?"

"Yes. Sure."

"Good." His small thin hands hung in the air on either side of the armrests. He wore a blue blazer, white trousers, and highly polished black slippers. A light blue ascot was folded perfectly at his neck and a white handkerchief nestled in the cuff of his left sleeve. "You have been playing mostly Bach, I understand. Any Mozart?"

"Not very much. Hardly any. The D Major Sonata."

"That's good. A clean slate, as it were. What exercises?"

"Scales, arpeggios, thirds, sixths, and octaves." Claude could read very little in the man's slightly imperious face except a sense of self-possession that the boy found somehow reassuring. "C. P. E. Bach. Cramer."

Mr. Fredericks nodded and then raised an index finger without lifting his arm from the armrest. "No more than three hours of practice a day. From now on."

Claude liked to practice, and for a moment he considered saying so.

"Three hours of work with total concentration," Fredericks said, "will be sufficient. More than that can drag you down."

"Yes, sir." In the back of his mind he thought he could always play jazz if he wanted to keep on.

"Now." Fredericks rose smoothly. "Let's go in."

It was a long, bright room with large windows and a set of French doors along one side overlooking the Hudson River. A pair of concert grands stood side by side at the far end of the room. As Claude followed Fredericks across the thick carpeting, he felt the silence of the room pressing gently upon him. There were no background sounds of any kind — no humming machines, no hissing radiators, no creaking wood. It was as if the entire room were frozen under a spell. Fredericks sat at one piano and waved Claude to the other. There was music on Claude's, Bach's Invention VI in E Major. The stand was folded down on Fredericks's, and the lids of both instruments were propped fully open.

"Play the first section, please. Ignore the repeat."

Claude ran his eye over the twenty bars, which he knew well, placed his hands on the keys, took a breath, and began to play. Five or six bars in, Fredericks said, "Wait. Stop. Let me hear it not legato. See if you can play it non legato."

Claude thought about it for a minute and began again, concentrating on the value of the notes, unconsciously pulling his shoulders in and moving his head closer to the keys. He played with extreme care, almost holding his breath. As he pressed and released the last isolated bass note, he was afraid to look up.

"Good," said Fredericks. "You *connect* the notes. No one is entitled to use legato unless he can connect the notes without it. You understand?"

Claude nodded.

"Actually, it probably doesn't matter if you understand. You seem to do it naturally, which is best of all. Do you sing?"

"No."

"It's good to listen to singers for that. Only the best, of course."

Fredericks straightened his back, lifted his chin, and played the same piece. Claude had not known what to expect, and was momentarily confused when Fredericks played at perhaps half the volume the boy had done. It seemed at first too soft, and Claude wondered if this was some instructive trick, but then, very quickly, as the lines flowed, he heard the exquisite control with which Fredericks released the music into the air. It was eerie. The piano seemed to disappear and somehow the lines themselves filled the boy's consciousness, the architecture of the music lucid in every small detail, the whole statement sealed, floating, and folding into itself, and into silence. Claude ached at the beauty of it. He wanted to leave his body and go chase the music into whatever hyperspace had swallowed it. Fredericks turned his head and the boy stared into his eyes, motionless, breathless, as if staring could somehow bring the music back.

After some time the faintest smile appeared on Fredericks's lips. "You see?" he said. "Easily, easily . . ."

Claude tried to speak but could not. He felt a strange calmness far back in himself even as his brain raced with the implications of what had just occurred. He'd played those twenty bars hundreds of times, heard Menti, Sturm, and even Weisfeld play them, and yet he knew that just now he had heard and understood them completely for the first time. He felt on the brink of something, as if every atom in his body were undergoing some subtle change, some minute realignment, to prepare him for entrance into a new world. He felt alive.

"Now," said Fredericks, "shall we work?"

Going back to the city in the train, Claude sat by a window and stared at the sky. Telephone poles whipped by with metronomic precision, but he was barely aware of them. His head was filled with Fredericks's instructions. Play the black keys with the long fingers, consider refingering any manuscript that does not follow that principle. Maintain as straight a line as possible between elbow, wrist, finger, and key, move arms laterally along the keyboard. Keep a loose wrist and shift smoothly through hand positions, keep the legato going through one perfect hand position after another. Never turn the hand when the thumb goes under. (Menti!) Keep the hand gently arched at all times. These technical matters were clear, and Claude had already felt in his body, during the first session, what it was Fredericks was after, and the boy knew he could do it. But the matter of dynamics — of what soft was and what loud was and what everything in between was — seemed a great deal trickier. The boy realized that whatever else was going on in Fredericks's ability to make such magically pure music, dynamics was a crucial element, and Claude had no idea if his own fingers, or his ear, were up to it.

"There are degrees of forte, certainly," Fredericks had said, and banged out a two-handed chord in the middle register so loud it made Claude's cheeks vibrate. "As I'm sure the admirable Herr Sturm has demonstrated to you." He whipped the handkerchief from his cuff, coughed discreetly, and replaced it. "But consider this: the louder it gets, the less important are the degrees of separation. How useful is the difference between a triple forte and a quadruple forte, after all? Not much. And then, you can only hit the thing so hard before the strings start breaking. No, it's the other end that particularly deserves our attention. The quieter you play, the more important are the degrees of separation. The human ear can discern the differences between triple pianissimo and quadruple pianissimo quite easily. N'est-ce pas?"

"What?"

"Oh, forgive me. Miss Rockefeller used to be my eight o'clock, and we sometimes spoke French. The point is, you look at the manuscript and you see various degrees of pianissimo, but they are only the crudest sort of guide. For us" — and here he had raised a finger in the air again — "there are ten thousand degrees of pianissimo."

Sitting on the train, Claude worried about that. Had Fredericks been exaggerating to make a point, or had he meant it? If he was serious, Claude was going to have to learn to play the piano all over again.

The main room of the basement apartment began to fill up with files and bundles of newspapers. She would stack the newspapers — a month of the *Daily News,* the *Wall Street Journal,* the *Post,* the *Herald Tribune,* the *New York Times,* the *Brooklyn Eagle,* and half a dozen more she bought daily — tie them with string, and pile them against the walls. When wall space ran out she set the bales elsewhere, and eventually the room could be negotiated only through a pattern of interlocking paths. She worked at the couch, with the typewriter on the table, surrounded by file folders, papers, stamps, envelopes, letters, news clips, and various reports and official-looking documents. She no longer went straight to work in the morning, but waited for the mail delivery, sorting through everything before she left.

Mystified, Claude would examine the white and manila envelopes that arrived from the Office of the Mayor, the Board of Estimate, the Deputy Commissioner of Trade, the Municipal Workers' Union, the Board of Education, the Office of the City Attorney, the Assessor's Office, and on and on. Letters from committees, various organizations, city councilmen, and others. He understood that these were responses to communications of her own, but what could she possibly want from the Parks Department?

Dear Emma Rawlings,

In response to your letter of the fourteenth instant, all questions regarding the collection of trash in Central Park should be directed to the appropriate office of the Dept. of Sanitation.

The budget information for the Bronx Zoo may be found in the Annual Fiscal Report of the City of New York.

Sincerely yours,
Sheila Mahoney
Public Information
Parks Department

And why, when she had received this letter, had she crumpled it up and thrown it angrily into the kitchenette (from where he had later retrieved it)? "Bullshit! Bullshit!" she had cried. He didn't know what to make of it.

One morning in the castle, after a year of lessons, Claude played the Mozart B Minor Adagio he'd been working on for two weeks. Fredericks nodded. "Coming along, coming along." Then Fredericks played it himself, and the boy shook his head.

"What?" Fredericks said in mock alarm. "No good?"

"It's beautiful. I just wish my fingers could, I mean, when I try to control them to that extent I can feel it just so far and then I can't feel any further. Touch. I'm talking about touch. At a certain point I hit a wall."

"Good."

"What do you mean? It's awful. It feels awful. I can't do anything about it."

Fredericks rose from the piano. "Let's go into the library." He surprised the boy by gently taking his arm. "It's good," he said as they moved across the great bright room, "because very few players ever get to the point where they realize the wall is there."

The sudden physical intimacy made the boy blush. Fredericks was a fastidious man, and the gesture was so out of character it seemed to suggest that Claude had risen to some new and higher status. "Then there *is* a wall."

"Of course," said Fredericks. "For all of us."

In the library Claude stood by the French windows while Fredericks went to his desk. The boy glanced at the bright river and then saw some movement outside on the balcony below. A short, slender young woman with black hair, wearing a red bathrobe, walked to the railing and paused there. She raised her hand to her mouth and took a puff of a small, thin cigar. The blue smoke drifted over the stone railing.

"Come here," Fredericks said. "Stand here." He held something in his hand.

The boy walked over and faced him. He received a glass ball about the size of a peach pit attached to a string.

"Hold it like this." Fredericks also had a glass ball. He held the string between thumb and forefinger, the ball hanging motionless below. The boy did likewise. "You will find there is an attraction between these pieces of glass," Fredericks said. "Like magnetism, even though they are glass."

Fredericks reached out and pushed Claude's glass ball in such a way that it swung in a circle. "Do not move your hand or your fingers. Remain absolutely still and let the ball swing. All by itself."

Claude obeyed, watching the glass ball go around.

Then, very gently, Fredericks swung his own ball so that its circle came within two or three inches of the path of Claude's.

"Now keep still and watch."

When, after a moment, the orbits of the two pieces of glass brought them near each other, Claude both saw and felt his ball move slightly out of its orbit toward the other one. It was quite distinct. A little jump.

"You see?" Fredericks said. "You held perfectly still?"

"Yes." Claude was amazed. "Magic. Is it magic?"

Fredericks took the glass balls and put them back in his desk. "Some people would have you believe so, but it isn't. It only feels like magic."

"Well, what is it, then? What made it do that?"

"You did."

"No, I didn't move. Not one bit. Anyway, I could feel it. I could feel a little tug when it jumped."

"You believed the pieces of glass were attracted to each other."

"Well, you said they, I mean, I didn't actually know whether —"

"Listen to me, Claude," Fredericks said. "This is important. It's *because* you believed."

"But that's like magic. You said —"

"I said *you* did it. You did it without knowing it. Tiny micro-movements in the pad of your thumb and the pad of your forefinger. Infinitesimally small movements below your level of physical awareness, magnified because of the length of the string, making the ball jump."

Claude looked away and stared into the middle distance for several moments. "Are you sure?" he asked finally.

"I'm absolutely sure. I'm positive." Fredericks moved back and sat on the edge of his desk.

Claude turned up his hand and looked at his fingers. He touched his thumb and forefinger together.

"You understand the implications?" Frederick asked.

"I'm not sure." Claude continued to move his fingers. "It seems so strange."

"It's the other side of the wall."

The boy looked up.

"I've just shown you that your fingers can do more than what you physically feel them doing." He made a little arc in the air with his hand. "The other side of the wall."

Claude thought about it. "Yes, but how? How do you do it?"

Fredericks got up from the desk and stood directly in front of the boy. "You must imagine the music in your head. Imagine it shaped and balanced the way you want it. Get it in your head and then believe in it. Concentrate, believe, and your fingers will do it."

"My God," Claude whispered.

"Anything you can imagine clearly, you can play. That's the great secret."

"So it goes beyond the body," Claude said.

"Exactly."

"How's the Wiener schnitzel?" Weisfeld asked.

"Good." Claude cut a piece, squeezed a little lemon juice on it, and popped it into his mouth. "Almost as good as Helga's."

Weisfeld put down his stein of beer. They sat in a booth in the Rathskeller, under a large fake boar's head on the wall. "I had a postcard from them. They've opened a donut shop in a little town called Boca Raton. They swim in the ocean every morning."

"Aren't they old for that?"

Weisfeld shrugged and ordered another beer. "Not so old, really. And it is warm down there."

"Boy, the food was good. After, she'd always ask me what I thought. Was the crust flaky enough."

"Yes. I had some wonderful dinners there."

"Mr. Fredericks says he knew the maestro."

"Of course he did."

"He says I'm lucky about the trust money because he's a very expensive teacher."

Weisfeld received a fresh stein. "He is the most expensive." He touched his mustache with a napkin. "Mr. Larkin was somewhat taken aback when I told him. But Fredericks is the best, I told him. The best in the country."

"I wonder what would have happened if I hadn't had him," Claude said. "I mean, by now I can't even imagine what would've, how I could've . . ."

"He saved you a lot of time," Weisfeld said. "And when he has a student with as much music in him as you have, he respects it. That only happens a few times, you know. Only rarely."

Finished, Claude put the knife and the fork, tines downward, on his plate. "I can't play like him."

"You're not supposed to. That's the last thing he wants."

"I know. He can tell when I . . . He stops me."

"Very good." Weisfeld nodded.

"He says we're almost finished."

Weisfeld drank some beer. He was slightly flushed. "And how do you feel about that?"

"It's okay." In fact, Claude was uneasy at the prospect. For over two years — interrupted only when Fredericks had traveled or appeared in concert, which was seldom — the weekly ritual, and the attendant preparation for it, had been the basic principle of order in Claude's life. The regularity of lessons with Fredericks, and work and practice at the music store, had been his lifeline. "It's okay."

"You can go back for a visit anytime if you want him to hear something. If you want an opinion, or whatever."

Claude nodded.

Weisfeld leaned forward. "But now you should start thinking about school. About regular school. This can't go on. You have to go to a good high school."

Claude's instantaneous reaction was fear. In his mind the huge, shadowy municipal institutions he had heard about seemed like engines of impersonal malevolence, dark prisons where his every weakness would call down great forces that would grind him to nothingness. He would get beaten up. To the teachers he would be no more than a number. He would be alone, and he would lose himself.

"Why? Why do I have to?" He heard the fear in his own voice, and that made it worse. He attempted to cover it by drinking some water.

"Lots of reasons," Weisfeld said. "Mr. Larkin is concerned, for one thing."

"He doesn't even know me."

"He knows more than you think. He's a good man, a very remarkable man, and he has your best interest in his mind. Believe me."

Claude stared down at his empty plate.

"You need to be with other children, you need to . . ."

Without meaning to, Claude clicked his tongue against the roof of his mouth — a sound of impatience, of dismissal.

Weisfeld jerked his head back in surprise. For several moments — moments that were extremely uncomfortable for the boy, who had not wanted to reveal so much — he said nothing. "I take it you disagree?" he said finally.

"I'm sorry."

"No, no. I understand. The whole thing scares you for some reason. That's part of it."

"I mean other kids . . . ," Claude started. "They just seem like kids, they just, they just — I don't know."

Weisfeld waited, as if to let the implication of the boy's inability to fully express his thought sink in. Then he sighed. "Claude, you're not the first young player to be in this position." He had the boy's attention now. "This is an old story, and a lot of people have thought about it. We've talked about this before. You want a good, balanced education. You want to go to college and find out as much about everything as you possibly can — the arts, philosophy, science, good and evil, all of it. The history of human thought, Claude. It will make you strong." He tossed down a kirschwasser, his eyes glistening. "And you're going to need it."

"What?" This was a new Weisfeld. The implicit threat was a brand-new way of talking. "What do you mean?"

"We all need strength." He nodded, as if agreeing with himself. "Life is full of surprises."

Claude sensed this was a retreat, so he pushed. "I think I'm strong enough," he lied. "I'm not afraid of surprises."

"You should be," Weisfeld said. And then abruptly he shifted in his seat and looked out over the room. "It is surprising to me — I mean, if I take the long view — it is very surprising to me that I'm sitting here getting drunk in a German restaurant." He gave a short bark of laughter. "Drinking German beer."

"You're not drunk. I've seen my mother."

"Yes, you're right. Not quite." He pushed the various glasses on the table away. "Time to stop."

7

Y OU MUST WEAR a jacket and a tie," Weisfeld had said. "Be polite, but volunteer nothing. They're hiring you to play the piano parts, just the way they hire people to drive their cars or serve the caviar."

"What's caviar?"

"Fish eggs. Roe. Considered a great delicacy. You won't be getting any."

"That's okay with me."

And so, at the age of fifteen, height five foot five inches, weight one hundred and sixteen pounds, dressed in a wool jacket, gray trousers, white shirt, and a blue tie from Bloomingdale's basement, Claude Rawlings stood at the corner of Fifth Avenue and Eighty-eighth Street at four o'clock in the afternoon and regarded the Fisk mansion.

Surrounded by tall apartment buildings, it was an architectural anomaly — a three-story building of gray stone set back from the street, with a slate roof, mullioned windows, and Doric columns framing the entranceway. There was a short curved driveway, arcing from the avenue to Eighty-eighth Street. He walked across its cobbled surface, past an empty black limousine whose license plate caught his eye. Number 57, with various official-looking badges and emblems of thick metal attached to its upper rim. Weisfeld had explained that Dewman Fisk was high up in city government, and that among his posts was that of deputy mayor. Claude climbed two steps to the door and rang the bell.

A uniformed maid opened the door. "Yes?" She was quite young. Puerto Rican, maybe, the boy thought.

"I'm supposed to be here at four."

"Yes, yes. Come in." She turned away.

She had a white bow tied at the small of her back, and the two ribbons that hung from it moved with her narrow hips as she walked through the foyer into a large, high-ceilinged room in which clusters of delicate-looking antique furniture stood in different areas around low, highly polished tables. There were flowers everywhere — vases of them, small and large, different shades of color for each bunch. Red, pink, salmon, white, and then, at one end of the room, near the fireplace, a profusion of various blues held in crystal and porcelain. Flowers of different shapes, bursting, drooping, fountaining up out of green ferns. "I change them every other morning," the maid said. "It takes two hours."

She walked to the end of the room opposite the fireplace and climbed three wooden steps onto a shallow curved platform. She went behind curtains that covered the entire wall. After a moment the curtains began to part, and he realized he was looking at a stage, complete, as he took the steps to the apron, with footlights. When the curtains were fully opened he saw a grand piano and some chairs and music stands at stage left. The maid emerged from the wings and indicated the piano bench. "Wait here. They'll come."

He sat in the shadows and watched her descend, weave her way through the flower-drenched room, and disappear through one of its many doors. From behind the piano he could see partway into another large room, opening off the first. Bookshelves. A long table covered with magazines. Two black leather chairs. Standing brass lamps with green shades made of glass. He could hear voices, although he saw no one.

He glanced through the music on the piano. A mélange of excerpts, transcriptions, reductions, and selections, mainly Mozart but also some Mendelssohn and Schubert. He could not find a full piece of music anywhere. He took care to leave everything in the order he had found it. Bending his head, tilting his right ear to the keyboard, he tried a quiet chord. The action was so stiff he barely got a sound. With the damper pedal down he played a few soft scales, put his hands in his lap, and waited.

He waited a long time. Snatches of high-pitched conversation, bits of laughter, and murmurs floated in from the other room. He began to wonder if the maid had told anyone he'd arrived. But then Mrs. Fisk emerged, followed by a strange-looking boy of seven or eight years. His head, covered with blond curls, was much too large for his body, and it bobbled as he moved, as if the weight were too much for the slender neck. His eyes were magnified behind thick glasses and moved lazily like great blue tropical fish. His arms were short and his waist very high. He was dressed in a brown velvet suit with a white lace collar, and he carried a small violin case.

"Good afternoon, Rawlings," Mrs. Fisk said, climbing slowly onto the stage. "I see you've found the piano." She flicked a wall switch and the air exploded into brightness. "This is my son, Peter Fisk."

The boy walked over to Claude and extended his hand. Claude grasped it — cool, limp, jelly-boned. The boy withdrew, his body moving stiffly. He went to the music stand, took out his three-quarter-sized violin, and slipped it under his chin. "Give me an A," he said, his voice unexpectedly full, like a mezzo-soprano's.

Claude played an A.

Mrs. Fisk sat down on one of the folding chairs. "Peter has been playing since he was four." Peter tuned his instrument rapidly, skimming the bow over the strings. Claude had very much hoped he'd be playing with Catherine, but his disappointment was muted by curiosity about this exotic creature who now looked up.

"The B-flat Mozart?" Peter asked.

"Yes. It's here on top."

Peter opened his music. "All right. Four-four. Ready. One, two, three, four."

Claude's hands went to the keys like lightning, caught the opening chord, and they were launched. It was a simple piece, a transcription from the Viennese Sonatinas, and Claude played easily, almost automatically as he shifted his attention to the violin, first in order to figure out why it sounded so odd. The boy could play — he was certainly playing the notes, with a thin tone and practically no vibrato — and yet it sounded completely mechanical. The time values were correct, but the notes did not flow into one another. It was one note at a time, laid out flat.

"Lovely," Mrs. Fisk said when they finished.

Claude was bewildered. The child hadn't made a single mistake, and he had even followed the dynamic notations, albeit crudely, and had obviously put in hundreds of hours on the instrument. But why and how could he have done all that work without the slightest musical feeling? Claude stared at the motionless boy, standing there like a machine waiting to be switched on, heard the few delicate claps from Mrs. Fisk, and in a quick, chilling flash understood. The boy was playing simply because he'd been told to play. His accomplishment was only slightly less amazing than that of a deaf person who had some-how, against all odds, learned to play by the senses of sight and touch.

It was pitiful. He felt a mixture of revulsion, respect, and, surpris-ingly to himself, protectiveness toward this robot child in the velvet suit, as pale as an orchid. Claude wondered if Peter ever went outside. People would certainly stare at him.

"What's next?" asked Mrs. Fisk.

And so they went through the pieces, one after another, Claude adjusting his playing to give the child the most support possible. Now and then, when he saw an opportunity — a few bars of solo piano — he would play with a bit of feeling, trying to nudge Peter toward flexibility, but the child gave no sign that he had heard anything. During the last piece of heavily edited Schubert there was a unison section, and Claude played with rubato to bring out the shape of the line.

Frowning, the child lifted his bow from the strings in mid-course. "What's that? I don't see anything," he said, peering at his music. "Aren't we supposed to be together in here?"

They both looked at Claude — Peter genuinely perplexed, Mrs. Fisk alert, expressionless. For a moment Claude was tempted to tell the truth, but even as he drew his breath he knew that the child wouldn't understand, and that the mother would doubtless hire somebody else to play accompaniment. "Sorry," Claude said, "my fault. Let's start again at the top of the page."

As they were playing, Claude heard the sounds of voices and of the front door slamming. Then, from the corner of his eye, he saw Cather-ine come into the room, glance at the stage, and continue on into the library. A very tall man entered a minute later, stopped, sat down on a chair, crossed his legs, and gave a little wave to Mrs. Fisk. As the piece ended, he joined her in brief applause.

"Well done, Peter," he called from his chair. Dewman Fisk had a rosy face, thin dark hair graying at the temples, pendulous earlobes, and quick pale eyes. His hands, now folded over his knee, were large.

"Thank you," said Peter, loosening his bow.

Mrs. Fisk got up and, moving carefully, stepped down from the stage to join her husband.

"How was the rehearsal?" she asked.

"Splendid." He stood up. "Balanchine says they're ready."

They moved together into the library.

Peter placed his instrument in its case.

"Did your teacher . . . ," Claude began. "Did you have trouble learning to sight-read?"

The child looked up. "No. Did I play wrong notes?"

"I didn't hear any."

"That's because they were correct," the child said, closing the case. "After I play a piece two or three times, I don't make mistakes."

"You play very well."

"Thank you."

There was an awkward silence, and then they climbed down from the stage. Peter moved to the library, and Claude, not knowing what to do, followed. He stepped into the room cautiously. The maid was serving tea. Mrs. Fisk sat in a wing chair, Mr. Fisk and Catherine sat on the couch, and Peter knelt on a small striped pillow at the low table.

"He said I could come to the studio and watch them run through the new thing," Catherine was saying eagerly. "The duet where she has to run away, and he wants to go with her."

"That's nice of him." Mrs. Fisk picked up her teacup with both hands.

Suddenly Catherine looked up and saw Claude standing motionless just inside the doorway. After a moment she gave a little laugh. "Look at his tie."

Mrs. Fisk whispered something Claude could not hear, and the girl turned her attention to a plate of small sandwiches, held her hand over them for a moment, and picked one. Her teeth were very white as she bit off a corner and gave a small toss of her head. Dewman Fisk appeared to be reading the afternoon paper, his smooth face expressionless. Mrs. Fisk lowered her cup and half turned in her chair. Without actually looking at Claude, her faintly trembling body in three-quarter profile, she said, "That was fine. Will the same time next week be convenient?"

"Yes." Claude was blushing because of Catherine's remark. He wanted to say something sharp to her, something to break her composure, but his anger was no more than a surface reflex. Deep down, he felt she was so beautiful she obviously had the right to say anything she wanted. Deep down, he felt gratified that she had noticed anything at all about him. It was a peculiar sensation.

"Very good, then," Mrs. Fisk said. "Peter, will you show Rawlings to the door, please?"

The child got up immediately.

In the hall Claude paused. "What's wrong with it?"

"What?"

"Your sister doesn't like this tie."

"Oh, she says things like that all the time. She's always trying to be so grown up. Anyway, she's only my half-sister. Her father died a long time ago."

Claude pondered this information. He resisted the urge to ask more about her, aware that Peter, dulled by familiarity, probably took her for granted. Also, he didn't want to give away the fact that she fascinated him. She would doubtless amuse herself by using it against him somehow.

At the door, just before Claude stepped out, Peter glanced at the tie in question. The blue eyes drifted upward.

"It may be too shiny," he said. "My father's ties aren't that shiny."

Claude understood that the movies were not real. They were fabrications, delightful concoctions, shaped and formed to achieve an effect. Life, on the other hand, simply happened. Movies were metaphors in various realities beyond his ken, and gave him the exhilarating sense of being lifted out of his own petty and narrow surroundings. He did not go to learn, but inevitably lessons from Hollywood seeped into his bones.

Westerns. Do not approach a campfire without first announcing yourself from a distance. Do not brag, bully, or lie. Do not draw on an unarmed man, shoot anyone in the back, or steal a horse. Be respectful to women, regardless of their situation in life.

War movies. Democracy is worth dying for. Germans are intelligent, arrogant, ruthless, and sadistic. Japanese are treacherous, cowardly, fanatical, and devoid of individuality. Russians are brave, emotional, and crude. Chinese are simple, domestic, gentle, and the keepers of ancient wisdom. Italians are childlike, the French weak, the British brave and noble. War could be conducted in a civilized manner. American soldiers are the best because of obedience to authority, without any concomitant sacrifice of individual initiative and courage.

Gangster movies. Crime does not pay. Low criminals are stupid and brutal. High criminals are greedy, reckless rebels against the beneficent forces of organized society. The police are good, unless corrupted from below by money or from above by political power. Women are weak, venal, decorative, and irrelevant. Guns, large automobiles, conspicuous consumption in public places, and familiarity with the uses of terror are potent symbols of real power.

Horror movies. Death is obscene. The unknown is dangerous. Destructive forces surround the visible world, and protection is afforded by religion, moral purity, light, and banding together in groups. Luck is an important factor. Courage is foolhardy.

Private-eye movies. The individual is isolated in a hostile world. Anyone may shoot anyone else in the back at any moment. Everyone lies. Greed prevails. It is necessary to be extremely careful at all times.

Cartoons. The weak can prevail over the strong through applied intelligence. Humiliation is intrinsically comic.

Claude went to at least three double features a week. The theaters were huge, with vaulted ceilings, two balconies, and large screens. Hundreds of people were scattered through the darkness. In the evening, especially Fridays and Saturdays, it could be hard to find a good seat in an audience of more than a thousand. He preferred the late afternoon, and the thrill — having entered in the daytime — of emerging at night, as if the world had recognized the compressed, high-velocity emotional rides he had just experienced, and transformed itself accordingly. He liked the familiar kinds of movies, variations on tacitly understood themes, but he particularly relished movies that attempted to define their own terms. These peculiar movies came along once or twice a week.

Up in the balcony, slouched in his seat, feet up, he peered down through his knees and entered fabulous worlds in which, for the most part, virtue was rewarded and love, delirious, puissant love, sacred and profane at the same time, conquered all. Romantic love was deeply interesting, not only because it promised an end to loneliness, but because it suggested an elevated state of existence, a transcendence. Sometimes when lovers kissed on the screen it meant little to him, but sometimes, when the people were right and the story was right and the music was right, he felt as if his heart would break. Aware of the hisses and catcalls from the remote children's section, hearing the snores of the fat man asleep in the next row, he nevertheless soared, flying out of himself toward the unbearable beauty of the kiss. When the images faded he would cover his face, as if to keep them a moment longer.

He stepped out of Loew's Orpheum into the early evening bustle of Eighty-sixth Street. On the sidewalk people walked quickly, shifting vectors, angling their shoulders, slipping through the traffic. He added himself to the side of the stream and moved toward Lexington Avenue, smelling beer, sauerkraut, and meat from the steam table as he passed a German bar, hearing Rosemary Clooney singing the oriental strains of "Come On-a My House" from the record store arcade, walking through the bright light spilling from the white interior of Fannie Farmer Candies. There was a stiff breeze, and men held down their hats. Paper swirled in the gutter.

He turned at the Automat and pushed through the revolving doors. Holding his change in one hand, he slid a tray along the chrome bars and looked into the compartments. Hot franks and beans in an oval dish. He dropped in a quarter, twisted the handle, and the door sprung open. Moving to the back of the room, he bought a hard roll, a glass of milk, and a cupcake. Someone had left a *New York Post* at an empty table, and he moved quickly to get it, putting down his tray in the center to establish his territorial rights. He ate unhurriedly, turning the pages of the newspaper with his left hand.

As he lifted a forkful of beans to his mouth, he saw a thin young man in a black topcoat, buttoned to the throat, approaching the table. The man carried a saxophone case and walked leaning forward, as if about to fall. He pulled up a chair and sat down, staring off into the middle distance. His long face was pale, the eyes heavy-lidded, his hair black with a pompadour over his brow, and brilliantined brushed-back sides in the style called a DA. The man sighed heavily and looked back to see an older man, also in a black topcoat, following with two cups of coffee. The older man also pulled up a chair from the next table.

"Drink this, for Christ's sake," the older man said.

They were sitting opposite Claude.

"I can't believe it, Vinnie." The older man's voice was pained. "What're you gonna do? Nod out on the fucking stand?"

"I'll be fine," Vinnie said, holding the case on his lap. "Polka. Um-pah-pah, um-pah-pah. See?" He gave a slow little giggle. "I can do it."

"Drink the coffee. We need this gig. We gotta look sharp. The owner's no dummy."

"Look sharp, feel sharp, be sharp." Vinnie raised the cup and drank. "Bong."

"Oh, shit." The older man looked down at the floor. "You were doing so good there."

"Don't be mad," Vinnie said.

"I'm not mad."

Vinnie considered this and said, "Okay."

The older man pushed forward the second cup of coffee. "This one too."

"I haven't finished the first one yet," Vinnie said. "Don't rush me."

During the long silence the older man stared at Vinnie and checked his wristwatch. Neither of them so much as glanced at Claude, who began carefully to peel the paper from his cupcake.

"You okay?" The older man asked Vinnie.

"Sure. I'll play my ass off."

The older man seemed to think for a moment and then make up his mind. "Okay. Stay here. Drink coffee. I'll come back for you, okay? You read me?"

"You're a good man," Vinnie said. "I love you."

The older man walked away.

Claude ate his cupcake and drank his milk, moving as little as possible. After a while Vinnie took some coffee, shivered, and leaned back in his chair.

"I love the Automat," he said, as if his friend were still there. "All the different things to eat, everything tucked away in its own special little box. Like the special little creamed corn all cozy in the creamed corn box, just sitting there waiting. And when somebody takes it out, another little creamed corn comes along to take its place. It's very nice." He reached up lazily and scratched his jaw. He began to hum softly. Claude was finished now, but he sat motionless. "All the brass shining like that," Vinnie said. "Nice and warm and cheerful. All the people happy, eating their food and not bothering anybody, everything smooth, everything mellow." His body gave an almost imperceptible jerk, his eyes widened for an instant, and he lowered his head to drink some more coffee. When he finished he unbuttoned his topcoat. He was wearing a tuxedo. He started searching his pockets, leaning this way and that, his movements slow and studied. When he finally extracted some change he stared at it, lying there in his palm, for some time. He picked out a nickel and placed it in the center of the table near the edge of Claude's tray.

"Listen," Vinnie said, "do me a big favor and get me a refill, would you? I'm a little under water here." His eyes took a moment to focus. His expression was gentle and he gave Claude a wry smile with the corner of his mouth.

Claude picked up the coins and the empty cup and went over to the coffee spout. He pulled the lever and hot black liquid came out of the mouth of a brass dolphin. He carried the cup back to the table, put it in front of Vinnie, and sat down again.

"So what's your story?" Vinnie asked. "Are you Italian? You look kind of Italian."

"No."

"That's how I got in the union. Because I'm Italian. I was just a kid and I screwed up the test, but he gave me a break. Sweet old goombah he was, that guy." He started searching his pockets, repeating all his previous moves. In his breast pocket he found what he was looking for, a drugstore inhaler. He took two quick sniffs. "Ahh." He shook his head as if to clear it, and put the plastic tube on the table. "You live around here?"

Claude nodded.

"I'm from Brooklyn." Vinnie said. "We're playing that German dance joint down the block. I could get you in. You like music?"

"Yes, I do. But I have to go home."

"Do you play?"

"The piano."

"Longhair," Vinnie said. "I bet you play longhair. I wish I could. A lot of that stuff is good. But I got the wrong ax."

"I like boogie-woogie too."

"Oh yeah? Well, it's the blues, and the blues, well, that's where everything starts." He picked up the inhaler, grasped the base with one hand, the tube in the other, and with a grimace, broke them apart. "You probably play F, B-flat, F, C, B-flat, and F. Am I right?" He examined the broken tube and the yellow cotton packing now revealed inside.

"Mostly I play it in C," Claude said.

"Yeah, C is okay." With two fingers, he carefully extracted the yellow cotton. "But F is the blues key." He dropped the cotton into his coffee and stirred it with a spoon.

Claude sensed it was better to remain silent about this strange action. Both of them behaved as if nothing of importance had happened. Vinnie sipped the coffee and then poured in some sugar and stirred it again. He pressed the cotton against the side of the cup with the spoon, released it, pressed, and released it. He drank some more. "You know Bird's changes to the blues?"

Claude had no idea what he was talking about. Birdchanges? "No."

"The bebop changes."

Bebop? He shook his head.

Vinnie pulled the *New York Post* across to his side. "You got a pencil?"

Claude patted his pockets. "No."

"Go get one."

Claude went to one of the windows at the central change kiosk and asked the lady for a pencil. She gave him one and made him promise to give it back.

For all his strange talk, Vinnie seemed more normal as Claude returned. His eyes no longer had that sleepy look, and his movements were crisper. He took the pencil and wrote in the margin of one of the pages of newspaper. He tore it off, folded it, and handed it to Claude. "Put this in your pocket."

Claude obeyed.

"Look at it next time you play." He drained his coffee and placed the cup in its saucer with exaggerated care. "Look sharp, feel sharp, be sharp," he said. "Bong!"

"I better go," Claude said.

"Yeah, sure. In a minute, in a minute. Tony's coming back." His face seemed paler now than before. "What can I tell you? Make sure you listen to Art Tatum. Fast, fast, fast, and he swings. Hands like snakes, you know? They open up like that, like when a snake opens its mouth, you know, wide, and then wider, like it's so wide it's impossible." He began to drum his fingers on the saxophone case in his lap. "Go up to Minton's and listen to —" He stopped abruptly, his mouth open.

Claude's peripheral vision seemed to close down until all he could see was the man's frozen face.

"Oh. Oh. Oh." Vinnie's hands went to his chest.

Claude didn't know what was happening, but the hair rose on the back of his neck. Vinnie's eyes were locked, staring into his own, and the boy saw the change, the instantaneous transformation as life left them. Even before the man fell forward, his head sending a spoon end over end to the floor, before the saxophone case slid sideways, before the faint tang of shit in the air, Claude knew he was dead. Unbelievably but entirely dead.

There was complete silence, but everything was going on as before — people eating, getting change, carrying their trays. A woman with a plate of pie walked by the table without noticing anything.

Claude understood that he had just witnessed an event of profound importance, utterly off the scale of his own experience or knowledge, but somehow he could not bring himself into focus. His mind seemed to be swimming aimlessly in the silence, going around in circles. As he got to his feet he stumbled, and held on to his chair for a moment. He glanced at Vinnie — whose skin had gone gray, the color of cement, his body still beyond stillness — and backed away a few steps.

Now, suddenly, as if a switch had been thrown, he could hear the sounds of the vast, open room. The low burble of a hundred voices, the clinking of plates, the sighing of coins falling down the chutes at the cashier's window. He saw the yellow pencil next to Vinnie's hand, moved forward to get it, and went to the kiosk.

He put the pencil on the counter.

"That man just died," he said to the woman, and pointed to the table. "He's dead."

The woman looked at Claude, at the table, and then back to Claude. "Dead drunk," she said. "I saw him come in."

"No. Really."

She cracked a roll of dimes on the edge of the counter and fed them into the change machine. "I'll take care of it."

The boy stood, waiting. Her maddening casualness suggested that something was slipping away. In his encounters with adults he was used to being barely visible, to being beneath notice — it was the way of things — but surely this situation was different. The very magnitude of the event ought to have ensured that he would be taken seriously. But, indeed, whatever dignity or power he might have gained from witnessing Vinnie's death was slipping away instant by instant. He felt cheated.

"You can go," she said. "I'll take care of it."

He walked toward the revolving door. A policeman entered and took off his cap. Claude pointed back to the table.

"That man there," he said. "I was sitting there and he died and fell

over like that. I told the woman in the change booth but she didn't
believe me."

The cop didn't speak at first. He was heavyset, with a square,
weather-beaten face. His gray eyebrows rose and then came down as
he looked across the room. "Okay. Wait here."

As he watched the cop go to Vinnie, Claude felt the first stirrings of
fear. Very rapidly he no longer cared about being taken seriously. The
cop half knelt at the table, reached out to take Vinnie's pulse, and
gently turned the dead man's head. Claude saw the fixed eyes, and saw
the cop close them, one at a time, with his thumb. As the cop rose and
looked back at Claude, the boy felt a wave of warmth and he heard a
sound like the ocean in his ears. He backed away to the revolving door.
The cop motioned him forward with his arm, but Claude turned,
pushed the brass bar, and ran out into the street.

The black topcoat was right in front of him. Big. Getting bigger.
Impossibly, the dead man was about to fold him into darkness. Claude
veered and bounced off his hip.

"Hey! Take it easy," Tony said. "What's the rush?"

Claude kept running, weaving through the people, who seemed to
him like mannequins frozen on the sidewalk. What he had heard the
black topcoat say was *Come Claude, come Claude* in a soft, intimate,
all-pervasive voice.

When he reached the northeast corner of Lexington, with the insula-
tion of the crowd behind him, he got control of himself and ducked
into the subway arcade. He sat in the doorway of a vacant shop and
waited for the storm in his body to subside. He understood that the
voice he had heard was both real, because he had heard it, and unreal,
because it was clearly impossible. It had not been Vinnie's voice, but a
voice of pure authority, from some other realm. Whatever threat it
might have represented was now gone. For a moment he had been at
the threshold of an immense black void, the voice calling him, but it
had only been a moment, and it was over.

The wind had picked up. It blew through the tunnel of the arcade
with a hollow moan, pulling at the sleeves of his army-surplus jacket.
He heard the Lexington Avenue express screeching to a stop down
below. As the people came up the stairs, he got to his feet and went out
with them. Dodging buses, cars, cabs, and a speeding, rattling newspaper truck, he crossed over to the southeast corner. A small crowd had
gathered near the spot where he'd once shined shoes.

His mother, standing on a box, her back to the wall, was addressing the crowd. She held a thick bundle of leaflets under her arm and passed them out as she spoke. He saw her great jaw moving, and the flash of her teeth, but in the wind he could not hear what she was saying until he elbowed his way in.

". . . being bled by corruption. Oh sure, the building inspectors, the fire inspectors, the cops, the sanitation workers, we all know about that. You'd have to be deaf, dumb, and blind not to know about that." Her face was blotched in various shades of red, and her eyes bulged. She spoke in a strong voice and threw some spittle. "But City Hall gets away with murder. The mayor is a jumped-up crook. Here are the facts, here are the names, the dates, and the places of just a few of the recent outrages." She offered the sheets of paper. A couple of people took them, one man without even looking as he strode past, but most did not. Some pages blew loose and rose in ever-ascending arcs out over the avenue. "Kickbacks from asphalt dealers. Illegal bids from favored service companies. Payoffs from gambling and prostitution direct to the mayor's office. It's all here." It began to rain. A cloudburst, sudden and heavy. People moved away. "Tampering with voting machines in four districts, and that's from the *Herald Tribune,*" she shouted. "Judges bought and paid for, all over this city. Contracts auctioned off in the political clubs. It's all here." She held out leaflets, but the people were gone, and those moving by with their coat collars turned up were almost running. She was wet, her hair plastered down and water running over her face. She held out a limp leaflet to Claude. "It's all here. Take it."

Claude moved forward. "It's me."

She looked at him, but she didn't see him. It was like the moment before she had turned on the man at the Hack Bureau. "Unless the people act to stop —"

"It's me!" he shouted. "It's me!"

She looked at him, and then very quickly to the left and the right. She stepped down from the box and picked it up. "You take the flag."

There was a small, cheap American flag beside her, leaning against the wall. The gold paint on the pointed arrow on top of the dowel had started to run. He picked up the flag. "What's this? Where'd you get this?"

"City ordinance," she said. "You need a flag."

She mumbled to herself as they walked through the rain. He offered to take the leaflets, but she pulled them against her breast. Her behavior had grown increasingly strange over the past few months, but now, at this particular moment, he was calmed by the sight of her — a big, strong woman completely absorbed in her crazed mission, doomed to failure, and yet powerful in her single-mindedness. She seemed indestructible.

"Benzedrine," said Mr. Weisfeld. "I talked to Mr. Kaminsky, the pharmacist at Whelan's. That's what's in some of those inhalers. So if you put all of it in your coffee and drink it down like that, it can stop your heart. Just like that your heart stops. It was an accident."

"But why did he do it? Why did he drink it?"

"He thought it would wake him up. Benzedrine is a stimulant. He had a bad heart, probably."

Claude had been terribly worried for days about running away from the scene. He'd hidden in the back room for a while, convinced that the police were looking for him, perhaps in concert with the FBI (Mr. Burdick knew all about him). So filled with guilt and mounting dread that he couldn't practice, couldn't sleep, and could barely eat, he'd finally gone to Weisfeld and confessed.

"Look," Weisfeld said now, as they sat at the counter sorting out cellophane packets of guitar strings. "I called them, I talked to them."

"Who?"

"The Eighty-third Precinct. The police. Sergeant Boyle, a nice man, very understanding. They don't need to talk to you. They're not looking for you. I explained you got scared and just ran. You know what he said? He said in your shoes he would have done the same thing. A dead person is scary."

Claude felt a flush of relief, as if constricted valves hidden away deep in his body had suddenly opened all at once and he was back to sweet normalcy. "I wasn't scared of him."

"They said he was a drug addict."

"It wasn't him. He was just dead and it wasn't scary like in the movies when they — he just stopped," Claude said, interrupting himself. "Like a puppet, and you cut all the strings, and it falls. It was later, when I was watching from the door, everything got weird. I don't know."

Weisfeld nodded. "You had a shock. It was so fast it took you a little while to catch up with it. I know about this." He paused, tilted his head back, and closed his eyes. "Somebody dies. We want to think it means something. We insist that it means something. But essentially it doesn't. It's meaningless, a meaningless mystery. You put it well. The strings are cut. That's it. The end."

"He was right in the middle of saying something."

"Deathbed speeches in novels. The soprano bares her soul and collapses on the divan. Citizen Kane and his Rosebud. That's what we want, I guess. Some message, some meaning expressed in the last moments. What better time for it all to make sense than at the end? But it doesn't make sense." He opened his eyes. "The last moments are the same as any other moments. There is no special wisdom." He looked at Claude with a faint smile. "That's what you saw in the Automat."

"When I try to remember what it felt like — it got sort of dark — it was me that did it, it was really me. The weird feeling."

"Sure," Weisfeld said.

"So he's just dead and that's all there is to it."

"Correct."

"He shouldn't have put that stuff in his coffee." In a moment of daring, Claude said, "You've seen people die."

"Oh, yes. Quite a few. But we'll talk about that another time. What did your mother say?"

"I was going to tell her. I started to, but she was mad about something. She's acting awfully strange. She doesn't seem to hear when you tell her something, like she's listening to something else."

"That's interesting." He stroked his mustache. "Give me a for instance."

He had not seen Mr. Fredericks for some months when he received a letter of invitation (mailed to him in care of Weisfeld's Music Store) for the evening of the fifteenth. He had never received a letter before. A large square envelope of heavy cream-colored paper, and inside a single sheet of paper, folded once, on which Fredericks had written with a thick-nibbed pen. Claude was to wear his best suit and wait outside the shop, where he would be picked up at seven o'clock for "an evening of adventure."

The boy posted himself fifteen minutes early, standing with his hands in his pockets, shifting his weight from one foot to the other in his excitement. The columns of the elevated obscured his view of the avenue, so that the cars and taxis emerged suddenly, lights blazing, to rush past. Mr. Bergman closed and locked the gates of his pawn shop, shaking them to make sure they were secure. An old man bent over with asthma, he sometimes came in to gossip with Weisfeld or to get an opinion on an instrument.

"So what's this?" he said when he saw Claude. "It can't be a funeral this time of day. Maybe the Stork Club?"

"I don't know where I'm going."

"But fancy, whatever it is."

"They're taking me someplace."

Wheezing, the old man glanced up at the windows above the music store, where Weisfeld lived in an apartment Claude had never seen. "Aaron?"

"No. One of my other teachers."

"Aaron should get out more. He's still young enough. It's not healthy." He walked away.

From the darkness under the el a white cat streaked onto the sidewalk and disappeared into a pile of crates in front of D'Agostino's Fruits and Vegetables.

The car was suddenly there at the curb. For all its size — wide, tall, with enormous headlights and a massive grille topped by a Winged Victory — it had arrived without a sound. The chauffeur emerged, came around the front of the car, and touched the brim of his cap.

"Good evening, Master Rawlings."

"It's you."

"Yes. I do the driving, usually." He reached out and opened the rear door of the car. Claude entered, and the moment it closed behind him with a soft click he was enveloped in silence, the scent of leather, tobacco, and perfume. The compartment was so large it felt like a room. Mr. Fredericks and the woman from the balcony sat deep in the rear seat. They were dressed in identical clothes, something like the tuxedos of the men in the Automat, but simpler. Fredericks nodded and Claude sat on an upholstered bench, facing them.

"Claude," Fredericks said, "this is my dear friend Anson Roeg. She is a writer." His arm was extended across the back of the seat, and he lowered his hand to touch her shoulder. "This is Claude Rawlings, my dear, the best pupil I've ever had. *Un enfant, mais quant à la musique il a une connaissance extraordinaire.*"

Claude felt a flush of pleasure at Fredericks's praise. As the woman leaned forward, her long pale face came into the light, serene and beautiful. He thought, as she reached out, that she wanted to shake hands, and so he moved forward and reached out himself, but she cocked her wrist upward and presented her palm. He automatically followed her gesture and their hands came together, palm to palm, finger to finger.

"We are the same size," she said, then broke contact and leaned back. At that moment he felt the car begin to move. Her hand had been soft, the gesture itself abruptly intimate.

"I'm delighted you could come," Fredericks said. "I've missed you. My eight o'clock is now a certain Mr. Du Pont, who plays like a typist. It's no way to start the day, I can tell you."

"That exercise for jumps really works," Claude said. "I wanted to tell you."

"What exercise is that?" she asked.

"Take any two-part counterpoint from Bach," the boy said, "and play it in octaves, in both hands."

"At the original tempo," Fredericks added. "You are continuing theory and harmony with Mr. Weisfeld, I presume? Give him my regards."

"Composition too," Claude said.

"Ah, composition. Yes, of course."

Bars of light drifted across the ceiling of the compartment, sometimes angling down briefly to catch one or the other of them in the back seat. Claude looked out the window and realized they were driving down Fifth Avenue. "Where are we going?"

"Carnegie Hall," Fredericks answered.

On Fifty-seventh Street they joined a line of limousines and taxicabs, moving forward bit by bit until they pulled to the curb in front of the hall. The driver got out.

"Well, I know Wolff is good," Anson Roeg said, "but what about the music? Is he going to play anything?"

"The 'Hammerklavier,'" Fredericks said.

The door opened and suddenly it was bright and noisy. Claude hopped onto the sidewalk. People streamed out of the night toward the broad steps, ticket scalpers shouted, small groups of elegantly dressed men and women gathered at the columns, looking out through the floodlit air at the converging crowd. Anson Roeg stepped from the car, followed by Mr. Fredericks, who said something to the driver and then walked quickly, almost running, to the entrance. Claude was instantly aware of people looking at Fredericks, their faces turning to watch him. A large woman in a cape and tiara nudged her companion. Someone waved. Two or three people even started to approach him, but he was too swift, making directly for the central doors. Roeg was right behind him. Startled, Claude ran after them, not catching up until he was inside, past the ticket taker, who nodded as he went by.

A tremendous din. People laughing and calling to each other. Some of the women very shrill, excited, almost screaming. It was uncomfortably warm and close. The crowd seemed to part just enough to let Fredericks through. He was still moving fast, up the stairs, past the usher with a wave of his hand. Claude snatched the offered program and followed them into the shadowed calm of the box.

"Shut the door," Fredericks said, whipping the handkerchief from his sleeve and touching his brow. Claude obeyed.

There were four chairs. Fredericks took one in the rear. "You two sit in the front."

Claude sensed an instant of hesitation in Anson Roeg. He waited until she picked a chair, and then sat down in the other. He placed his hands on the red velvet banister and took a deep breath. His heart was beating so hard he could feel the pulse under his chin. Roeg, very close by his side, emanated the scent of lemon and tobacco.

The stage was empty except for a long, black, highly polished grand piano. In contrast to the darkness of the stage, the orchestra was filled with color and movement, row upon row of women in bright costumes of every hue and texture, the pale blue dazzle of jewelry, the white flash of arms and necks. It was like some huge impressionist painting sprinkled with the black points of the men in their tuxedos, still as ink in the larger swirl of color.

"Where did you get that suit?" Roeg asked, leaning her head even closer.

Claude could not remember for a moment. "Bloomingdale's."

"I like it," she said. "Do you like it?"

"I guess. I just asked the guy for a suit. It was in the basement and they didn't have very many. He picked it out."

"I see." She nodded. "*Trouvé.*"

Claude thought of checking the label, but decided not to risk it. "That's it. *Trouvé,*" he said.

The house lights dimmed and the crowd noises imploded into tense silence. From stage left — opposite the box in which Claude sat — a figure emerged and strode to the piano, making no acknowledgment of the great wave of applause that greeted him. Lank blond hair fell to his shoulders and his eyes glittered with unnatural intensity. He sat, sweeping back the tails of his coat, and regarded the keyboard. A single muted feminine cough from somewhere in the auditorium hung briefly in the air. Victor Wolff swayed gently on the bench for several moments, raised his hands into the air like talons, pounced, and the first great chords of the sonata filled the hall.

Claude entered the music instantly, hearing its clarity, following each new thread as it was introduced and woven into the ongoing structure, everything dense and lucid. His awareness was split, most of it taken up with the propulsive tension of the music itself — the thrilling emergency of it — but, as well, he was watching the player, watching the hair fly as the head was thrown back, watching the expressions of agony, euphoria, anger, and gentleness flow across Wolff's face with astonishing speed, watching the body slump and the face disappear behind a curtain of hair, watching the swaying, listing, and dipping of his shoulders, hearing the occasional hiss, moan, or grunt forcing itself out. It was frightening.

During the long slow movement, almost unbearably attenuated, Anson Roeg bent her head again, as if to whisper something in Claude's ear. His hand came up so quickly it nearly struck her. "I'll lose it, I'll lose it!"

She leaned away.

When, after forty minutes, the structure was complete and the final celebratory fugue washed over him like sweet rain, he felt in its release a sense of exaltation so strong it was all he could do to remain in his seat. When the applause began he stood up, clapping hard and fast.

Laughing, he turned to Fredericks, who had moved his chair to the deepest part of the box to sit sideways, without a view of the stage. Fredericks was staring at the ceiling, biting his lower lip. He began to nod as if in assent, and when he became aware of Claude, he smiled and stood up.

Victor Wolff walked off the stage. Just as he reached the wings he appeared to stumble, and there was a collective gasp from the crowd as he reached out and held on to the curtain for an instant. From the angle of their box, Claude, Fredericks, and Anson Roeg saw Wolff step behind the curtain into the shadows, where he fell, half turning, into the arms of the two men and a woman who stood waiting there. One of the men dropped the glass of water he had been holding out for the maestro.

"Oh, really," Anson Roeg said. "He's at it again."

"What's happening?" Claude whispered, and turned to Fredericks.

"Don't worry," he said, patting Claude's shoulder. "It's nothing. He gets overwrought. I'll just pop backstage and brace him up. Brandy and sugar. Be right back."

Claude sat down and watched the group recede, Wolff walking now with his arms over the men's shoulders. The box door clicked shut as Fredericks left.

"Is he sick or something?"

Anson Roeg moved to a rear seat. "I used to think he did it on purpose, but apparently he can't help it. Something happens to him in performance."

"His face. His face was . . ."

"I know," she said. "Come back here and take off that jacket. I want to see it."

Claude stepped up to the rear of the box, out of the light. She extended her arm and wiggled her fingers. "Give it to me."

He slipped off the jacket and handed it to her. She examined the cloth and the lining, and then got up and took off her own jacket, thrusting it into Claude's hands. "That's from Paris, and it's very, very expensive."

Claude couldn't think what to say. "It feels very nice," he managed.

"Do you have a tuck?" she asked.

"What?"

"A tuxedo. Formal evening wear. No? Well, you're obviously going to need one. I'll give you mine. A trade. But we have to do it right now." She undid her bow tie and began to unbutton her shirt. "The whole works, but right now."

Claude was bewildered. He thought for a moment that she might be going mad, having some kind of attack brought on by the general excitement, but in fact she was quite calm as she removed her shirt, revealing a broad, pink elastic-looking band that encircled her body at chest level. Claude looked nervously out into the hall.

"Don't worry," she said, unbuttoning her pants, "nobody can see us. Hurry up."

He began to take off his shirt.

She slipped off her shoes, stepped out of her trousers, and stood in her underwear. "Come on." She laughed. "Shake a leg."

He stripped down, aware of her body bumping against his own as they exchanged articles of clothing. He felt the residual warmth of her as he pulled on her trousers, smelled again the lemon and tobacco as he put on her shirt. Her shoes fit him perfectly.

"Your tie," she said, and stepped up to tie the soft bow at his neck. She was smiling, close, her cheeks flushed. "Isn't this fun?" she whispered.

It had happened so fast as to leave him dizzy. "I guess."

"Let's go." She opened the door and stepped out into the light. As he moved to follow her, he became aware of how comfortable his new clothing felt, snug and yet not restrictive, seemingly without weight, smooth against his skin. She took his arm and they ambled twice around the full curve of the corridor, a promenade through the crowd.

"People are looking," Claude said.

"Yes, they are," she said, and he could hear the satisfaction in her voice.

When they returned to the box Fredericks was there, showing no surprise when he saw them.

"Quick work," he said to Roeg with a wan smile.

"How is he?" Claude asked, and just then a great roar filled the hall. Wolff strode to the piano.

Once again he seemed electric, larger than life. As he began to play it was with such confidence it seemed impossible that anything could go wrong. Nor did it. The B Minor Sonata of Franz Liszt, climbing through the enharmonic modulations like a knife through butter. During a sequence of incredibly fast octaves, Fredericks leaned forward and said, "They say he shakes the octaves out of his sleeves."

Claude laughed. That was exactly what it looked like. It was fierce, dark music, and Wolff tossed his hair and threw himself into it, elbows flying. The audience seemed to explode at the end, swirling and shouting.

As he played Scriabin he looked to be a wild man, lurching in euphoric abandon. Claude kept a cool enough head to notice that the music itself was nevertheless executed with clarity, the lines ringing out in high relief. Wolff took his bows and women streamed down the aisles to cluster at the foot of the stage, throwing flowers, clapping with their hands high over their heads, laughing and calling up to him. He played two quick, dazzling encores, and then, after several minutes in the wings listening to the ovation, wiping his neck with a towel, he came out, walked sideways to the piano with his hands in the air, sat down, and played a bravura arrangement of "Stars and Stripes Forever."

Pandemonium as Wolff took a long final bow. On his way to the wings — the women flowing with him, below him, following him like some thick, undulating school of fish — he stooped to snatch up a bouquet lying on the floor. With a quick smile he lofted it toward them and slipped away.

A dozen pairs of arms reached up. Claude's eye followed the flowers as they sailed over the women to the front seats and were snatched out of the air by a figure he recognized, with a delicious shock, as Catherine. It *was* her standing there, laughing with delight as she displayed her trophy to Dewman Fisk, who leaned back in mock alarm as if the bouquet were a bomb.

"What is your mood?" Fredericks asked Anson Roeg.

"Nibbles," she said.

The waiter stood at the edge of the banquette table, pencil poised over pad.

"Veuve Cliquot," Fredericks instructed. "Borscht." He made a circling gesture with his finger to indicate the table. "And then a tray of good little things — mushrooms, the grated black radishes, and then blini. A bit of caviar. I leave it to you."

"Sir." The waiter gave a small bow.

"Enough to satisfy the appetites of youth."

"Sir." The waiter moved away.

The restaurant was crowded and noisy as patrons poured in, still excited from the concert. A long, narrow room, brightly lit. Fredericks's reserved table had the advantage of being set back in a corner, out of traffic, while affording a full view. Anson Roeg's eyes darted as she noted those present, sometimes announcing them to Fredericks.

"Isn't that Kirsten Flagstad? Ah! There's Rubinstein." Her voice was calm. "Phoebe Saltonstall. Judge Foote."

"What did you think of the Liszt?" Fredericks asked Claude.

"It was amazing. Those double thirds, all those leaps, the crossovers — he played it like it was nothing."

"I mean the music. The sonata."

"There was so much. I've never heard it before. I'd like to hear it again."

"You've never heard it?" He was incredulous.

"Well, the radio. They never played it."

"You don't have a phonograph?"

"Henny and Constance," Roeg said, still preoccupied.

"No. Just the radio."

Fredericks shook his head as he unfolded his napkin. "I'll tell Weisfeld to speak to Larkin. They have the long-playing records now. Quite remarkable. You should be listening to everything at your age, everything."

Roeg suddenly looked at Claude. "You know, when I was young I could hear better, understand better, or faster or something. One simply *gets* it. You should be listening. In an organized fashion."

"The tuxedo looks good on you," Fredericks said, and turned to Roeg. "*Et toi, ma chère. Qu'est-ce que c'est que ça? La nostalgie de la boue? Une gamine de New York? Enfin, tu es adorable.*"

"*Je m'amuse,*" she said as the champagne arrived. "*Voilà, Monsieur Fisk et sa belle jeune fille.*"

Claude did not understand, but he had already spotted them walking down the aisle. Catherine held her bouquet. Fisk nodded, waved, and now and then stopped to shake hands. He seemed to know a great many people.

Claude caught his breath, hoping they would come all the way down the room, but they took a table near the center. As Catherine sat down she glanced in his direction, but gave no sign of recognizing him.

"Don't gulp it," Roeg said softly. "This is good wine."

"Sorry." His mind was spinning. He wanted Catherine to see him in this splendid company, in his new tuxedo with its appropriate matte-black bow tie. He thought about going to the men's room, but it turned out to be in the wrong direction. Could he simply approach the table? No, he didn't know what to say and would only look foolish. He understood her to be someone in whom an attitude of scorn — in her gestures, her words — was practically second nature, and even though he sensed it wasn't very deep (how could it be, when the beauty of her soul lit up her face like that?), he feared it nonetheless. He ate his food without tasting it, and watched her, seeing nothing else.

When they left after a single drink, he leaned back and sighed inadvertently.

"Yes," Roeg said, misunderstanding emptiness for satisfaction. "The food is wonderful here."

In the Rolls, they rode for a long time in comfortable silence.

"I invited you for two reasons," Fredericks said as they turned from Park Avenue onto Seventy-ninth Street. "Wolff is probably the best pianist alive, and not just technically." He leaned forward in his seat. "But that is *despite* the theatrics. Despite them. Do you understand?"

"Yes."

"He is so good he manages to play better than everyone else even with all the foolishness." He sank back. "Never allow yourself such antics. Never."

"I won't." Claude felt slightly foolish, since the figure of Wolff, like some kind of mad vampire at the keyboard, had in fact thrilled him to the bone. "I won't."

8

LOOK AT THIS." Claude handed Weisfeld the thick spiral-bound notebook. Its cover was deep, glossy blue with the words THE BENTLEY SCHOOL in small gray letters in the corner.

"Where'd you get it?" Weisfeld asked, opening it.

"It was on the floor under my seat at the Grande. He must have dropped it."

"What's playing?" Weisfeld shifted his weight on the stool.

"Greta Garbo and Melvyn Douglas in *Ninotchka,* and an English movie called *Green for Danger.*"

"Intelligent handwriting," Weisfeld said, turning pages. "A notebook. Ivan Andrews. Nice graphs here."

"I read it. Stuff about mythology. A long thing in French I couldn't read. A section on Japanese poetry. Biology with drawings and diagrams. It's interesting."

"It's supposed to be a very good school."

"Private school. Costs a lot of money, I guess."

Weisfeld closed the book and drummed his fingers on the cover, watching Claude. "No doubt." He straightened up. "There's a lot of work in here. Why don't you go over there and give it back to him. Take a look around. See what you think."

Claude took the notebook back. "We need some more ukuleles," he said. "We've only got one left. I don't know why people buy them, they sound so awful."

"I'll make a note. Thank you." Weisfeld watched for some reaction from the boy, who simply turned away and went to the back of the store.

But several days later, on an impulse, Claude walked over to Eighty-fourth and the East River, where the phone book indicated the Bentley School was located. It was a wide, four-story building of red brick, one side facing the river. He stood on the sidewalk for a moment, looking up at the gleaming white casements of the windows, at the flags hung from short poles jutting out from the wall on either side of the entrance. The street, a dead end, was quiet and free from traffic. He climbed the steps and went in.

A man in a quasi-military uniform sat behind a large desk reading a newspaper. He had a white handlebar mustache and thick, disorderly gray eyebrows. He glanced up over the paper and then put it down. "Can I help you?"

"I'm looking for Ivan Andrews. I think he goes here."

"May I ask what you want with him?"

"This notebook. He left it in the movies."

The man's eyes dropped for a split second, taking in Claude's old tennis shoes and bare ankles. "You can leave it here with me. I'll make sure he gets it." He extended his arm.

Claude was tempted, but something — perhaps the hint of disdain in the man's manner — stopped him. "I think I'd like to give it to him. Myself."

"I see." The man gave a little nod, as if he understood all about it. "Looking for a tip, I suppose." He got to his feet.

"You can suppose what you want. Just get him."

The man recoiled in surprise.

Claude was hot with anger. He turned away, went to a bench against the wall, and sat down, staring at the marble floor.

The man came around the table, walked halfway to the bench, stopped, and glared at Claude. "How dare you," he sputtered. "How dare you walk in here and . . ."

Claude raised his head and stared into the man's eyes, saying nothing, motionless, his gaze unwavering. After several moments the man spun on his heel, went back past the desk, and around a corner. Claude could hear his footsteps on the stairs.

As Claude calmed down, he looked around with a certain amount of curiosity. He stood up, crossed the foyer, and took a step down into a paneled room with dark green leather furniture, bookcases on the walls, displays of silver trophies, and a rack of newspapers hanging sideways on slender wooden rods. It did not feel like a school. He went to the tall windows and looked out at the street. An elderly woman, holding the arm of her gray-haired nurse, walked slowly past on the opposite sidewalk and entered a brownstone.

A discreet cough alerted him. He turned to see a young man in a tweed suit with a round, florid face, curly brown hair cut rather long, and quick blue eyes that seemed unnaturally bright.

"I'm looking for a student named Ivan Andrews," Claude said.

"You have found him." The young man smiled. "I know what you're thinking. Too old." He had a slight British accent. "It was the war. Buzz bombs. Shipped to the country and all that. Time out." He looked at the notebook under Claude's arm.

"Then this is yours." Claude held it out.

Ivan stepped forward, took it, rifled the pages, and gave a sigh of relief. "Wonderful. I can't thank you enough."

"What is this place? What's it like?" Claude asked.

Ivan looked up sharply. "Would you like a cup of coffee?" He glanced at his wristwatch. "It's the least I can do."

"Sure. Okay."

"Splendid. We'll go up to the faculty lounge. Chances are it'll be empty just now."

They passed the man at the desk, who did not look up, and mounted the stairs.

"It seems very quiet for a school," Claude said.

"Wait till the bell rings."

Ivan led the way to the lounge and opened the door. The room was indeed empty, strewn with newspapers and overflowing ashtrays. They drew coffee from an urn and sat by the window.

"If you're a student, how come you get to come in here?"

"My status is unique," Ivan said. "That is, I teach as well. Introductory Greek. Old Dr. Ashmead got a little deep into the sherry one afternoon and broke his hip. They didn't have anyone to take over his class. I had years of Greek in the UK, so . . ." He gave a shrug. "Now what about you? What grade are you in?"

"Ninth. But I don't always go. I don't know about school."

Ivan's curly eyebrows rose. "What? How old are you?"

"Fifteen. How old are you?"

"Nineteen. But good heavens, man, what are you thinking of? You have to go."

"So I've been told. Do you like it here?"

"Here?" He cleared his throat. "Here? The Bentley?"

"What do you think of it?"

"Well, it's first rate, of course. It's famous. It's very good," he said quickly. "It's, er, quite expensive as well."

"My teacher said something about scholarships. Do you have scholarships?"

"Your teacher? I thought you said —"

"My piano teacher," Claude said. "Something about scholarships and you don't have to pay."

"That's right." Ivan stirred his coffee, staring down into the cup for a moment. "A few. Very difficult to arrange. You know, special students, mathematical prodigies, sons of alumni who died in the war, that sort of thing."

Just then the door opened and a tall, thin, stooped-over man with horn-rimmed glasses swept into the room and strode to the coffee urn. "Andrews," he said with a nod.

"Sir," Ivan responded.

"And who do we have here?" the tall man said without looking.

Ivan opened his mouth, hesitated, and then looked at Claude.

"Claude Rawlings," Claude said.

"He was asking about scholarships," Ivan said.

"Oh, was he?" The tall man lighted a cigarette, took his coffee, and half sat on the windowsill, his leg swinging gently. He looked at Claude for the first time.

"Aren't you on the committee, sir?" Ivan asked.

The tall man didn't answer, but continued to examine Claude. "Scholarships are for people with special gifts and abilities." He took a sip of coffee. "Do you have any special gifts and abilities?"

"Yes," Claude said.

The leg stopped swinging. "Such as?"

Claude looked at Ivan, who sat motionless, his cup frozen in the air. Then he looked at the tall man. "The piano," he said.

There was a long silence. The tall man sighed and extinguished his cigarette. "All right, Andrews. You caught me at the right time. Let's take him down to the auditorium and see about this."

Andrews blushed.

On the way downstairs, as they followed the tall man, Claude leaned toward Ivan and said, "Don't worry. This is going to be fun."

The bell rang as they approached the floor below street level, and boys burst into the hallways with their textbooks and notebooks, coming out of classrooms talking and laughing, but in an orderly fashion for all that. They wore jackets and ties, and quite a few stared at Claude in his sneakers, baggy trousers, undershirt, and oversized Eisenhower jacket. "An urchin," he heard someone say. "Andrews caught an urchin."

The auditorium was small, perhaps a hundred seats, but there was a stage larger than the one at the Fisk mansion, and even a shallow U-shaped balcony. The piano, a beat-up Knabe baby grand, was off to the side, below the stage. The tall man waved his arm to indicate the instrument.

"What is an urchin?" Claude asked Ivan.

"I'll explain later," the older boy said.

Claude sat down at the bench and regarded the keyboard. So familiar, that black and white pattern. He felt a mild, comfortable thrill. No matter how weird or mysterious the surroundings, whether the comfortable basement of Weisfeld's Music Store, the spooky living room of Maestro Kimmel, the dim chaos of his own room, the brittle splendor of the Fisks', no matter where he was, when he sat down at the piano the world around him simply didn't matter. His physical relationship was fixed. All else was transitory. He was *located*.

It flitted through his mind to play something flashy. The last movement of the Chopin B-flat Minor Sonata, for instance, about as fast as anything he'd ever come across, but it seemed like giving too much away. And he would need the music. Instead, he found himself playing Bach's little Fugue in G Minor, not technically difficult but a strong and solid piece. At the third entrance of the three-note motive, back in the tonic, he let himself add some fire, as Herr Sturm would have it, and even a very slight, very smooth accelerando. He built to the finish and lifted his arms.

Ivan, who had been looking at the floor, raised his head and smiled.

The tall man said, "Who are you?" and then wheeled on Ivan. "Andrews, is this a prank? Where did you get this boy?"

"I've never seen him before today, sir. I lost a notebook and he came here to return it, no more than half an hour ago."

"What?" He seemed almost angry. "You mean he just walked in?"

"Yes, sir."

Claude said, "I wanted to find out about scholarships."

The tall man was momentarily speechless. Ivan stood waiting and no one seemed to know what to do, so Claude played Chopin's Etude no. 5, op. 10, easily, as Mr. Fredericks had taught him.

The tall man turned out to be Dr. Morris, who taught history, and who made Andrews responsible for walking Claude through two days of tests.

First, a repeat performance of the Bach and the Chopin for Dr. Satterthwaite, head of the music department, a grim, chunky man in his forties whose square face remained entirely expressionless during the playing. It was a different piano this time, a Steinway upright in Satterthwaite's classroom. At the end Satterthwaite turned to Dr. Morris.

"What do you want to know?"

"Your opinion, obviously."

"About what?"

"Oh, come on, George," Morris said, pursing his lips impatiently. "His playing. His playing. How good is he?"

"We've never had anyone near his level." Satterthwaite turned toward the door. "He plays quite a lot better than I do. Better than I could ever hope to." He opened the door and left.

"Well, good heavens," Ivan burst out. "You'd think he'd want to shake hands or something. Ask a few questions."

"Andrews!" said Morris.

"Sorry, sir," Ivan said.

Later, outside the door to a small office where Claude would be left alone with the Stanford-Binet, various aptitude tests, and drills, Ivan gave him a few words of advice. "These things are all nonsense, actually, so don't be intimidated. Go through the multiple choice quickly the first time, answering the easy ones. Then go back for the more difficult. Leave the impossible ones for the end and just fill in any answer."

"What?"

"You're not penalized for a wrong answer, so you might as well put something down — A, B, C, or D. You might get lucky."

"Oh, I see." Claude nodded. "Thanks."

"See you at four." Ivan gave him a pat on the shoulder.

The next day, a gray-haired woman showed him a series of elaborate inkblots on cardboard panels and asked him what he saw in them. Claude enjoyed it — the woman's manner was calm and reassuring. "Good," she would say, or "Fine," or "Very good," as if rewarding him for effort, when what he was doing was as easy as breathing. When he'd gone through the entire stack of panels she gave him a blank one, and a pencil. "Now I'd like to ask you to draw a person."

He looked at the blank panel. He did not pick up the pencil beside it.

"Please draw a human figure."

"I can't draw," he said.

"That doesn't matter. This isn't about how well you can draw. Please give it a try."

He knew whatever he did would look foolish. Childish. "I'd rather not, if you don't mind."

She waited a moment, and then took back the panel. "Okay. That's all right. We're finished now."

Ivan was waiting outside in the hall. "How did it go?"

"Okay, I guess. I saw a lot of bats."

"Bats? Oh, dear." When he saw Claude frown he said quickly, "I'm kidding, I'm kidding. I saw butterflies."

"You took that test?"

"Oh yes," Ivan said. "They give it to everyone." He gave a little snort of laughter. "Weeds out the barmies."

"What's a barmy?"

"A crazy. Not like you and me, my boy."

A week later, after a brief interview with Dr. Phelps, the ancient palsied headmaster, Claude was admitted to the Bentley School with a full-tuition scholarship and an additional grant with which to buy textbooks.

Al hunkered down at the curb and examined the flat tire of the cab. He tightened the valve cover.

"You got the key?"

Claude took it from his pocket and handed it over. "The cop told me it's been here more than a month. He knows me. He says the city can tow it after a month and we better move it."

"Unh-huh." Al went to the trunk, opened it, and began rummaging around. "So your momma just stop working, is that it?"

"I guess so."

"That's a shame. Good cab like this. Good medallion." With a grunt he hauled out the spare tire. "Spare's all right." It bounced on the asphalt. "You hold it while I get the jack. What's the matter? Is she sick?"

"No." He felt the satisfying weight of the tire.

"Well, then?"

"I don't know. She acts kind of crazy. Cutting up the newspapers. Writing letters. Handing out pamphlets and stuff."

"Did she get religion? I've seen that."

"No. It's all politics, but it doesn't make any sense. I mean, some of it does, but I don't understand why she's doing it."

"Unh-huh." He slipped the jack under the car, pumped it a few times until it caught, and then moved around to loosen the bolts on the wheel. Each bolt creaked as he struck the tire iron with the heel of his hand. "This wheel ain't been off in a *long* time. Look back there and see if she got any oil. A squirt can maybe."

Under some rags Claude found a wooden box filled with tools, old parts, and a copper oil can. Al applied a few drops to each shaft and took off the wheel. He put on the spare and jacked down the car. He unscrewed the valve cover, put some spit on the tip of his index finger, and touched the top of the valve.

"What's that for?" Claude asked.

"If it's leaking, that spit'll swell up." He watched for a moment. "It ain't leaking." He screwed the cover back on.

They put everything in the trunk and got in the front seat. Al put the key in the ignition, adjusted the choke, and tried to start the engine. It barely turned over, and Al stopped immediately. "The battery run down. Shit."

"Well, we can leave it." Claude watched as Al stared out the windshield, his fingers tapping the wheel.

"The street run downhill a little bit," Al said finally. "What the hell, let's try it."

Together, Claude in back with his feet braced against the fender of the car behind, Al by the open driver's door, pushing the frame with one arm and handling the wheel with the other, they rolled the cab away from the curb and out into the street. After the initial resistance of inertia, it was surprisingly easy. Al was a slim man, but strong. He jumped in behind the wheel and closed the door.

"Okay. Push!" he yelled.

Claude pushed, leaning forward, both arms fully extended, and the car began to pick up speed. Just as Claude began to have to run, Al engaged the gear and Claude bumped up against the trunk. The engine sputtered, coughed, and started. Al drove down the street a ways, then pulled to the curb, brake lights flashing, engine racing. Claude ran after the car and got in the front seat.

"Terrific!" he said.

"The trick is to pop it into second gear," Al said, milking the accelerator. "First is no good."

"What now?"

"Drive around. Charge up the battery." Al pulled out into the street. "Might as well go uptown and get the tire fixed for cheap."

At the corner they took a left and went up Third Avenue, in the central lane under the elevated.

"You ever tell your momma about me?" Al asked.

"Sure I did."

"That stuff in the dumbwaiter back when you were a little kid. You tell her that?"

"Of course not. I told her about you keeping the piano, and helping me with the shoeshine stuff. Teaching me cards. Like that."

"What did she say?"

"Say? She didn't say anything." Claude was slightly puzzled. "What would she say?"

"Nothing," Al said. "All right then, that's fine."

At Ninety-sixth Street a woman hailed the cab as Al drove by.

"Should we put the flag down?" Claude suggested.

"Why not?" Al reached out and pulled it down. The meter started ticking.

Now they were in East Harlem, the late afternoon streets crowded with people. Men sat on stoops, kids played off-the-point or stickball on the side streets, women hung out the windows, and the air was filled with shouts, snatches of jazz, gospel music, and occasionally the sharp, hot beat of samba. A funky, loose energy suffused the avenues, a kind of social electricity flashing through groups of people clustered at the corners, standing in front of the candy stores, leaning against parked cars, pitching pennies, drinking, talking, laughing.

Al drove toward the East River, past warehouses, past a large excavated area behind a chain-link fence, and pulled up in the shadows under an overpass.

It was a small junkyard. A couple of rusted-out car bodies, a three-legged tub washing machine, piles of old tires, scrap iron, and a small lean-to shed made of wood and nailed-on metal signs. An obese black man sat on a mailbox, staring down at a dismantled automobile generator spread out on the sidewalk before him. He picked up a part and began to scrape it with his fingernail.

Al carried the tire and laid it down next to the generator parts. "Got time for this?"

The fat man got up and went into the shed.

Al and Claude sat down on a salvaged car seat placed up against the side of the shed. Al lighted a cigarette. Overhead, cars sighed on the highway.

The fat man came out with some irons and a large rubber mallet. He examined the tread of the tire, rolling it, and then let it fall. He levered an iron between the steel rim and the tire, broke the bead, and tapped the iron delicately around the circle. He was quick, and worked without any wasted motion.

"So how long she been acting crazy?" Al asked.

"I guess for a while. Hasn't paid the rent for three months. I saw that in a letter she just threw away."

"That ain't good."

"And they taped some kind of notice on the door. She tore it off."

Al smoked in silence and then flipped the butt into the street. The fat man came over with the inner tube and held a section between his hands. "Little slice. Glass, most likely."

"You got hot patch?" Al touched the spot with his finger.

"Don't need no hot patch. Do a cold patch right, it'll be fine." He rubbed the tube on his grimy coveralls and went back to the shed.

"She on relief?" Al asked.

"I don't think so. But I don't know."

"Well shit, man. Don't you ever talk to her?"

Claude picked some stuffing out of the seat. "Not much, I guess. I'm not there."

They sat in silence for some time. The sky over Harlem was turning purple.

"I'm going to school now," Claude said. "I got into this fancy school."

"Is that a fact?"

"I like it."

"Well good, then." Al scratched his chin. "You can hold your own."

The fat man presented the repaired tire. "Fifty cent," he said. Al paid and they got back in the cab, whose engine had been left running.

"Let's go see her," Al said.

Claude was surprised, but said nothing as they rode downtown.

They descended the iron stairs and Claude paused with his key in the lock. "It looks kind of . . ." He half turned to look up at Al. "I mean inside. It's ah . . ."

"Open the door."

Claude pushed it open and they entered. In the gloom they saw the stacks of newspapers, boxes of files, and piles of reference books from the library. It was a warren, the paths strewn with old magazines, envelopes, and papers of every kind. The air was musty, as if in a cave. Emma sat at the kitchenette counter, under a single light bulb with a plastic shade like a Dutch collar, scissors gleaming in her hand as she cut up the *Daily News*. She did not raise her eyes until Claude stood right in front of her. He put the key on the counter.

"Al fixed the cab."

She shifted her gaze. "Al," she said without expression. At times now she talked in a flat, toneless voice, almost as if she were speaking without volition. Other times she yelled, or talked at a tremendous clip like a speeded-up movie. "Yeah, Al," she said. "Okay."

The slim man nodded, watching her.

"I've been very, very busy." She put down the scissors.

"Unh-huh." He pulled up a stool and sat opposite her, forearms resting on the counter, hands folded.

"It's hard to straighten it out," she said. "You have to look at everything. Most of it is lies, a whole lot of different kinds of lies they put out, but if you stick at it, you begin to see the patterns. People don't understand."

"I understand," Al said.

"Most people don't care."

"That's a fact," he said. "They don't."

A peculiar silence held. Claude felt an absence of tension as Al and his mother sat there like two old people on a park bench, who might say something or might not. There was a sense of everything moving slowly, an odd peacefulness in the air.

"The cab runs fine," Al said.

"They put me on suspension a while back. A frame-up. Just politics. Politics and lies."

"Claude tells me you stopped working."

She looked at the boy, and once again Claude had the strange feeling that she didn't really see him. "He sure can play. You ever hear him play?"

"Yes, ma'am. I have."

"Call me Emma."

"All right."

"He's got it," she said. "They're helping him because they know that."

"Yeah, well, he's still gonna need his momma."

Claude flushed.

Emma gave the faintest smile and shook her head. The boy didn't know how to read the gesture. It could be denial, but also bemused acceptance. He glanced at Al, whose eyes did not move from the woman's face. "You in trouble," Al said.

She remained motionless, staring down at the counter.

After a long time Al said, "How you going to make your way, Emma?"

The question hung there. Claude was astonished at the whole situation — at Al's directness, his mother's silence, the way in which these two strangers acted as if they'd known each other for years. He felt like a child. At the same time he was so curious he actually held his breath.

He saw her tears, falling from her motionless head to the counter. His astonishment gave way to something like nonbelief as he saw her reach out and place her hands over Al's. She still did not look up. Now he could see a faint trembling in her shoulders.

"Claude," Al said, "your momma and me gonna have a little talk. Why don't you go down to the corner and get yourself a Coke for a while? Okay with you?"

Stunned beyond speech, Claude simply nodded, and after a moment moved away, across the room and out the door.

9

THE PUERTO RICAN MAID, whose name was Isidra, carried the large tray bearing the tea service and placed it on the low table in front of Catherine on the couch.

"Where's the cinnamon toast?" Catherine asked. "I expressly ordered cinnamon toast."

Isidra gave a small shrug.

"Well?" Catherine's voice was sharp.

"I don't know this toast." She spoke reluctantly, her ordinarily pretty face fixed in sullenness.

Claude, sitting on the floor on the opposite side, broke in without thinking. "It doesn't matter." He looked over at Peter, also on the floor, at the end of the table, for support.

"Mmm," said Peter, his head wobbling.

Catherine glared down at Claude. "Stay out of this. You're a guest. You're *barely* a guest." She turned to Isidra, who stood stolidly, staring at the mantelpiece. "Well then, bring us some biscuits. The British kind in the long brown box."

Isidra left.

"Insolence," Catherine said, raising the teapot. "Nothing but insolence. She wouldn't dare if Dewman were here." With slow, almost studied movements, she served Peter, Claude, and then herself. She sat back on the couch and took a small, thoughtful sip. She wore a simple white cotton blouse with half sleeves and a dark plaid skirt. Claude could not take his eyes off her — the smooth porcelain perfection of her forearms, the faint touch of rose in her cheeks (from anger?), the hair so black it seemed wet, and above all the dark eyes. He could not tell — could never tell — if she was aware of how intently he studied her. For more than half a year he had waited in vain for the slightest sign of recognition.

"I'm going to give a soirée," she announced.

Peter slurped his tea. "What's that?"

"An evening of light entertainment. Some music. A brief dramatic interlude on stage. A *tableau vivant*. You and Rawlings will start it off."

"I told you I'm quitting," Peter said. "I don't want to play anymore. It's boring."

"Just this once. For me." She sipped again, shifting her glance to Claude over the rim of her cup. "Do you think he should give up the violin?"

Claude hesitated, wondering if it was some kind of test question. He was perfectly prepared to lie to give her the answer she wanted, but he couldn't tell what she wanted. "Well, why do it if he doesn't like it?"

Isidra entered with a plate of biscuits. She put them on the tray and withdrew.

Catherine picked up a biscuit. "If he stops, you won't get to come here anymore." She took a neat bite.

"Oh yes he will," Peter said. "*I'll* invite him."

Claude had in fact agonized over this very point. He'd done everything he could think of to keep Peter amused, bringing in little pieces (à la Weisfeld years ago), pop tunes, snippets of jazz, and folk music, but the boy seemed unable to get any pleasure out of it. He approached everything perfunctorily. "Turkey in the Straw," "How Much Is That Doggie in the Window?," "Clair de Lune," and "Bolero" were all ground out with listless accuracy. As Claude grew more fond of the precocious boy, he began to feel guilty at the way he was using him. As well, it wasn't often that Catherine so much as said hello. She seemed constantly preoccupied, her whole manner suggesting that higher, more important, more adult matters had a previous claim on her time and attention.

"So," she said, "five minutes of music to set the mood. Rawlings will pick something."

"And what is the mood?" Claude asked.

An infinitesimal crumb clung to her bottom lip. As Claude stared, his body quickened. He felt a tingling sensation and blood roared in his ears. He imagined taking her lip gently between his teeth, picking off the crumb with the tip of his tongue, feeling the heat of her head on his face, inhaling her scent — all of this in a split second so powerful it made him dizzy. "The mood," she said, catching the bit of biscuit with her own red tongue, fast as a snake, freezing his heart, "should be wistful. Simple. Elemental. Almost sad. It will introduce the myth of Daphne and Apollo. I'll need your help onstage, but don't worry, you won't have any lines."

"I don't want to," said Peter.

"I know. But you have to."

"When?"

"They're giving a dinner party."

Claude, emerging from his fantasy, heard only the last part of this. He wondered at her confidence, because Mrs. Fisk had been ill for some weeks, confined to her bedroom. White-uniformed nurses were on round-the-clock duty, and once the doctor himself had walked through the living room during a session. Peter had explained that his mother had retreated like this, for weeks at a time, for as long as he could remember.

"What's wrong with her?" Claude had asked.

"First it was TB. We couldn't go into that part of the house, and the nurses wore masks. Now it's because she's delicate." The way Peter had said "delicate" made it clear he was repeating it without understanding it, the way he did with music. "I don't remember the TB very well. I was little then."

Sipping his tea, Claude got an idea. "What about a trio? Piano, violin, and flute?" He would be in charge of the rehearsals, of course, and the thought of having that small bit of dominion over her was thrilling. He would be gentle, but firm.

She glanced at him, alert, for all the world as if she'd read his mind. "I'll consider it," she said crisply.

Weisfeld and Ivan sat on opposite sides of the counter, next to the harmonica case, while Claude waited on a customer up front.

"So tell me," Weisfeld asked quietly, "how's it going with him over there?"

"I would say extremely well. He's getting high marks in everything, apparently. He seems to have read a great deal."

"I mean with the other boys. The social part of it."

Ivan frowned for a moment, thinking. "He's a bit standoffish. What's the American word? A loner. But people respect that. Some of them seem slightly awed, in fact."

"He doesn't tell me much about it," Weisfeld said.

"Oh, it's fine. Really."

"What about this urchin business? He mentioned it back at the beginning. He wanted to know what the word meant, and I had to drag it out of him where he'd heard it."

"Well, that's what they call the tough kids around First and Second avenues." Ivan gave a quick, rueful, apologetic smile. "The school is quite old. Something that just hung on, I suppose. Remnant of the nineteenth century."

"They don't . . . they wouldn't . . ." Weisfeld's voice trailed off.

"No, no," Ivan said quickly. "Absolutely not. I mean to say, of course he's a bit exotic to most of them, but he's awfully clever, and they see that. And then there's the music. He almost never does it, but all he has to do is sit down and play, and suddenly twenty people are there listening."

"Does he need anything?"

"I don't think so."

"Are his clothes all right? Does he dress right?" Weisfeld stroked his mustache nervously.

"Mr. Weisfeld," Ivan said, "believe me, everything is fine."

"Good, good." Weisfeld nodded his head. "I'm glad to hear it. You're a fine young man. He's lucky he met you."

"No luckier than me," Ivan said.

Weisfeld studied Ivan for a moment. "This is good," he said.

Claude came down the aisle and rang up a sale on the cash register. "Ukulele madness," he said. "I don't understand it."

Weisfeld shrugged.

"Arthur Godfrey?" Ivan offered.

"Take your friend downstairs," Weisfeld said to Claude. "Show him your studio." There was the faintest spin of self-mockery in the word "studio," discernible only to Claude.

Claude led the way as they descended to the basement. "It's funny, my room at home is always a mess." He clicked on the light switch at the bottom of the stairs. "But I keep this organized."

The space had evolved over the years. Only a small portion, to the rear of the building, where they now stood, was used for storage. The rest had indeed become a sort of studio, albeit without natural light. The walls had been whitewashed, the cement floor covered with cheap beige carpeting to absorb sound ("Remnants," Weisfeld had said; "a guy in Brooklyn going out of business; he practically gave it to me"), and now pine bookshelves crammed with music stretched along the far wall. Fluorescent lights hung from the ceiling. It was a clean, orderly place.

"Here," Claude said, going to the first worktable, "I read scores." A straight-backed wooden chair. A Zenith phonograph. Neat piles of long-playing records and carefully stacked columns of music — piano, orchestral, and chamber. He moved down to the next worktable. "Here I write." Pencils, pens, bottles of India ink. A manuscript in progress lying half open. He crossed to the gleaming Bechstein and gave the case a little rub with his elbow. "And here I play."

Ivan strolled by, touching things lightly. "This is wonderful," he said.

"I practically live here," Claude said. "It's hard to leave sometimes."

Ivan nodded.

"Even copying — you know, writing out parts for people — I can lose track of time down here. It's terrific." He pointed to a blackboard in the corner. "Mr. Weisfeld taught me harmony on that. Theory, other stuff."

"How long has this been . . . ?"

"Oh, God. Years." Claude sat down sideways on the piano bench. "I can't remember how old I was."

"And he just gave you all this?"

"Yes."

"Remarkable."

"And the piano was left to me in a will by Maestro Kimmel, the Hungarian composer. I used to practice on it in his living room when I was a kid."

Ivan went to the bookcases. He gave a small sigh. "I envy you. You know what you want and you're going after it. I feel like I'm just thrashing. I get excited about something, and then a few months later I get excited about something else. I just dip in here and there. Typically British, I suppose. The truth is, I don't know what I want to do."

Claude looked down at the floor for a moment. Then he turned to face the piano. "Let me show you something. It's really neat. Can you read music?" He moved to the bass end, leaving room for Ivan, who sat down beside him.

"I had recorder lessons years ago," Ivan said.

"Okay. This is baby simple." He pointed to the music he'd written out. "It's just this phrase over and over, except here it's E and here it's E-flat." He played the twelve-bar sequence rapidly. "See? It's called 'Blues in the Closet.' "

Ivan played it, haltingly but correctly. "What're all those funny symbols underneath, there?"

"That's jazz notation. They don't write everything out. They do it that way. They're all sevenths. Now play the melody again, and I'll play the traditional blues harmony."

Ivan stumbled at the start, but then got it right. Claude played simple dominant sevenths, three of them, spread out over the twelve bars.

"That's fun," Ivan said. "Let's do it again."

When they'd finished, Claude pointed at the symbols. "I met a jazz player and he gave me these. A saxophone player named Charlie Parker thought this up. Play the melody again and listen to the difference."

This time Claude played a series of shifting chords, a pattern of major sevenths moving down to the subdominant, and then another cycle of fifths starting in the minor, back down to the tonic. Despite the fact that he was playing two chords to the bar, for a total of twenty-four versus the traditional three, it fit the melody perfectly. A rich harmony, filled with different colors and propulsive energy.

"Good heavens!" Ivan cried. "What did you do? That's wonderful. Do it again."

Again they played it through together. "See how it fits?" Claude asked.

"Like magic," Ivan said.

"What's really amazing is it works with every blues line. All of them. The simple and the complicated." He played the Parker chords against a nonrepetitive blues melody called "The Swinging Shepard Blues," and then against a tricky melody of Parker's invention. "Works every time," he said. "Instead of just staying on the tonic for four bars, waiting to go to the subdominant, he sets up this ride and *carries* you there. And I love the change from major to minor. They call it bebop."

"I've heard of that. I thought it was supposed to be wild — wild music."

Claude laughed. "Oh, they do tricks with the instruments, and there's so much movement in the harmonics and stuff. But really it's straight out of Bach. I mean, Bach could easily have written that blues harmony."

"You're kidding."

"I'm serious. In fact, I don't know why it took so long. Somebody could have done it fifty years ago. But then Parker is incredibly inventive. His stuff is full of counterpoint and cycles. It's baroque, really."

Ivan stood up and went over to the phonograph. "You haven't had Dr. Satterthwaite yet, have you?"

"No. I have to do all the required courses. I can't take any music for a while."

"You should have some interesting discussions. I heard him talking about jazz once in the teachers' lounge. He thinks it's barbaric. He doesn't think it's music at all, just noise."

Claude thought for a moment. "That's strange. Of course it's music. I wonder why he would say that?"

"He's a bit of a stuffed shirt," Ivan said. "Icy. The way his lips are always pressed together, as if he's angry about something." He started going through a pile of records. "Have you got any bebop in here? I'd like to hear it."

Claude sprang up. "Sure. I've got some seventy-eights of Parker. I'll put it on. You'll love it."

Most of the furniture in the living room of the Fisk mansion had been removed, and six large round tables, each with a white cloth and a setting for twelve, had been placed at the end of the room near the stage. The men wore dinner jackets, the women long dresses, and the air hummed with their voices, their laughter, and the clink of silver, china, and crystal. Candlelight made their faces glow and their eyes shine. Maids in black uniforms with short white aprons moved continuously back and forth, carrying plates, bowls, and large dishes of food. Two men in black, less hurried, served wine, hovering at the shoulders of the guests.

Claude, dressed as instructed in his tuxedo (the same that had once been Anson Roeg's), sat at a smaller table for four on the periphery with Peter and two large men named Dennis and Pat, the mayor's bodyguards. They ate steadily, making no attempt at conversation with the boys, their eyes scanning the room, coming back always to the central table where Mrs. Fisk sat with the mayor, her father Senator Barnes, and others. Dewman was at the next table with Balanchine, a few of the top dancers from the ballet company, and Nelson Rockefeller. Peter had pointed them out to Claude.

"And see that girl in the gray over there," he said now, pointing with his fork. "That's Betsy Lafarge. From the side with the name but no money. She's at Brearley with Catherine. Dicky isn't paying her a bit of attention."

"Who is Dicky?" Claude asked.

"Dicky Aldridge. Dumb as a stick, but he's at Princeton." Peter moved his head very close to his plate, peered down through his glasses, and cut a small slice of his beef Wellington. "He'll probably get drunk. He almost always does."

"This is good," Pat said to Dennis.

"It's okay," Dennis said. "But there's no gravy."

"Never had this before, with the crust and all," Pat said.

Through all the hubbub Claude suddenly heard Catherine's sharp laughter. She sat between Dewman and Nelson Rockefeller, a glass of red wine in her hand, her head tilted back. As she lowered it, smiling, Claude saw the hollow in her throat, whiter than the pearls around it. Now she was talking quickly, making gestures with her free hand, seeming to address the table at large. Some of the men leaned forward, polite and attentive. Claude felt a pang of jealousy.

"I wish I was older," he said.

"I don't," said Peter. "Everything's just going to get worse."

"You can say that again," Pat said, surprising them.

Claude had been waiting for an opportunity to address the men. "My mother says the mayor is crooked. Is that right? Is he?"

Dennis had a bit of roasted potato halfway to his mouth. He stopped, raised his eyebrows, and then completed the gesture. "Is that your mother sitting there with him?" he said, chewing. "Talking so nice? Throwing this nice party?"

"That's not my mother," Claude said.

"That's *my* mother," Peter said.

"Oh, I see," Dennis said, nodding to Claude. "And where's your mother, then?"

"She's not here, but she says he's crooked."

"Politics." Dennis touched his mouth with his napkin, and would say no more.

"Well, you haven't answered," said Claude.

Dennis sighed and looked away, but Pat leaned over the table, speaking softly. "Sure he's a crook, lad. He's the mayor of New York City." The two men laughed.

Claude looked down, flushing.

"There's one honest man at that table," Pat said. "Senator Barnes. And look how His Honor toadies to him."

"He's my grandfather," Peter said.

"Is he now?" Pat sucked his teeth. "Well, that's something to be proud of."

"If he's a crook," Claude went on rashly, "how can you work for him?"

Pat raised his wine glass in a mock salute. "The answer to that question is, we don't work very hard." Again the two men laughed, and this time Peter laughed with them. Claude gave it up.

He saw Catherine flit over to her mother's table and then back to her stepfather's. There was an odd quality to her gaiety, a certain brittleness, a sense of tension as if she were wound up too tight, her eyes and teeth flashing in the candlelight. She caught Claude's eye and indicated the stage with a quick toss of her head.

"Time to go," Claude said.

"But I haven't finished my ice cream." Peter sank his spoon into the parfait glass.

"Okay, but hurry up."

Now, with a great bustle of comings and goings, one flock of maids cleared the tables while another served coffee. It seemed there were as many maids as guests. The wine stewards moved along gravely, serving champagne. A rolling cart of variously shaped bottles — brandies and liqueurs — was brought in from the library. As Claude and Peter started toward the stage, the toasts began.

Dewman Fisk rose to toast his father-in-law, Senator Barnes, as the devoted father of three beautiful daughters, as a distinguished lawyer, and, despite his retirement, as the "continuing conscience of the Senate." George Balanchine rose to toast both the mayor and Dewman Fisk for their noble and enlightened efforts in support of City Center and the City Ballet, making the point that the cooperative mix of private philanthropy and municipal support would provide an example for the rest of the country. Nelson Rockefeller rose to toast the hostess. A few others spoke, but Claude stopped listening when he reached the piano. He set up Peter's music on the stand as the boy opened his violin case.

Claude had been unable to convince Catherine to play the flute. "I'll be too busy," she had said. He'd masked his disappointment. After a good deal of thought, and recognizing the expressive limits of Peter's playing, Claude had picked an extremely simple, and he thought elegant, piece by Purcell called "Music for a While." He'd transcribed the countertenor melody of the song for Peter and instructed him to play without vibrato, so as to approximate the sound of the fretted violins of the period. At the first rehearsal Claude had realized the wisdom of his choice. It was early music, pre-Bach, cyclical in form and contrapuntal in style. It had only to be played flatly and accurately to tick along like a Swiss watch, revealing its delicate structure and cool lyricism all by itself. Interpretation was not necessary.

Claude and Peter sat together on the piano bench, waiting, watching the glittering scene. After the toasts, everyone seemed to start talking at once. Blue cigarette smoke spread like cirrus high above the guests. Catherine got up from her side, closing the door behind her.

"It's funny how far away they seem when you're up here," Peter said.

"Nervous?" Claude asked.

"No." He seemed, indeed, quite calm. "I told you Dicky would get drunk. Look, he spilled something. He went to your school, you know. He plays lacrosse. Big goon. He has a crush on Catherine, but she won't even talk to him."

"Who *does* she talk to?"

"No boys, that's for sure," Peter said, and Claude felt relief. "You know how stuck-up she is."

"Yes. I do."

Dewman Fisk stood and tapped the side of his glass for silence. "And now," he announced, "a brief period of entertainment from the children." Scattered applause. Tappings of glasses in approval. "First, my son Peter will play the violin, after which time Catherine will present a short *tableau vivant* drawn from classical mythology." Much applause, especially from the ballet dancers. "Peter, you may begin."

With a sigh, Peter rose, took up his position near the curve of the grand piano, adjusted the music on his stand, tucked the violin under his chin, and tuned up rapidly to Claude's soft A. The child had an accurate ear, at least, for which Claude was grateful. Pointing at the crowd with his bow, Peter shouted out, " 'Music for a While,' by Henry Purcell." The room fell entirely silent, except for distant noises from the kitchen.

The moment he laid his fingers on the keys Claude was oblivious of his surroundings, aware only of Peter, into whose magnified eyes he stared fixedly. The feel of the keys, the topography of them — so familiar, so constant — launched him into a trance, like an infant at his mother's breast or a true believer before the moment of communion. He paused, imagining the music in his mind, and then began to play. Four bars of introduction, a nod to Peter, and they were launched, the stately bass figure ascending smoothly, the top line of the piano fitting the free melody of the violin, the inner voices moving effortlessly, all of it spinning into the languid air. Peter played confidently, not bothering with the music. Claude heard the words to the bittersweet melody in his mind:

> Music,
> Music,
> For a while,
> Shall all your cares beguile.
> Shall all, all, all,
> Shall all, all, all,
> Shall all your cares beguile.

It was going so well Claude introduced the slightest rallentando as they approached the cadence. Peter followed with uncharacteristic smoothness, and then gave a lopsided smile as they held the last chord. "Terrific," Claude whispered when it ended.

Peter put his violin on top of the piano and turned to the audience to acknowledge the applause. He placed his forearm rigidly across his waist and bowed twice. Then he stepped back and swept his arm up to indicate Claude. This formal gesture got a little laugh through the applause as Claude half stood at the piano and nodded to the crowd. Mrs. Fisk came forward to wait at the foot of the stage as Peter descended, folding him under her arm, kissing the top of his head, and shepherding him back to her table, giving quick squeezes that hunched up his shoulders.

Suddenly the stage lights went out. Claude sat in the darkness and watched all the lights at the opposite end of the room come on.

Catherine, barefoot, wearing a white knee-length toga and a green cape, ran from the dressing room and leaped onto a coffee table in front of the fireplace.

"Hark!" she cried, and all heads turned in her direction. "Hark to the story of Daphne and Apollo!" She spread her arms, her voice ringing out strongly. "I am Daphne, and my father is Peneus, god of the river. He allows me freedom to do what I want, to run in the deep woods, my hair full of leaves, my legs and arms cut by brambles and thorns, my heart wild as I hunt, like Diana. I am free!" She jumped gracefully from the table, ran to the side of the room, and mimed shooting arrows in the general direction of Central Park. Then she froze, staring at the audience. "What is that noise?" From the corridor to the kitchen came the sound of running (Claude knew this was Charles, the chauffeur, running in place, having picked up his cue). "It is Apollo! Chasing me!" she cried, and ran in a zigzag pattern toward the tables.

"Do not fear" came the muffled shout of Charles. "Stop and find out who I am. No rude rustic or shepherd, I am the Lord of Delphi, and I love you."

"I know," said Catherine, addressing the audience as she strode back and forth before them, her eyes glittering. "I know the message of the nymphs to Prometheus. May you never, oh never, behold me sharing the couch of a god. May none of the dwellers in heaven draw near to me ever. Such love as the high gods know, from whose eyes none can hide, may that never be mine. To war with a god-lover is not war, it is despair." Now she ran, legs flashing, through the tables, weaving in and out toward the stage. From the pantry, Charles increased his tempo. This was Claude's cue to go to the wings, which he did. Isidra was on her knees, her right hand on the handle of one of two long, blue cardboard cutouts shaped to represent waves, which stretched across the back of the stage to the opposite wing, where another maid knelt in a similar posture. Isidra looked up, her expression entirely blank, and Claude nodded.

"As fleet as I am, he is a god and he will catch me sooner or later," Catherine cried as she ran up the steps to the skirt. She screamed, and it raised the hair on Claude's arms. "Help me, Father, help me!" She extended her arms to the rented scrim, which represented a river, and Isidra began pulling and pushing the handle. The two long cutouts passed back and forth in opposite directions, creating the illusion of water. "My father is too deep in the river to hear me." Now her movements to stage center became stylized, slow motion. "A dragging numbness comes upon me." She stopped and faced the audience. "Now my feet send roots into the sandy earth. Bark encloses me. Leaves sprout forth. I have changed into a tree, a laurel."

She grasped the edges of her cape and slowly raised her arms. Slender laurel branches had been sewn into the material. "Apollo watched the transformation with grief," Catherine said. " 'O fairest of maidens, you are lost to me,' he cried. 'But henceforth with your leaves my victors shall wreathe their brows. You shall have your part in all my triumphs. Apollo and his laurel shall be joined together wherever songs are sung and stories told.' "

This was Claude's cue, but it took him a moment to react, so fascinated was he by her image. She had swept through the recitation with a kind of recklessness, an abandon that now seemed to infuse her with power. Her small white figure under the lights seemed to radiate some fierce and intangible energy. When she turned her head, looking for him, her gaze was so intent, so focused, it felt almost like a blow. Startled, he looked around at his feet for the wreath, found it, picked it up, and proceeded onstage. He approached her slowly, holding the wreath before him, bringing it to her outstretched hand, which she then laid upon it. He could see drops of sweat at her temples, glistening there, her cheeks flushed, her lips slightly swollen.

"Thus the wreath," she cried, her dark eyes sharp, seeming almost angry, "is carried to the champion."

A buzz in the audience as Claude bore the wreath down the steps, across the open space, past the first tables and up to Dewman Fisk. The man's face seemed even more long and melancholy, as if his head had been pressed from either side by some great vise. His eyes were dull, unfocused. As Claude placed the wreath on Fisk's head, he thought he saw a faint welling of tears.

As the applause started, Claude remembered to step out of the way, out of Catherine's line of sight. "I want to see him," she had said. "And you watch his lower lip. See if it quivers." It was not quivering.

Catherine stepped backward and the curtains were drawn jerkily, two or three feet at a time, until with a final swing they joined.

Claude did not speak to Catherine again that evening. When she rejoined the party, still dressed in the toga, the green cape (with the laurel branches removed), and new gold sandals, she was surrounded by a knot of men, pressing her with champagne and conversation, and he could think of no way to approach her.

Mrs. Fisk and Peter withdrew, presumably to retire. Senator Barnes, tall, white-haired, with very light blue eyes, drifted into the library with Dewman, the mayor, Nelson Rockefeller, and a dozen other men. The ballet dancers, the other guests, and Catherine with her entourage milled about in the living room. Claude tried to catch her eye to wave goodbye, but she was constantly in motion, talking and laughing with great animation, spinning from one face to the other.

The candles were beginning to gutter, and as the staff began discreetly to clean up, Claude went to the cloakroom for his coat. Balanchine was there, staring into a mirror and rubbing the hair back over his ears. He caught Claude in the glass.

"That was well done, young man," he said. "Very professional."

"Thank you, sir." Claude left, crossed the foyer, and slipped out the front door. He buttoned his coat up to his neck and walked home.

10

T HAT WINTER Claude saw a movie called *A Place in the Sun*, with Elizabeth Taylor and Montgomery Clift, and was swept away. He fell in love with Taylor, and, without knowing it, with Clift. The story — poor boy falls in love with beautiful rich girl, but the relationship is doomed because of his previous affair and impregnation of a poor factory girl (Shelley Winters) — struck him as profound and tragic. His heart seemed to twist as he saw the two young people, before things got complicated, flirting over a billiards table, water-skiing on a bright lake, riding horseback through the woods, dancing, kissing. He was drawn back to the Loew's Orpheum again and again, until he could play the entire movie in his mind, from the first frame to the last. (The only fly in the ointment was the soundtrack: sentimental strings, unimaginatively arranged, playing a schmaltzy love theme with a two-bar melody that didn't go anywhere. After a while he didn't even hear it.) It never occurred to him that there might be a connection between the movie, which had the power to make him weak at the knees, and Catherine, who could do exactly the same thing. It did not occur to him that his adolescent desire for Elizabeth Taylor was mixed up with a yearning for the rich, secure, gentle, and civilized world in which the Taylor character and her family lived. This, he imagined, was the real world, the world as it should be — secure, love drenched, and safe. There was an almost unbearable beauty to the image of Taylor languishing sadly under a lap rug in a bay window, autumn leaves swirling in the air behind her, dreaming of her lover in his jail cell. As well, Claude was moved by her father's tactful concern.

When the movie crossed the street over to the Loew's Eighty-sixth for a second run, Claude took Ivan to see it, forgoing the balcony to sit downstairs, very close to the screen, in which, had he been able to arrange it, he would undoubtedly have wrapped himself.

Afterward, outside on the sidewalk, Claude still deep in the movie's spell, Ivan thought it better to say nothing for a while. They walked up toward Prexy's.

"What'd you think?" Claude finally asked.

"I enjoyed it. The script was intelligent. Good direction, good acting."

"Isn't she beautiful? I used to think Jean Simmons — did you see her in *Blue Lagoon*? Just incredibly lovely. But now I don't know." He gave an apologetic little laugh. "I can't get this movie out of my system. I've seen it four times now."

"It's very romantic," Ivan said. "Much more so than the book. Dreiser is interesting. Possibly the clumsiest writer that ever put pen to paper in terms of style. Just awful. But the ideas and the structures are wonderful. There's a part when he's working in a big fancy hotel. It's not in the movie. Somehow the hotel becomes a symbol for the city and the whole hierarchical capitalist system. It's marvelous. You'll like it. Not in the same way as the movie, of course."

"I know it isn't real," Claude said. "But it gets to me."

"Movies can do that."

Claude was seldom home, but it became clear that Al was now a frequent visitor. If the intensity of the first encounter between Al and Claude's mother had been a mystery, no less puzzling was the way he seemed to be helping her, guiding her with great patience back to something like normalcy. It had taken only a couple of weeks to persuade her to get back to driving the cab for at least part of the day, with the late afternoons and evenings reserved for her "project," as they came to call it.

One night he came home to find them drinking beer at the kitchenette counter (she had stopped keeping whiskey in the apartment), working with pencils and paper, drawing up budgets.

"He ain't as bad as some of them," Al said, referring to Mr. Skouras, the landlord. "Now you at least making the rent, he pulled those eviction papers. You chip away at that back debt twenty dollars a month, I bet he'll go for it. Give you the time."

"Yes, maybe," she said. "But that means driving ten or twelve hours a day again. I'd have to give up the project."

Al looked thoughtful.

"I'm getting the goods on those crooks. I don't want to stop now."

"I can see that." He nodded and rubbed his thumb on the side of his bottle of Pabst Blue Ribbon. "You put in a lot of work here."

Claude had sensed that telling his mother he'd actually been in the same room with the mayor or that he'd talked to the man's bodyguards would only excite her unnecessarily, perhaps setting her off on some manic spin. The thought of her showing up at the Fisk mansion, hurling accusations and demanding justice, made his blood run cold.

"Tell you what," Al said. "How about another driver? Keep that medallion on the street, making money two shifts."

"Oh, sure. How am I going to find an honest hackie? I'd get robbed, and the way they drive, it would ruin the car."

"I used to hack," Al said quietly. "I got a chauffeur's license. Kept it up, for some reason."

She put down her beer and stared into his fox-like face. "You mean *you*? You'd do it?"

"Sure. For a while. Till you get even. Four or five hours a night. The usual split."

"Well, that would be great." She smiled. "Great."

"Then it's settled," Al said. "Let's go over the numbers again, see how they come out now."

Claude had gotten so used to the towering piles of newspapers, magazines, files, and cardboard boxes of correspondence that he only gradually became aware that they seemed to be getting smaller, the paths between the stacks growing wider. He interrupted them one afternoon as they sat on the floor, Emma with a ledger, Al methodically going through a large mound of papers spilled out between them. He would pick up five or six papers at a time, glance over them, and hand them to Emma one by one.

"This is cement contracts," Al said.

She took the paper and, twisting, dropped it into one of a number of large numbered cartons behind her.

"These two are the sanitation department."

She repeated the gesture, dropping them into a different carton.

"What's going on?" Claude asked.

"This stuff is all mixed up," Al said. "We're getting it organized."

"For the archives," his mother said with satisfaction in her voice.

"The what?"

"The archives," she repeated. "It was Al's idea."

"Sure," Al said. "Lot of important stuff in here. Got to save it for the future." He looked up at Claude. "You know. History."

All at once Claude understood. He knew perfectly well from previous conversations that Al considered the hoarding of all this printed material to be an expression of Emma's disturbed state of mind. "Got to wean her away from it," he had said, "like a junkie off horse." Claude was moved by the man's seemingly inexhaustible patience, going through thousands of pages of trash as if it were important material. Al watched Claude carefully. It was a delicate moment, an invitation to live out the necessary lie, to treat Emma, temporarily at least, like a child, and a sick child at that. Al's face betrayed nothing but an extreme alertness. Claude gave the faintest nod.

"Moving it over to my building," Al said, busy again. "Got a safe place there."

"My archives." Emma gave a little laugh. "On Park Avenue."

"I take 'em two or three at a time in the cab. Everything numbered. Emma puts it down in the book."

"Can I help?"

"No, no," Emma said quickly. "We've got a system."

Satterthwaite's office was a small cubicle off the music room. The man himself, now that Claude had a good look at him, had an odd appearance, seeming, with his blue-white skin drawn taut and shiny over his face — so taut Claude imagined someone behind the man, with his knee in Satterthwaite's spine, pulling the skin at the back of his head — his slightly bulbous eyes, his lips blue, like some large fish.

"It says before I can apply for your composition class I have to take harmony," Claude said.

"Yes." The faintest trace of a lisp.

"I've had a lot of harmony already. And theory."

"From whom?"

"Mr. Weisfeld. You know Weisfeld's Music Store on Third Avenue? He started teaching me years ago."

"And the internationally renowned Mr. Fredericks? A bit there too?"

The delivery was so flat and emotionless Claude could not tell if irony was intended. Had he thought it was, he would have gotten up and left the room. After a moment he said, "Well, it came up all the time. He assumed I knew harmony, and mostly we worked on interpretation."

"Do you?"

"Do I what?"

"Do you know harmony?"

"Well, yes, I guess I do. I mean, I'm sure I don't know everything but . . ."

"Do you have an hour? Right now?" Satterthwaite got up and went to a filing cabinet.

"I guess so. Sure."

As Satterthwaite pulled out a drawer with his short arms, even his body seemed fish-like. His feet, in black shoes, heels touching, toes pointing out at a wide angle, were like fins. With the curve up to his wide waist, closing then to his narrow shoulders, and the head very close to the body, he looked like a dolphin standing on its tail. He extracted some papers from a file and handed them to Claude. "This is the final examination from last year's harmony class. You may do it in the next room." He glanced at his wristwatch. "Return in one hour."

"Okay. That seems fair." Claude took the exam papers.

"Fair?" Satterthwaite said, turning, his hands folded at the small of his back, to look out the window. "Fairness has nothing to do with it, Mr. Rawlings. It is a matter of *requirements.*"

Claude went into the other room, took a desk near the piano, and went to work. The first set of questions instructed him to identify a long list of musical terms relating to scales, modes, and their harmonic properties. He flew through these. Next, a series of chords to be identified in the context of various key signatures, including second and third inversions. Then he was asked to analyze some modulation series from Mozart, Bach, and Haydn. Only one chord, in the Mozart, was somewhat ambiguous due to the lack of a root, but because the previous chord was clearly a C, he called it a G, with a ninth.

The last question made him smile: "Western music uses twelve tones. There are twelve tones on the piano — not eleven, not thirteen or fourteen. Why? Why twelve?" He remembered the precise moment in the basement of the music store so many years ago when Weisfeld had explained it to him. Now, glancing up at the clock on the wall, he realized he'd used up only fifteen minutes, so he decided to try to impress Satterthwaite.

The overtone series (he wrote), also called the harmonic series, is determined by nature. The piano string at low C vibrates at 64 per second, but also segments of that string vibrate separately at the same time, the pitch going up according to the length of the segment — two halves, three thirds, four quarters, until they get too small to matter. One-half length of the low C vibrates at 128 per second, or an octave higher. That is the first overtone. One third the length of the low C creates a G above the second C. That is the second overtone, and the interval is a fifth. Now the overtones keep going up, but the one that really matters is the G, because it is the loudest, and the closest to the tonic C. So nature says if you take any note as the tonic, its closest relative will be a fifth above, the root of the dominant.

If you go in a straight line from tonic to dominant, and then make the dominant a new tonic going to *its* dominant, and keep on going *on a tempered piano* (he very much enjoyed remembering to put in this last bit, and even underlined it), you get C, G, D, A, E, B, F#, C#, G#, D#, A#, F, and C again. That makes twelve tones before you come back to C, and that's why there are twelve instead of some other number.

He took the pages in to Satterthwaite, having used only half the allotted time, and placed them on the desk. Satterthwaite looked up from his book. "Finished? Check your box tomorrow."

"Yes, sir."

"You've done Fuchs, I suppose? Sometime in the distant past?"

"Yes, sir."

"Fine." He went back to his book.

They often walked up to the luncheonette on First Avenue for cartons of coffee and donuts, which they would take down to a bench overlooking the East River. Ivan talked incessantly, so intent on his ideas Claude sometimes had to guide him past fire hydrants and ashcans like a blind man.

"So of course it had been building for some time," Ivan said, "but then fifty years ago everything changed. Just like that!" He snapped his fingers. "And fifty years is nothing, historically speaking. The blink of an eye. Most people still don't know it happened."

"They know about the atom bomb," Claude said.

"They know it worked. They're vaguely aware that there's some sort of connection between mass and energy. But it's just a bomb. I'm talking about the big picture. Of course, once you get into this stuff you have to read in about a dozen different directions — physics, cosmology, history of science, philosophy, things like optics. It's fascinating, but I still sometimes feel as if I'm jumping all over the place. Just the other day I found out that in terms of size, man is apparently in the exact center of the observable universe."

"What do you mean? Watch it! Don't step in that."

"The largest thing we know about is the red-giant star. The smallest is the electron. We're in the middle — we're just as much larger than the electron as the red giant is larger than us."

"Hey, Copernicus would've liked that."

"Yes, he would. On the other hand, *I* don't particularly like it. It seems such a coincidence."

Claude pushed open the door to the luncheonette. "So it's a coincidence. Didn't you say it's a coincidence that the moon is exactly the right size to cover the sun in an eclipse?"

They sat on stools and ordered coffee and donuts to go. A skinny old man filled the cartons right in front of them.

"Yes, well, that's an oddity, but there's no place to go with it. This other matter" — he made a quick humming noise, which he sometimes did when chasing down a thought — "Look, you go down and down and there's the atom, protons, electrons, and it doesn't matter if they're little balls or wave phenomena or whatever. Heisenberg comes in and you can't look at anything smaller because the beam of your fancy flashlight is going to knock the little thing away or change it or something. So you're stopped at that end."

The skinny old man had the order ready, but he stood motionless, watching Ivan.

"At the other end you've got the red giant. But where are we looking from? From Earth, right? Looking out at the visible universe, everything speeding away from us, the farther away the faster the speed. Doesn't the question of scale enter here, possibly? Suppose we could somehow get so big we got *out* of the universe — forget about the curvature of space for a moment — you know, if we got out we could look back, or down or something, who knows what we might see? But we're topped at that end too."

The old man put the coffee containers, each with a napkin and a donut on top, on the counter.

"Maybe," Ivan said, reaching out, "everything is in the middle, from its point of view. Maybe there's no middle."

They were out the door and on the sidewalk before Claude said, "Hey, we didn't pay him." He went back in and gave the old man fifty cents. "Sorry."

The man nodded. "Tell me something. Do you understand what he's talking about?" He seemed genuinely curious.

"Not all of it. I usually get the drift, though."

"That must be some school you boys go to. I get 'em in here all the time, but that fella takes the cake." He moved down the counter, shaking his head.

"He thinks you're nuts," Claude said as they walked toward the river.

"Sure he does. He thinks a ten-pound cannonball falls faster than a one-ounce marble too. He'd bet money on it." Ivan quickened his step. "It's been three hundred and fifty years since they proved that every-thing falls at the same rate, and that fellow still doesn't know it. But then, even Newton, most elegant of thinkers — no, I take that back, *second* most elegant of thinkers — even Newton, although he knew it, didn't know what to do with it. You know his explanation?"

"No, I don't."

"He just sidestepped it. He'd worked out damn near everything else. The principle of inertia, the three laws of motion, all that, and it was really beautiful. But his law of gravitation? The cannonball and the marble? I just read a description. How did it go?" He stopped dead in the street, raised his head, and stared at the sky, repeating from mem-ory: " 'The mysterious force by which a material body attracts another body increases with the mass of the object it attracts. If an object is small, its inertia is small, but the force that gravity exerts on it is also small. If an object is big, its inertia is great, but the force that gravity exerts on it is also great. Hence gravity is always exerted in the precise degree necessary to overcome the inertia of any object. And that is why all objects fall at the same rate, regardless of their inertial mass.' Lincoln Barnett."

"You mean you memorized that?" Claude said, his voice rising. "You remember it word for word?"

Ivan started walking again. "No, no," he said impatiently, "it's just a trick. I can see the page in my mind. Sort of read it again. It's useful sometimes, but it doesn't mean anything."

"Wow."

"But you see how he fudged it? That's some kind of a coincidence, gravity adjusting to inertia like that. No experiments to back it up. And what about gravity acting instantaneously over millions of miles? Inverse of the distance notwithstanding. Instantaneously? Like nothing else in nature? Einstein didn't believe it."

"Is that why he —"

"That and a lot of other things. All the tag ends of this and that, little discrepancies, various conundrums like absolute motion. We say something is going a thousand miles an hour, but what if the thing it's *going* on is going ten thousand miles an hour in a different direction?"

"Subtract?" Claude suggested.

"And the solar system is moving, and the galaxy is moving, and the universe is expanding? There isn't any fixed point. There isn't anything stationary to measure from. You see the problem?"

They reached the promenade and sat on their favorite bench. The day was bright and crisp, the river glittering in the sun. For a few moments they ate, drank, and regarded the scene. Behind them they could hear the shouts of boys playing basketball behind the high wire fences of the Bentley School playground.

"Einstein was only six years older than I am when he saw the new system," Ivan said. "And it's taking everything I've got to even begin to understand it."

"Don't worry about it," Claude said, licking his fingers. "You should hear some of the music Mozart wrote when he was six and seven."

"The trouble is, we're so thoroughly trained by what we see directly." He spread his arm to indicate the vista before him. "The banks of the river. The river. That tug with the barges going upstream. The sunshine. Clouds up above. It's our little system and it's hard to push one's imagination beyond it."

"So what did he say about gravity?"

"It's the same as inertia. You know when you go up in a fast elevator? When it's accelerating and your stomach goes *bloop?* Well, everything in that elevator gets pulled down equally, regardless of its weight. Your stomach or the change in your pockets, no difference."

"But that doesn't work. They're standing upside down in China. The earth can't be accelerating in two different directions."

"It can, actually, but that isn't relevant. The elevator image is what he calls a thought experiment. It starts getting very complicated as he builds them. I'm working on it, but you get some wild stuff. Everything is related. Matter is just congealed energy. Energy — light, radiation, et cetera — is just, uh, released mass. Space itself is affected by the mass in it. It sort of bends around heavy stuff, ergo light bends as well."

"What do you mean? Space? Emptiness? Emptiness bends?"

"Yes, I know. It's hard to imagine because we can't visualize it. But the fact is, there's only one constant, unchanging thing in the universe — the speed of light. It's the same everywhere. It doesn't change if the source is coming towards you or going away. It always moves at 186,282.4 miles per second. It helps me to not even think of the speed, but to just think it *is*. I mean light *is*."

"You've lost me," Claude said.

When Claude had gone to his school mailbox for the harmony exam, he'd been surprised to see it unmarked, with only one notation at the bottom of the last page: *accepted for composition,* in Satterthwaite's severely slanted hand. Nor had any mention of it been made since. All the more remarkable, Claude thought, because there were only two students, himself and a moody, self-absorbed math whiz named Platt. Twice a week they sat, one seat away from each other, in the front row of the music room, watching Satterthwaite drift back and forth in front of the blackboard, lecturing with his slight lisp, filling the air with chalk motes in rapid spasms of erasure.

Then one day — the big day, Claude was later to think of it — the startling news was revealed. Satterthwaite wrote $I \times V I$ on the board.

"This," he said, tapping the board with the chalk, "represents the music of the classical period and almost all of the romantic period. I, establish the tonic; x, develop harmonies as long as you like; leading to V, the dominant; and returning to I, the tonic and closure. Tonal music. It has prevailed for more than three hundred years. This is what you've been doing in your little exercises up to now." He went to his desk and sat on the corner. "But as you have no doubt noticed from my daily analyses of the romantics on the board, there is a progressively more impatient pressing against the bounds of tonality rising through the latter part of the nineteenth century. More and more work at the edges of the system. Do you see that?"

"Yes," said Platt. "Definitely."

Claude nodded.

"So things were building up, and then, all at once, about fifty years ago, everything changed." He snapped his fingers, exactly as Ivan had done. "Like that!" The smile on his tight face was almost eerie. "Schönberg!"

Silence. Satterthwaite raised his hands in the air, folded them as if in prayer, touched the end of his nose, and said again, more softly this time, "Schönberg."

And so, in the next few classes the story was told. Schönberg's early traditional work. His brave leap to atonality and the long period of grappling with its theoretical implications, culminating, finally, in the twelve-tone system of composition. The greatest and most exciting advance in the history of music, according to Satterthwaite.

"You must understand that tonality is nothing more than the way we have been trained to hear. Assonance, dissonance, these are matters, in a certain sense, of fashion. Nothing more. We have been trained into tonality, and the new music can train us out of it. Someday, when the larger and purer music has opened our ears, we will hear everything differently. You understand what I'm saying? We will hear differently. And that, gentlemen, is what this class is all about. I will lead you out of your tonal prejudices into an entirely new world. The world of the future."

Both boys were mesmerized by the change in their teacher, from a distant, sarcastic figure to a man seized by a vision. They glimpsed a kind of messianic prophet breaking through the cool façade, and for a moment it scared them, it was so abrupt and powerful. But, almost as if by an effort of will, the fire in his eyes was suddenly extinguished and he was back to his old self, moving to the board.

"So, let us begin. We start to use a new vocabulary. The tone row, for instance."

It was raining outside, so they lounged in the common room, on opposite couches, their feet up on the low table in between.

"Say that again, please," Ivan requested, pulling at his right eyebrow, trying to see the hairs, his eyes crossed.

"What are you doing?" Exasperated, Claude made a clucking sound.

"I'm listening, I'm listening. Say again."

"Well," Claude said, "you write what he calls a set. You use all twelve tones in any order you want, but no tone can appear more than once in the set."

"Why not?"

"If you use a note more than once, it might suggest a tonality. Like, that's the tonic. The point is to avoid *anything* that suggests tonality."

"Aha. I understand, vaguely."

"And then, get this. As you go along you can use the set the way you wrote it. You can use it upside down, backwards, or backwards upside down."

"Sounds like Bach, a bit."

"But only those ways," Claude said. "And anyway, the whole point of Bach's system was to reconcile chromaticism and tonality. There was a reason for his so-called rules."

"Why do you say 'so-called'?"

"Because he broke them all the time. Whenever he wanted. These rules are strict."

"At least they're simple."

"Not that simple," said Claude. "Once you've made a set, you're allowed to state it beginning on any one of the twelve tones."

"Hmm."

"You can state vertically, in chords, or horizontally, like some weird melody. It gets complicated. But the thing is, I don't see what the big deal is. I don't understand where the rules have any reason behind them, except to avoid tonality."

"A negative *raison d'être*."

"What does that, I hate it when you speak French, what does . . ."

"Sorry, sorry. A negative reason for being. Avoid tonality and be forced into the new way of hearing you were talking about. Maybe it *is* a big deal. Maybe they think some new kind of hyper-harmony will emerge? Sounds very idealistic. Like Marx saying the State will wither away."

"It just feels wrong somehow," Claude said. "The whole thing."

Claude's daily routine during this time was highly structured, having come about quite naturally. It gave him a sense of security. Interruptions, unexpected events, or unforeseen demands on his time could make him irritable. He woke in his cot at five-thirty every morning — to the sound of the Big Ben alarm clock he'd gotten from Weisfeld to catch the train to Frank's Landing in the old days — ate cereal in the dark and silent kitchenette, went up Third Avenue to the music store, entered with his own key, and went down to the basement for two hours of practice on the Bechstein. Scales. Exercises to warm up, to get the fingers supple, the arms and shoulders moving smoothly. ("Not just a digital exercise," Fredericks had said. "They are beautiful. They can be played beautifully." Claude had discovered the truth of those words.) And then an hour or so of sight-reading. To the right of the Bechstein's music stand was a large and ever-changing pile of music — where both Claude and Weisfeld tossed manuscripts of all kinds — from which Claude would blindly pull something, play it, and then move it over to the pile on the left of the music stand. Then forty-five minutes to an hour of concentrated effort on whatever special piece he was working on at the time. At eight-thirty Weisfeld would open the door at the top of the stairs and cry, "Good morning, good morning!" Claude would then finish up and ascend for the coffee Weisfeld brought down from his quarters in large mugs. They usually sat on stools by the cash register, or sometimes up front looking out at the street. By nine o'clock Claude would be at school. Except for the time he spent with Ivan, he used every available minute — free periods, lunch, part of gym, assembly — to read, prepare for his classes, or do homework. The other boys, most of them relaxed, good-natured, given to larking about at every opportunity, seemed nevertheless to respect his privacy and did not tease him. Indeed, sometimes when they passed him as he worked in some corner, or sitting on the stairs, they would lower their voices, nodding as they passed. He knew a few of them by name, but most only by their last names, as they were addressed in class: Baldridge, Keller, Wilson, Abernathy, Cooper, Garcez, Peabody.

At four he was back in the store, waiting on customers, arranging the stock, sweeping the floor or doing whatever else was needed. Occasionally Weisfeld would go out for short periods, coming back with a book or some groceries. Now and then he would unlock the door to the second floor and go upstairs for a nap. Claude could hear the creaking of the floorboards as he moved around up there.

He usually ate supper at Wright's, the Automat, or one of the cafeterias on Eighty-sixth Street. He had a favorite meal at each establishment. Then he would return to the store — Weisfeld most often having retired for the day — and go down to the basement to listen to records, copy scores, play the piano, compose (both at the piano and at the worktable), and read manuscripts and books. He was home by eleven and asleep in his cot by a quarter past. There were interruptions — the movies, weekend wanderings with Ivan, and sometimes he would run into Al and Emma having a late supper as Al came off shift.

Claude had noticed that the kitchenette was now scrupulously clean and orderly, and that there were some new cooking utensils. Al, it turned out, was a good cook.

"I don't know how you do it in such a tiny space," Emma said one night.

"Just keep it organized," Al said with a shrug. He shook a frying pan, turned a knob, peered into a pot, and began to set out dishes. "Try a little taste?" he asked Claude.

"Sure."

Al turned his back and went to work.

Emma, with a regular-sized bottle of beer, was in a cheerful mood. "We did well today. We both had trips to Idlewild, and Al picked up two cases of oil uptown at half price."

"Remember that guy under the overpass?" Al said. "Ran into eight cases somehow." He gave a little laugh. "He's all right, though. Might get him to do a ring job. The car could use it."

"How is Mr. Weisfeld?" Emma asked. "I saw him in the street. He always looks so pale."

"He's fine. He just doesn't go out much."

"Well, give him my regards. Thank him again for all he's doing. I still can't believe you're in that fancy school."

Al turned and presented the food. Shaved ham with redeye gravy, greens with butter, and hash brown potatoes with bits of onion and green pepper. All three of them fell to.

"Damn, that's good," Emma said.

Al presented four biscuits that had been warming in a pot on the hot plate. "Make biscuits in a pot. I used to watch my momma."

"Where is your momma?" Claude asked, savoring a bite of ham.

"Oh, she dead. My daddy too. Long time ago." He ate fastidiously, giving the food his complete attention for several moments, and then took a sip of beer. "It's some story," he said, lowering the bottle. "Like in a book."

"What happened?"

He ate some more, then looked out into the middle distance. "They was out in the field, chopping cotton. The sky was getting dark and the bossman, he standing there in the wind, feeling a few little bitty drops of rain, he get mad and starts telling everybody to work faster. See, he wants to make the quota and go on back to the house. He got this little leather stick he's always swatting in the palm of his hand, you know? Ain't a real horsewhip, it's more like a lady's horsewhip. So he starts moving through the rows, hitting people on their feet, on their ankles, shouting at them hurry up, he ain't got his hat."

"My God," Emma said, sitting up.

"Well, that bossman, he start hitting my momma's feet, and he don't know my daddy's in the next row. Now my daddy, he was a big man, and I mean big. They called him Bear. His name was Sam but everybody called him Bear. He rose up and told the bossman stop hitting my momma. Bossman call him a no-account nigger and hit him right across the face with that leather stick." He stopped, ate a bite of food, and looked first at Emma, then at Claude. "Now, you got to remember my daddy standing there with the cotton knife right in his hand. Bossman ain't got no time to unbuckle everything and get out his gun. Can't do it if my daddy make a move. By now there's people standing around watching, see what's gonna happen. It's raining. My daddy throw his knife on the ground. Bossman try to go for his gun, but my daddy is on him in a flash, just pounding away with his great big fists look like two smoked hams. He just beat the Jesus out of that man, sloshing around in the mud and the rain, bringing him down. And my momma screaming at him to stop, pulling his rope belt as hard as she could, trying to get him off that white man." He took another sip of beer and stared at the bottle. "So all that hollering brought another bossman, come over from the other side of the field to see what's going on. Now this one has his gun *out*. He lifts it up and points it straight at my daddy. My daddy just stand there, Momma behind him on her knees, moaning. Now everybody waiting for him to pull the trigger, and he's just about to when suddenly a bolt of lightning comes out of the sky with thunder like the end of the world, and that lightning go *straight to the gun*. Can you beat that? It goes straight to the gun, like it was aimed. Course, I suppose it was the iron really, but anyway that second bossman drop dead as a stone."

Both Claude and Emma had forgotten about their food and sat still as statues. Al took some greens on his fork.

"So what happened?" Claude asked. "I mean, your parents?"

"The Klan got them two nights later. Strung them up by the river."

There was complete silence. They stared at Al for what seemed a long time, until the faintest wisp of a smile appeared on the black man's mouth. Emma immediately burst into laughter and almost fell off her stool.

"What? What?" Claude cried.

Now Al was laughing, nodding his head.

"Oh, you had me," she said, wiping tears from her eyes. "You had me good."

"What?" Claude repeated.

"Just funning, boy," Al said gently. "A little entertainment. Just a way to pass the time."

"You mean . . ."

"My momma died of sugar in the blood. My daddy was a drunk, broke his head on the toilet in the back of a bar one night. That's the way it really was."

Claude had buried (but not, of course, completely extinguished) the memories of his early childhood — the vague nausea, the loneliness, weakness, and vulnerability. Fear of those old ghosts drove him, without his knowing it, into a dependency on ritual, and into a highly compartmentalized way of life. If there was anything remotely like a center to his existence, it was Weisfeld and the studio below the store, but his mother was separate, school was entirely separate, his love for Catherine was both hidden and separate, the movies were a world unto themselves — and it was as if he were a slightly different person in each setting. He intuitively sensed that this was a good thing, that the compartmentalization worked to protect the most valuable and personal source of strength he had, music. Only when he was in music, awash in it, could he feel truly secure. Only music had the power to lift him out of himself and relieve him of the burden of himself. There were moments with Catherine, moments in the movies, moments while reading a book or chasing down ideas with Ivan, moments of silence in the mysteriously calming and strengthening presence of Weisfeld — but these were evanescent, transitory echoes of what he got directly from music.

At school he did almost everything he had to do right there on the premises. He would come early or stay late if necessary, adjusting his schedule to maintain the compartments. His high grades he took as a confirmation of this strategy.

Thus he became uncomfortable when Satterthwaite's twelve-tone challenge began to leak out of the compartment of school and into the rest of his life. He found himself playing Schönberg on the Bechstein, listening to Schönberg on the phonograph, and studying scores in an increasingly tense state of frustration tinged with fear. He understood the mathematical and structural nature of the work, but that was all he understood. He was not learning to hear in a new way, and if there was music in there, he was missing it. He said nothing about this for months, until one morning when Weisfeld asked an innocuous question about school.

"I should have skipped Satterthwaite's Music Three," the boy said.

"Really?" Weisfeld raised his eyebrows. "Why is that?"

"It's all twelve-tone." Claude looked down. "The other kid is a math whiz, and he loves it, can't get enough of it. I hate it. It's driving me crazy."

"Why?"

"It doesn't seem to matter what it sounds like. I mean, they don't really seem to care. It's all just structure. I don't even bother to play the stuff I hand in. I write it out in study hall and don't even try to hear it in my head."

"Which would be difficult in any case," Weisfeld said. "Satterthwaite admires Schönberg?"

"Schönberg is God."

"A certain amount of talk about purity?"

"All the time. And the word 'free,' he uses that a lot and gets excited."

"I see." Weisfeld watched the boy for a moment and then stared upward, beginning the slow stroking of his mustache that he did, unconsciously, when he was thinking. Claude knew when to remain silent. The thinking on this occasion went on for an unusually long time. Finally Weisfeld got up and said, "Let's go downstairs."

When they reached the basement Weisfeld turned with a smile. "Remember Fuchs? Counterpoint when you were just a little squirt?"

"It was fun."

"You got all hot — I remember it, your face actually turned red when you weren't allowed to use parallel fifths. Boy oh boy, you were steamed. 'Why not? Why not?' you'd asked. You loved the sound of them."

"But you explained it. It made sense. Give up that sound and the lines will fit better, and you get other sounds."

"Let me see something you've done in twelve-tone." Weisfeld went to the piano.

Claude went to his worktable, rummaged around, and came back with a single sheet of music. "It's awful," he said.

Weisfeld held the paper in his hand and studied it for several minutes. He traced each bar with his fingertip, occasionally giving a small nod or a barely audible grunt. Then he put the paper on the music stand and looked at it for another moment. "This is not awful. That little rhythmic figure in the second bar, the way you fool around with it here and spread it out over all of this. And then backwards. That's clever, doing it with the rhythms as well as with the notes. What's the tempo? You haven't marked it."

"I don't know. Allegro, I guess."

Weisfeld leaned forward, put his hands on the keyboard, and launched into the piece, playing firmly. As the motive was developed, dissonances flew left and right, thick as firecrackers at Chinese New Year, and the piece moved forward without a tonal center, without any home base, making Claude feel slightly queasy. All it had, as Weisfeld finished, was an odd kind of lilt, like a cross between a waltz and a march. To Claude's ear it didn't really end, it just stopped.

"So," Weisfeld said. "Not bad. Runs out of gas, sort of, but not bad at all."

Claude pulled out the chair from his worktable and sat down. "I just don't get it."

"It's inventive. You follow the rules. You're thinking."

"But it doesn't sound like anything!" Claude sounded like a child — ready, almost, to cry. "It's all over the place. I can't control it. I'm not *allowed* to control it." He slumped forward, looking at the floor, his head in his hands.

"Ahh," Weisfeld sighed, as if the boy had said something important.

"What do you mean, ahh?" Claude asked wearily. "I don't know what you mean."

"It's all right." Weisfeld got up. "Go to school now, before you're late. Let me think about this and tonight we'll have a talk. We'll close early and take a walk in the park. Okay?"

Claude nodded.

The very fact that he'd mentioned the matter to Weisfeld made Claude feel a good deal better. At school that day — it was a Thursday and he did not have Satterthwaite — he'd even cracked a joke in American history. A rather slyly delivered pun on 'seamen' and 'semen,' which everyone got immediately, had even won a grudging guffaw from the teacher.

Weisfeld surprised him by closing the store almost as soon as Claude got back. The boy couldn't remember the last time he'd closed early. They walked to the park in a comfortable silence and made their way to the gravel path around the reservoir.

"You're not a kid anymore," Weisfeld said, walking slowly with his hands behind his back. "You're on your way to becoming a well-educated young man, and we're getting into deep stuff here. I can't just *tell* you, you know what I mean? So I'm going to ramble. My thoughts. Maybe right maybe wrong. Maybe useful maybe not. I've been thinking about it all day because I know this music makes you uneasy. It maybe even scares you a little. That is understandable, but unnecessary, really. Unnecessary."

Some people rode by on the horse path. Then a young woman, dressed as if for a fox hunt in an English movie, walked along leading her horse by its bridle. Every now and then she'd turn her head and speak angrily to the animal.

"Satterthwaite says it's the future of music," Claude said.

"With all due respect," Weisfeld said, "nobody knows the future. Not about music, not about anything. All we can do is guess, believe me." He stared at the water through the chain-link fence, his small feet making soft crunching noises as he walked.

"People are attracted to systems. It's human nature. They're always looking for systems, hunting them down, thinking them up. Not just about music, about everything. Sometimes it's good, sometimes it's not so good."

"Like what?"

"You've heard of Karl Marx?"

"Communism."

"Right. But not at first. A brilliant man. Reads everything — economics, history, anthropology, philosophy, everything. A moral man too. He wants to make things better. So he creates a system. I mean an intellectual system, an analytical system, like a tool you can use. He covers everything, the system can explain everything in economics, all you have to do is look it up. People start to build on it, develop it and so forth, and what do you get? Where do you end up?" He paused and shot Claude a glance. "You get Stalin, that's who you get. One of the greatest monsters of all time."

"But didn't he help beat Hitler?"

"So? Two monsters fighting. Plus, in the beginning they played footsie. But let's get back to the question of systems. That's what I want you to think about. The urge to make systems. Mr. Schönberg is not alone, I can tell you."

"Is his system good or bad?" Claude asked.

"Wait. It isn't that easy. You think if it was that easy I wouldn't tell you right away?"

"Sorry."

"Now for a good system you could say the evolution of scientific method. Do they talk about that in school? Scientific method?"

"I've heard it," Claude said, wishing Ivan was with him.

"Beautiful stuff. You've got the experiment, it has to have a control. You've got Ockham's razor — if there's two answers, you take the simple one. Other stuff, but in general it's a system and it works. Human knowledge about science is expanding so fast it's exploding, practically. So that looks like a good system. You don't get Hitler or Stalin, you get penicillin."

"But music *has* a system," Claude said. "You taught it to me. It *has* a system."

Weisfeld nodded. "Very good. A very good point." He raised a finger in the air and then reclasped his hands behind his back. "Almost always a new system takes the place of an older one. Once they thought earth, air, fire, and water, that's it, that's everything. But it couldn't hold, so eventually it's carbon, oxygen, hydrogen, and so on. Chemistry. Once they thought God made everything in seven days and there it was, man, the animals, fixed, unchanging, forever. But *it* couldn't hold, so eventually it's Darwin, evolution, and the survival of the fittest. You see?"

"Newton couldn't hold," Claude said, "so then there's relativity."

Weisfeld stopped walking. "Exactly! This you learned, I presume, from your friend Ivan."

"He's trying to understand it. Space bending. Time changing with speed, all that stuff."

"He mentioned it." Weisfeld began walking again. "A nice young man. A very lively mind."

Claude experienced a guilty twinge of jealousy, but only for a second. Ivan could not, after all, play the piano. Moreover, Claude was proud of Ivan, proud to have him as a friend, and therefore proud that Weisfeld thought highly of him. As they walked along the northern rim of the reservoir Claude felt a sudden wave of love for Weisfeld, a kind of melting sensation in his chest. He moved closer, and Weisfeld, without breaking stride and in the most natural way, took his arm.

"Can tonality hold?" Weisfeld said. "That's something to think about. Is it really a prison, or is there plenty of room left? Is Schönberg jumping the gun? Is the new system really bigger and better, or is it, in the end, smaller and worse. Will it go anywhere? These are things to think about."

"But what do *you* think? That's what I want to know."

"What I think doesn't matter so much. I'm not the one who has to deal with it. You are. The new generation. You have to find the answers inside yourself. And don't be hasty. Remember, almost all the young composers are writing twelve-tone. Almost everybody."

They walked in silence for a while as Claude thought about it. "Maybe they're just trying it out," he said finally.

"Perhaps. And that might not be such a bad idea."

"You mean —"

"Don't be afraid of it. Learn it. Work hard. Do it seriously and try to get what you can out of it. Keep an open mind, and if in the end you decide to throw it away, you'll be doing it from strength."

"Oh, God," Claude sighed.

"One thing I'm sure of. *Play the pieces.* Play what you write, on the piano, and listen hard. So it's weird. Who cares? Listen as hard as you can to the new sounds, even if you don't think you're controlling them, which seems to bother you so much. Concentrate. You might begin to hear more" — he searched for the word — "more widely. Maybe, as good as your ear is, who's to say, maybe, under pressure, you'll hear more deeply a little bit? Is that possible?"

Claude looked ahead and realized with surprise that they had gone all the way around the reservoir. Weisfeld stopped at the path from which they had entered. "Okay?" he asked.

"Okay." Claude nodded, slowly kicking a stone. "But it won't be easy."

"So what else is new?" Weisfeld said. "You want easy? Play the ukulele."

In fact, almost immediately it became less difficult. Because of Weisfeld's words Claude was able to stop fighting with himself. Satterthwaite's messianic certitude no longer seemed threatening, only eccentric, and the boy, who had once been worried that twelve-tone was what he had to get *to,* now understood it as something to get *through.* It made all the difference. He pushed himself, working late into the night, motivated now by the idea that once he had thoroughly explored the system, he would be free to move beyond it. This was an act of faith, since he did not know what, if anything, lay beyond it. He found himself increasingly interested in structure, caught up in a growing awareness of ever-widening, seemingly limitless structural possibilities. He wrote piece after piece, trying each time for a new architecture, a new form. He became mildly obsessed with metrical and rhythmic effects, overlapping time signatures, jazz beats, Latin syncopations, and the uses of silence. In the absence of harmony, he paid attention to texture in the abstract. He created patterns with dynamics, with hand-plucked strings, pedal technique, and anything else he could think of.

And he listened. He composed mostly at the worktable, popping over to the Bechstein now and then to see if something was physically playable or to check a motive or a rhythm figure. But when he had a piece written to his satisfaction he would take it to the piano and play it — at first very slowly, often so slowly as to be out of tempo — and listen with all the concentration he could muster. He felt oddly passive, hearing his own work as if from a distance. The strange sounds contained in a progression of unrelated intervals. The eerie, dense chords, like black stones in a Zen garden. Notes skittering in all directions. Everything up in the air without a net.

Sometimes, even with a purely atonal piece, he could hear fragments of some unwritten, hallucinatory, tonal substructure running along underneath, as if played by a string section of ghosts. When this happened — and it was always by chance, beyond his control — he became excited, carried away with an only slightly guilty pleasure. Once he played such a section for Satterthwaite and asked him if he heard anything else behind the stated sounds.

"Like what?"

"Oh, I don't know," the boy said. "Sometimes I hear chords when there aren't any chords. In my head, I mean. Like there, bars twenty-three to twenty-six."

"Play it," Satterthwaite said, bending his head to take his brow in his hand.

Claude played the four bars.

Satterthwaite lifted his shiny face. "I hear only the notes."

"Okay."

"If you are hearing something more," Satterthwaite said tentatively, "it's probably your brain trying to pull it into tonality. Disregard it. You are doing wonderful work, young man. Very pure, very adept. Stay on the high path. Don't be sucked down, even in your head."

"Yes, sir," Claude said, knowing full well that if this was impurity, he wanted more of it.

In the music store late one afternoon, daydreaming while cleaning the glass of the harmonica display case, an odd thought popped into his head. How much could Satterthwaite hear? Claude realized that he had assumed, because Weisfeld and Fredericks could hear everything, that Satterthwaite could also. Fredericks had taught Claude not to be afraid of missed notes or wrong notes, pointing out that they always cropped up at one time or another and that there were more important things to worry about, but at the same time he never failed to hear them. Miss even a single appoggiatura in the middle of a high-velocity bravura passage and Fredericks would hear it. Weisfeld as well. Claude rubbed the glass until it was practically invisible, and a subversive idea formed in his mind. He began to replace the harmonicas when Weisfeld came down the aisle.

"What is it?"

"Nothing," Claude said.

"You look like the cat that swallowed the canary." He continued on to the back of the store.

Claude wasn't sure that what he had in mind was possible, but when Weisfeld closed the store the boy started down to the basement to find out.

"I'm going to the cafeteria with Mr. Bergman," Weisfeld called. "You want to come?"

"No thanks. There's this thing I have to do. I've got an idea."

"Okay. If you go out, don't forget to lock."

Downstairs, he pulled up a stool and turned the light on over his desk. He dragged out the old blackboard and set it up where he could see it easily. Then he found some charts and tables he had drawn up and copied them on the left side of the board in white chalk. He also transcribed, from memory, a twelve-bar series of chords, once in the first inversion and again in the second. He sat down on the stool, arranged manuscript paper, a soft lead pencil and a block of India rubber in neat order, stared at the board, and began to think.

He wrote nothing for perhaps half an hour. Then he reached for a piece of scrap paper and made a few doodles, put them aside, then stared at the board again. Suddenly he leaned forward over the desk and began writing notes on the staves. He worked slowly, raising his head often to consult the tables on the board, sometimes tapping out a figure on the edge of the desk with the pencil, or simply going still and staring at nothing while he worked something out in his head.

He erased often. Sometimes he would cross out two or three bars with angry slashes and move down the paper to start again. Sometimes he had to throw away the whole piece of paper and pull a fresh one. He worked with total concentration, unaware of the little sounds he made — sighs, impatient clicks of the tongue, faint umms of pleasure, soft hisses. At some point he heard Weisfeld return upstairs, but he ignored it and kept on working.

Gradually, enough bits and pieces emerged, and held, for him to sense the general shape of the first four bars, which would contain all twelve tones, without a unison or a repetition. He worked it out so as to include a certain four-note motive he was familiar with. When he had the complete tone row, he double-checked the math and began to explore the upside-down and retrograde forms.

At one point he almost lost heart. He'd written himself into a corner. There seemed no way to use the retrograde row against the original without a number of fairly strong tonal effects creeping in. He fooled with it a dozen different ways, but as soon as he excised one tonal effect another would crop up somewhere else. It was like trying to pick up liquid mercury with your fingertips. Then he saw something. If he broke the original row into halves — a modest impurity even by Satterthwaite's standards — and used the second half upside down, the tonal intervals were avoided.

He pulled a fresh sheet of paper and began writing out the piece, polishing as he went along. His excitement grew as he saw that the first part of the experiment — that is, this particular twelve-tone piece — was going to work. He forced himself to get up, stretch, and breathe deeply a few times. He knew that when he got excited he could make mistakes, and for his idea to prove anything at all the piece had to be perfect, or very close to it. He bent his head, put pencil to paper, and continued.

When he was finished he put the piece to the test — the second part of the experiment — and jumped up with a shout of exhilaration. He walked around the room a couple of times and ran upstairs into the shop. He went to the door leading up to Weisfeld's quarters and knocked loudly. No response. He knocked more loudly and then heard a thump, followed by the sound of breaking glass as something fell to the floor. Then more thumps in quick succession. Suddenly the door was pulled open.

Claude jumped back involuntarily. Weisfeld, clad in a sleeping gown, his hands trembling, his eyes wide but unfocused, sweat on his face, chest heaving, lurched forward. "They're coming," he cried, and with astonishing strength swept Claude off his feet and ran toward the back of the store.

"Mr. Weisfeld! Mr. Weisfeld!"

At the rear wall Weisfeld let go and began pushing aside some cardboard boxes. "The door! Where's the door? They won't see us." He seemed possessed, deep in some nightmare, and Claude was terrified.

"Mr. Weisfeld!" the boy yelled.

Finally, his hands flat on the empty white plaster, Weisfeld straightened up.

"It's me . . . It's just me, Claude."

The man's entire body shuddered. He turned around, pale as wax, and seemed to see the boy for the first time.

Claude felt tears spilling down his cheeks. "I'm sorry, I'm sorry, I was just working on, I wanted you to hear, I forgot where, I'm sorry I forgot I'm sorry."

Weisfeld looked around as if orienting himself, then lowered his head. After a moment he kicked a cardboard box. Claude recoiled. Weisfeld rubbed his head with both hands and gave a great sigh. "It's okay," he said. "Everything is perfectly okay now. I'm sorry if I alarmed you."

"I just forgot. I never should have —"

"Shhhh," Weisfeld said softly, making damping motions with his hands. "Calm down. Relax. What time is it?"

"I don't know," Claude said, pointing at Weisfeld's wristwatch.

"Oh, yes. It's four o'clock in the morning. What are you doing here? Is something wrong?"

"No, no. I was working downstairs. I lost track of time. I'm sorry. I'll go now." Claude turned away.

"Wait a second, wait a second." Weisfeld moved forward and touched the boy's cheek and then his shoulder. "Something important, yes? What is it?"

Claude felt nothing but remorse. "I wrote a thing," he mumbled. "I got all . . ." He paused and shook his head. "It doesn't matter."

"Sure it matters. It's music. Let's go down." He took a step and stopped. "Look at me here, in my nightshirt." He smoothed out his sleeves. He looked back at the door he'd come out of and then turned to look at the wall. He remained motionless for several minutes.

"Mr. Weisfeld?"

Weisfeld gave a little shake of his head. "Amazing," he said, and pointed at the wall. "In the farmhouse, that's where the door was. The secret door." He lowered his arm. "Amazing."

On the way to the basement Weisfeld said, "So what is it? You wouldn't knock on my door for nothing. Something wonderful?"

"I don't know," Claude said. "It was hard. It's probably crazy."

"I'm all ears."

Weisfeld sat at the worktable, facing the piano, and Claude played the piece. It was tightly structured music, the sound limpid, the colors pale pastels with only brief flashes of dissonance.

"Play it again," Weisfeld said, and came over to stand behind the boy and read the manuscript. "Very interesting," he said after the last bar. "I see it's twelve-tone, but somehow it has a flavor —" He paused, stroking his mustache. "There's a quality. I don't know. It sort of feels like it's in the middle. I don't know what it is. I'll have to listen to it some more. I can't quite put my finger on it. It's beautifully worked out structurally. Very clear." He reached down to play a couple of bars with his right hand. "That in there. Very good. Intricate but clear." He straightened up, still thoughtful.

"Okay, just one more thing." Claude got up and Weisfeld followed him over to the phonograph, which was on, a record spinning on the turntable. Claude adjusted the volume knob and said, "When I go back to the piano, drop the needle at the beginning. I'll come in at the twenty-fifth bar."

"What is this record?"

"Charlie Parker. The bebop player I told you about."

Weisfeld reached forward for the tone arm. "I've got it."

Claude went back to the Bechstein and Weisfeld lowered the needle. The sharp sound of Parker's alto saxophone cut the air with a twisting, syncopated blues line, repeated after twelve bars. At the twenty-fifth bar two things happened: first, the pianist on the record began to play the cycle of fifths based on Parker's bebop changes Claude had been given in the Automat, and second, Claude began to play the twelve-tone composition he'd been working on all night.

In a very few seconds Weisfeld understood what was going on and jumped up from his chair. The two fit together harmonically, as if the bebop were accompaniment for the twelve-tone, or vice versa. His mouth opened in astonishment.

Claude played the piece twice, then came over and turned off the phonograph. "The thing is," he said, "it follows the twelve-tone rules. But I made it out of the overtone series from the roots of the chords on the record. Fifths, sevenths, and ninths, mostly. Sometimes I had to go farther out. I mixed them up, of course, but it's all based on harmony, really. Do you think he'll hear that?"

Weisfeld laughed out loud. He bent over and slapped his knee-caps, letting out a couple of whoops before regaining control of himself.

Claude smiled nervously. "So is it tonal or atonal?"

"It's wonderful, that's what it is," Weisfeld said, rubbing his hands. "I wish the maestro was here for this. He would have —" He broke off and took a more serious tone. "Listen, Claude. This is brilliant. I'm not kidding you. Brilliant. What led you to do this?"

Claude blushed. "I was curious. I didn't know if it could be done. And if it could be, I wondered if Mr. Satterthwaite would hear it. You know, if he'd suspect something, the way you did."

"Ha! Well, show it to him. Play it for him. Let *him* play it."

"You think that's okay? Just show him and not say anything about the . . ." He gestured toward the phonograph.

"Sure it's okay?" Weisfeld laughed again. "It's a great idea. Tell me what he says."

"Excellent," Satterthwaite said, lifting his hands from the keys. "Mr. Platt? Anything strike you about this?"

Platt, who had started off strong at the beginning of the semester, no longer seemed particularly interested in music. Chess had become his passion, and he had the preoccupied air of someone continually working out games in his head. "Uh . . . no, sir. It sounds fine."

Claude squirmed nervously in his seat.

"He doesn't hear it," Satterthwaite said.

Claude waited.

"Mr. Platt. He has broken the tone row into two halves for the development. Only a mild heresy, and not without precedent. Berg, for instance. You should have noticed that."

"Sorry, sir."

"Mr. Rawlings? Experimenting?"

"Yes, sir." Claude relaxed.

"Very good. A certain amount of play is certainly allowed."

"Thank you, sir." Now that he'd brought it off, Claude felt uncomfortable and almost wished that he hadn't done it.

After class, Satterthwaite asked him into his office.

"The semester is almost over," Satterthwaite said, arranging himself behind his immaculate desk. "You have moved forward with astonishing speed, frankly. I believe you have promise as a composer. Very definite promise." He stared at the boy, his eyes widening. "I am prepared to continue with you, outside of class, on an informal basis. Private study, and of course there will be no fee. You are precisely the kind of young musician who can carry the new music forward, continue to build on the foundations laid down for us by the master, and open the ears of the next generation. This is an exciting and important responsibility, Mr. Rawlings."

Claude wished he were at the movies, or sorting saxophone reeds at the store, or working on double thirds at the keyboard. He wished he were anyplace else other than where he was. He swallowed hard and wondered what he was going to say. Satterthwaite's taut face, his wet eyes, his thin smile, seemed to be growing larger, like a slow zoom close-up at the RKO.

"I'm very —" Claude cleared his throat. "I'm very flattered, sir. It means a lot to me that you think I might have some talent."

"Oh, you have it."

"Yes, sir. Thank you." He briefly considered telling the man the truth. Tonality was natural, alive, and the means through which to express an infinite variety of emotions. Twelve-tone was nothing more than an idea, and a negative idea at that. A pipe dream. Claude knew he might be wrong, but that was what he felt. Twelve-tone made him positively claustrophobic and thus far had never touched his soul. But Satterthwaite's benevolent, calm faith might well have been all the man had, and Claude could not bring himself to challenge it.

"I'd like to," Claude said. "It's been fascinating. I'd like to very much, but I have to work on my repertoire. I've fallen too far behind."

Except for the disappearance of the thin smile, Satterthwaite didn't move a muscle. "Your repertoire?"

"Well, yes sir. That's how I plan to make my living."

Satterthwaite got up and went to the window, staring out, bent forward slightly, his fingers on the sill.

After some moments of silence Claude said, "I'm really sorry. I wish —"

"Thank you, Mr. Rawlings," Satterthwaite said. "I understand. That will be all."

He didn't turn around as Claude made his escape.

Running downstairs, Claude felt his concern for the man — the novel sensation of feeling sorry for him — peel away rapidly, as if he were shedding some heavy, uncomfortable overcoat. By the time he pushed open the door and hit the street he was buoyant, exhilarated by a sudden sense of freedom, sweet as a winter apple. The sun was shining, and the world was full of promise.

11

B UT YOU *must* come," Ivan said as they entered the hall. "It was great fun last year."

"I'm too busy," Claude said.

"Oh, really. Make time for it."

"And I can't dance."

"Any lummox can dance. Just move your feet around in a square."

Claude was surprised to see a letter in his box — a real letter from outside the school. He drew it out and turned it over. When he saw her name he almost dropped the envelope. It took him a moment to get up the nerve to open it.

Dear Rawlings,
   You may escort me to the mixer. Come to the house at 7:30. Charles will take us in the Packard.

                                                              Catherine

"What is it?" Ivan asked.

Claude handed him the letter.

"Hmm," Ivan said as he read. "The tone is a bit imperious, wouldn't you say? Who is she?"

"A girl."

"Well, I assumed as much. Catherine who?"

"I forgot she goes to Brearley. Somehow I just don't associate her with —"

"You don't mean Catherine Marsh? Senator Barnes's granddaughter? This is from her?" He was astonished.

Claude looked up sharply. "You know her?"

"Well no, not really." His chubby face frowned. "I know *of* her. Good heavens, Claude, she's a famous beauty. Boyish hearts breaking left and right. She won't give anyone the time of day, and here she is writing you to be her escort."

Claude studied the letter again, admiring her fluid, vaguely sensual hand. "I suppose I'll go."

Ivan gave a bark of laughter. "I should hope so! You'll be a hero. Now how on earth did you meet her?"

As he approached the mansion, stepping onto the curved driveway, he became concerned about the time. Was he too early? Also, would she have thought his postcard rude? After a dozen drafts of a letter, each of which seemed sillier and more wooden than the last, he had thrown them all away and sent a postcard. He'd written just *7:30* and his signature. Better to err on the side of simplicity, he had thought, than to make a fool of himself.

Isidra opened the door. As he stepped inside she put her hand on his arm. She showed him a small cross made of dark wood, perhaps an inch high, holding it in front of his face, and stared at him intensely.

"You take this," she said, slipping it into his breast pocket. "It will protect you."

Claude was bewildered. Spluttering out his thanks, he realized from her expression that this was no light gesture on her part. "It keeps away spells," she said.

Spells? What was she talking about? He put his hand over his breast pocket, and she turned and walked away.

Peter was in the living room, and seemed not to have grown an inch nor added a pound since Claude had last seen him. "Come on," he said, pulling Claude's sleeve, "you've got to see this."

They entered a long hall. "Where are we going?"

"My playroom." The boy stepped into a room and turned on the lights. "I used to have electric trains in here."

A huge low table under special lighting dominated the room. Claude moved forward and gazed at the multicolored map that was its surface — North Africa, from Morocco in the west to Cairo in the east, with the island of Malta bright orange in the blue-green of the Mediterranean Sea, which ran across the top of the table. In wooden boxes lined up along the edge were lead soldiers, tanks, ships of various sizes, airplanes, and field artillery, all in different colors.

"Rommel is black. The Italians under his command are yellow, because that's what they were," Peter explained. "The British are blue and the Americans are white. You can play out all the campaigns, but my favorite is the summer of 1942. We finished it last night, but it took three whole days. That's why the board is empty now. We haven't decided what to do next."

"You play with Catherine?"

"No, silly. With my mother. She's awfully good with the books. Dewman even got us some secret stuff from the War Department. Those folders over there." The boy pulled up a kitchen chair and sat down by Casablanca. "I'm always General Rommel." He reached under the table, pulled out a German officer's cap, and put it on. It looked to Claude only slightly oversized.

"Is that real?" he asked.

"Sure. And all that other stuff too."

Claude went to the shelves. Books, olive-drab folders, maps, a bayonet, gas mask, Luger pistol, various medals, and a German helmet. A silver death's-head medallion on a small velvet cloth.

"Rommel was a genius. He was going to sweep right across and take Cairo. After that, south, and enough oil to go on forever. It should have worked, it really should."

Claude came back and stared down at the table, thinking. "Why didn't it?" he said, stalling for time.

"Malta." Peter pointed. "The British. He told Hitler to take it, and he was right. But Hitler was worried about the Russian front. He wasted everything. He was good in the beginning, but then he got stupid, or crazy or something."

Now Claude noticed a flag or pennant hanging on an old lampstand behind Peter's chair. "Peter, how much do you know about the war?"

The boy's huge eyes swiveled in surprise behind the lenses. "I know everything about this part," he said rapidly. "I know the campaigns, the ordnance, the time schedules, the troop movements down to patrols, practically. The supply lines, the chain of command, the strategy. I know it all. We play it out right here."

Claude went to the lampstand. "I meant the whole thing." He

reached for the lower edge of the cloth. "Do you know about the concentration camps? The gas chambers?"

"Gas chambers? For what? You mean fuel storage?"

Slowly Claude lifted the cloth to reveal a small flag with a black swastika in its center.

"Peter!" Mrs. Fisk's voice came sharply from the doorway. "I thought I asked you to entertain Rawlings in the library. I'm quite sure I did."

"I just wanted to show —"

She interrupted. "Rawlings is much too old for toy soldiers, dear. Now come along."

"Yes, mother." He got up and she left the doorway, but not before turning out the lights. "Oh, rats," Peter said, moving through the gloom. "Anyway, it's much more fun than electric trains."

Claude followed, his mind spinning. The swastika had been a shock, leaping out at him like something alive. But for Peter it was obviously not of great importance. Just one of a number of props in an elaborate game. Mrs. Fisk, on the other hand, had seemed eager to get him out of there. And why hadn't she told Peter the truth? Did she think he was too young to know about such monstrous evil? Then why did she let him surround himself with the symbols of that evil? It didn't make any sense.

As they entered the living room Catherine appeared at the top of the stairs in a dark blue velvet dress trimmed with lace. As she lifted her arm to the banister, the light caught a thin bracelet of gold on her wrist. She descended slowly, with Dewman Fisk several steps behind her.

"There you are, Rawlings," she said.

"Hi."

"Ready to *cut the rug?*" She accentuated the last three words, made a little circling motion in the air with her forefinger, and laughed.

Mrs. Fisk busied herself with some flowers. Peter threw himself into a large armchair and pulled his knees up to his chest. Dewman came over and shook Claude's hand with mock gravity. Then everyone seemed to be frozen for a moment. There was silence and a curious tension in the air. Claude could hear the soft rustle of the flowers as Mrs. Fisk moved them.

"Let's go," Catherine said.

The Packard was waiting in the driveway. Charles held the door open and they got in. Catherine pressed herself into the corner, sitting sideways, slipped off her black pumps, and folded her legs up onto the seat under her. She stared out the window as they drove down Fifth Avenue.

"I've never been to anything like this before," Claude said after a long time.

"You're at Bentley. It's part of it."

"I wasn't going to go, until I got your letter." He reached up and held the leather strap behind his window. "You look very pretty."

"You think so? In this ridiculous dress? I look like some little girl out of the Brontë sisters."

Below the lace collar he saw the swell of her breasts. "Then why did you wear it?"

Instead of answering, she straightened out one leg and put her bare foot in his lap. He looked at it and then glanced up to see the back of Charles's head behind the glass separating the compartments.

"Don't worry about him," she said. "He can't hear us. Now tell me if my foot is pretty."

He astonished himself by wrapping his hand around her heel. With his other hand he gently encircled her ankle. Unable to speak, he looked up at her. Her expression was attentive, curious, as if watching an experiment in chemistry class. He returned his attention to her foot, which seemed perfectly ordinary, a trifle pudgy. He wondered if she felt his erection underneath it, wondered how she could not.

Very slowly she moved her big toe. "You can put that in your mouth if you want."

In the midst of the soft roar of hot blood suffusing him, his head swelling up, his throat tightening, some part of his mind nevertheless kept operating with a particularly sharp clarity. Her suggestion seemed incomprehensible, grotesque, insane, and frightening, while at the same time intimate and, for reasons he could feel but not understand, shockingly erotic and wonderful. For a split second he considered bending his head.

"No," he said, dazed. And then, foolishly, "Not right now."

He let go of her foot and she removed it slowly and carefully. She watched him for a moment and then looked out the window.

"There are people," she said, "who would give anything for the opportunity. Literally crawl on their knees. Can you believe that?" Her tone was calm, reflective.

"I guess," Claude said. "Sure."

.   .   .

Charles guided the Packard around the arc at the end of the street and pulled up in front of the River Club. He started to get out, but Catherine had already opened her door and stepped onto the sidewalk. Claude followed.

Other couples came down from the avenue and moved through the glass doors into the crowded vestibule. Catherine saw them bunched up at the chaperones' table near the entrance to the ballroom and reached back for Claude's arm. She turned to the right and led the way to the iron fence beyond which they could see the river, black as oil. She watched it for a while, her hands on the fence. They could hear laughter, cries of greeting, and high excited voices behind them.

"You know what this is, don't you?" she asked.

"The mixer? It's a dance."

"It's an upper-class marriage market, you idiot. They start early, when you're just a kid, and it goes on year after year. The dance lessons, mixers, coming-out parties — all of it so people will marry inside their class. I think it's vulgar, really. It's more hypocrisy, and they're not fooling me."

"I never had dance lessons," he said. "As you'll soon see."

"At least you know the piano. Most of those jerks in there don't know anything except how to dance and how to spike the punch."

It seemed to him an extraordinarily significant moment. A compliment, freely sprung from those perfect carved lips. A compliment, however faint, at long last. It was so precious to him he immediately moved to cover it up, to go on as if nothing had happened, lest it be taken back.

"I don't know," he said. "I've met some really smart people at Bentley. One guy in particular is the —"

"I said *most,* not all. There are exceptions, certainly."

In the silence it was now possible to savor her recognition of him, to feel the after-echo, like the spinning away of some beautiful chord. Watching her in profile — the slender white neck, the black wing of hair over her cheekbone, the clean line of her brow — he fell into a sort of trance, holding on to the moment, trying to pull it into himself. She turned her head and looked at him, first with an expression of mild annoyance, but then, relenting, with a hint of pity. "Let's go in," she said.

As they approached the chaperones' table to give their names, he was aware of attention from the crowded ballroom. Quick dance music from a small orchestra shimmered in the air. Couples glided across the floor with impossible smoothness, as if on roller skates. Faces turned as Catherine and Claude walked in, and a group of senior boys gathered around the punch bowl stood frozen for an instant and then rushed forward.

"Lester Lanin," Catherine said. "Good old reliable Lester."

"Who's he?"

"The bandleader. That skinny little man hopping around up there."

Claude looked around for Ivan. "I wonder if my friend . . . ," he began, but Catherine was gone, swept onto the dance floor by one of the seniors. Holding her close, moving with an almost violent grace, he danced her through the crowd and out of sight toward the opposite side of the room. Claude, who had imagined her by his side all evening, was thunderstruck.

"That's the way it works," said Ivan, coming up behind and giving him a clap on the shoulder. "You won't see *her* for a while."

"But we just, I mean, it was two seconds, I didn't even —"

"Punch," Ivan said. "Time for punch. Follow me."

A very large bowl of cut crystal was half filled with pink liquid and a block of ice. Ivan poured out two cups with the silver ladle and handed one to Claude. They sipped.

"Is it spiked?" Claude asked.

"I don't think so." Ivan smacked his lips. "Not yet."

Claude ate a cookie, trying to catch a glimpse of Catherine. Most of the people on the floor danced expertly, but Claude was gratified to see a few couples moving woodenly on the fringe of things. He recognized Platt, the math whiz, marking off the same square again and again, out of tempo, with a tall bony girl at arm's length. She stared stoically over the top of his head. Catherine and her partner burst briefly into view. Claude felt a mild apprehension at the speed with which she moved. Ordinarily she held herself with a certain authority, a calmness, and this seemed reckless, out of character. He felt she was being forced.

"She dances well," Ivan said.

Claude and Ivan went over to the bandstand and watched the musicians. A septet — rhythm section and four horns — with Lester Lanin calling out the tunes, which flowed one into the other without a break. "They don't use music," Claude said. "And watch how he flashes them the key signatures. See that! Three fingers down, three flats." They listened and watched until the end of the tune. "Look. One finger up.

One sharp. G major." As the new number began, the saxophones, trumpet, and trombone blended neatly.

"They're pretty good," Claude said, surprised. "They play together at least."

"Peppy," said Ivan. "Quite peppy, as usual."

"You've heard them before?"

"They play all these events. All the Social Register stuff." Ivan drained his punch.

"What's the Social Register?"

"There's Bitsy Ingalls," Ivan said, moving away. "I believe I will ask her to dance."

Claude, feeling self-conscious, went back to the punch bowl and took an inordinate amount of time serving himself. As he turned to look at the dance floor he saw Catherine dancing with another boy, and then yet a third boy cut in and waltzed her back into the crowd. Bearing his glass cup carefully, Claude moved to the wall and sat down on one of a line of empty chairs. The punch was surprisingly good, tart and slightly fizzy.

"I know who you are." A stocky girl with red hair and freckles swept her skirt behind her knees with one arm and sat down beside him. "You're Rawlings. Catherine told me." She was boyish, to the point that he somehow sensed her lack of comfort in the frilly clothes, and resolutely cheerful.

"Oh, yes," he said, hiding his pleasure at the thought that Catherine had actually mentioned him to someone else. "Hi."

"Brigett McMann. Are you going to play the piano?"

He hadn't even thought of it. For an instant he allowed himself the fantasy — the familiar comfort of the keyboard, the self-assertive rush he would feel knocking out, say, *Rhapsody in Blue* and watching their jaws drop — but he quickly squelched it. "Er, no."

"Well then, let's dance." She somehow eased him onto his feet before he knew what was happening. She put her hand on his right shoulder.

He was nervous, and yet in the back of his mind was the notion that he had to dance with Catherine at least once, and that he might as well try to get the feel of it with this girl, whose hand he now clasped. The band was playing "I've Got You Under My Skin" at a fairly brisk clip.

After a moment she said, "Is this something special?"

"What do you mean?"

"Well, I mean we're just standing here."

"Oh." He looked down for a second. "No, I'm trying to figure out, I'm trying to catch the —"

"Put your left foot forward." Brigett pulled him with gentle pressure. "Then to the side, then back. That's it." She smiled broadly. "Then start all over. Yeah. That's it!"

They began to dance. Responding to hints communicated through her hands, he began to get the hang of it and speeded up his movements until he caught the tempo of the tune.

"Terrific," she said, and moved in a bit closer. There was still plenty of air between their bodies, but now it was easier to turn. He marveled at her adroitness, how she anticipated the few little variations he began to introduce. It seemed like magic.

"Terrific," she said again. "Forget about me. Do anything you want and I'll follow. Really."

"You mean it?"

"Absolutely. I know what I'm doing."

Feeling giddy, he tried a full turn and they made it without missing a beat. He could hardly believe it, and almost immediately did it in the opposite direction.

"Whee!" she said softly, light as a feather. "Isn't it fun?"

They smiled at each other, and he felt a sudden rush of gratefulness to her. A complete stranger, Brigett had brought him through this dreaded ritual easily and comfortably, as if it were nothing at all.

"I love to dance," she said, after somehow reading his body in such a way as to lead him, without his knowing it, into a particularly nifty move. It was as if she knew what he was going to do before he did, and got there ahead of him. "They say I'm the best dancer at Brearley." She laughed at her own daring.

Claude was intoxicated by the fact that he was really dancing, not just going through the motions, but dancing, the way they did in the movies. They kept on for tune after tune, and he believed he was cutting a fine figure. Eventually the music stopped. She gave him a pat on the shoulder.

"Have to go to the ladies'," she said. "Let's do it again sometime."

"You bet," he said, flushed. "Thank you."

She moved away, transformed back into an ordinary, stocky girl with red hair.

· · ·

In the small men's room, he edged around a group of upperclassmen lounging by the marble washbasin drinking from small flasks. One of them offered his curved silver vessel. "Scotch?"

Claude took it and pretended to drink. A few drops entered his mouth and he almost coughed. "Thanks." He returned the flask and went to the urinal.

"I believe I am in love," one of the boys was saying, "struck through the heart like Romeo on the plaza."

"On the plaza?" another voice asked. "Was it the plaza?"

"Wherever it was."

A third voice, thick from whiskey: "Oh, it's just boobs. I'm sick of them and their precious boobs."

"Jenkins, you're an animal," the first voice said good-naturedly.

"A drunken animal," someone else added.

"I'm not going to be led around by my nose," Jenkins said.

"Ah," said the first voice, "would that she would only touch my nose." General laughter. "I'd follow her anywhere. Oh, yes, yes, take my nose!"

Claude zipped up and made his way back to the ballroom. He sat down on the edge of the bandstand and listened to the trombone player doing inside harmony. The music was slower now, with fewer people on the dance floor.

"Time to do your duty," Catherine said, surprising him, appearing from over his shoulder.

He stood up instantly. Avoiding his eye, she moved into his arms and they began to dance. The very abruptness of her nearness shocked him into silence. Unlike dancing with the other girl, this seemed intimate, the closeness of her body overwhelming his senses. His hand at her waist felt the curve of her body, and when the blue velvet shifted a millimeter under the light pressure of his fingers he became aware of her skin, of her smooth, hidden flesh. She was warm from dancing, emanating a faint scent like hot peaches. She moved in closer, her breasts touching him, and once, as he began a turn, he felt, for a delirious instant, the whole length of her body against his own.

"You can dance," she said. They were the same height, their faces very near. Still she did not look directly at him.

"I'm learning," he managed to say.

"Well, I guess I'm disappointed," she said. "I was imagining it would be like dancing school when I was a little girl. You know, one, two, three. Baby steps for baby feet."

He didn't know what to make of this remark.

"Oh, it's all right," she said, as if sensing his confusion. She saw something behind him and then he felt someone tap his back.

"No," Catherine said.

"Cutting in," said a voice behind Claude.

"I said no, Bobby." She put her cheek against Claude's. "Shove off." Her breath exploded in his ear, and then gently, whispering as they danced, "What a jerk." After a moment she took her cheek away.

He was surprised to find she was not as good as Brigett. Ivan had complimented Catherine as they'd watched her being swept away so firmly by the tall boy with the slicked-back hair, but now Claude discovered that with a tentative dancer like himself she was not so light on her feet. Rather than anticipating his moves, she was a fraction of a second late. There was something perfunctory to her dancing — it reminded him of the way her half-brother played the violin — and he could tell she took no particular pleasure in it. For himself, he cared about nothing but the chance to hold her, to be close to her, and this made him feel guilty, as if he were taking advantage.

When the music stopped he looked around for Ivan, took Catherine over for introductions and a final glass of punch. After some small talk Catherine said to Ivan, "I like England. That is, I've never been there, but I'd like to go."

"It's cold and damp, and the sun sets at four in the afternoon, but I like it too," he replied.

"Was it true about the buzz bombs? As long as you hear the buzz it's all right, but if it stops, you jump under a park bench or something?"

"That's what they say. I don't really know from my own experience. I was quite far from London, actually."

She laughed. "That's fun, the way you say 'actually.' "

Ivan smiled. "It's pleasant to be able to amuse someone without expending any effort. Just by being one's self, as it were."

There was a brief silence. Claude felt uncomfortable and found himself blurting out a question he had previously decided not to ask.

"Don't you think it's funny," he said, trying to get her to look at him, "those war games Peter is playing with your mother?"

She did look at him, with a hint of sharpness. "Toy soldiers," she said.

"But the swastika. The stuff he says about Hitler."

"Oh, don't be so bourgeois. He's just a little boy."

Claude wasn't sure what she meant by bourgeois, so he said nothing.

"It was a pleasure meeting you," Ivan said. "See you anon, Claude."
He walked away.

"He's the one you think is clever," Catherine said.

"Yes."

"You're probably right. Let's get out of here."

In the darkness of the Packard her face was pale and luminous.
"Where should we drop you?"

He didn't want to leave her, but he also didn't want her to see where
he lived. "Are you hungry? We could get a hamburger at Prexy's."

"Maybe another time," she said. "I'm expected at home. My grandfather will be there. They all went to the theater and he's supposed to
be disappointed I didn't come."

"Oh." His mind spun emptily.

"What should I tell Charles?"

"Eighty-sixth and Lexington. I'm starving."

She leaned forward and rolled down the glass a few inches. "Eighty-
sixth and Lexington, Charles."

"Yes, miss. Will we be parking?"

"No. I'm going on home."

"Very well, miss."

As she rolled up the glass partition she turned to look at Claude,
head tilted, a faint smile on her lips. "Your first dance. You'll never
forget it."

"I guess not," he said. "I guess I won't."

"Well, you were perfectly charming. You did very well. Thank you
for taking me." She sat back, folding her hands on her lap.

They rode uptown in silence. He was dismally aware of the passage of each block. Eighty-third, Eighty-fourth, Eighty-fifth, closer and
closer to the moment he would step outside the car and she would
simply ride away, as if jettisoning both him and her memories of an
unimportant evening.

"There's just one . . . ," he started to say as the car pulled up. He
grasped the lower part of his face in a reflexive nervous gesture, covering his mouth.

"What?"

He lowered his hand. "Why did you ask me to take you?"

"Oh, I don't know. A whim, I suppose," she said, a bit too quickly for him to believe her, a bit too flip.

"There must have been some reason," he said, looking down at the floor of the car. He held himself entirely still, as if giving her plenty of time to answer.

"Well," she said after a while, "I certainly don't belong there. I don't belong at any of those things, but sometimes I go, and I pretend. I picked you because you don't belong either. You come from nowhere, and you haven't any money. We're different from them," and a touch of anger entered her voice, "for different reasons. So is that enough?"

He was on dangerous ground. He didn't know why, but he could feel it — some charged, electric quality to her candor, something fast and threatening in her manner, as if at any moment she could reduce him to the status of a little boy, a child like Peter, whose Nazi games were without significance in view of his youth, ignorance, and innocence. Claude clung fast to himself, to the significance of his desire, to his knowledge of sublime forces on the other side of the wall, to the heat of his own body. Weisfeld and Fredericks strengthened him, like angels on his shoulder, and he was able to nod, slowly and calmly, to shake her hand, which disarmed her, and to get out of the car.

Two nights later he was in the balcony of the Loew's Orpheum, working on a pair of girls from Sacred Heart. One of them was smoking a cigarette, and as soon as he leaned forward from his row to theirs to ask for a match, they all knew what was up. The girls whispered to each other, giggled, and a book of matches was offered over a shoulder.

Ordinarily he would have been a good deal more circumspect and gradual in his approach, waiting for a hint or two of indirect encouragement, but he was in a state of great tension, something approaching desperation, and it made him reckless. He climbed over the row and sat down next to the smoking girl.

The other girl gave a little gasp. "You going to let him do that?"

"It's a free country." The girl with the cigarette was fifteen or sixteen, with curly hair, small ears, freckles, and a slightly pug nose. She stared directly at the screen.

He put his left foot on the back of the empty seat below him, and his right arm over the back of her seat, touching her lightly.

"You're a bold one," she said, blowing a thin stream of smoke with pursed lips and then turning to glance at him. She had chubby cheeks.

"Mary, what are you doing?" the other girl whispered in a high, tight voice. "What would Sister say?"

Mary turned back to the screen, took another puff of her cigarette, and said, "Fuck Sister."

Claude felt, simultaneously, a great rush of relief, a sense of expansion and lightness, as if he were about to float into the air, casting off some mysterious ballast, and at the same time a thrilling shock of sexual energy so powerful his legs began to tremble, even, for a brief moment, the skin of his face.

"Well, I'm going," the other girl said. "I'll watch the rest downstairs. It's just what I said, we should never have come up here in the first place."

"Okay." Mary was calm. "See you later."

They watched her step stiffly down the aisle, turn, and disappear.

"Miss goody-goody," Mary said. "Are you from Saint Ignatius?" She turned to look at him again.

"Yes," he lied.

"I thought so."

Moving his head forward slowly, he kissed her. Her mouth was warm, and soon he felt the quickness of her tongue, the touch of her hand on the back of his neck.

He had necked with girls in the movies before, long sessions of negotiated tenderness, gentle pressing, gentle demurral, but Mary was different. She was fierce, and he found himself ascending into fierceness himself, discovering at each level greater strength in her to accommodate the quickness of his passion. They bruised their mouths, they bit, they wrestled and pulled against each other in a frenzy of lust. Eventually his hand was in her slick vagina. They feasted for hours, until, both of them dizzy, she broke away, exhausted.

"Come with me," he said. "Come with me somewhere where we can —"

"No, no. I won't do that."

"We could go in one of the boxes."

"I won't do that," she said again. "I've got to go."

"My God, don't go. Okay, we'll stay here. Don't go."

She straightened her clothes and stood up.

"Wait," he cried. "When will I see you again? Where can we . . ."

But she was off, moving fast over to the aisle, down the steps, and away.

12

As CLAUDE came around the corner one spring afternoon, his jacket slung over his shoulder, he was surprised to see Mr. Fredericks's Rolls-Royce parked in front of the music store. He quickened his step and ran across the avenue at an angle, giving a wave to the Negro chauffeur who sat behind the wheel. The little bell tinkled as Claude entered the shop, but neither Weisfeld nor Fredericks, deep in conversation by the cash register, looked up until he was almost upon them.

"Ah, here he is," said Fredericks, reaching out to touch Claude's cheek, making him blush.

"It's good to see you, sir."

"You see?" Weisfeld said from behind the counter. "Getting taller. Putting on some weight. Pretty soon shaving, Vitalis, the whole *mishe-gaas.*"

" 'For never-resting time leads summer on to winter and confounds him there,' " Fredericks quoted.

"Gentlemen, you're embarrassing me," Claude said.

"All right, all right," Weisfeld said quickly. "Go on downstairs. Mr. Fredericks wants to talk to you."

"I'll be down in a moment," Fredericks said.

Claude descended, wondering what was up, what they could possibly be talking about that they didn't want him to hear. From the cigarette butts he had noticed in the ashtray — Fredericks's special

Turkish brand — he guessed they'd been at it for some time. He went to his worktable and neatened up the surface, moving things back and forth until Fredericks came down.

"The famous Bechstein," he said, glancing around and then approaching the piano. "I played it many times in his living room." He sat sideways on the piano bench, facing Claude. "What are you working on at the moment?"

"I started *The Sunken Cathedral* last week, and I've been reading through Debussy. Also the Chopin B-flat Minor Sonata for a long time now."

"Good. Anything else?"

"Well," Claude said, shifting his position, "I've been trying to play some jazz. Improvising on chord patterns. There's a player named Art Tatum I like a lot."

"Yes, I know his playing," Fredericks said. "Rachmaninoff once said he wished he could play as well as Tatum."

"I've transcribed some of his runs for exercises."

Fredericks nodded, leaned forward, and clasped his hands between his knees. "I've been talking to Mr. Weisfeld about an idea I have." He paused for a moment. "You know, of all the music we worked on, you and I, the Mozart Double Piano Concerto seems to stand out most vividly in my memory."

"K. 365, in E-flat Major."

"Yes, I thought we went rather far with it in a fairly short time. Something very nice happened. What is your recollection?"

"Oh yes," Claude said, feeling a prickly kind of excitement, "it was wonderful. The way it would be so strong, and then suddenly it would be fun, and then into the minor. I loved it. I still play it. By myself, of course."

"Good. Now I should give you some background. A few friends of mine have a summer music festival up in Massachusetts. The idea is a student orchestra working with professional conductors, various instrumental workshops and classes, seminars on composition, orchestration, that sort of thing. All very informal. More or less continual performances of one sort or another going on right through the summer. You get the idea?"

"Yes, sir."

Fredericks raised his head a fraction and looked directly at Claude. "I've agreed to do a benefit for them in June. I thought we might do the Mozart Double Concerto with the student orchestra." He held Claude's eye. "You and me, that is."

Claude became aware that his mouth was open. He closed it and swallowed. Fredericks was silent, waiting, but Claude could not speak. Fredericks's words were repeating and repeating inside the boy's head, so loud they drowned out thought. He swallowed again.

"What do you think?" Fredericks asked.

"I can do it," Claude blurted out. "Yes. Oh, sure, yes."

"I'm delighted." A faint smile. "It's settled, then. Now, as I said, it's all very informal, but we want to do the music justice."

Claude nodded.

"It would be nice to have more time," Fredericks continued, brushing a mote from his sleeve, "but we'll have to make do. We'll be using the Breitkopf and Härtel edition, and I suggest you take a very close look at the orchestral music with Mr. Weisfeld. We didn't do much of that before, and it's important. Study it."

"Yes, sir."

"I can manage four piano sessions with you. I'll let you know the dates. The first will be devoted to the twenty-two bars after the entrance. Now, I know you'll probably be playing the whole thing night and day, but remember, first we'll be digging into those twenty-two bars. We'll get them right, and the rest will follow."

"I understand."

"Excellent." Fredericks stood up. Claude jumped from his chair and they shook hands. "I'm looking forward to this," Fredericks said. "It's such an elegant piece."

They went upstairs to find Weisfeld in the front, staring out the window. "It's a lovely day out there today," he said, as if, for some reason, surprised.

"All is arranged." Fredericks opened the door and the bell tinkled. He looked up at it. "E-flat! How appropriate!"

From inside they watched him enter the Rolls, which pulled away from the curb like a great black ship gleaming in the sun.

"Well," Weisfeld said as they stood shoulder to shoulder, "this is quite a development."

"I can do it. I can do it."

"Of course you can. He knows you can, or he wouldn't have suggested it."

"With an *orchestra*," Claude whispered.

"With Fredericks!" Weisfeld reminded him. "Maybe the best Mozart player alive."

"I can't believe it," Claude said. "I mean, just like that? Just . . ." His voice trailed off.

"It's the way things happen sometimes."

For several minutes they stood in silence, watching the street. Claude felt a brief electric shiver over his whole body, the hair on his arms standing erect. "Oh, my God," Claude said suddenly, panicked.

"What?"

"I forgot to ask him what part I'm going to play, one or two."

"We discussed it," Weisfeld said. "The second part. The lower one."

Claude blew up his cheeks and released the air. "Okay. Okay, good."

"It's the part Mozart played," Weisfeld said.

It took a day for everything to sink in, and the next night Claude and Weisfeld talked it over after the shop closed. There was the Mozart, and the need to drop everything else to work on it — the orchestral score, the structure of the concerto itself, analysis of both piano parts, and the time-consuming work of getting the music into his hands, getting it physically memorized so as to be ready for the subtle business of interpretation during his sessions with Fredericks. But there was also school, and the end of the school year approaching with a full load of exams, papers, and the like. Claude was an A student with the odd B now and then, and Weisfeld was insistent that the boy do nothing to erode his progress. He pointed out that college was almost upon them, and that the boy would need both high grades *and* the piano to get the necessary full-tuition scholarship to a first-rate institution. "I know it probably doesn't feel like it," Weisfeld had said, "but this is really more important than the concert. There will be other concerts." Secretly, Claude was relieved to hear him say this, not because he agreed about college necessarily, but because it took some pressure off in terms of the Mozart. Weisfeld would be satisfied if Claude got through it decently, as long as he also did well in school.

With pencil, paper, and ruler they drew up Claude's present daily and weekly schedule — a fairly elaborate document as it stood — and moved around various blocks of time, amending the kind of work to be done within them. As the plan emerged Claude wanted to add an extra hour, early in the morning, at the Bechstein. Weisfeld was skeptical, worried about the possible effects of less sleep, but reluctantly agreed to a trial period, reserving the right to put an end to it if he thought it was affecting the boy's strength. They drew up two copies of the schedule and Claude went home.

For some time now, after having changed the alarm clock on the floor by his cot from five-thirty to four-thirty A.M., Claude found himself waking spontaneously at exactly one minute before the alarm would have gone off. He rolled over, reached down, and pressed the button by feel. Then he switched on the light by reaching high for the wall switch.

Moving silently, he got dressed, turned out the light, opened the door carefully, and went to the kitchenette. He fixed himself some cornflakes and sat down to eat in the dark. He watched the fan-shaped window beyond which, as he finished, dawn began to break. He put down his spoon and sat motionless, his mind empty as the gray light filtered into the room.

Then he heard a faint click, instantly recognizable as the knob mechanism on the door to his mother's room, out of sight around the corner. After a moment a figure appeared, fully dressed, tiptoeing to the front door, cap in hand. It was Al.

Claude stopped breathing. If he could have willed his heart to stop beating he would have done so, so eager was he for Al to get out the door without noticing him. But as if by sixth sense Al turned his head, saw Claude, and froze.

Neither one of them moved. It was an eerie moment, as if a movie had gotten stuck on a single frame, arresting the illusion of life. Then Al looked down at the floor, gave a little sigh, and came over to the counter. He put his cap down and sat on a stool. He raised a finger to his lips, with a tilt of his head to indicate Emma's room.

"Morning," he said very softly.

"Morning," Claude said, no louder.

"Well, I told her, I said, 'If he don't know already, we ought to tell him.' But she can't make up her mind." He drummed his fingers on the counter. "It don't matter now." He watched Claude's eyes.

The boy knew that something was expected of him, but he felt unsure of himself, plunged headlong into these adult matters. He found himself actually thinking about what he should say. What was being asked of him?

"I have to get up at four-thirty now," he said. "It gives me another hour for the Mozart."

"All right," Al said.

"I mean that's how come —"

"Claude," Al said, "you know I care about her a lot. A whole lot. Do you know that?"

Claude nodded.

"She's a good woman." He continued to speak in a murmur. "She been lonely."

"She had to stop those discussion groups," Claude said. "That man Eisler warned her, and I guess he was right, because then there was all that trouble. Then she started getting crazy."

"She told me."

"She didn't do anything except drive him around. She wasn't in any Communist conspiracy. The whole thing was ridiculous."

"I know that." He leaned forward. "She was just lonely. Uptown, a person would probably go to church, get some strength from the brothers and sisters, but this ain't uptown, and she ain't no sister."

"I think she's been a lot better since she met you," Claude said.

"I hope so. I believe she is." Al paused. "We've been talking. You understand, we've been talking to each other from our hearts."

Suddenly, for no reason that he could understand, Claude felt a wave of sadness, an utterly abstract, pure, and elemental sadness, washing over him. At the same time he felt a distinct but mysterious sense of relief, as if some hitherto unsuspected weight had been lifted from him, announcing its presence only by its disappearance. For an instant he was totally confused, but then he regained control of himself. "Good. That's good," he said.

Al watched him for a long moment and then nodded his head. "The thing is, we have to be careful. People don't like mixing."

"I understand."

"It could look like we're sneaky, but we ain't. It's just we have to be careful."

"I won't say anything."

"No, no." His voice rose slightly. "I don't mean you. You tell anybody you want. It might even be good you tell somebody — long as you trust them. I mean the neighbors, the landlord, the Hack Bureau, like that. That's all I mean."

"Okay."

They sat in the gray light as if waiting for something, in tacit agreement that more words were necessary and yet the words weren't coming. After a long time Claude got up.

"I have to go," he whispered.

A frown appeared on Al's narrow brow, but then it went away. "Yeah. Time to work. See you later."

Claude walked the quiet streets to the music store. The stillness reassured him, and the rhythm of his stride, by its very familiarity, seemed to suggest that it was okay for the time being to put Al and his mother out of his mind. He fingered the key in his pocket, eager to get into the store, down to the neatness and clarity of the studio where the Bechstein waited with timeless, infinite patience.

As the weather warmed Claude and Ivan resumed their old habit of occasionally eating at the bench by the river. Ivan had just finished a long description of Schliemann's discovery of the buried city of Troy, which had been presumed to be mythical, waving his Coca-Cola bottle with enthusiasm as he explained how the great man, a relative amateur, had the audacity to take the classical poetic sources literally, and had been led right to the spot.

"I love it when somebody comes in from the outside and confounds the experts," Ivan said. "It's so delicious."

"Hmm." Claude took a bite of his bologna and cheese sandwich.

"I say, old chum, you've been rather quiet the last couple of weeks. And looking a touch peaked. Is everything all right?"

"Have I?" Claude was surprised. "It's just I've been working. I'm fine." Impulsively, he decided to share his secret. "I'm going to play the Mozart Double Piano Concerto in June."

"Oh, splendid," Ivan said casually.

"No, I mean I'm going to play it in a concert, with an orchestra and an audience. At the Longmeadow Music Festival."

"Good heavens!" Ivan said, catching on now.

"With Fredericks," Claude said, turning away to throw the rest of his lunch in the trash barrel.

"Your debut. And with him!"

"Yes."

"I see, I see, I see. Well, this is tremendous. I'm so happy for you." His round face broke into a smile.

"Yes, it's a great chance." Claude paused. "Don't tell anybody, will you? I don't want to tell anybody yet."

"When in June?"

"The tenth, I think."

"Blast! Blast and double blast. I sail for England on the seventh."
He leaped up from the bench and strode back and forth. "Maybe I
can change it. The trouble is, I'm going with my uncle, but maybe I
can —"

"Don't worry about it," Claude said. "It's no big deal. A student
orchestra way up in the boondocks somewhere."

"Ha! Tell that to yourself if you need to. But don't expect *me* to
believe it. I know what it is."

Claude stood up and they began to walk back to school. "Just don't
spill the beans," he said.

If there was tension building in Claude — stomach pains and short
episodes of diarrhea, a tendency to break the pencils he habitually
rolled in the fingers of his right hand, exasperation when he had to wait
for something or stand on line, sudden headaches, a tic under his left
eye late at night — he was barely aware of it, and in any case it seemed
of no importance. But it all went away when he worked with Weisfeld.
It was like the old days. As if they had all the time in the world.

They sat together at the Bechstein, gazing at the Breitkopf & Härtel
edition of the full score. "No one would claim," Weisfeld had said at
the outset, "that this is a tremendously deep, profound, earthshaking
piece of music. The spirit is more like a game. I'm not talking frivolous,
naturally. I mean a kind of elegant, subtle game that once in a while
gets a little serious. Almost despite itself, maybe. But if you miss the fun
in this, well . . ." He gave a shrug. "They say he wrote it to play with
his sister."

"Is that why he played the second part?"

"There isn't a great deal of difference. Maybe he liked the sonority
better down here. Remember, he wasn't playing a full-sized piano. Up
above, it could be it sounded more feminine. Who knows? But definitely there's some high-level fun going on here. Between the orchestra
and the pianos, between the pianos, between the players and the
audience. It's a dazzler."

They had spent more than a week breaking down each of the three
sections into its component parts, and then another week putting them
back together. Weisfeld concentrated on the orchestral score, identifying the themes and lines that would flow into the piano parts, noting
those parts that were merely supportive.

"In here, for instance." Weisfeld pointed to the ninety-sixth bar of the opening allegro. "The violas with those sustained whole notes — the F — and then the violins add to it, like everybody's holding their breath so that here" — he moved his finger to the right — "you get the crescendo, and then this is just pure joy. You play with joy in here. You see what I mean? The strings help set it up."

During another session he stopped at the fifty-fourth bar of the andante. "Look at that oboe! The sustained C! It's special, because you're going into this special section down here. Down here it's practically opera. The second oboe comes in two measures after the first, playing a D a seventh below, and then the resolution to B-flat, you see? That painful clash against your B-flat appoggiatura? Wonderful. You play Fredericks's part and I'll play yours." He counted off the beat, sang the C in a soft thin voice, and they played eight bars to the letter break. Jumping in so fast at a technically difficult passage, Claude had missed a note or two, but Weisfeld didn't mention it. "That's a real highlight in the whole concerto, as far as I'm concerned. But you see what Fredericks says."

Now, at the Bechstein, they looked at the opening bars for the orchestra. "You're going to be excited," Weisfeld said. "The orchestra sound all around you, so strong you wouldn't believe it, so strong you've got to remind yourself you're sitting there with a job to do. So you concentrate, listen to them, focus on them."

"Okay."

"I'm going to tell you what to listen for. When you go out there and sit down and everything's going so fast, I want you to remember to listen to what they do with *this* note." He pointed to a grace note in the fifth bar. "This one." He played the fourth, fifth, and sixth bars. "Dut-dut-dut dah-dah-dah *duh*-dah dah dah."

"Okay. The B-flat. I got it."

"The reason is, people can play that several ways. They can play it fast or slow, and if you listen it'll give you a hint how the conductor is going to approach those shapes. Slow gives you one kind of impulse, fast gives you another, and if you can get with their impulse immediately, so much the better."

"Okay. I'll remember."

"It doesn't mean you have to repeat it when *you* play it, but you'll know what you're coming off of."

Claude played the three bars several times, tipping the B-flat first one way and then the other.

"See?" Weisfeld asked.

"Yup." Claude said with a smile of pleasure. "Right there. Right at the start."

"Okay. Now I want to show you something in the rondo."

On the train Claude read Stendhal's *The Red and the Black,* required for a Bentley Great Books course, with complete attention. The story of Julien Sorel and his rise from the company of his doltish brothers at the provincial sawmill to the drawing rooms of the rich and powerful fascinated Claude no less than would have the wide, winged head of a cobra swaying before his eyes at roughly the same distance as the book he held aloft with both hands. He almost missed the stop at Frank's Landing.

Everything seemed smaller — the town, the trees, hedges, and houses. It did not seem as long a walk to Fredericks's mansion. The sun caught a window on the highest turret, blazing more brightly than fire, and the gravel of the driveway crunched once again under his feet. He felt well prepared.

The great hushed room with the French doors and the pianos had not changed. Only the light, since it was later in the day, angling in thick mellow shafts over the polished instruments.

"The entrance," Fredericks said from his piano. "Letter A. The trills. Not loud, but firm." He played the trills in his part, using both hands. "Go ahead."

Claude played.

"We want," Fredericks said, "an even sound. Rounded, rolling smoothly. Let's do it together."

When the unison trills were satisfactory, Fredericks called Claude's attention to the subsequent two grace notes. "Softer, but distinct. Distinct. It's the first sense of direction, so be distinct, rolling to the grand unison E-flat." He played the whole passage three times, then listened to Claude. "Good. I remember your instincts with this. Good." They played it together, breaking off the E-flat crisply.

"Yes," Fredericks said, looking at the music. "It's a grand announcement of the root of the tonic. A bold announcement no one could miss. I think of a tall, periwigged, powdered, ruffled personage at the door to the ballroom rapping his great stick. 'E-flat!' he shouts."

Claude laughed.

Fredericks looked over. "Of course, we're not supposed to think of pictures, are we," he said with a quick sly glint, "like a couple of fat burghers. I take it back."

"Too late," said Claude. "I'm impure. I won't be able to get it out of my mind."

"We'll see. Now these sixteenth notes, this running shape. It isn't easy, because we have to play together with phrasing. The whole thing descends, but let us ever so slightly emphasize the higher notes. See if we can phrase together."

They spent the better part of an hour on the first four bars. Claude felt it coming together and was grateful when Fredericks kept on having them play it anyway, until it sounded utterly seamless. Claude had the illusion that he could reproduce it at will, even by himself, back in the basement.

"Now this melody," Fredericks said. "I've got it first. Dut-dut-dut dah-dah-dah *duh*-dah dah dah." He played it rapidly. "Watch that B-flat appoggiatura to the A."

"Mr. Weisfeld told me to listen for that in the orchestra, bar five."

"Mr. Weisfeld is, as usual, correct. I'll be listening to them also. But you should pay a bit more attention to what I do with it, since you have to play it yourself ten or eleven bars later. You're responding to my statement, most immediately, whatever else you're doing."

"Okay," Claude said. Maintaining his concentration, he was on edge, but comfortably so, willowed by a balmy, gentle sense of contentment, something like what he felt after an especially good meal.

"But let's go back now." Fredericks played the first variation, which began with the same three staccato quarter notes, although this time a tone above. "You see how he plays with our expectations? No *duh*-dah this time. He just marches right up dah-dah dah-dah dah to the half-note C, and that delicious hesitation, and up to D, and then, with the decoration, our old friend E-flat. How cunning he is, how artful!" For an instant Fredericks seemed to forget Claude's presence. He played the two sequences together. "Great care with the first," he said, "and the second is an invitation to be a bit fanciful, a bit expressive. Do you hear it?"

"Yes. There's room. There's space."

"Exactly. I'll play through now to your entrance. Then let's keep going till the tutti."

Fredericks played, then Claude, then Fredericks, and then Claude to the end of the solo section.

"Good," said Fredericks. "In these exchanges we want to preserve the identity of each player. You picked up on a certain — what should I call it? — a certain eagerness toward the end. You might amplify that the tiniest bit. We're eager to join them, *n'est-ce pas?* My trill, your trill, and then *boom,* they're sawing away like mad. You're closer, so you get to be even a shade more eager. Let's try it again from the very beginning. Letter A."

They met every other day, for a total of four sessions. Fredericks seemed to forget about his schedule, and twice Anson Roeg had to come into the room to remind him he was expected somewhere. He grew increasingly demanding with Claude, although never impatient.

"We must agree on how we're going to do these left-hand chords. They shouldn't sound blocky."

Or: "Favor the lower note on these descending mordants."

Or: "We have to keep it flowing in here. This whole page. Those thirds must flow like single notes. Again!"

Or: "This is very dramatic. Orchestral almost. Try for some power. Kick it. Get on top of it."

Claude's notations began to fill the white spaces of his score. He scribbled down so many he had to introduce underlining and exclamation points to differentiate between their degrees of importance.

"These bars of parallel tenths. They'll sound better if we favor my piano just a bit, just a shade."

Or, toward the end of the middle section: "The game here is to make it sound like one piano. The mood is playful, and we should hand it back and forth without the audience knowing who's got it. You see? Like a magic trick."

Claude was particularly impressed when Fredericks made a casual remark about a low grace note, in Claude's part, five bars before the end of the andante: "He was after sonority here. That was the lowest note on his piano. The bottom key. A vast, sonorous, spacious sound across the whole keyboard." It was as if Fredericks felt Mozart was alive, in the next room perhaps, and Claude in turn felt himself to be the recipient of special secrets, special mysteries carried down through time, unchanged and vigorous. When he left the great house it was necessary for him to collect himself, to remind himself to stop at the corners, watch where he was going, and try to remember the shortest route to the train station.

.   .   .

School was ending, and when he reported to Mr. Weisfeld that he'd gotten straight A's, he was wrapped in a brief but exuberant bear hug.

"I'm proud of you," Weisfeld said, his eyes glinting, holding him by the shoulders with straight arms. "I know it's been hard with so much, but believe me it was worth it. Perfect marks at Bentley! They'll pay attention to that, they'll pay attention."

"It wasn't anywhere near as hard as when I first went there." Claude said. "You get the hang of it, and Ivan sure helped."

Weisfeld was actually rubbing his hands together. "So now you've got, what, a week and a half before you go up there? You can play as much as you want. This is terrific. You can get more sleep."

"I will."

"Relax a little. We'll have some schnitzel, maybe. See a movie, maybe, one night."

Claude was pleasantly surprised, and instantly resolved they would sit in the orchestra, well away from the action in the balcony. "Great," he said.

The plans for the concert had been explained to him in the library of the mansion by Anson Roeg, who had handed him his railroad tickets. Claude was to leave on Tuesday by train for Springfield, Massachusetts, where he would be met and driven to Longmeadow in time for dinner. Wednesday he would rehearse with the student orchestra, Thursday Fredericks would arrive from Boston for a single full rehearsal, and Friday at three P.M. the concert would begin under the great tent. Since Fredericks was to arrive from Boston by rail, Anson Roeg, Weisfeld, and any guest Claude might want to invite would be driven up in the Rolls on Friday morning, to return the same night.

Claude had brought the matter up with his mother.

"I can't do it," she said. "I know it's important, Claude, but don't make me do it."

"Okay," Claude said. "That's okay."

"I take swells to Carnegie Hall all the time. I wouldn't know what to say. Let me just stay here with Al and you can tell me all about it, you can tell us both."

Even with some mild encouragement from Al she had remained adamant. "On top of everything else I'm too big. I'd stick out like a sore thumb."

"What you talking about," Al said. "You ever see some of those opera-singer ladies?"

"Did you ever see Kate Smith? It doesn't matter. I'm going to stay right here. Claude understands."

And so, a few days later, in the basement of the music store, Claude put aside the scores on his worktable and composed a letter to Catherine Marsh. He went through two drafts on notebook paper before copying it down on heavy stationery he had bought at Woolworth's.

Dear Catherine,

On June tenth, at three o'clock in the afternoon, I will be performing Mozart's Double Piano Concerto in E-flat Major, with Charles Fredericks at the Longmeadow Music Festival in Longmeadow, Massachusetts. I should add that this will be with a full orchestra. I guess you know that lots of people think Mr. Fredericks is the best player of Mozart. Even better than Victor Wolff. Also he hasn't played a recital in a long time, so this will be a big event. It will certainly be big for me!

I would like to invite you. If you can come, Mr. Fredericks's driver will pick you up in the Rolls-Royce Friday morning at your house (I will already be at the Festival). But then I can ride back with you Friday night. I really hope you can come. Please call me at Weisfeld's Music Store, ATwater 9–0418. If I'm not there, please leave a message. I hope you will let me know soon so I can arrange everything about the Rolls-Royce.

Sincerely,
Claude Rawlings

He sealed the letter, went upstairs and got a three-cent stamp out of the cash register, affixed it carefully, and mailed it at the corner box. It would be delivered, he knew, the next morning at the earliest, or the next afternoon at the latest.

Five days later, as Claude left to meet Ivan at Bentley and say goodbye, Weisfeld held the letter out to him from behind the counter. The address had been crossed out with a slash of blue ink, and someone had written *Return to Sender*. He turned the envelope over several times. It did not appear to have been opened.

"What does this mean?"

"I don't know," Weisfeld said.

"Did she do this?"

"I don't know."

"I can't believe she wouldn't even read it." Claude kept looking at the envelope, the blue slash, the unfamiliar handwriting. "This is strange," he said, finally putting it in his back pocket. Weisfeld shrugged.

Claude walked over to the Bentley School. Halfway there, he stopped at a corner and pulled out the letter for yet another look, put it back again, and crossed the street. For days he had been waiting for her response, looking up every time the phone rang, and now he realized he had been waiting for nothing. Passing a newsstand, he resisted the urge to kick out the table and send the papers flying.

Ivan awaited him in the faculty lounge and poured him a small glass of sherry. "The headmaster gave it to me. Said if I was going to Cambridge I might as well get used to it. Cheers."

"Cheers," said Claude, and took a sip.

"Well, God knows when I'll see you again. Possibly never." He sat down on the leather couch, legs sprawling. "But it's been fun."

"I never thanked you properly for all the help." Claude went over to the window.

"Working hard on the Mozart?"

"I . . . I . . ." He took a breath. "I invited Catherine Marsh to the concert, but the letter was returned unopened and I can't figure it out." Staring out at the street, he eventually became aware of the silence behind him and turned to face his friend. "What?" Claude asked.

"You haven't heard?" Ivan gave a small cough behind his hand.

"Heard what?"

"Everybody's been talking about it for days. I thought you would've heard. All very dramatic. It seems she's eloped with somebody from the Harvard Business School and gone to Australia. Just like that. Didn't even warn her family. Gone."

(Many years later, in the wings of a theater in Cleveland, Claude was to be knocked half unconscious by a falling board. Sunk to his knees, he was to feel not pain but a sensation of discontinuity in time, as if lifted out of its flow entirely and then, *click,* back in, feeling uneasy and unsure about what it was he was back into. He would later connect that moment to what he felt now in the faculty lounge.)

"Are you sure?"

"Nobody seems to know much about this fellow except his father owns an aluminum company. That's why Australia. The bauxite. John Dogge, I believe his name is — with two *g*'s and an *e*."

"When . . . ," Claude began. "How long?"

"I don't know. The story is, they took a train to San Francisco, caught a Matson liner, and were married by the captain the first day out." He drank some sherry, watching Claude. "Like something out of a bad novel, isn't it?"

"My God." Claude fell into a chair.

"I know you fancied her," Ivan said. "I'm sorry."

"She's only seventeen."

"Well, that's old enough, old chum. They grow up faster than we do." He got up and approached with the bottle, topping up Claude's glass. "Drink."

Claude did so, and Ivan topped the glass again. "That's enough," Claude said.

"Now don't be downhearted our last time together," Ivan said. "Life is long and rich. We are young and there will be many girls. I know it sounds insensitive, but it's true."

"Yes. Of course."

They talked of other things.

The station wagon, an old but well-kept-up Ford with the words WHITE FOX INN burned into the wood under the side windows, was parked beside the station. As Claude approached, the driver, a short, wizened old man in overalls, scanned the crowd behind the boy, moving a toothpick from one side of his mouth to the other. Claude walked right up to him.

"You Rawlings?" the old man asked.

"Yes."

"I thought you'd be older." He removed the toothpick and reached for Claude's small suitcase. "Hop in."

As they drove out of Springfield, into the hills and the soft late afternoon sunshine, Claude saw fields, farmhouses, cows, and low stone walls. He watched with attention, since he'd never been out of New York City and its environs before.

"The reason I thought you'd be older," the old man said, "is you're staying at the inn with the big shots. The kids stay in those old houses on Perkin's Road. School bus picks them up. You must be important, I guess."

"I guess," Claude said.

They rode in silence the rest of the way. The White Fox Inn was a large, three-story building with a broad wooden porch stretching almost its entire length. People lounged in the shade, talking, reading newspapers, even playing cards at bridge tables. No one seemed to notice as Claude and the driver climbed the steps and crossed the threshold into the lobby.

At the reception desk another old man — who could have been the driver's brother, so close was the resemblance — touched his bow tie and turned the registration book around. The lobby smelled of apples and vinegar.

"Rawlings," the driver said. "One bag." He placed it on the floor, turned, and left.

"Please sign here," the clerk said. "You have 203. That's right across the hall from Mr. Fredericks. Just go up the stairs and turn left. The bellboy's off helping his brother find a cow."

Claude signed.

"Dinner's in there at six-thirty." He gave a nod toward the dining room in back. "I guess you know everything's been paid for already."

"Thank you."

"You know how to get to the farm?" Catching Claude's blank expression, he added, "Where the festival's at?"

"No."

"Okay. Walk out the door, take a left, turn right at the first street, that's Perkin's Road, and it's about a quarter mile."

His room was high-ceilinged, with two windows facing a lawn, a stand of tall trees, and a lake behind. There was a four-poster bed with a tufted white bedspread, a bureau, and a writing desk. He found a small closet, and a bathroom with an enormous tub on cast-iron legs. He went back and lay on the bed.

Taking several deep breaths, he closed his eyes. His body still felt the motion of the train and the station wagon. He was tired and wound up at the same time, his mind casting around. He thought he might go over to the festival after dinner and see if he could find a piano somewhere, lock himself in, and play. He had done almost nothing but play since his meeting with Ivan.

On a sudden impulse he went into the bathroom and, with a great clanking, rattling, and knocking, filled the deep tub with the hottest water he thought he could stand. He undressed and lowered himself inch by inch, gasping at the sweet pain. It was possible to lie fully stretched out, the back of his head against the porcelain, immersed to his chin. The warmth crept into his body, ever deeper, and his mind fell still, hypnotized by the slow, steady drip from the faucet.

After some time he heard the drip as a tempo, and he heard the high, clear voice of Alfred Deller in his head. *Music, music, for a while, shall all your cares beguile.* Claude fingered the notes of the accompaniment on the bottom of the tub.

He ate alone in the nearly empty dining room, served by a gray-haired woman who wore a hair net and kept her white socks rolled at the ankles. The meal was good — thin slices of pot roast with gravy, mashed potatoes, glazed carrots, peas, and iced tea. He ate steadily, surprised to discover how hungry he was. After she'd cleared the table, the woman in the rolled socks came back with a piece of cherry pie à la mode. "Try this," she said. "I made it."

It was excellent, tart and fruity with a light crust.

He went back to his room, lay down for what he thought was going to be a few minutes, and fell asleep. He woke in the middle of the night, undressed, and climbed between the sheets to sleep the clock around.

Early the next morning he stood in front of the administration building — a large farmhouse converted to office space, studios, a library, living quarters, and classrooms. The assistant director, a wire-thin woman named Mrs. Chatfield, had greeted him with obvious relief even as she shouted instructions to the front office, answered the telephone, and pulled out drawers at her desk.

"Marvelous," she'd said, "you're here. One less thing to worry about." She flashed a brief apologetic smile and handed him a three-ring binder full of mimeographed material. "Everything's in there. Maps. Schedules. All the events. Felix will show you around. Felix!" she shouted.

Now, standing in the sunshine, Felix, a fast-talking, effeminate young man in his twenties, pointed with a languid arm. "Three hundred and fifty-six acres. Twelve buildings. The big performance space is behind us, near the lake. A sort of natural amphitheater. Major rehearsals over there, in the old cow barn. I'd show up early if I were you."

"Okay."

"You want me to take you around? I've got a composition seminar in forty-five minutes, but there's time."

"Thanks. I'll just wander."

"Fine." He went back into the building.

Claude walked along the main path toward an enormous, solitary elm tree. There was a rough-hewn bench underneath it, where he sat down and opened the three-ring binder. He could not shake a feeling of unreality — the birds singing above him, the wide, impossibly blue sky, the smell of new-cut grass, the rustling leaves, the background of deep silence, the sense of space. The binder seemed to contain an anti-dote: facts, lists, times. Descriptions of activities. He read slowly.

At first it was bewildering. What was the difference between a class and a seminar, a rehearsal and performance preparation, a lecture and a demonstration? Most of the music referred to he recognized, if not by the piece itself, then by the name of the composer, but who was Christian Sinding? What was Jacques Ibert's Capriccio? What was the Thuille Sextet? What were the ongoing auditions? Auditions for what?

The days were jammed with classes, meetings, and rehearsals. Grad-ually it became clear that a great deal of what was going on was aimed at the afternoon and evening performances. Performances of one kind or another seemed to be almost continuous in different buildings and settings. It took Claude five minutes of riffling the pages to discover that the student orchestra had been working on the Mozart Double Piano Concerto under someone named Vladimir Popkin for an hour a day. It seemed a short time, but as he correlated information he saw they were working on a number of other pieces as well.

He raised his head and was surprised to see people moving around the previously empty landscape. A young man ran clumsily with a thick pile of manuscripts in his arms. Two women strode briskly with violin cases. Groups of people ambled every which way, talking, laugh-ing, arguing as they moved over the grass. Nearby, a young woman lay down on her back and turned her face to the sun. Everyone seemed to be wearing white — skirts, pants, shirts, even a few hats in various shades of white. Two men in identical cream trousers sat on a split-rail fence, white sleeves rolled up, swinging their legs as they talked. One of them sang a phrase, tracing the shape of the melody in the air with his forefinger.

Claude became uncomfortably aware of his blue suit, green tie, and heavy black Florsheim shoes. He took off his jacket and tie. At least his shirt was white, and brand new. He rolled the sleeves to just below the elbow, like the men on the fence.

After an hour of walking the grounds he came upon the amphithe-ater, which was empty. An enclosed stage, rows of benches under a large canvas of army-surplus khaki, and a gently rising hillside of cropped meadow. As he stood looking down on it a flock of large black birds flew silently overhead toward the lake behind the stage. It would be like playing outdoors, he thought, wondering how much he would be able to hear.

He'd asked Weisfeld once why it was that after an hour or so of playing, the Bechstein sometimes seemed to warm up, even to get "hot," more sensitive, more responsive, easier to play. With a violin or a horn it made sense, but the piano was huge, weighing more than half a ton, and the action, after all, was mechanical. Weisfeld had thought for a moment, his deep-set black eyes staring at the ceiling. "I don't think the piano changes," he said. "I think it's you. Lots of echoes down there. Differences in humidity and the like. Probably sometimes you focus in on the acoustics more precisely, and it feeds back into your fingers. I bet that's it."

Now, walking along a path that curved through a cluster of small buildings ("sheds" on the map), Claude heard the sound of a piano. He located the shed and went in through the open door. To his surprise it was a single room, the walls lined with music stands, gongs, bells, a xylophone, a set of kettle drums, and folding chairs. Under a window, his head and shoulders caught in a bar of sunlight, a gangly, blond young man was playing a grand piano with unusual ardor, bobbing and weaving, humming, lifting his arms now and then in dramatic arcs. ("All nonsense," Fredericks had said of such air-sculpting. "Show biz.") His blond hair appeared white in the sun. He broke off abruptly.

"Well, what do you want?" he asked. "A triangle? The clack sticks? Whatever it is, get it and leave me alone. I don't have much time." He ran his hand through his hair. Even his eyebrows were white.

"I'm sorry," Claude said, stepping back. "I didn't mean to interrupt."

"Oh, it's all right," he said with a sigh. "Who are you, anyway? I haven't seen you."

"I just got here. Claude Rawlings."

"Well, I'm sorry to be — wait a minute. Rawlings? Are you the one playing with Fredericks?"

"Yes. The Double Concerto."

The man's attitude underwent an instantaneous transformation. He rose from the piano with a broad smile, his teeth white and regular as Chiclets, and came forward with his arm extended. "Dick Denby," he said as they shook hands. "Well, well."

"Was that Beethoven?" Claude asked.

"The Quintet, opus sixteen. We're playing it tonight in the South Barn."

Claude went over and glanced at the score. "I've heard it, but I've never played it."

"Fairly easy," Denby said. "Not like the late stuff. Have to stay on your toes in the rondo, though. It clips along."

"Well, I'll let you get back," Claude said.

"No, no," Denby said, touching Claude's shoulder lightly. "I was just about to break. We're having a picnic. The winds, I mean. You must join us, please. They'll be thrilled."

Claude hesitated. There was something forced about the man's heartiness, and he had the kind of bland, blond good looks that made his face hard to read. All the same, Claude was hungry.

"Wonderful," Denby said, taking silence for assent. "Claudia's bringing a really good pâté."

Shortly afterward, Claude found himself sitting on the edge of a large plaid blanket spread in the dappled shade at the rim of the amphitheater bowl. Dick Denby lay, legs crossed at the knees, with his head in the lap of Claudia, a dark-haired, black-eyed girl in a white dress who played, apparently, the oboe. Claudia was very long, and she'd kicked off her sandals to wiggle her toes, the nails of which were painted red.

"So, how are your reeds, sweetie?" Dick asked. "Are they okay?"

"Don't joke," Claudia said. "You don't have to make the notes. You don't know what it's like."

"You can say that again," said Jerry, the bassoonist, all elbows and knees, with a sharp chin and slightly protuberant eyes, like a young Ichabod Crane. "No offense, Claude, but it's true. Pianists can't imagine the tyranny of reeds. It can drive you nuts."

"I know." Claude pulled his knees up to his chest. "I work in a music store. I've had some very picky customers when it comes to reeds."

Marty, the clarinetist, and Roger, a florid and heavyset French horn player, opened the hamper and began setting things out on the blanket. They were all four or five years older than Claude, and all of them studied at the Curtis Institute of Music in Philadelphia during the winter.

"Pâté," said Roger. "A Camembert. Celery. Olives."

"Pears," said Marty. "Apples. Wine. Bread."

"Oh, goody." Claudia pushed Dick's head from her lap without ceremony and grabbed a paper plate.

Everyone fell to, chattering, passing food, holding out their cups for wine. Jerry offered some to Claude. "A little chablis?"

"Thanks, but I'll pass. I've got a rehearsal pretty soon."

"Very wise." Jerry nodded.

"I love to watch you eat," Dick said to Claudia dreamily. "Those big romantic bites."

"Watch it, buster," she said.

"That little muscle working away underneath your cheekbone, changing the shadow. Your delicate oboist's fingers holding that olive like some fabulous black pearl. It's beautiful." He picked up a pear, examined it closely, and took a bite.

Claudia ignored him. "Try the pâté," she said to Claude. "It's got truffles."

"I'm not going to open the last bottle," Jerry said. "We have to perform."

Groans from Marty, Roger, and Dick.

"Good man," said Claudia.

Like a huge cricket, Jerry rearranged his limbs as he turned to Claude. "Okay, you haven't done any competitions, you don't go to Juilliard, so how did you get here?"

"He asked me."

"Fredericks? But how did you get to Fredericks?"

"I studied with him."

There was a pause. Marty finished a sandwich and said, "I thought he only took rich —"

"Marty!" Roger interrupted. "You've got Camembert all over your chin!"

"I do?" he said, bewildered, touching his face.

"And how," Jerry went on, "did you get to Fredericks?"

"Oh, that was Mr. Weisfeld." Claude looked at them. "He was my first teacher. He owns the music store."

"You mean where you work?" Dick asked.

"Yes. On Eighty-fourth and Third."

Claude watched them all watching him, as if he were expected to say more, and then glancing at one another with blank faces when he didn't. Claudia gave a low laugh.

"That's it?" Dick asked.

"Well, yes, more or less," Claude said. He didn't feel like telling them about the maestro, Mr. Larkin, the studio, and all of that. "Why? What's wrong?"

Jerry looked down. Dick selected another piece of fruit. Marty and Roger began putting things back in the hamper.

"Nothing," Claudia said finally. "People will be curious, that's all. A festival like this . . ." She gave a sigh. "Well, there are a lot of very ambitious musicians here. All sorts of gossip. And Fredericks is famous. This is a big deal." She waved her arm to indicate the hillside, the distant stage. "There'll be thousands of people. All over the place. And some important people sprinkled through. You can bet on it."

He was aware they were all looking at him again. "By ambitious, you mean . . ."

"Jobs, careers, who you know," she said quickly. "The pecking order. It's all people talk about."

"Well," Dick said, "I wouldn't go that far."

"Ha!" said Roger.

Claude thought about it. "I don't know what to tell you. That's what happened."

Now they all reassured him, talking over one another.

As they folded the blanket, Claudia said, "Come hear us tonight in the North Barn. Chamber music. A small audience. It should be good."

"Yes, come," the others said, as if slightly ashamed of themselves, eager to make amends.

Claude arrived at the rehearsal shed during a break. People milled around on the lawn near the entrance, and he was aware of a few glances as he went inside. The shed was half stage and half open space where musicians stood talking, some of them with their instruments, a few playing little runs or phrases. Claude made his way up to the stage. Vladimir Popkin, a rumpled white-haired man in his sixties, was bent over the podium examining a score. He looked up quickly, his hanging cheeks — reminiscent of those of the actor S. Z. Zakkles — swinging bluish wattles. "You must be Rawlings," he said in a heavy accent. "Is true?"

"Yes, sir." At lunch they had told him that Popkin was concertmaster of the Chicago Symphony.

"Good, good." He tapped the score with a broad finger. "Here it is. Tell me what he wants."

Claude stepped forward and opened his own score, resting the edge of it on the bottom lip of the podium. Popkin, smelling of sweat and cloves, pressed up close to Claude's shoulder. "Okay, we turn pages. Tell me tempo — where he slows up, goes fast. Tell me dynamics. Aha! I see you have notes like that. Eggselent! But so many notes I can't see the music!"

They went through the score rapidly, Popkin making exclamations, grunts, and tooth-sucking noises. Claude's quick comments were accompanied by the sound of Popkin turning pages. "So," he said at the end, "nothing radical. He plays like it is. You think?"

"Yes, sir. He pays a lot of attention to phrasing."

"But of course." Popkin turned and gave a great shout. "Come children! Come, come. Time to play."

Quite a few people climbed onstage, going to their chairs, arranging their music. Not a full orchestra, but a lot of people.

"I only see one piano," Claude said.

Popkin didn't seem to understand.

"I mean, who's going to play *his* part?" Claude asked. "Where's the other piano?"

Popkin wiped his brow with the sleeve of his shirt. "There is other piano. I can bring it out and conduct from other piano if you want. Not so good. I thought you play both parts, yes?" He raised his busy eyebrows expectantly.

Claude looked down at the score in his hand, his mind racing through the music. He would have to reduce some things. There would be some awfully tricky counterpoint.

"Leave out what is impossible," Popkin said.

"Okay," Claude said, "I'll try." He moved away to the piano, stumbling over the leg of a music stand. "Sorry."

"That's okay."

Dimly, Claude was aware of a girl with green eyes smiling at him, holding her violin on her knee.

"Okay, children," Poplin shouted, rapping the podium with his baton in a brisk tattoo. "Mr. Rawlings, give us an A, please."

When it was over, he was astonished to find that more than an hour had gone by. The sound of the opening bars had electrified him. The power of the orchestra, the dense texture, the colors, the clarity of the different voices, all combined for an effect so strong it felt, for the first few moments, almost crude. He played by reflex. He missed the thirty-second note in the fifth bar of the solos altogether, the one Weisfeld and Fredericks had talked about, and simply cruised through with everyone else until the first crescendo at bar twelve, when he was able to collect himself and concentrate on what he was doing. The sensation had been something like stepping onto an escalator without paying attention. But once oriented, he played with confidence, and was disappointed when Popkin broke things off at the solo.

"Horns!" Popkin said. "This is Mozart, not Mr. John Philip Sousa. Keep it light, like the sunshine, like a good musgatel. Strings, make clear the staggatos. Again. *And* one, *and* two . . ."

It became clear that this was a rehearsal for the orchestra. Time after time Popkin cut him off only a few bars into the piano part, or started him only a few bars before a tutti. Popkin gave Claude no directions, making all his remarks to the ensemble. The rehearsal ended and they had not played the piece entirely through. Claude felt like protesting. There were several segments of piano and orchestra he felt needed more work, and he was certain Fredericks would have agreed.

As the players got up for a break — chairs clattering, music rustling — Claude went to the podium.

"This part in the allegro," he said, flipping pages, "here in the rondo, and this part in here. We should work on those."

"Yes, yes." Popkin nodded. "No more time today. They have to do the Brahms next, and then something . . ." He looked through a pile of music. "Something else here somewhere. Where is it?" He looked away, then back at Claude as if surprised to find him still there. "Rehearsal tomorrow with Fredericks," he said. "We do it then."

Slightly exasperated, Claude nodded and turned away. The green-eyed violinist stood in front of him.

"How did we sound?" she asked, giving a little flip of her head.

"Swell," Claude said. "Very good. Really."

"We've worked on it more than anything else." She had a sprinkling of freckles across the bridge of her nose.

"Well, I guess . . . ," he began. The girl had a straightforward air, a kind of candor in her gaze that made him self-conscious. "Well, Fredericks, I guess," he said.

"You bet. We practically fainted when Dr. Popkin told us. Is Fredericks hard? You know, a pill? Like some of them?"

"Oh no, he's very kind," Claude said. "Sometimes he pushes, but it doesn't make you feel bad."

"Well, that's good to hear," she said, and turned away. As she started down the steps she said, "I could tell you wanted to play more. From the back of your neck."

Claude had bought a pair of white tennis shoes and two pairs of white socks at a general store in Longmeadow. They did not have any pants, however, and that had been a disappointment. At the inn he mused over the problem during dinner — pork chops stuffed with prunes, baby carrots, and potato dumplings — and mentioned it to the lady with the hair net when she served him pie (blueberry this time).

"I need a pair of white pants," he said.

"What on earth for?" she said. "They'll just show the dirt."

"They all wear them."

"Over at the farm? Well, they got them in the city. You can't get white pants in Longmeadow."

"I know," Claude said.

She shook her head and made a soft clucking sound. "You look fine. Eat your pie." She left.

It was dusk when he got to the North Barn. The walk after dinner had refreshed him, and his new shoes made him feel light on his feet. He looked down at them, pleased at their brightness. People were moving through the entrance and he joined them, into the shadowy interior where he immediately sought out the men's room.

When he opened the door he heard a woman's sharp voice. "Can't come in now." Then he saw the flushed face of Claudia. The others from the quintet were crowded behind her in the small room. "Oh," she said, "it's you," and waved him in. He advanced. They were gathered around Dick Denby, who lay pale-faced with his back against the wall. He had apparently vomited in the toilet, and he wiped his mouth with the back of his hand. His eyes were glassy. Everyone seemed to be talking at once. Claude noticed that Denby's hands were trembling.

"I can't," Denby said to no one in particular, "I can't."

"Of course you can," said Jerry, the bassoonist, lowering his gangly frame to get down on one knee. "You've done it dozens of times in front of a lot more people. Certainly you can."

"It's all in his mind," said Marty, the clarinetist, and gave a sudden giggle.

"What are you laughing at?" Roger was furious, gesturing with his

French horn. "Kribbs from the Chicago Symphony is out there. Mc-Taggart from Cleveland! Grimes from Boston! Have you lost your mind? This is a catastrophe!"

"Dick," Jerry said gently, "tell us what's happening. Let us help."

"I can't. Everything sounds funny and looks funny. I think I'm going crazy."

"You spineless creep!" Claudia shouted.

"We're on in ten minutes, people," said Marty.

"You worthless sack of shit!" She bent over Denby to shout it in his face, trying to get him to look at her.

"You're not helping," Jerry said, shaking his head.

"That's it, then," said Marty. "I'm packing up."

"I have to go home," Dick said mechanically, his voice devoid of emotion. "I have to take a hot bath."

"Dick," Roger said, "think about it. Give in this way and there'll be psychological damage. You have to beat it now. Otherwise, before every concert, before every appearance . . ."

"I have to go home," Dick repeated.

Claudia stood erect and took a deep breath. "Yes, go home. Spend the rest of your life playing tennis at the Merion Cricket Club. It's all you're good for." She picked up the score from between his legs and thrust it at Claude. "All right. You do it. An emergency. You do it."

Marty said, "Now wait a minute."

"No rehearsal?" Roger cried. "He just sight-reads it? Are you kidding? It's better we don't play at all."

Claudia was staring intently into Claude's eyes. "No, he's good. He's got to be good."

"I don't know about this," Marty said.

Claude took the score, broke away from Claudia's gaze, and looked at it. A few flecks of vomit marred its cover. He went to the stall and got some toilet paper and wiped it clean. A definite sense of excitement began to stir in the back of his brain.

"It could be awful," Roger said. "How do we know?"

"It's an emergency," Claudia said. "We'll announce it. People will understand."

That was all Claude needed. "I'll do it," he said.

"Oh, God," Roger moaned.

"Oy vey!" Marty said.

Claudia put her hand on Jerry's shoulder and the bassoonist looked up. "What do you say?" she said. "Let's just do it."

There was a moment of silence while Jerry regarded Claude and bit his lower lip. Very slowly, a trace of a smile showed at the corners of his mouth. "What the hell. Let's see what happens."

And so the arrangements were made. The string quartet who were to have played Bartók during the second half were prevailed upon to play first. Meanwhile Claude studied the score, with Dick Denby's sketchy notations, in the front seat of Roger's Studebaker. During the last available ten minutes, Jerry sat with him and went over tempos and phrasing.

"What we're doing is insane," Jerry said as he reached up to turn off the dome light.

"I know," Claude said, and they both laughed.

In the sudden silence following the last abrupt volley of notes ending the piece, the first thing Claude heard was the awestruck voice of the girl with the green eyes, her breath in his left ear. "Wow!" she said. She had stepped forward from the audience when Claudia had asked for a volunteer to turn pages.

And now the applause started. Claude looked at the faces of the other players, all of them smiling. Jerry giving him a thumbs-up sign, Claudia blowing him a kiss. As he stood up from the bench he realized that the applause from the sixty or seventy people in the audience was very spirited, punctuated by the odd shout. Claude made his way around the piano to stand with the other players. As they all bowed, more or less simultaneously, the audience got to its feet and continued to applaud.

"Terrific," Jerry said out of the corner of his mouth. "We did it."

"Thank God," said Marty.

"Amazing," said Roger.

Facing the audience, Claude felt a sense of relief. He had missed dozens of notes, played a few wrong ones, rushed the tempo of the third section out of nervousness, and had not quite matched the phrasing of the horns on several occasions. But the piece as a whole had been executed clearly, its shape unambiguous. Parts of it had even been beautiful, and, remembering those moments, he allowed himself to be swept up in the general enthusiasm.

A second bow.

"I knew it," Claudia said. "I had a feeling."

A third and final bow.

"Where's Dick?" Claude asked as they all thanked him and began moving out to their friends in the crowd. No one knew. "On the way to Philadelphia, I hope," said Claudia.

Quite a few people from the audience came up to Claude and offered compliments. "You really never played it before?" asked a short man with a white beard.

Claude made his way outside and took several deep breaths of the balmy air. There was the barest sliver of moon hanging over the trees, and the dark sky glinted with innumerable stars, more stars than he had ever seen. He felt extraordinarily alive, cleansed somehow, his body light and humming. He felt fresh.

The dark shapes of people fanned out in all directions. Behind the barn, car engines started, and beams of light appeared to the left and right like a panoply of arms. A single figure approached him from the center of the shed.

"Here." It was the girl with the green eyes. "Don't forget this." She held out the score.

"Thanks." He put it under his arm. "And thanks for turning pages. Your timing was perfect."

"My pleasure," she said. "It was something to see."

They stood in comfortable silence. He could see the pale orb of her face, but it was too dark to make out her expression.

"Well, I better get back to the inn," he said.

"Are you driving?"

"No, walking."

"Me too. I'll come along with you."

"Okay. Sure." Now he could catch a faint lemony scent as she came up to his side, close, almost as close as she would to take his arm.

There was a path along the side of the road, and when it narrowed her shoulder would touch his arm. He felt buoyant, almost dizzy, and everything he saw — the trees, the stars, the wooden bridge over the creek — pleased him in some simple, mysterious way. At the same time, even though no words were being exchanged, he was aware of a tacit tension growing between them. They seemed to be talking without talking, and strange as it was, it felt natural, inevitable.

It was almost a shock when, turning the corner toward the inn, she spoke. "My name is Eva."

"Claude," he said. "It's nice to meet you." He felt a little foolish, and as he turned to smile she put her hand on his arm and they stopped in the middle of the sidewalk.

"Could we get a cup of coffee or something?" she asked.

"I bet we can." He found himself bending his head forward, like one of the actors on the great screen, again with an odd, graced sense of inevitability, to kiss her. Her lips were warm and he closed his eyes, lost in sensation.

Then she was smiling, and she took his arm, and they began walking again.

The lobby of the inn was entirely empty, even the reception desk. The dining room was closed, and dark through the glass doors. For a moment he stood, her warmth up against his side, unsure what to do next.

"I guess . . . I guess . . ."

"It doesn't matter," she said.

"We could go up," he said, amazed at himself, as if the words had passed through him from some powerful agency, as if he'd been seized by magic. He held his breath.

"Yes," she said. "Let's do that."

They climbed the stairs and went to his room. She didn't leave until just before first light.

"You look like you could use this," the waitress with the hair net said at breakfast, pouring him coffee. "What'd you do last night, tie one on?"

For a split second he thought she knew, but then he realized she meant drinking. He shook his head and looked down at his plate. "No," he said, spreading his napkin on his lap. "The truth is . . . the truth is, I feel very good. I feel great."

"Well, fine," she said.

And it was true. He'd spent half the night making love with Eva, and the world seemed like a brand-new place. Everything seemed newly minted — the salt and pepper shakers, the sun coming in the window behind him, clattering sounds from the kitchen, his own slender hands. He felt so good he imagined his happiness to be radiating outward from the confines of his body, and he marveled that the waitress didn't seem to notice it. And the Beethoven! He felt the music again. The Beethoven! He had to concentrate to eat his breakfast.

When she came back to clear up she said, "The chef has some white pants you could borrow. They won't fit, though."

He rose from his reverie. "I'm sorry?"

"The white pants you wanted."

It was like a memory from weeks ago. "Oh, yes. The pants. Thanks. Thanks for asking. I mean, for going to all that trouble."

"They won't fit."

"It's okay. I don't need them. It turns out . . . I'm . . . everything's okay," he spluttered.

"Good," she said. "Supposed to tell you you've got a message at the desk."

He approached the reception desk with trepidation, various embarrassing scenarios running through his head. The old man looked up, his milky blue eyes sharp and steady.

"Morning," he said.

"Morning."

"They say stop in at the administration. You got some telegrams."

"Oh, fine," Claude said, instantly relieved. "Thanks a lot."

"Good breakfast?"

"Absolutely. First rate. Delicious."

"We do good breakfasts."

"You sure do. The food is great," Claude said. "Dinner too. Just great."

"We aim to please." The old man picked up a toothpick from a glass and slipped it between his lips. He pushed the glass forward. "Want one of these? Mint. Got a mint flavor."

Claude accepted one and moved away. Now that he appeared to be safe, he wondered about the telegrams.

On his way to the farm he looked up at the sky — great, billowing white clouds hanging motionless under the blue — and for no reason at all broke into a run, relishing the air against his face. His new white tennis shoes gripped the surface of the path as he flew effortlessly along, slapping at the leaves now and then.

He was out of breath when he reached the administration building. Mrs. Chatfield wore a different sweater but the same pearls, and the same half glasses midway down her slender nose. Telephones rang, people came and went with pieces of paper, and she held a pencil sideways in her mouth as she rummaged through her drawers.

"*Voilà.*" She handed him two yellow windowed envelopes. He opened the first, which read:

Unavoidably delayed here. Have notified Popkin. Show him what
we want. Look forward to performing with you tomorrow.

                                                    Fredericks

Claude would have to do the second rehearsal alone. He felt a flutter as
he realized the extent of his responsibility, but he also remembered
exactly those places he had pointed out to Popkin, so he at least knew
where to start.

"Fredericks can't come to the rehearsal today," Claude said to Mrs.
Chatfield.

"These things happen all the time around here," she said with a sigh.
"I'm sure it will work out."

He found a chair against the wall, sat down, and opened the second
telegram.

Some time to get the flu. Doctor insists bedrest. I will be thinking
of you tomorrow. Play loud maybe I'll hear it.

                                                    Weisfeld

Claude stared at the paper for a long time, his eyes going over and
over the strips of tape bearing the words. He did not know what to
think, aware only of a sense of disappointment, a kind of slowing
down within himself.

"Something wrong?" Mrs. Chatfield asked.

"My teacher has the flu. He can't come."

"Fredericks?" she said, half rising in alarm, her glasses, held by a
black cord, falling to her chest.

"No, no. My first teacher, my real teacher. Mr. Weisfeld."

She sat back down. "I'm sorry to hear that," she said, sounding
relieved. "That's a shame."

"Can I call him on the telephone?" He got up and went to the desk.
He wrote the number on a scrap of paper and handed it to her.

"Well, I'm not supposed to," she said, reaching for the receiver, "but
if he's not well . . ."

She read the number to the long distance operator and handed the
phone to Claude. After some time he heard the soft burr of the ringing
on the other end. Then he heard a woman's voice. "Hello?"

Claude was confused. "Hello. Is Mr. Weisfeld there, please? This is
Claude."

"He's asleep, Claude. I was just on my way out. This is Mrs. Keller
from next door."

"Oh, hi. Hi, Mrs. Keller." It seemed odd to be talking to her, odd to think of her in the music store. "Is he okay? I got a telegram, it just says the flu."

There was a brief pause. "That's right. The doctor's been. He just has to rest and he'll be fine," she said. "It's nothing serious. When're you coming back? He told me you're up in the country someplace."

"Tomorrow. Tomorrow night." He switched the phone to his other ear. "But he's okay?"

"I'm sure he'll be up and about by the time you get back."

"Good," Claude said. "Okay. Well, thank you very much, Mrs. Keller."

"You're welcome."

Claude hung up the phone, thanked Mrs. Chatfield, and went outside. He walked down the path and sat at the same bench under the big tree. Weisfeld could not come, would not be with him in the wings, and Claude felt slightly askew, slightly adrift at the prospect.

"Is this your first time?" Eva had asked in bed.

"Yes."

"Not me," she said cheerfully, and kissed him.

He did not question the fact that he was only mildly curious about her. He knew she would go back to San Francisco, back to the conservatory, her parents, and her golden retriever, and that he would never see her again. He also knew it was the right time of the month for her to make love, because she had told him. She had asked him very little about himself.

From the first — their silent walk, the kiss on the sidewalk, their shared delicious sense of breaking the rules on the way up to his room (she had even giggled once, into her hand, as he'd fumbled with the key) — he'd known perfectly well that this was not what he'd read about in *Romeo and Juliet,* or the sonnets, or what he'd seen in the movies or read in novels. This was not transcendent. But he very much liked her. She was good, she was generous, and in her courage she had been the agent of his release. She would never know how much it meant to him to be free of his virginity, and he could never tell her because, in truth, what had happened to him seemed far more important than what had happened to her. Hence there had been few words during their long, voluptuous night of physical intimacy. At times they had been languorous and tender, at times they had clung ferociously like two kids on a roller coaster. He did not really know her, but he felt he owed her the world.

Now, as he came upon her in the rehearsal shed, he felt an instantaneous shock — an electricity of pleasure up his spine — at the simple sight of her. It caught him completely by surprise.

She smiled. "Let's sit for a second."

Musicians milled around but no one seemed to pay them any particular attention. Popkin was fussing at the podium.

"Let's do it again," he said, "tonight."

"Ah, you are a hungry lad, Claude."

"Yes. Yes I am." He could not take his eyes from her mouth. "God knows I am."

"We'll see. You have beautiful dark eyes, you know."

"I'm glad."

"But," she said in a new tone, "in here it's all business. I will forget about you, and you will forget about me, and the only thing that counts is the music."

"How can I do that? You'll be sitting right behind me, staring at my neck." He was bold enough to tease.

"I won't." She leaned forward a bit. "Claude, I'm serious. I swear I won't even look at you. This is serious. We can't screw up the performance. We have to be professional." She looked down and shook her head. "I'd never forgive myself," she said, sounding genuinely alarmed.

"It's okay," Claude said. "It is, really. When I get to the piano something happens to me. I don't know how to describe it. It's like I'm there, but I'm not there. I go into some kind of zone or something. It always happens, so it'll be okay. I promise."

"Just forget about me up there — tomorrow afternoon *especially*."

"Mr. Rawlings!" Popkin shouted. "Come up here, please. We have to talk!"

"So," Popkin said as Claude joined him, "he says you know what he wants. So what does he want?"

There was a certain amount of irritation in his voice, and so Claude thought carefully. "I sure don't know everything he wants," he said, "but if you don't mind going to the piano, I can show you some of the phrasing."

They moved to the grand. Claude opened his score while Popkin stood over his right shoulder. Starting at the beginning, and reminded by his copious notes, Claude went through the five or six places he remembered from the previous day as most likely to bother Fredericks.

"This note shouldn't be so quick," he said. "He told me to watch it.

He's after the smoothest possible shape, with a light legato." He played the phrase and Popkin grunted. "Here," Claude continued, "this forte shouldn't be so forte. More of a swelling up, sort of." He turned pages. "This sounded kind of limp yesterday. He wants it spirited. He used the word 'virile.' " He turned more pages, going over the material and playing when necessary. Popkin made him repeat sections now and then. Claude was aware of the players taking their seats, talking quietly to one another, occasionally glancing up.

"We try," said Popkin, and he returned to the podium. "Everybody here? Good. From the beginning." He raised his baton and gave the tempo.

It was once again a thrill to hear the sound, but this time Claude forced himself to listen closely. Popkin let them play four bars and stopped them. He nodded to Claude, who understood, and played the bit with what he thought was the correct phrasing.

"You see?" said Popkin. "Rounder. Not so fast with the appoggiatura. Let me hear it as a note."

The orchestra played.

"Strings, strings!" Popkin interrupted. "Do it like the horns! They've got it right. Listen to them. Horns! Just the horns now. *And* one." The horns played. "Good, good," Popkin said. "Now the strings alone." The strings played. "Better. Now everybody. *And* one."

They progressed through the piece, playing in fits and starts, isolated sections again and again. It was grueling work, taking a great deal of concentration and total alertness. The room was growing uncomfortably warm. Popkin's shirt darkened and sweat rolled down his pendulous cheeks. Some piano keys became slick.

After about an hour, working on part of the middle section, Claude suddenly stopped. The orchestra straggled to a halt. Popkin looked at Claude with surprise. "Something?"

"It's just, it's just . . ." He twisted in exasperation. "It isn't clear. It isn't focused. We do something five times and it still sounds blurry. What's the matter?"

There was a moment of silence, and then Claude heard some shuffling of feet, some quiet hisses, and a boo or two from some of the students watching the rehearsal.

"Ten minutes!" announced Popkin, and waved for Claude to follow him offstage. Claude felt as if he'd been hit in the stomach. The hisses and boos were like sucker punches, all the more powerful for being completely unexpected. He turned to see Eva's back as she walked away.

In the gloom behind a flat, Popkin put his arm over Claude's shoulder. The man no longer smelled of cloves. "Listen," he said, "first time playing with a big group. Right?"

Claude nodded.

"Many, many people," Popkin continued. "Each one a separate people. Not like one piano, two pianos, everything precise, all the notes already made, all you do is press the key."

"I'm sorry," said Claude.

"No, no. Understandable. Absolutely," Popkin said. "But this is good because you learn. You learn right away. Today. Now." He lifted his arm from Claude and wiped his own brow with it. "Is different, orchestra. Great slow beast, powerful beast. Patience is necessary. Very much patience to control such a big animal." He found a folding chair and sat down. "Difficult business. You do a little bit here, then a little bit there, then back to over there. Little by little, you understand? And it gets better. It doesn't get perfect but it gets better, believe me. Fredericks knows this, don't worry." He put his elbows on his knees and held his chin in his hands. "You know the octopus?"

"The octopus? Sure."

"What do you call the long things? Long arms like snakes?"

"Tentacles."

"Okay, tentagles. Some tentagles playing fiddles, some tentagles playing different horns, different reeds, big drums, little drums. All those tentagles wiggling around, playing like crazy, trying not to bump in. You see? Is magic. Is a miracle they play music! So we go very easy with the octopus. Big dumb beast trying hard, he shouldn't get confused, he shouldn't get angry. We go easy. We say nice octopus. Sometimes we say beautiful octopus. Sometimes to the audience we say this is my dear, dear friend the octopus, please clap for the octopus. You see?"

Claude felt ashamed of himself. "Yes. I understand. It won't happen again."

"Is natural," said Popkin, rising. "Back to work."

Claude walked back in with his head down. Just before lowering himself to the bench he turned to the orchestra. "I'm sorry," he said. "I didn't mean to —"

Popkin interrupted from the podium. "Fredericks isn't here. Remember how much pressure is for this young man. Is not easy. Now we play. We are together, we are all in this together. We will do this."

Claude didn't know how much of it was in his mind, but the rest of the rehearsal — still working on fragments — went better. Once he did not expect a quick response, he began to hear how the phrasing seeped into the sound of the orchestra bit by bit, like shapes solidifying in mist. He felt grateful to Popkin, and made a point to go and shake his hand when it was over.

"They all hate me, I guess," Claude said. "Well, so be it." His head was crooked against the headboard. Eva lay beside him, her cheek on his shoulder. When she spoke he could feel her warm breath on his chest.

"I wouldn't say that," she said. "They assumed you were experienced. I mean the way you play, and Fredericks picking you. After you left, Popkin said you'd never played with an orchestra before. Some of them felt bad when they heard that."

"I'm glad you came. I didn't think you would."

"Music is music, but this" — she kissed his nipple — "is this. And it's our last night."

"Yes. I go back tomorrow too." He was astonished at how quickly he'd gotten used to lying naked in bed with a naked girl. He felt as if he'd been doing it all his life, so natural did it seem. They'd made love twice in as many hours, less rushed but no less powerful than the previous night. His body, which had seemed, in the act, like a rag doll in the hand of a giant, now floated calmly in the darkness, warm and serene. He drifted.

Later, they both woke to the sound of voices in the hall outside. Bumping of luggage. Key in lock. Muffled talk, instructions, hushing noises.

"They're here," Claude said.

Eva sat up. "Fredericks?"

"Anson Roeg too."

She slipped out of bed, went quickly to the door, and knelt down to peer through the keyhole.

"What are you doing?" Claude whispered.

She waved her hand in the air behind her. She stayed at the keyhole for several moments, until the noises stopped, and then tiptoed back to bed.

"Again," she said, with rapid kisses across his chest. "Again."

.   .   .

"One should eat lightly before a performance," Fredericks said as the food was rolled into his suite on a little cart. The young waitress draped a cloth over the table and set three places. "I took the liberty of ordering," he went on. "Consommé, toasted cheese sandwiches, and mineral water. Will that be enough for you, my dear?" he asked Anson Roeg.

"Of course."

They took their places and unrolled their napkins.

"The food is pretty good here," Claude said.

Fredericks took a sip of soup. "Lemon," he said to the waitress. "Some cut lemon."

"Yes, sir." She bobbed in a half curtsy and left.

"That's sweet," Anson Roeg said.

"What?" Fredericks looked up.

"Her little curtsy. We could be in Austria."

"Austria before the war." He touched his lips with his napkin. "You can bet they don't curtsy now. Not to us, at any rate." He ate fastidiously. "So, Claude, have you been enjoying yourself?"

"Yes, indeed." Claude nodded, trying not to smile.

"My apologies for yesterday. It was unavoidable. What do you think of the orchestra?"

"I guess it'll be okay. Dr. Popkin really worked them. It's hard for me to judge."

"Just so," he said. "We heard about the Beethoven this morning. It's the talk of the festival."

"Very courageous of you," Roeg said with a trace of archness.

Claude blushed. "Well, I just thought, what the hell."

"Indeed," she said.

"I mean, *he* sure couldn't do it. He was shaking."

"Did you have any time at all to prepare?" Fredericks asked.

"Forty-five minutes. I sat in a car with the score, and then maybe ten minutes with the bassoonist, going over it. He was great."

"Good," Fredericks said. "They say you brought it off quite well."

"It was scary, but it was fun."

Anson Roeg leaned forward a bit and stared into his face. "You're different," she said.

"My dear?" Fredericks asked.

Claude stared into her gray eyes, trying not to show his feelings, which were that he agreed with her.

"Something," she said. "Something's different. He has a certain air about him, a certain . . . I don't know, but he's different."

The waitress re-entered and served lemon wedges.

"The Beethoven," Fredericks suggested. "Trial by fire."

"Perhaps," Roeg said.

"Do you feel different, Claude?" Fredericks asked.

"I guess I do, yes. I'd have to say that. It's been an amazing couple of days. Feels like weeks." He realized he was eating too quickly, and slowed the pace.

Fredericks put his napkin on the table and gazed out the window. "A beautiful, calm summer afternoon. A fine day to play Mozart."

"I hope Mr. Weisfeld is all right. I've tried twice to call him," Claude said.

"It's just the flu," Roeg said. "He'll be fine, and you shouldn't worry about it." She reached up suddenly and grabbed Claude's chin to hold his face for a close examination. "What *is* it?" she said as if to herself, exasperated.

Claude could not stop the slow smile from appearing on his slightly swollen lips. Her eyes came up from his mouth and he saw the shock of recognition. Her head jerked back a fraction of an inch. "Oh," she said, taking her hand away.

"What is it?" Fredericks asked.

"Nothing," she said.

"You've been reading Yeats again," he said.

"That must be it," she said, and finished off her mineral water. "Yes, that's it."

As they drove slowly to the amphitheater shell Claude saw an entire hillside of people scattered over the grassy expanse with blankets, sun umbrellas, folding chairs, pillows, and picnic hampers. Nearer the stage the crowd was denser, and the rows of benches were completely filled.

"Good turnout," said Roeg.

"Hmmm." Fredericks was reading a newspaper.

The Rolls glided silently through the parking area — hundreds of cars in neat rows on the meadow — and pulled up behind the shell. An attendant ran forward to open the door of the car while another held open the rear entrance door to the building.

Anson Roeg got out first, followed by Claude and then Fredericks, who stretched his arms and took a couple of deep breaths before going inside.

Mrs. Chatfield and her assistants greeted Fredericks effusively and led the way to the green room, where Popkin and a number of others immediately surrounded him. Claude felt Anson Roeg take his elbow and lead him to an empty area in the corner. Couch, table, a few chairs. They sat down.

"He'll get rid of them in a few minutes," she said, retrieving a silver case from her purse. She withdrew a small brown cigar and held out a silver lighter to Claude. He accepted it and took a moment to figure out how it worked. Flashbulbs were going off. Claude lit her cigar.

"Thank you," she said, and took back the lighter. She leaned back on the couch and sent a thin plume of blue smoke toward the ceiling.

"Is it always like this?" Claude asked.

"This is nothing," she said calmly.

Eventually a buzzer sounded and the room began to clear. Fredericks came over, with Popkin at his elbow. "So you do the Brahms now. That is, what, fifteen minutes?"

"Very close," said Popkin. "You will get two buzzes, then you come." He reached out and caught a young man in a white coat by the sleeve, never taking his eyes off Fredericks. "You would like something? Coffee? Tea? Perhaps the lady? Something?"

"A pitcher of water and three glasses," said Fredericks.

Popkin nodded to the young man, who went to get it. "Fine," he said. "I see you out there." He caught Claude's eye. "You do good."

Claude didn't know if it was a prediction or an instruction, but he thanked him anyway and reflexively touched the wooden cross on his chest, under his shirt.

Finally they were alone, sitting three around the table with their glasses of water before them. Fredericks folded one leg over the other as, very faintly, they heard the beginning of the Brahms.

"You know that stock he talked me into," Fredericks said, "the pet-food company? It went down four points."

Anson Roeg tapped some ash into the ashtray. "People must have heard you bought it."

"Exactly." He gave a small laugh. "If I want it to go up, I should sell."

Claude started to run down the Mozart in his head, repeating the first phrase several times. He closed his eyes and gave himself over to the sense memory of playing the music, of the sound of it, the feel of the keys, the changing positions of his hands. He was a hundred bars in when suddenly he lost the thread. His eyes snapped open. He stood up and began to pace, humming to himself to find the place where he'd stumbled.

"Claude," Fredericks said, "sit down."

"What?"

"Come back and sit down."

Claude obeyed, noticing that Anson Roeg was rummaging in her bag again. What was that? A deck of cards?

"Stop thinking about the music," Fredericks said. "Do not think about the music before you go on. It's too late. There is nothing to be gained, and it will only make you nervous."

Anson Roeg was shuffling the cards.

"Do you know how to play gin?" Fredericks asked.

"Yes." Al had taught him.

"Fine. We play a half cent a point. You may deal, my dear."

"I'm two dollars up on paper," Roeg reminded him.

"I know. Now make a column for Claude."

And so they played gin rummy, in silence except for the odd remark. While Claude was shuffling — the soft sound curiously reassuring — someone opened the door, peeked in, and closed it quickly. Claude dealt.

When the buzzer sounded Fredericks said, "Wait a minute. Let's play this out, we're close." He threw down a four of hearts. Roeg picked it up, rearranged her hand, and discarded a seven of clubs.

Claude picked up the seven. "Knock for two," he said, placing the fan of his hand on the table, upside down so they could see it.

"A club run?" Fredericks laid down his cards. "But you sloughed the jack!"

The young man in the white jacket opened the door, stepped in, and held it open. "Gentlemen," he said.

Fredericks and Claude stood up.

"I'll be in the wings," Anson Roeg said. "I have to tally up the score."

Fredericks and Claude followed the young man down a corridor.

"Why did you slough the jack?" Fredericks asked.

"Well, the queen was dead."

"It was?"

"The second or third discard," Claude said.

"Really. I should have remembered that."

It was bright at the end of the corridor. They paused for a moment.

The stage was flooded with sunlight, angling in from over the top of the hill. The orchestra, and Popkin, were in shirtsleeves.

"Off with your jacket, Claude." Fredericks removed his own and dropped it to the floor without looking. Claude did the same. Then they walked onstage.

Claude glanced briefly at the audience — what seemed like thousands of people making sharp movements that he eventually recognized as clapping — and then found the piano. With a kind of tunnel vision he stared at the instrument, which grew larger as he approached. It filled his consciousness as he sat down, and then, almost with a click, he saw Popkin, Fredericks, the orchestra, and Eva staring at the floor. His ears opened as the applause faded. He took a deep, sighing breath and the music started, instantly there, like some enormous flower blossoming out of nothing in a nanosecond, big as a house. The air was thick with music.

After the staccato chords of the tutti, after the heartbeat rest of silence, when he and Fredericks laid in their double trills as one, together shaped the grace notes and announced the unison E-flat with the same firm touch, after the bar and a half of descending sixteenths flowing like grains of sand in an hourglass, Claude removed his hands from the keyboard and listened to Fredericks play the next eleven bars. It was clear, spirited, and apparently effortless. Claude found himself playing the response, an octave below, with willful concentration, consciously controlling the sense of euphoria he felt building in his breast. It was launched, it was loose, it was free, and they would play right through to the end, a great sailing ship running with the wind.

Trading off with Fredericks, he felt almost outside himself, listening to the magic flow, the shift of colors, hearing the pulse, watching his hands do their amazing work. As he shaped the music in his mind and played it, he felt Fredericks shaping and playing right along with him, their souls joined in harmonious enterprise, like two old friends who can talk without words, who can communicate a thought even before it has fully emerged, because the same thought is nascent in the other. Claude knew he was on the stage, at the piano in Longmeadow, Massachusetts, but at the same time he was somewhere else, somewhere he could not describe even to himself — nor did he have the faintest urge to, so heavenly did it seem. Watch it! Watch it! Listen! Concentrate! Here it comes. Here it is. *This!*

·   ·   ·

They took their bows facing full into the sun. Claude watched Fredericks from the corner of his eye and copied his movements. The applause from the benches and the hillside sounded like heavy rain, and he could hear the orchestra behind him tapping their music stands. Popkin embraced Fredericks, and then Claude, and the two pianists went into the wings.

Anson Roeg stood with a towel in each hand. She gave one to Fredericks and tossed the other to Claude. "You're drenched," she said to Fredericks. "It must be a hundred degrees out there."

"Thank you, my dear." He wiped his face and neck, and opened a couple of buttons on his shirt. He looked at Claude. "I hardly noticed, it went so well, I thought. How about you?"

"I wish it had gone on forever," Claude said.

"It was exquisite," Roeg said. "There's no other word."

"I wonder if there's a shower in the green room bathroom." Fredericks held the front of his shirt with two fingers and flapped it in and out.

"No," Roeg said. "We'll have to wait till we're back at the inn."

"Well then, let's get through this as fast as we can. I don't like to see people like this."

As they walked down the corridor various people backed up against the walls to let them pass. They were all clapping. Fredericks nodded and waved his hand as he went by. Someone touched Claude on the back and said "Bravo."

More flashbulbs as they entered the green room. People thrusting programs to be signed. Claude followed Fredericks's lead and scribbled his signature on a dozen or so.

"Where's Popkin?" Fredericks asked.

"He's coming," Roeg said.

The short man with the white beard who had asked Claude about the Beethoven stepped out of the crowd and shook hands with Fredericks. They put their heads together and talked for a moment, but Claude could hear only the end of the conversation, when Fredericks invited the man to come back to the inn with them.

Suddenly Popkin was there, his dewlapped cheeks flushed, his eyes bright. "Wonderful," he said to Fredericks. "A joy! I've never heard it better. I hope the children did not get in your way."

"They did well," Fredericks said. "My thanks, and tell them I said so."

"Here is the wunderkind!" Popkin hugged Claude. "Very good, very good. He helps me also prepare the orchestra. But you played like an angel!"

"Thank you, sir." Claude repressed the urge to wiggle free, and was finally released. "And I'll remember about the octopus."

"Time to go," said Roeg.

They made their way slowly through the crowd, signing a few more programs, and went out the rear door. A small crowd applauded as they emerged, and opened up before them as they went to the Rolls.

Suddenly an astonishingly loud, high-pitched whistle cut through the air. Claude turned his head to see Eva, twenty yards away, removing her fingers from the corners of her mouth. She stood on the bottom step of an orange school bus. She put one hand on the door frame, jutted her hip in a little vamp, and blew him a kiss. Blushing and laughing at the same time, Claude returned the gesture. Eva smiled and disappeared.

"Mystery solved," Roeg whispered to him as they entered the Rolls.

It was blessedly quiet inside the enormous automobile. Claude and the gentleman with the white beard sat on the jump seats.

"Claude," Fredericks said, "this is my manager, Otto Levits."

"Sir," Claude said as they shook hands.

"Perhaps if you have a few minutes," Levits said, "after you clean up. I'd like to discuss something with you."

13

On the sidewalk in front of the music store, Weisfeld looked up at the gray, overcast sky. "It's getting darker. Maybe I'll roll the awning out a couple of feet." He reached for the iron pole.

"Here," Claude said, "let me do it." He took the pole, connected it, and rolled out the awning.

"Good," Weisfeld said. "I just did the windows a couple of days ago." He flipped the sign on the door to read BACK SOON and tried the lock. "So," he said, turning to Claude, "you're sure. You've made up your mind."

"Yes."

"I didn't talk you into anything? It's your life, after all." He put on his beret.

"It's what I want to do. It makes sense." Claude saw the cab coming even before the quick toot of the horn. "Here she comes."

Emma Rawlings pulled up at the curb and they got in the back.

"Good afternoon, Mrs. Rawlings," Weisfeld said. "It's nice to see you."

"My pleasure," said Emma. "I'm gonna have to put the flag down, but don't get nervous, because it doesn't count."

"Whatever you say."

"Al couldn't come?" Claude asked.

"Nope. They're welding a boiler at his building, so he has to be there."

She drove west to Madison Avenue and then took a left downtown. The hack stand in front of the office building was empty and she pulled into it. "Just like last time," she said. It began to rain, and people on the sidewalk moved in close to the buildings, edging around each other as they walked. Weisfeld, Emma, and Claude got out of the cab and entered the building.

Going up in the elevator, Emma ignored the operator and asked Weisfeld, "I guess it must feel pretty good, huh?"

"I'm sorry?"

"Well, you were right about him. The stuff he did up in the country? You were right from ten years ago, practically. It must feel good."

"Hey," Claude said. "I'm standing right here."

"It feels good." Weisfeld nodded with a small smile.

"You deserve it," she said.

Claude was relieved when the operator pulled the gates open.

Nothing had changed. Mr. Larkin's eyes were still clear and blue, and he had not aged at all. Everything in the room was exactly as it had been. Otto Levits rose from his chair at the conference table to be introduced to Emma, and they all took their places.

"Claude," Larkin said, "first of all my congratulations on what I've heard was a brilliant performance."

"Thank you."

Larkin paused to arrange some papers. "We are here, as you know, to formalize the agreement establishing Mr. Levits" — he gave a nod to the bearded man — "as the manager and agent in matters musical for Mr. Rawlings." Another nod. "I understand from Maestro Fredericks, Mr. Weisfeld, and Mr. Levits that a good deal of discussion about Claude's future has taken place, and that there has been, shall we say, a meeting of the minds. Is that your understanding, Claude?"

"Yes, sir."

"And I take it that you have yourself thought long and hard about these matters?"

"Ever since —" Claude stopped himself. "I was going to say ever since the concert, but really, we've been talking about it for a long time." He looked at Weisfeld. "I mean we have, really, thinking back."

"Yes," said Weisfeld.

"Good." Larkin gave an encouraging smile. "It seems to me this might be a good time for Claude to share his thoughts with us, now that we're all here together. I admit to a certain personal interest. Just very informally, if you will."

The room fell silent. Everyone looked at Claude, even his mother. He resisted the nervous urge to begin talking immediately, and watched the rain on the window for a moment, gathering his thoughts.

"The most important thing to me is music," he said. "And the more music I do, the clearer that is. I want to play and I want to compose. Music will never run out. It'll never disappear. So that's what I want to do with myself." He felt a slight lump in his throat and coughed into his hand. "But I also think," he said, talking a bit faster, "that to become the best musician I can be, I have to do other things besides music. I'd rather go to college, if I can, than to conservatory. I want to read, and find out about stuff, all kinds of stuff." His eyes found Weisfeld's. "It isn't because I think I'd be a freak if I did nothing but play. I don't think I'd be a freak, as a matter of fact. I mean, I know it can happen, but I don't think it would happen to me. But I'm thinking of Ivan, you know, and how much fun it was. Maybe in college there'll be something like that."

"Ivan?" Larkin asked.

"A friend at school," Claude said.

"An extremely bright young man," Weisfeld added. "Off to Cambridge, I'm afraid. *Cambridge* Cambridge."

"I see," said Larkin.

"So I want to do both, if that's possible," Claude finished.

Otto Levits cleared his throat. "From my point of view it is possible. In fact, it is desirable. I think of the long term with my artists, Mr. Larkin. Everyone knows this."

"Quite true," said Weisfeld. "So we're talking balance. Carefully planned appearances during the school year, spread out, not too much traveling, never around exams. This way he can make enough for his living expenses. In the summer, maybe a little more. We can work it out."

"And this is feasible, Mr. Levits?" Larkin asked.

"Of course. It's what Fredericks wants, and he'll help if necessary."

"What about competitions?"

Both Levits and Weisfeld shook their heads.

"He doesn't need all that craziness," Weisfeld said. "He's already got a sponsor."

"Between us," Levits said, "we have the necessary connections.

Competitions are for people from Nebraska who don't know anybody. I agree with Aaron."

Larkin nodded. "Good. Mrs. Rawlings, the document requires your signature, as Claude is not yet of age. Do you have any questions?"

"You're going to get him jobs?" she asked Levits.

"Yes."

"And you're going to keep on watching out for him?" she asked Weisfeld. "Look, I was in vaudeville a long time ago, but I don't know anything about this business."

"Yes," Weisfeld said. "Rest assured."

"Then if it's okay with Claude, it's okay with me."

Larkin brought the document around the table for everyone to sign, including Weisfeld as witness.

"Can he make enough to pay for college?" Emma asked.

Weisfeld handed back Larkin's fountain pen. "That might tip the balance. We're going to try for scholarships. He got A's at Bentley, after all."

"It's a good question, Mrs. Rawlings," Larkin said. "I'm glad you brought it up. Have you given any thought to where you might like to go, Claude?"

"Uh, no. I thought I'd talk to somebody at Bentley. There's a person you're supposed to talk to. I just didn't have time."

"Harvard," said Weisfeld.

"Columbia is good," said Levits.

"I don't know much about it," Claude said.

Larkin stood behind his chair, his forearms relaxed on its back. Claude noticed the length of his hands, envying them. Hands that big could handle long tenths. "Talk to your advisor," Larkin said, "and perhaps you might consider some of the very best of the smaller schools."

Claude was aware of a certain heightened alertness in Mr. Weisfeld, who leaned forward a bit. "What do you mean?"

"There is sometimes a greater degree of flexibility, a more sensitive awareness of each student as an individual, if you see what I mean. At a place like Cadbury College, for instance, the course of study can be practically tailor-made."

"I never heard of it," said Levits.

"Cadbury?" Weisfeld looked up at the ceiling. "Is that Pennsylvania?"

"Yes, between Philadelphia and Princeton. A small Quaker institution with four hundred and thirty young men enrolled at the moment. A first-class college. I'm on the board, as a matter of fact."

"I see," said Weisfeld.

"Yes." Larkin brought his hands together. "And since it's a matter of public record, I should perhaps mention that I'm a member of the scholarship committee."

"Oh," Weisfeld said, and Claude noticed him smile.

PART TWO

14

FOUR AND A HALF years later Claude was reading Gibbon's *Decline* in his carrel in the Boyd Library at Cadbury College when he became aware of a young woman nearby in the stacks. She was trying to find a book. Her profile struck him immediately — fine-boned, aristocratic, and somehow familiar — and when she turned he felt a slight disappointment. She was not quite as beautiful as he had imagined. Nevertheless he could not take his eyes off her.

"What happened to the GS seven hundreds?" she asked. "It just stops at six ninety."

"Across?" He suggested the opposite shelf.

"No." Her voice was wonderful, with a breathy rasp around the perfect elocution. She wore a tartan plaid skirt and a cashmere sweater.

"Ah." He closed his book and stood up. "Maybe the side shelves. They start over here."

Although Cadbury was a men's school it was not unusual to see young women from nearby Hollifield College around the campus. Hollifield was an elite Episcopal school, rumored to be superior to Cadbury, which did not stop the girls from coming over to take certain advanced courses, or from dating Cadbury boys. The schools enjoyed what was called a special relationship.

"Here they are," she said, and knelt to read the numbers. The gesture moved him for some reason, a combination of trust — since she was only inches away from him — vulnerability, and unselfconscious grace. "Here it is." She extracted a volume and glanced up. "Marvell. Have you read him?"

He nodded. "Heady stuff." She had large, gentle brown eyes set wide apart, her expression at once soft and alert.

"He's beautiful," she said simply.

"Are you at Hollifield? Sorry to sound like the movies, but you seem familiar."

"I do?" She gave a soft laugh. "Yes, well, I'm almost never there on weekends, so you must have me mixed up with somebody else."

"I guess so."

They stood for a moment, neither one of them moving.

"I thought I'd go down to the coop for some coffee," he said.

"That sounds good."

During his early years at Cadbury, Claude had dated several girls from Hollifield, but few of these arrangements had lasted more than a couple of months. One girl had been put off by his general air of seriousness, his inability to lose himself in the communal frivolity of a big weekend or a football game. Another — a tense, intelligent scholarship student from a working-class neighborhood in Philadelphia — had intrigued him both before and after her stunning revelation that she was a lesbian. It had taken him a while to believe her, and a while to absorb the shock. He knew that in trusting him with her secret, given the conformist mores of the times, she was doing something dangerous, and this had made her all the more attractive. But even the blindness of his lust could not stop him from the eventual realization that love with a male was, for her, quite impossible. A couple of other girls had simply toyed with him, which, because of his naiveté and pride, had taken him longer to recognize than it should have. He still couldn't figure out why they'd bothered. By his senior year he'd stopped going to Hollifield altogether. He had surprised himself with his impulsive invitation.

In the deserted coop they bought coffee and sticky buns and sat by a window. They chatted about school, a movie they'd both seen, the metaphysical poets, President Eisenhower, the Quaker practice of fifth-day meeting, and several other safe topics, with Claude increasingly aware of how pretty she was and of how quickly her mind worked, with a kind of light wit that called no attention to itself. Rather, she seemed inclined to mask it, whether out of modesty or a desire to test her listener, he could not yet tell. He made sure to let her know he saw it, and to establish that he was himself up to speed. He made her laugh several times.

By the time they left the coop and strolled across the lawn to the bicycle rack, it was clear to both of them that they would see each other again. Yet it was only now that they exchanged names. Hers was Priscilla Powers.

"But everybody calls me Lady," she said. "It stuck from when I was a kid."

During the whole hour they had spoken of nothing of particular importance, asked no personal questions, and more or less avoided references to their lives outside school. This seemed entirely appropriate to Claude, who had slipped easily and gratefully into the egalitarian society of Cadbury, in which it was not important where one had come from. A quiet idealism glowed on both of these small, protected campus worlds — islands of optimism within the larger security of calm, prosperous postwar America.

As she mounted her bicycle, Claude asked, "What dorm are you in?"

"Chesterton," she said.

"Can I give you a ring?"

"That would be nice." And she was off down the path, pedaling briskly, her brown hair pulled by the wind.

For the last two years the college had bent its rules and allowed Claude to live off campus. He had two rooms over a small laundromat, directly across the street from the great stone pillars marking the entrance to the college grounds. He had argued that he needed instantaneous and continuous access to the piano in order to practice, work on his repertoire, and prepare for the recitals, accompaniment jobs, and chamber music performances he did about once a month. The dean had reluctantly agreed and, upright Quaker that he was, made a point to warn against the insidious dangers of a bohemian lifestyle.

In fact, Claude was accused by his friends of being somewhat of a straight arrow. He continued his habit of rising early, and most often put in two or three hours on the rented Chickering grand before the machines began to rumble downstairs as the laundromat opened. His days were carefully structured, balancing his musical and academic studies with composing, jazz, and a mild enthusiasm for basketball. He took most of his meals at Founder's Hall with the other students.

But as he saw more and more of Lady, he began to shift things around. They took long walks through Cadbury's extensive and bucolic grounds, studied together in the huge vaulted library at Hollifield, went to the occasional movie, or met for hamburgers at the local diner. The first time she'd come to his rooms, for afternoon tea (a very Hollifield thing to do), she'd been surprised by the piano.

"Good Lord. What's this?" She walked over and put her hands on the lid. "It takes up half the room!"

He'd told her very little about himself, having mentioned music only in passing, without hinting at its importance. "I play," he said simply. "I'm a musician."

"I thought you were an English major."

"I am, I am."

Over cups of Earl Grey he explained about Weisfeld, Fredericks, Larkin, Levits, and the master plan.

"You mean you studied with Fredericks?" she asked in amazement. "*The* Fredericks?"

"Oh yes, for quite a while."

"Well aren't you the slyboots." Lady raised her cup. "Saying nothing all this time." She seemed pleased.

What he learned about her came in bits and pieces spread out over several weeks. She was from New York City, had gone to Spence, and enjoyed something like celebrity status at Hollifield as an A student, coeditor of *Horizons,* the school paper, president of the Student Council, and captain of the field hockey team. Nobody at Cadbury seemed to know much about her, since Claude was the first Cadbury boy she'd dated, but he could tell, from the almost palpable admiration she continually received from Hollifield girls coming up to talk to her (unable to mask their curiosity and surprise at the presence of Claude), that it was a different story at Hollifield. She dealt with her status with a kind of patrician modesty, as if it were of no great importance. He noticed how generous she was with people, how carefully she listened to them.

"Why do you go home every weekend?" he asked her once.

"Oh, my family," she said.

"What about them?"

"They like me to come home," she said, and changed the subject.

At night they would ride their bikes to Chesterton, her dorm, well before the eleven o'clock curfew, when the lantern man would lock the gates. Under an arch, behind a tree, or in any shadowed private place, they would lean their standing bodies together and surrender to the voluptuous warmth of each other's mouths. She was slightly taller than Claude, and she would sometimes get up on her toes, her arms around his neck, and take over. Despite his avidity — the hot, sweet pain of his body — he never rushed her. He felt the softness of her breast for the first time only when she guided his hand, her thigh hard between his legs, her mouth at his forehead. "Mmm," she hummed. "Mmm."

Half delirious, drowning in sensation, Claude would come awake at the lantern man's ritual cry of "Closing. Closing, ladies and gentlemen. Closing." A last kiss and they would move to the gate, barely aware of the other couples emerging from the darkness.

"See you tomorrow," Lady would say, going through.

"Tomorrow." Trembling, he would break away, never knowing where he'd left his bike, moving through the roar of his blood, his groin aching as if from a blow.

For the first couple of years after her departure Claude had, instinctively and without volition, wiped the image of Catherine from his memory. Only after a long time could he afford to let a few stray thoughts of her into his consciousness, like a man taking tiny sips of a potentially dangerous elixir. Fragments came back to him — a frozen gesture, a scrap of conversation, the edge of a distant emotion — never lasting more than a second before floating away. He could be in mid-sentence talking to someone. He could be tying his shoe, doing scales, or writing an exam. Eventually these fragments were stripped of any physicality whatsoever and became simply pure emotion, pangs so swift he barely noticed them.

But one day, two months after meeting Lady, while eating lunch in the bedlam of Founder's Hall, laughing at a joke one of his friends had just told, he felt without warning a complete awareness of her, a dense and weighty sense of Catherine, of Catherine-ness, exploding in his soul like the swift circular penumbra of light moving from the center of an atomic bomb bursting on a movie screen. His knife and fork fell from his hands.

"Hey, Claude. What's up?" asked his friend Charley.

"You okay, buddy?" The face of another friend, Dan, loomed before him like a balloon.

"It's nothing," he was finally able to say. "Nothing. I just remembered something."

"Spooky," said Charley.

"Pass the tuna fish," said Dan.

After lunch they all went out onto the lawn for Frisbee. Claude threw himself into the game with fervor — running, catching, leaping — distracting himself so he could pull himself together.

Later, unable to sleep at one in the morning, watching the sky through the square panes of the window at the foot of his bed, he saw a star move. It was quite definitely moving against the static backdrop of the other stars. He grew increasingly excited. A distant spaceship, as in *Astounding Stories*? (His magazine collection was still in the back room of Emma and Al's basement flat, stacked on top of the white piano.) A flying saucer moving slowly? The very fact of picking out that particular point of light with his eye seemed to bring it closer. Suddenly it moved sideways and Claude jumped to a sitting position. He felt he was looking at something that had never been seen before. He was convinced of it. There was a telephone beside his bed, and with rapid movements he got the number of Dr. Greene, his astronomy professor, and called him.

"Hello?" The voice low, sleepy, and wary.

"Dr. Greene, this is Claude Rawlings. I'm sorry to bother you, but there's something moving in the sky. I've been watching it through my window. It's really moving. Sideways even."

Perhaps a half minute of silence.

"Dr. Greene?"

A brief, soft, but unmistakable sigh. "Okay. Which way does your window face?"

"West. It's due west."

"I see. Did the object move quickly?"

"No, it's still there. I can see it."

"Is it moving now?"

"I'm not sure," Claude said. "But it was before. I saw it."

"Please describe your window."

"It's just a regular old window," Claude said impatiently, "small panes, four on top, four below, like a grid."

"Do you have pencil and paper handy?"

"Sure." Underneath his intense excitement he was puzzled. Why didn't Dr. Greene get up and look for himself?

"Fine. First, pace off the distance between where your head was and where the window is. Second, calculate the angle, in degrees, at which you viewed the object by drawing an imaginary line from the pillow to that pane in the window through which you viewed the object, as against the horizontal floor line. Got it?"

"Yes, sir." Claude collected the figures and was chilled by his awareness of what Dr. Greene might mean. Working together on the phone, they computed the numbers, including a measurement of approximately how far the object had moved since Claude first noticed it. It was now in a lower pane, as seen from the bed, perhaps an inch below the wood strip. Step by step — angles, distances, rotation of the earth, solar orbits — they worked out the inexorable and pedestrian truth.

"What you're looking at is Mars," said Dr. Greene.

"Oh, my God," Claude mumbled. "But what about the sideways it did, I mean, I saw it go sideways," he said.

"A bubble or imperfection in the pane of glass," Dr. Greene suggested.

His last hope gone, Claude knelt and pressed his forehead to the edge of the side table. "I'm terribly, terribly sorry, sir. I feel like the stupidest man on earth."

"That's all right, Mr. Rawlings," said Dr. Greene, an elderly man who tended toward formality. "Isn't it interesting how close the figures are despite the lack of measuring tools? It shows how much you can do with a pencil and paper. See you in class."

Mortified, Claude said goodbye and hung up the phone.

Lying back in bed, he found himself thinking about Catherine. In retrospect he realized that what he had felt, after the initial shock of her disappearance, had been shame. In fact, for years he had been living with a drawn-out, half-buried feeling that wasn't all that different from what he'd just experienced with Dr. Greene. Mortification. How could he have been so self-deluded? Her snobbery and disdain had been right out in the open, and yet he had stupidly thought he could overcome them. He squirmed in his bed. His own excitement, his own yearning for the miraculous, had distorted his perception. He had seen a spaceship where there was only Mars, and he had seen an end to loneliness where there was only a flighty, stuck-up girl. So in fact, he told himself, nothing had really happened. It had been an illusion. He wasn't a kid any longer, and he would discard those useless memories, as he had discarded so many others. He closed his eyes, thought of Lady, and went to sleep.

·   ·   ·

Living off campus had not led Claude into bohemianism, although he was never too sure what the man had really meant. Candles in Chianti bottles? Irregular hours? Taking opium like Coleridge? (Except for a few people in anthropology, no one at Cadbury had yet heard anything about marijuana.) General slackness? Claude had actually worked harder the last two years of college than he had the first two. But now, close to graduation, it seemed that his living arrangements had perhaps speeded things up with regard to Lady. It was strange to think of it that way, but he did.

A large, half-sprung blue couch, which he'd inherited from the previous tenant, sat between the piano and the front windows. Initially, he'd used it while reading scores as his LP's were playing, but eventually Lady's weekday afternoon visits became more frequent, and they would lie there together.

"Muffy's engaged to Harry," she said one afternoon, her chin on his chest. They had paused after a long session of necking.

"Good," he said. "They've been together a long time."

Remaining faithful to one's steady was greatly admired at Cadbury and Hollifield. "Hmm," she said, "seems like everybody's getting married after graduation."

He opened his eyes to look at her, but her manner was casual. "What do you think? A quarter of the class?"

"More like a third at Hollifield," she said.

They were children of their time, and neither one of them thought there was anything odd about these statistics. Rather, the numbers suggested that their friends and fellow students were indeed the good, responsible people Claude and Lady had taken them to be. In the abstract, getting married seemed not only incredibly romantic, but grown-up as well. A serious thing to do, a commitment to optimism and faith, carrying on the grand tradition their colleges had taught them.

The blue couch tested them for more than a month. They kept their clothes on, but their hands and mouths were all over each other. Claude managed to sustain control of himself, but the effort was driving him to distraction. He would reach a point of saturation, his body strained to the limit, lips tender and engorged with blood, pelvis aching, penis numb and hard as oak, heart shaking his chest — and he would pull back, rolling off the couch away from her and onto the floor.

And then one evening, as she lay with him on the blue couch, her brown hair hanging free against his temples as she dipped her head to nibble his mouth, she suddenly reached down with her hands, lifted her skirt, unbuttoned his jeans, took him out, adjusted her underwear, and sank down on him with a shivering moan. He blossomed out of numbness into the sweet warmth of her.

"Don't come," she whispered, "don't come, don't come," as with excruciating slowness she moved up and down. It had happened so quickly — all at once he was inside her — it took his mind a moment to catch up with his body. He controlled himself as long as he could, and then with great speed pushed her hips with the heels of his hand and ejaculated into the air. She fell back onto him, clinging with all her strength. Stunned, they lay together in silence for a long time.

The next evening they were back to necking with limits. She would not take off her clothes and go to bed with him, but insisted on the blue couch as if nothing had happened. As the weeks passed and it became clear to Claude that even her safe time of the month wasn't going to change anything, he began gently to press her. But she didn't want to talk about it. She did not argue but simply stood mute, distracting his attention with kisses. Claude could sense her increasing fascination with the turmoil in his body, an almost experimental curiosity about the forces she had the power to unleash. He could see the wonder in her eyes. Eventually their lovemaking fell into a kind of pattern, a tacit understanding. They would neck for hours, and when he could stand it no longer, she applied her hand and her mouth, and he would climax. This calmed his body, but left him always with an odd, enervated sense of emptiness, a confusing mixture of satiation and longing, of gratitude and hidden resentment.

A number of events had conspired to make Claude late. Very late. The basketball game had begun half an hour after it was supposed to, and had gone into double overtime. Claude was the shortest man on the senior intramural team, but he was the playmaker, the strategist, and the third-highest scorer, and hence invaluable in the championship game against the juniors. Toward the end, in an attempt to speed things up, he'd attacked the basket recklessly, weaving between the taller players to throw up hooks, fingertip lobs, and left-handed lay-ups, taking the defense by surprise. His teammates egged him on, ribbing him good-naturedly when he missed. They kept feeding him the ball, rather than the reverse, until the buzzer sounded with the seniors two points up. High spirits. Horsing around in the showers. Illegal consumption of contraband beer behind the field house.

When he got home to change, the telephone was ringing. Otto Levits had chosen this moment to go over Claude's schedule for the next month — two concerts in Philadelphia and one in Princeton — and to describe at length the human and musical idiosyncrasies of the people he'd be playing with. For the third time Levits asked if Claude still wanted to do a certain important engagement that clashed with Cadbury's commencement exercises, and for the third time was reassured. Finally the old man rang off.

Pedaling hard on the way to Hollifield, standing up for speed, Claude felt the cuff of his freshly pressed khaki pants catch in the bicycle chain just before he crashed into a hedge. It took time to extricate himself and sort things out, cursing all the while.

Flushed and disheveled, he arrived at the great lawn behind the Hollifield library and leaned his bike against a tree. Under an enormous striped canvas tent several hundred people sat on folding chairs looking up at the platform, where the last of the graduates were filing past to accept their diplomas. As the names were read out over the public-address system, small groups of people in the audience would pop up, applauding, sometimes giving a shout, and then sink down again. It was a fine, clear, balmy spring day.

Claude walked behind the audience and made his way along the edge of the tent toward the front, where groups of young women in their robes and mortarboards stood milling about. He caught sight of Lady, encircled by her classmates, talking animatedly, turning to look into all their faces. He felt a surge of pride and possessiveness. She was a lovely, good, and serious person, and everyone knew it. She seemed to glow among her friends. He waited some distance away until she noticed him, broke away with a laugh, and came to him. Smiling, she took his hand and pressed up against his side.

"Did you like my speech?"

"I just got here," he said, pointing down to his frayed cuff. "Going too fast. I fell off my bike."

Now she noticed the scratches on his wrist. "My goodness. Are you okay?" Her raspy voice worked its magic, making him almost dizzy.

"I'm fine. I'm sorry."

"Oh, it doesn't matter. The girls gave me a big hand, though, and that was nice." She raised her arm to shield her eyes as she looked at the stage. "At least you'll hear Grandpa."

He had forgotten. Lady was the third generation of her family to attend Hollifield. Her grandmother was dead, but her grandfather had apparently given a great deal of money to the college and was scheduled to speak.

"Where are your parents?" Claude asked. He was curious, since Lady almost never mentioned them.

"In the audience somewhere. The other side, I think. Oh, good. President Hunter is going to introduce him." With a gentle pressure on his arm, they moved closer to the platform and sat down on the grass. Some small children ran by and one of them dropped a program. Claude picked it up and held it out, but the little boy had already turned away. As the slightly cracked voice of Dr. Hunter came over the PA system, Claude spread the program on the ground between his knees. He glanced at it casually until his eyes locked on a name. For a moment his mind raced emptily. Then he looked up to see Senator Barnes approach the microphone. Lady applauded with her hands high in the air, and then turned, smiling, and stopped when she saw Claude's face. "What is it? What?"

"Your grandfather is Senator Barnes?"

"Yes. Him. Up there." She frowned. "I must have mentioned it."

"No," he said. "I would've remembered." He kept his tone calm and light, instinctively concealing the confusion he felt. There was a touch of fear — Catherine, who had so recently haunted him from the inside, was now doing it indirectly from the outside, threatening somehow to expose his shame. Lady was, he finally figured out, Catherine's first cousin. On the face of it an incredible coincidence, and yet somewhere below the level of reason, spookily apt. He stole a quick glance at Lady and felt a moment of unreality as he discerned a faint resemblance, a family resemblance in the eyes and the brow. It both chilled and attracted him. He wanted to hear Lady's voice, the breathy rasp that was so much her, so distinctively her. "Is your stuff packed?" he asked.

"Most of it's already in the station wagon." There was laughter and applause for something Senator Barnes had said. "Isn't he marvelous? They say he was the best speaker in the Senate."

Claude caught the odd phrase from the platform, but he was too jittery to string them together. He lay back, supporting himself on his elbows, and stared blindly at the crowd. He wondered how long he could safely go without telling Lady he had met her grandfather before, and that he knew the Fisk mansion and its inhabitants well. Not very long, he decided, but perhaps the senator would settle it.

But the senator did not. His speech finished, he came directly to Lady and embraced her, raising his arms from his sides, stooping forward. Her hands rested on his hunched old man's back. "Congratulations, my dear," he said, cheek to cheek. "I'm proud of you. Pleased as punch, as Hubert would say." His eyes flicked rapidly over Claude, then closed for the last moment of the hug.

"This is my friend Claude Rawlings," Lady said.

Senator Barnes shook hands. It was clear he didn't remember Claude. "Cadbury man, are you? Fine school. Spoke there some years ago."

Claude decided to plunge ahead. "I believe we've met before, sir. Very briefly, years ago, at the Fisks'."

"At Dewman's?" The old man tilted back his head to look through the bottom of his glasses.

Lady looked at Claude in amazement.

"Yes," Claude said lightly. "I was the piano player accompanying Peter when he played the violin at a big dinner party there. Balanchine was a guest, and the mayor."

"By George," Barnes cried, "that was the night Catherine surprised Dewman with a crown of weeds. She was hell on wheels, that girl." He turned to Lady. "Where is she? Still in Australia?"

"I don't know. They don't talk about her." She was still looking at Claude. "This is strange."

"I guess so." Claude shrugged. "It was a long time ago."

Senator Barnes took her arm. "Let's find Mater and Pater, Lady, before these blue-haired women get their hooks into me. I can feel it building."

Frowning, Lady led them both across the lawn.

Ted and Linda Powers made a handsome couple, standing just outside the tent under a large elm. She was a small, trim woman with delicate features and a vaguely flapper cut to her graying hair. She smiled when she caught sight of her father and daughter. Ted Powers was tall, square-jawed, and solid — something like a darker version of Randolph Scott, Claude thought, although without facial mobility, which gave him a guarded look. He wore a three-piece suit and a striped tie.

"You were both wonderful." Linda stepped forward to give them each a peck on the cheek. She fluttered between them. Ted nodded and stared out over the crowd.

Lady made an attempt to introduce Claude, but was cut off by the arrival of some people eager to shake the senator's hand. Claude felt Ted and Linda Powers's eyes lock on to his own for the briefest possible instant. Linda turned to talk to an elderly woman. Ted pulled out his pocket watch and pondered the time.

"Let's go," Lady whispered in his ear. "I want to get that picture out of my room before somebody pinches it."

As they walked to Chesterton, Claude expected Lady to question him, but she did not.

"I'm going to miss Hollifield," she said. "I'm going to miss it a lot."

"These places are like heaven on earth," Claude replied. "We've been lucky." He did a spontaneous cartwheel and brushed the grass from his palms. "But on the other hand, the world awaits."

"For you, maybe. You know what you want to do."

"So will you. It'll come."

She sighed. "I know what I *don't* want to do, which is go back to Seventy-third Street with my parents. But that's what I'm doing."

"Come live in a garret with me," he said, "if you can stand listening to the piano four hours a day."

She stopped and looked at him. "You'd do it, too."

"Of course!" He smiled. "Why not?"

They continued walking. For a dreadful moment he considered himself to be entirely false — smiles, cartwheels, bravado, when in fact he felt confusion. He sensed it would be dangerous to admit any sort of weakness to Lady, who spoke often of her own ambivalence, which she hated, and of his apparent certitude, directness, and faith in himself, which she loved. But as graduation approached he had felt his own past coming up behind him. During all the years of strolling across green lawns to ivy-covered buildings, of easy fraternity with his class-mates, of being part of the benevolent Quaker world, of wearing button-down shirts, he had deliberately put his origins at a distance. An occasional remark about having been a shoeshine boy, delivered casually, may have passed his lips, as if he had no fear of those memo-ries. But to no one, and certainly not Lady, had he ever mentioned the nausea, the sense of being invisible, the loneliness and misery of his childhood. He had been entirely helpless, and of that he was ashamed.

With the possible exception of Weisfeld, no one knew that music had saved him, allowed him, as it were, to squeak through. Cadbury graduate or no, he knew that, thus far, without music he was nothing. Without music he would be that vague, weak child again, as insubstantial as a wisp of smoke. Sometimes, playing chamber music in a drawing room, or accompanying a singer in a hotel ballroom, he felt like an impostor. He knew he was a good player, and yet at some deeper level he was amazed to be getting away with it.

Lady's room evoked, as always, an erotic thrill. The angling light, the faint scent of her, the very walls bringing up countless hours of afternoon lovemaking. Even with her things gone, the mattress bare in the tiny bedroom, her books, clothes, and knickknacks boxed up and taken away, even in the startling emptiness he felt his body quicken.

"Good," she said, looking at the lithograph. "Could you take it down?"

It was a Braque, but not cubist. A young girl sitting at a windowsill, her hair to her waist, her small breasts partially exposed. Her expression was one of resigned sadness, and of innocence. Lady had bought it one summer on a trip to Paris. Claude stood on the bed and gently lifted it from the wall.

"She knows some secrets," Lady said.

"You can say that again." He got down from the bed and impulsively gave the girl in the picture a soft kiss.

"Lady?" It was the voice of Ted Powers at the threshold. "We're ready."

With Claude carrying the lithograph, they followed him through the hall, out the main door, through the arch, and out to the street. Ted went to the driver's side of the station wagon, reached in, and got the keys. He opened the tailgate and said, "Put it in there, on top." Claude obeyed, and Ted closed the gate and went behind the wheel without looking at Claude.

Behind the station wagon was a large black limousine. Claude turned to see Lady taking a last look at the dorm. Her mother rolled down the station wagon window. "Will the back seat be all right, dear?"

"Sure." She looked at Claude, who came forward.

"Well," he said.

"You'll call me tonight?"

"Yes."

From inside the station wagon her father had reached over the seat and opened the rear door. Lady got in, started to pull the door shut, and then paused. Through the glass Claude could see her face, the look of vexation. He was backing away when she suddenly popped out of the car, skipped over, and threw her arms around his neck. "Give me a kiss," she said, moving her face close to his. "A long one."

He did so, feeling the soft press of her belly.

When she broke away he saw the stunned, immobile faces of her parents. She got in and the station wagon pulled rapidly from the curb. Then came the limousine, Senator Barnes alone in back smoking a cigar. The old man gave Claude a barely perceptible nod as he passed.

15

AT HIS ACCUSTOMED PLACE behind the counter, Mr. Weisfeld coughed, leaned back on his stool, and turned a page of the *Herald Tribune*. "It says here they're thinking about tearing down the el."

Claude, having replenished the stock of number 3 valve oil, slid the drawer shut. "The Third Avenue el?"

"It's getting old, apparently."

Claude turned to look out the front window. "It's hard to imagine what it would look like." He picked up a broom and began sweeping the back aisle.

"Stop with the make-work," Weisfeld said. "Sit for a minute. You're making me nervous."

Claude obeyed, taking his stool by the harmonica case. "There'd be more sun."

"After all these years I wouldn't be able to go to sleep at night without the trains." Weisfeld folded the paper. "You're jumpy. You've been jumpy for weeks. What's up?"

"Jumpy? Really?"

"How's it going with the song cycle?"

Claude was composing a set of songs based on Blake's *Innocence* and *Experience*. "I got past a big problem this morning. I wish I knew more about the human voice as an instrument, though."

"Don't worry. These days they can sing anything. Just keep going. What about the girlfriend?" For some reason Weisfeld rarely referred to Lady by name. Claude thought he was merely teasing.

"Terrific," Claude said. "I'm going out to their house on Long Island this weekend."

"Don't forget to bring a house present for the momma." Weisfeld yawned. "Something tasteful. A little different. A can of marrons glacés maybe. Gristede's has them."

Claude remembered his first visit to the townhouse on Seventy-third Street. A brownstone. He'd gone down three steps from the sidewalk and pressed the bell. Through the heavy wrought-iron door and the glass behind it he saw, as the lights went on, a tiny room with a floor of veined marble. A sort of lobby, empty except for a gold-framed mirror on the wall, a small half table below it, and a coat rack. A second door, six feet away, opened and Lady emerged, shooing back a uniformed maid even as she smiled through the wrought iron at Claude. She pulled open the heavy door and Claude entered.

"Now don't be put off by all this grandeur," she said. "It doesn't mean a thing. Believe me."

They went through the second door. He sensed the kitchen to the rear. Heavy, dark oak door frames, doors with polished brass fixtures leading to unseen rooms off to the left. Straight ahead, the staircase, deep maroon runner, a brass strip gleaming on every step. A heavy silence as he followed her up, dark portraits lining the wall, her ankles glinting.

At the top they turned onto the landing. Oriental rugs. An antique chair and desk with a telephone, a few leather books, a brass lamp, and a copy of the Social Register. A series of small oil landscapes in elaborate gilt frames. Lady strode forward and opened the door to the brightness of the living room.

As she stepped aside he saw French windows. Ted Powers was seated in an armchair beside the couch, reading the paper, a drink at his elbow and a tan cocker spaniel at his feet, and Linda Powers sat at a small antique secretary with her back to him, writing a letter. There was a feeling of stasis, as if the room and everything in it were a painting, or a stage set five seconds before the curtain.

"Here's Claude," Lady said cheerfully.

Their white faces turned.

"What is marrons glacés?" Claude asked Weisfeld.

"Chestnuts. Candied chestnuts. Very fancy."

Earlier that summer, in fact at the very first opportunity, Claude had brought Lady to the store, to meet Weisfeld and to show her the studio. Weisfeld had donuts and coffee ready.

"I've heard a great deal about you, Mr. Weisfeld," Lady had said. "Claude says he owes everything to you."

Weisfeld smiled and patted her arm. "Claude is of course wrong. He owes maybe to God, but not to me. But he was right about you. I can tell that already."

Weisfeld had given her a rather longer than necessary tour of the shop, chatting easily about the instruments, his customers (some of them famous!), and throwing in an occasional humorous anecdote. Claude went along behind him, moved by Weisfeld's politeness and solicitude. He'd been nervous, for no reason he could name, about their meeting.

"I like him," Lady had said downstairs in the studio. "He's sweet."

Claude could not really fault her for this banality. Weisfeld had in fact seemed somewhat guarded to Claude, falling back on the humble but sophisticated European Jewish shopkeeper role that had served him so well with his Park Avenue clientele, and about which Claude and Weisfeld had sometimes joked.

"He's . . . ," Claude struggled. "He's complicated. The war . . ." It was too much to explain. "He's a wonderful teacher. I wish you could know how good."

"I believe you," she'd said.

Now, Weisfeld got up and took the keys from the shelf under the register. "So, should we take a look?"

He and Claude left the store, locked up, and walked to the corner. It was a hot afternoon, and beads of perspiration formed on Weisfeld's brow almost immediately. He looked up at the el.

"I bet they'll do it," he said. "The street is wide, you know, wider than it looks. They'll take up the cobblestones and pave it over." He wiped his head with a handkerchief. "May be good for business."

They walked west on Eighty-fourth Street past a couple of buildings to number 186, an old tenement. Weisfeld climbed the stoop and paused at the top, breathing heavily, coughing into his handkerchief. "Mrs. Keller told me about this. Mr. Obromowitz — I've seen him around — anyway he's got bad rheumatism or something, so he went out to Arizona someplace because it's supposed to be good for rheumatism. People will believe anything."

They entered, went past the mailboxes, and unlocked the inner entry door. "So he's going to try it, but he doesn't want to let go of his room in case Arizona doesn't work out. We're talking a month-to-month sublease, off the books." With the same key he opened Obromowitz's door. "Not bad. First floor, in front, at least."

It was very simple — a bed, bureau, table, two chairs by the front window, a hot plate and half refrigerator against the rear wall, and a small bathroom in back. The room was dominated by an entire wall of books, floor to ceiling. Thousands of books.

"Wow," said Claude, moving forward. He saw fiction, history, biography, philosophy, poetry, art books. Complete sets of Dickens, Conrad, and the *Encyclopaedia Britannica*. Books in German, French, and Hebrew. "What does Mr. Obromowitz do?"

"He was a lens grinder, I believe," Weisfeld said. "Before the rheumatism."

The place was scrupulously clean. "This is perfect," Claude said. "I'll tell Mrs. Keller right away."

Weisfeld nodded. "Thirty-five dollars a month. It's a steal."

The Chinese waiter smiled and made a little dipping motion before clearing away the plates and bowls — an astounding number of them, and all of them empty.

Emma burped quietly into her napkin. "Excuse me."

"Well *I* sure ain't gonna be hungry in an hour," Al said. "Mercy!"

"So how did it happen?" Claude asked.

"You remember Mullins? The doorman?"

Claude nodded.

"A mean drunk. Just got worse over the years, and getting to be an old man, really."

"He used to run the elevator when I practiced at the maestro's."

"Well, he got promoted to doorman. So one day he's on his break, dead drunk on that ratty old couch they use over by the storage rooms. I wake him up when it's time — I used to do that, you know, trying to be nice — and when he gets halfway up he gets the heaves, and pretty soon there's a mess on the floor. Since we just ate I won't go into details. Later, when he comes down from his shift, he wants to know why I ain't cleaned it up. I say I ain't cleaned it up because I ain't the one that done it. He say he going to get me fired."

"Mick trash," Emma said, her eyes narrowing. "Jumped-up mackerel snapper, pimping for the rich."

"And?" Claude asked.

"And that's what happened." Al leaned back and spread his long, tapering fingers across his belly. "I got fired."

"But, but, I mean how . . . ," Claude started.

"Doormen got a union, Claude. Mullins big in the union. Saperstein hated to do it, I believe the man, he truly hated to do it, but he had to. Told me he'd been trying to get rid of Mullins for years, but he'd lose his job if there was a strike."

"So you lose yours," Claude said.

Al shrugged. "Gave me three months pay."

"After fifteen years," Emma said.

The waiter brought tea and fortune cookies. Al poured three cups. "They're going to oil anyway. Don't need no coal man. But listen, we're doing all right. Got the down payment and the loan for another medallion. We'll have two cabs working, everything'll be fine. Be better this way."

Claude shook his head. "You're amazing."

"What?" Al wanted to know.

"I mean, you're not even angry. That's terrible what they did. It's outrageous."

Al turned his head and looked out the window, his body still and his face expressionless. After some time he said, "How do you know I'm not angry?"

Flustered, Claude fooled with his teacup. "It's just you seem so — I mean you don't seem . . ."

"I'm angry. I just don't give in to it." He sipped his tea and then put it down. "Stuff happens all the time. What'd you call it? Outrageous. Outrageous stuff make you so mad you can just burn yourself up with it. You got to decide if the mad runs you, or you run the mad."

Emma leaned forward with her big arms on the table. "It doesn't mean you roll over for everything, but you control yourself."

Claude looked at his mother's calm, wide, plain face, so different now in relative repose from the red, trembling, popeyed image he remembered from his childhood. She had changed in so many respects she seemed almost a different person, more easily given to gentle laughter, more temperate in the way she moved her large body.

"You're right," Claude said. "It makes sense."

"Anyway, things are changing," Al said. "I do believe. You see those people walking up and down with signs in front of Woolworth's on Second Avenue? Half of 'em white kids. They picket Woolworth's up *here* for what's happening in Woolworth's down south. Now that's something new."

"The movement." Claude nodded. "People at school talked about it. Nonviolent resistance to bring about social change. It's based on Gandhi and the independence movement in India."

Emma broke open her fortune cookie, read the slip, and snorted. " 'With age comes happiness.' Thanks a lot."

Al looked at his and hesitated a moment. " 'Your children are your greatest wealth.' I guess that means I'm flat broke."

"Mine is good," Claude said. " 'A journey of a thousand leagues begins with one step.' "

"A league? What's that?"

"Three miles," Claude said, proud of himself. "Roughly three miles."

In the back of his mind he'd thought it would go the way it went in the movies. When Elizabeth Taylor's father realized his daughter was in love with Montgomery Clift, he went out of his way to be nice to the young man, welcoming him to the fold despite his origins. Claude had been moved by that detail when he'd seen the film — a powerful mix to get both the girl *and* a good man as a surrogate father — and had in fact gotten teary during the episode. In dozens of other films dealing with similar situations it was always the young man's skill, courage, intelligence, and basic decency that counted. Further, Claude, who had polished his manners at Cadbury, had made it a point to be always on his best behavior with Mr. and Mrs. Powers. He called them "sir" and "ma'am," never went first through a door, controlled a tendency toward excitability in conversation, and in every way attempted to act like a gentleman. He even found himself remembering some pointers from old Franz. But it had not gone well when, after half a dozen dinners at the Seventy-third Street townhouse, Mr. Powers had suggested they stay at table for cigars while the ladies repaired to the other room. Claude had refused a cigar from the box opened before him by the Filipino maid, but had accepted a second glass of wine.

"I suppose you know," Mr. Powers said when they were alone, "that Lady has turned down young MacDonald's offer of marriage."

Startled, Claude looked up. Mr. Powers's square, handsome, vapid face was without expression as he stared at his cigar. "Yes, sir," Claude said.

Arthur MacDonald was the reason Lady had come back to New

York on weekends during college. Two years out of Yale Law School, he was, according to Lady, "sweet, thoughtful, dull, and a stuffed shirt." She had seen him, she said, because she'd had nothing better to do.

"The MacDonalds are old family friends," Mr. Powers said, "and Mrs. Powers and I are fond of Arthur. We're disappointed it didn't work out."

Claude didn't know how to respond, because he didn't know why Ted Powers was telling him what he was telling him. This situation had occurred a number of times, various remarks of Powers falling like lead. Surely at this moment the man could not expect commiseration, Claude thought. What does he want me to say?

"That was what we'd planned on," Powers said.

Claude's mind darted this way and that, searching for an opening but finally spinning in confusion. He said nothing.

"Lady will have many responsibilities in life." A slow puff at the cigar.

"I'm sure she will, sir." He had no idea what the man meant.

"Arthur could have helped her. He understands those kinds of things."

Claude could only look at his wine glass.

"Now what kind of responsibilities do you figure *you'll* have?" Powers asked. A trace of Montana had crept into his speech. He'd said something between "figure" and "figger." Lady had not given Claude much information about her father. She spoke of him rapidly and scornfully as a dimwitted self-pitying bully (Claude had felt a mixture of shock and glee at her words) and presented his history as if it were of no importance. He'd been born on the largest cattle ranch in Montana, which had been held by his family for generations, had "grown up in the saddle," come east to go to Dartmouth, where a large donation from his mother had assured his acceptance, met Linda, married her, and done nothing since, according to Lady, except for a soft officer's job in London during the war. "That man is nothing. The most important thing he does is cook dinner on the maid's night off."

"But doesn't he have a job?" Claude had asked.

"He has an office. He keeps track of family investments. Does the income tax. It's a fraud."

Somehow Claude could not believe it was that simple. He looked down the long table. "My responsibilities will have to do with music. I should tell you about that." He had been surprised by a household so completely empty of music — no phonograph, no radio except in the kitchen, no instruments of any kind with which to break the silence. He'd never heard anyone so much as hum a tune within these walls. To do so would have seemed almost disrespectful. So Claude went slowly and carefully with Mr. Powers, telling him how he'd started with Mr. Weisfeld as a child, describing his other teachers and what he'd learned from them, emphasizing the importance of practice, scales, exercises, and a daily routine, waxed eloquent (he thought) on the mysterious power of music to move both the mind and the soul, and told of his ambitions as a player and composer. Everything he said felt remarkably sound, remarkably good, and even exciting in the abstract. He felt himself flushing with emotion.

Mr. Powers smoked his cigar and said nothing for a long time, staring at the ceiling. Finally he extinguished his butt, jabbing it energetically in the ashtray. "So you want to be an artist, is that it?"

"Yes, sir. Exactly."

"That's for women."

The remark was so blunt and so ridiculous Claude couldn't believe what he'd heard. "What?"

"You heard me." Mr. Powers got up from his chair. "It's for women. Women and pansies." Without another word he'd left the room.

Now Claude sat at the window of the Long Island Railroad carriage and watched the flat land drift by. At his feet was a small suitcase, a rather expensive item given to him by Otto Levits for his overnight engagements. "It's important to look good when you go someplace to play," Levits had said. "You're a performer, a serious artist. Shoes shined, suits pressed, quality accessories. It's a gesture of respect." Inside the suitcase were a change of clothes, some Bartók scores, a paperback edition of *The Great Gatsby,* and a round tin of marrons glacés.

As the train pulled into the station at Ashton he realized he was simultaneously jiggling his knee and gnawing on a fingernail. He stopped instantly, as if rebuked. A strange mood was upon him — a mixture of romantic and erotic excitement, apprehension about Ted and Linda Powers (particularly since he knew Lady had forced the invitation), simple curiosity, and a certain amount of repressed and unacknowledged anger. He was both thrilled and slightly sickened.

He stepped off the train and saw Lady standing in the sunlight on the platform. She wore tennis whites, a green ribbon in her brown hair, and sunglasses. Her long, perfect, tanned legs seemed even longer as she skipped to his side. "Hi, cutie!" She gave him a quick kiss. "Got your shining armor in there?"

"No, but I did bring a bathing suit."

"Super. Let's go."

It was a British sports car, dark green, with a leather strap over the hood and the top folded down into a recess behind the jump seat. "Ouch! It's hot," she said as she got into the leather seat and grabbed the wheel. She pulled out of the lot with a splash of gravel. "This is the village," she shouted as they accelerated down a street lined with small Tudor buildings housing shops with tasteful signs. Tall elm trees threw dappled shade. They passed a movie theater, and then a white church with a slender steeple. Soon they were on a winding country road between fieldstone walls, speeding under a canopy of green.

"Mother's off having tea," Lady cried. "Father's playing golf, thank God."

"I brought a house present," Claude shouted.

She geared down, double clutching with finesse, and turned the long nose of the car into a break in the wall. An ascending driveway, rising to a gravel turnaround and the house, sitting alone on the top of the hill. Claude had a moment of déjà vu. A large, white, two-story clapboard house with green shutters and trim and a portaled entrance-way. The lawns, flowers, and shrubbery were tended to a point past perfection, lending the scene a tinge of unreality. It was the movies that made him think he'd seen this house, this impeccable setting, for indeed he'd seen its like from the balcony of the RKO many times. It was the sort of house within which might be found Walter Pidgeon, Greer Garson, or Ethel Barrymore. It made Claude feel better just to look at it.

"You're in the guest quarters," Lady said as they got out of the car.

They went through the front door into a wide hall. The living room was on the right — furnished with antiques and oriental rugs, much like the house on Seventy-third Street — dining room and kitchen off to the left. They walked straight across to a rear door and emerged onto a flagstone patio. There was a trellis, a small white building, and a swimming pool in the middle of the lawn, screened on two sides by rows of hedges. The clear blue-green water sparkled in the sun.

"The servants are in back," Lady said, opening a screen door, "and you're in here."

A bright room with hunting prints, a bureau, two small armchairs, and a four-poster bed. He put down his suitcase.

"This is very nice," Claude said.

Lady went to the bed and sat on the edge. "Comfortable bed." She fell back and threw her arms out to the side.

"Is it safe here?" he asked.

"Oh, absolutely," she said, her soft, breathy rasp more pronounced than usual. "Nobody comes in here."

He kissed the inside of her elbow and worked his way up to her mouth. She closed her eyes and accepted the weight of his body, her hands light on the back of his neck.

Later in the afternoon they swam in the pool. Claude lolled in the warm water while Lady did laps, her body moving smoothly and efficiently. Eight strokes, turn, eight strokes, turn, again and again until, breathing hard, she climbed out and lay on a towel. Claude spread one on the grass beside her and lay on his back, closing his eyes against the brightness of the sky. After a while he thought she might have gone to sleep, and he was just about to turn and look when she spoke.

"What's the difference between somebody who knows how to play the piano — I mean lots of people can play anything you put in front of them — somebody like that as against what you do, or Fredericks, or the famous ones."

Surprised, he opened his eyes and stared up at the blue dome. Lady had often asked him about how a concert had gone, or what sort of people he'd played with, or played for, or how much money he'd made, or what Minneapolis was like, but seldom more than that. It was as if his music were a given. "That's not such an easy question," he said.

"No?"

"Well, there are various levels. The higher you get, the harder it is to put into words, actually. Eventually it gets pretty mysterious."

He turned to find her watching him. He got up on his elbows. The side of her head was flat against the towel, her brown eyes steady. The afternoon air had become still and he heard bird cries in the distance, ascending loops like a child's doodles. Water lapped in the gutters of the pool. "I guess the first thing is control," he said. "No, that's wrong.

The first thing is probably the hand-eye thing. The way most kids are taught, there's so much emphasis on the eye, on the ability to sight-read, they become sort of input-output machines. You know, they just listen for mistakes, they don't listen for anything else. I was lucky. Right from the beginning the sound seemed so powerful and interesting I paid a lot of attention. Different key signatures meant my hands would assume different postures, and then those postures felt like emotions. C is a bright key, for instance. Cheerful. E-flat is darker, with more longing. It's like colors, almost. Anyway, there's something in there about the hands, a kind of feedback to deep inside you while your hands are moving and sort of tracing out the emotions there in the different key signatures, right there in the keyboard. I think you've got to have that right at the start." He turned on his side, facing her. "You sure you want to hear all this?"

"Yes. And I already know something about your hands."

"Then there's control," he went on, not picking up on her remark as he warmed to his subject. "*That* you have to work for, and it can take a long time. Dynamics, for instance. That's loud and soft. Take a single note and play it, then play it ever so slightly softer, then take it down by precisely the same increments all the way to silence."

"Can you do that?"

"Oh, yes. That stuff is basic. You play legato, staccato, and all of that and a lot more has to do with touch, with your ability to control the interaction of your body with the instrument. Your hands and the keys. You develop touch to the physical limit. You can be a pretty good player at that point. Most people don't go any further."

"Why not?"

He sat up and hugged his knees. "I don't know. Any number of reasons, I guess."

She shifted onto her back. "The sun feels good."

"Some people just never get past the written music. In a certain sense it's only black marks on paper, and of course you pay attention to it, but you have to remember there's actual music behind the black marks. Somebody played some music, or heard it anyway, and *then* wrote it down. Notation, well . . ." His voice trailed off for a moment. "I mean some of Bach, for instance, you just have the bare notes. No instructions, nothing. You have to be able to imagine the way he wanted it, and then play it that way. And he wrote before the piano was invented."

She gave him an encouraging sound, to indicate she was listening even though her eyes were closed.

"The thing is — and Fredericks showed me this — once you get to a certain point you can sort of forget your hands. It becomes mental, in a way. You go into a kind of trance of concentration, imagining what it's going to sound like, feeling it in your head, and somehow that's exactly what happens. It feels almost like magic. It feels so good sometimes you can hardly stand it. I mean, you know, you're playing and there's a resistance, you're pushing against it harder and harder, and then you break out into the clear. Just like that you're through and there's no resistance and you just sail along and it's like pure thought turning into pure music." He plucked some grass and let it fall. "You have to train yourself to keep your concentration, otherwise you can get so happy you just go over the top. It's wild."

He turned his head to look at her and felt a twinge of disappointment. She was asleep, her breath deep and even, her mouth slightly parted. He glanced up at the silent house, and then down at her body. He felt a sudden sexual urge, so swift and sharp he found himself recoiling from her. After a moment he got up and slipped back into the pool.

As he carefully removed a white shirt from his suitcase he was surprised to see his good-luck piece lying in a corner of the bag. He stood perfectly still, trying to figure out how it had gotten there. It was supposed to be with his cuff links, studs, and bow tie in a drawer at Obromowitz's — all the fancy stuff for formal dress performances in one place. Sometimes, for a really big job, he would carry the little wooden cross in his breast pocket. And yet here it was, all by itself. A mystery. He picked it up, rubbing it with his thumb, then put it back in the suitcase.

When he'd finished dressing he went into the bathroom and checked himself in the mirror. The blue blazer he'd gotten for three dollars at the Cadbury thrift shop looked fine. His teeth, as he leaned forward with a grimace, were as white as any movie star's. His black curly hair was perhaps a bit too thick and a bit too long, but not outrageously so. He buffed his brown loafers with a towel and decided he was presentable. Cocktails, Lady had said, at five-thirty in the living room.

Outside, as he walked across the grass, his eye was caught by the swimming pool. The light from the lowering sun fell at a steep angle, and the water was almost too bright to look at. As he approached the edge of the pool the brightness waned. In the still air the water barely moved and he stood watching the minuscule ripples on the surface. The surface held his eye.

Then, with a sensation almost like falling, his gaze was drawn through the water to the bottom of the pool. A smooth green expanse, two thirds in shadow, but with the last third covered with a fine net of shadow lines, a kind of gently wavering grid. It took him a moment to realize he was watching an intricate pattern thrown by the surface ripples, a pattern so regular it seemed unnatural. A strange, silent tableau, inexplicably beautiful. He stood staring down.

"Claude!" Lady called from the French doors. "What are you doing?"

"Nothing," he said, starting toward her. "It was the light." He waved to indicate the pool. "The shadows." He quickened his pace.

"I think swimming pools are vulgar, don't you? I don't know why he built it," she said as Claude joined her.

"Your father?"

"No. My great-grandfather. He gave them this place."

Inside, Linda Powers put down her pen and rose with a distracted air. "Ah, there you are. I can't seem to find my . . ." She looked back at the desk. "Well, never mind. I had tea with Bunny, dear. She says she looks for you at the club, but you're never there."

"I was there this morning," Lady said.

"Well, do be nice if you bump into her. She's been awfully good about the drive this year. Now, what was I —" Her voice broke off as the maid arrived. "Drinks! What would you children like?"

"Gin and tonic," said Lady.

"That sounds good," Claude said.

"Three gin and tonics, Maria. And the usual for Mr. Powers. Thank you, dear." There was a brittle, avian quality to her attractiveness — the quick, glittering eyes, the short bursts of speech. "Sit down," she said to Claude. "And thank you for the marrons. Sinfully rich."

"You were kind to invite me," Claude said, swiveling his head to include her husband. Ted Powers sat at the other end of the room over what appeared to be a very large jigsaw puzzle. He gazed down at the board with his chin in his hand.

Lady sat on the couch, rolled her eyes at Claude, picked up a magazine, and began flipping pages.

"Lady tells me you studied with Fredericks," Linda Powers said. "So you must have met Anson Roeg. In fact, it was Bunny who lent me a copy of *Secret Meetings*. We're all deliciously scandalized, of course." A quick smile. "But is she really so, ah, is she, er . . ."

"Eccentric, Mummy," Lady said. "That's the word."

"Yes, exactly. Eccentric?"

The maid arrived with a tray of tinkling drinks. Claude was served first, and was grateful for the interruption. His loyalty to Fredericks was almost as fierce as that toward Weisfeld, and he felt unaccountably nervous when talking about them to people who didn't know them, as if he couldn't do them justice, or worse, as if his reluctance might be construed as disinterest. The truth was, he loved Fredericks, but no one wanted to hear that. They wanted gossip.

"She does smoke cigars," Claude said, "but they're quite small. Not much bigger than cigarettes."

"One hears about her clothes," Linda Powers said.

"She wears pants all the time, as far as I know."

"Is she . . . er . . . mannish? That is, the way she behaves?"

Claude stared into his gin and tonic, which was the color of the water in the swimming pool. "She's practical. She takes care of a lot of stuff for him, arranging things, remembering things. But I wouldn't say mannish. In a funny way the clothes call attention to the fact she's a woman."

Lady put down the magazine. "That's interesting. Why do you say that?"

"She's always struck me as feminine." Claude shrugged.

"People say they're inseparable," Linda Powers said.

"I guess they are."

There was a silence, and Claude knew Linda wanted him to elaborate, but he chose not to. He felt awkward, and he was aware of the silent presence of Ted Powers.

The tray of gin, tonic, ice, and lime had been left by the maid at a side table. Lady and Linda went periodically to freshen their drinks. Ted stayed where he was, served every now and then by another maid, who also passed hors d'oeuvres. Claude could hear the ticking of the ornate clock over the mantel. It seemed a very long time before they were called in to dinner.

Mr. Powers and Claude sat at the ends of the long table, while Lady and her mother faced each other across the middle. Mrs. Powers kept up a line of light chatter, addressed mostly to Lady. Over soup Claude learned that Ernesto, the new gardener, seemed to be working out. Julio, the previous gardener, had been better, but he had died the previous summer of a heart attack. Linda had undergone the shocking experience of finding him face down in the flower bed. Over veal cutlets and asparagus it came out that Bunny had given five hundred shares of Pepsi-Cola to the Heuval Foundation, of which Mrs. Powers was the president. The foundation was dedicated to educational and proactive projects for unwed mothers. It ran four shelters in New York and Boston. Ted Powers, it turned out, had shot eighteen holes with a score of ninety, and had observed Judge Aldrich cheating on the approach to the fourteenth, kicking his ball from the edge of the rough onto the fairway. Over dessert, Linda Powers announced that someone referred to as Noodle was having her gall bladder removed.

"Do you have plans for tonight?" Linda asked Lady.

"We're going to the movies." Lady put down her napkin and rose. "Actually, we should get going."

"In the village?"

"Yup."

This was news to Claude, but he followed Lady's lead and they slipped out.

"I'm sorry," Lady said as they got in the car. "I just had to get out of there."

"Did you mean it about the movies?"

"Why don't we?" she said, pulling out onto the road. "It's supposed to be good. It's called *Some Like It Hot.*"

The theater was surprisingly small — perhaps twice the size of the children's section at the RKO — and completely filled. They were lucky to get two seats in the second row, which opened up at the end of the coming attractions. The crowd buzzed with anticipation, and then fell still as the movie began. Claude and Lady held hands, leaned back, and gazed up at the screen.

In a very short time Claude was laughing. Soon after he was laughing helplessly. The farcical situations seemed to build one upon the other until he had to wipe his eyes with the back of his hand. Lady would chortle every now and then, patting Claude's leg, without taking her eyes from the screen, when he seemed on the verge of losing control of himself. In the midst of his paroxysms Claude felt a sliver of fear as he perceived the remote edge of outright hysteria. He would quiet down for a few minutes, but then surrender to laughter because it seemed to cleanse him, to pull out the knots in his soul and leave him breathless and blessedly empty. When the lights came on, Lady looked at him with a smile. "Are you okay?"

"I couldn't help it," he said. "It must be the funniest movie ever made."

"It was good." She looked at him with curiosity, a muted version of the look she sometimes gave him during sex, and then turned away to collect her things.

Outside, in the warm night air, they moved through the fanning crowd to the car.

"Tony Curtis surprised me," Lady said. "I usually can't stand him."

"The pace of it was terrific. The whole thing had a jazzy kind of rhythm, and of course they were supposed to be musicians, which makes it even better."

When they reached the car a group of young people passed by on the sidewalk. "Lady," a girl called, "are you going to Caroline's?"

"What?"

"Caroline's having a party. Are you going?"

"Maybe." She gave a little wave and got in the car. As Claude followed he noticed her glance at her watch. She started the engine with a roar and tapped her index finger on the steering wheel.

"Who's Caroline?" Claude asked.

"I play tennis with her sometimes at the club. Bryn Mawr. Slightly strange. Her mother's dead and the rumor is she hasn't seen her father for years. She lives with her old nanny in this huge mansion. We should go for a drink just so you can see it." She threw the car into gear and pulled away. "Are you game?"

"Sure."

The road was dark. Trees, hedges, and fieldstone walls slipped in and out of the car's tightly focused headlight beams as Lady swept through the curves. After perhaps a mile she slowed and turned through two enormous stone pillars and an open iron gate. The white gravel driveway led between an avenue of trees, curved to the right through what Claude sensed to be a series of landscaped parks, topped a gentle hill, and curved to the left, where Lady stopped the car and turned off the lights.

Above them, the open dome of stars. Ahead, as his eyes became accustomed to the dimness, he saw the faint luminosity of the gravel road gently winding down a rolling lawn to a small cluster of lights surrounded by a vast blackness. Behind the blackness was Long Island Sound, beginning to glint now, just enough for him to see the outlines of a great house. They sat in silence for a minute, and then she turned on the lights and drove down the hill.

There were six or seven cars parked haphazardly in the circular driveway. Lady pulled in beside a gleaming chopped and channeled hot rod. They followed a flagstone path and climbed the wide steps to the front door. It was partially open and they pushed through.

Claude heard the thin sound of a scratchy record of a tune called "Harbor Lights" and moved forward in the marbled hall until he found the source. Lady stepped in front of him as they entered an enormous ballroom with chandeliers hanging from the curved ceiling. Three or four couples danced a slow fox trot, and a few people were outside leaning on a stone balcony, looking into the night. A long bar had been set up next to the French doors, and a girl in a blue dress accepted a glass of champagne from the ancient bartender.

"Caroline!" Lady said. "We heard and we came. I hope that's all right."

Caroline's skin was chalk white. Her round face and the softness of her arms suggested a trace of baby fat. Her eyebrows were thin and very dark, and her small mouth was painted a vivid deep red. "Of course," she said, suddenly smiling. "I left a note for you at the club."

Claude shook her hand, struck by the nervousness in her brown, downcast eyes.

"Have some champagne," Caroline said. "Patrick brought up a case, but most of them are drinking beer, for some reason."

Clusters of antique furniture lined the walls. They sat at the nearest group of chairs. The rest were empty. The music came from an old leather-cased portable phonograph set on top of a grand piano.

"Cheers," said Lady, lifting her glass. "Is there an occasion?"

"No," Caroline said. "I just thought . . ." Her voice trailed off. She sipped her drink. "A lot of them are down at the boathouse."

"Where's Buzz?"

"He drifted off somewhere."

Lady watched Caroline for a moment, then turned to Claude. "Get us a bottle, would you? Something to nibble on as well?" A fast wink. Then she moved her head closer to Caroline and began to talk.

Claude understood. He got up and walked out onto the balcony.

The people who had been there had moved down to the end, in the direction of the boathouse. He saw a flare as someone lighted a cigarette. He heard a splash, and some muted cheers and laughter from the pier. As he went back inside something landed on his wrist, and he felt a sting at precisely the moment he slapped at it. A small insect, and a tiny smear of blood. With a nod to the old bartender, he took a bottle of champagne and small bowl of pistachios and carried them over to Lady and Caroline, whose heads were still bent in conversation. He put the bottle and the bowl on the table and backed away as Caroline, oblivious, wiped a tear from her eye.

The phonograph played Nat King Cole, and the dancers continued to shuffle, each couple in a different part of the room. Claude moved to the bar. He picked up a glass of champagne. "Do you know what kind of piano that is?"

The bartender leaned forward and placed his gnarled fingers on the ivory linen. He had narrow shoulders and a thin face blotched with broken veins. "A Steinway, sir. I remember the day it was delivered. Spring of 1925."

"It's a concert grand," Claude said, unable to keep a touch of reproach from his tone. He was sure no one played it.

"They ordered it for the first big party of the season."

"For a party?"

"Oh, yes. They took their parties very seriously back in those days, if I may say so." His milky blue eyes took on a spark of mischief. "Wild and woolly, sir. Quite a treat for me, just off the boat. Very entertaining once I got used to it."

Claude laughed. "I bet!"

"Hundreds of people," he said, looking out across the nearly empty room. "Bless me if they didn't drink. Cocktails of every description. Very popular at the time, cocktails. We had a staff of nineteen, and four of us could make any cocktail they might name — the sidecar, rob roy, gin fizz, Manhattan. The sazerack with absinthe, and stingers. There were dozens of them. Very pretty, too, with the different colors. The ladies in particular seemed to enjoy the colors."

"What's a stinger?" Claude asked.

"Ah, well," the old man said with enthusiasm, and quickly reached under the table for two bottles. Claude watched as he deftly iced a glass, mixed the drink in another, poured, and served. "Brandy and crème de menthe, sir. Very smooth."

Claude tasted. "This is good. I like it."

The old man glanced at Lady and Caroline, and then, not bothering to ice a glass this time, made one for himself. He sipped it with a bulbous pinkie in the air, and then placed it on the bar. "They were wild. Do you see those chandeliers, sir? I remember a party with a young lady swinging on one and two gentlemen on the other. It was a contest, and believe it or not the young lady lasted the longest."

"Up there? How'd they get up there?"

"Human pyramid. Drunk as lords, every one of them. The pyramids kept breaking down and they'd all land in a pile, screaming and laughing." He drank some of his stinger. "Funny how they were . . . very formal in some ways, with team captains and a timekeeper, and yet there she was up there, buck naked."

"What?" Claude was shocked.

"Always something new. You never knew what to expect. Once at a tea dance a bunch of them rode right in here asking for mint juleps. We kept horses then. Came through the French doors clippety-clop. Stayed in the saddle, drank them down, and rode right out again. That was a big hit. Care for another, sir?"

Claude had finished his drink almost without noticing it. He held his glass out, feeling a slow flush of warmth spreading from his upper chest. The old man made two more stingers.

"They were like children, in a way," he said. "Very excitable, running every which way, throwing themselves into things. Wonderful spirit, really. Out there on the great lawn at two o'clock in the morning playing croquet. We had to follow them around with lanterns. Oh, yes, it was quite different being in service in those days."

The mint was smooth on Claude's tongue. "But didn't it, wasn't it, I mean, suppose you just wanted to sleep, and then you had to —" He broke off, waving his glass.

The old man frowned and looked down, pursing his mouth as if considering the question. Then he sampled his drink. "Oh, they knew who was up for it, sir. I was young, and to tell you the truth I enjoyed myself. It was just so wonderfully silly sometimes. You know, they'd press-gang us into the teams when they needed people. All those games, I didn't understand the rules half the time but it didn't seem to matter. I had to spend half an hour in a linen closet with a movie star one time before they found us. I can't remember her name, but we split a bottle of Dom Perignon sitting on the floor. I remember her perfume."

Suddenly the old man's lively eyes went flat. He half turned and busied himself rearranging glasses at precisely the moment that Lady came up and touched Claude's shoulder. "This is terrible," she whispered, steering him to the end of the bar. "It's so sad. Practically everyone's down at the boathouse. People haven't even said hello to her. They're just floating around. Half of them are townies, I bet. Caroline may be a little odd, but she deserves better than this. What's that you're drinking?"

"A stinger," he said, and finished it.

"Watch it. They pack a wallop."

"I'm beginning to see that," he said. "What does Caroline think?"

"Oh, she doesn't know what to think, poor thing. Or what to do, for that matter."

"What would *you* do?"

"I don't know. Pack it in, I suppose."

Claude felt a pleasant, warm humming in his blood. He stared up at the chandeliers.

"What are you looking at?" Lady asked.

"The chandeliers," he said abstractedly and moved forward.

The phonograph hissed emptily. He picked it up with both arms and lowered it to the floor. He opened the top of the Steinway to the second position and swung up the stick. At the keyboard he played a series of barely audible fifths and then sat down at the bench. The instrument was in good tune, with a heavy action. He thought for a moment, extended his arms, and played the last section of *Rhapsody in Blue*. The piano had a big tone, the notes tightly focused from the hardness of the hammer felts, and when Claude leaned into the fortes the entire ballroom was filled with sound. People began to drift toward him.

He was determined to be as flashy as possible and to play loud enough for the sound to bounce off the French doors in the direction of the boathouse. When he'd finished the Gershwin he launched without pause into James P. Johnson's "Carolina Shout," tearing off the left-hand stride leaps at a dangerously quick tempo. He could feel energy radiating in all directions, as if the piano had become incandescent. More people moved toward him, and he was dimly aware of people coming in from outside. He played "Ripples of the Nile," an old stride barnburner by Lucky Roberts he'd first heard as a child when Al's friend Mr. Oliver had played it in the Park Avenue basement. The texture of the keys began to change very slightly as the dry ivory absorbed the sweat from his fingertips.

Now, in the grip of a reckless exhilaration, he embraced every stride tune he could think of, keeping up the pulse, playing through mistakes as if they'd never happened, faking bridges when he had to, his hands flying, his body moving like a warm, oiled machine. He became aware that people were dancing, and he began blending Art Tatum into Fats Waller into Jelly Roll Morton in a continuous avalanche of jazz. He rocked back and forth and poured it on, his mind now empty of everything but the music. He felt he could play forever, but the sweat got in his eyes and he stopped after an elaborate up-tempo arrangement of "Is You Is or Is You Ain't my Baby?"

The entire room, crowded now with forty or fifty people, burst into applause, whistles, and shouts. "More, more!" they cried, and Claude waved acknowledgment with one arm while trying to clear his eyes with the other. Lady and Caroline came up over his right shoulder.

"It's so great!" Caroline said, kneeling at the end of the bench. "It's just fantastic. Everybody's dancing and having . . ." She seemed to lose her breath. "Please, please play some more." Lady smiled beside her.

Claude nodded.

From his left, a white towel was thrust into his hands and he saw the bartender placing first a napkin and then a rather large glass on the corner of the piano. "First rate, sir. Absolutely first rate. I took the liberty of making you another." He gave a brief nod and withdrew. Claude wiped his face and neck, took a sip of the stinger, slipped off his jacket, and to a general roar of approval, rolled up his sleeves. Then he began to play some serious boogie-woogie.

As Lady pulled away from the mansion, Claude gave a great, shuddering yawn and leaned his head back on the seat. The cool air was delicious against his body, which felt supple and entirely relaxed, as if he'd been playing full-out basketball for hours. "It must be late," he said.

"It is," she said.

"I shouldn't have done it, but it was fun."

"Why? Why shouldn't you?" She sounded almost aggrieved.

"Performing is serious, it's serious business, you don't just . . ." He waved a hand in the air. "I wasn't prepared. I horsed around. When they started calling out tunes I just faked the harmonies. I was being silly."

"But it was a *wonderful* thing to do," Lady protested. "It saved everything. Caroline was ecstatic."

"Well, that's nice, anyway."

"People loved it."

"Good." He wanted to drop the matter.

As if catching his tone, she said, "Well, I can't understand why you'd regret doing something like that. As if you were some kind of a snob or something."

"It's hard to explain," he said. "It's not that big a deal, really, it's just hard to explain to people. Forget it, it's nothing."

They drove the rest of the way home in silence. When Lady pulled into the driveway and saw that the lights were on downstairs, she murmured, "Uh-oh."

"What's the matter?"

"I don't like those lights."

"Why not?"

"It's not in the pattern," she said. "The pattern is one Scotch and soda for her, two for him, and then upstairs with ginger ale to their respective bedrooms. It never varies."

"Separate bedrooms?" Claude knew of such arrangements from the movies, but that was usually for older people, or people living in castles or great mansions like the one they'd just come from.

She'd gone quite still, sitting up straight, staring at the house. "Oh, yes," she sighed, and then, bitterly, "He came down one night about fifteen years ago and caught her making out on the couch with John O'Hara. I don't think they've touched each other since."

"Holy shit," he said, stunned both by the information and the fact that she would tell him.

She shrugged.

"You mean John O'Hara the writer?" he asked stupidly.

The front door opened and they could see the silhouetted figure of Mrs. Powers, her back bent slightly, her body moving with a jittery energy, holding the door frame and looking out at them. She turned away and retreated into the living room.

"Oh, Christ," Lady said, getting out of the car.

Claude followed her into the house. As soon as Lady appeared at the threshold of the living room, there was a muted keening sound from her mother, who was pacing back and forth, one hand at her chest and the other fluttering around her head. "Oh, God, God. Where have you been? We've been frantic, absolutely frantic."

Lady started to speak, but then simply looked down at the floor and slowly shook her head.

"Your father's been calling the hospitals. He's been so terribly worried. Practically out of his mind with worry. That fast car you insist on driving doesn't even have a roof. I tell you we've been frantic, not knowing what to do. It's almost three o'clock in the morning!" She turned away as if to sob.

Somehow, instantly Claude knew that the entire performance was fraudulent. Something had been going on in the house for quite a while, and the woman had worked herself into such a state she no longer knew what she felt, so intent was she on acting out the role of a distraught mother. Moreover, he sensed that she knew this but didn't really care, intoxicated as she was by her own histrionics. She wiped nonexistent tears from her cheek, lifted her head stoically, and seemed to plead with soft eyes. Initially alarmed, Claude was now only stunned by this weirdly unapologetic dishonesty. It was almost as if the woman expected applause, eerily reminiscent of Mr. Powers's expectation of a response after one of his gaffes.

"Where were you?" Mrs. Powers asked again, sounding exhausted.

"Caroline Howard gave a party," Lady said.

"Well, you could have called. You could have given some thought to us, after all." Mrs. Powers had not looked at Claude once. "It wouldn't have —" She broke off, lowering her forehead into her palm.

"All right, Mother." Lady turned and froze.

Claude followed her gaze. A man's legs, waist, silver belt buckle, arm, hand, and fingers (holding a glass of amber-colored liquid) were visible on the stairs. The rest of Mr. Powers's motionless body was hidden by the ceiling. He had presumably heard everything.

"Are you coming down, Father?"

There was a long silence. Mrs. Powers sat down in the living room. Claude watched Mr. Powers's legs. Finally they moved.

"I have nothing to say to you." Mr. Powers went back upstairs.

"What is this?" Claude whispered. "What's going on?"

Staring up at the empty stairwell, Lady held up a hand to quiet him.

She appeared calm, her face composed. Claude noticed a tremor in her hand. "I'll have to sit with her for a while now," she said. "You'd better go to bed. I'm sorry. I'll see you in the morning."

"Of course," he said, feeling an instant of guilt at how glad he was to be able to escape the house and its strange, thick atmosphere of hidden struggle.

Back in the city, Claude deflected his confusion and uneasiness about the weekend by immersing himself in work. Four or five hours at the Bechstein, two or three hours writing (the song cycle, a piece for piano), copying, score reading, harmonic analysis, and various other tasks. The very familiarity of the basement studio was soothing, leading him back into himself.

Eventually, over a lunch of corned beef on rye, pickles, and cream soda with Weisfeld in the back of the store, Claude found himself briefly describing the weekend — leaving out his impromptu performance at the party — and then going on at some length about the bizarre behavior of Mr. and Mrs. Powers. "And the next morning," he said, puzzled, "it was as if nothing had happened. She was chatting over coffee, he read the paper, and they went off to play tennis. Lady and I took a swim and I caught the train. It was spooky. And I swear to God, the whole weekend I don't think either one of them actually looked at me. You know, really looked."

"Yes," Weisfeld said. "I think I understand."

"You do? Well, what is it?"

"The parents don't want to see you, they don't want to look. If they don't look, then you're not there." He took a bite of his sandwich and watched Claude struggle with the implications. And it *was* a struggle. Down deep, Claude was aware that he didn't know very much about people — nor, for that matter, about himself — and often couldn't understand their actions. At college people had repeatedly surprised him by taking extreme positions, getting into fights, goofing off in their studies, getting drunk for days, all for no apparent reason. Between his sophomore and junior years one of his classmates — an interesting fellow with an impressive knowledge of art, music, opera, and modern poetry — had killed himself in his parents' garage. Claude had heard the rumor that the boy was homosexual, but he still could not fathom why he would take his own life. From his earliest years Claude had been alert to danger on the outside — the threat of circumstances —

and had developed, in his vulnerability and weakness, a protective screen of pride, tenacity, and self-absorption. He had never been able to afford thinking about danger from the *inside,* from within one's self, and as a result was prone to take people at face value, to assume they were what they presented themselves to be. He was naive. (Lady was perhaps the obverse. At college she had been impressive in her ability to read between the lines with all sorts of people. "Professor Albertson is aggressive because he's short," for instance. "He resents people for being taller than he is." It would never have occurred to Claude, although he recognized its truth the moment she told him.)

"But what have they got against me?" Claude asked. "I didn't do anything."

Weisfeld sighed. "You're seeing their daughter."

"What's so terrible about that?"

Weisfeld ate for a while and seemed to be thinking about what he was going to say. He drank some cream soda and put the bottle down with exaggerated care. "Maybe," he said, "people in that social circle, it's possible they want their daughter to marry let's say a nice boy who happens to be a Roosevelt, a Harriman, a Rockefeller, or the Duke of Kent or something fancy like that. You know, it's possible."

Claude was suddenly nervous. He did not want to entertain the suggestion. "Oh, that was the old days." And then it popped out of his mouth before he could stop himself: "This is America."

Weisfeld nodded. "Absolutely."

"I just mean the class system is supposed to be more fluid. I hated sociology, but I remember a whole chapter about the effect of the war on the class system," he babbled, trying to cover up. "Everything's different now."

"Sure," Weisfeld said. "And in some cases different but the same. Like you redecorate a room, but it's the same room. You put a mute in a trumpet, but it's the same horn. People don't talk about class and social background the way they used to, but that doesn't mean they've forgotten about it."

Claude drummed his fingers on his knees, a sour expression on his face. He remembered Catherine's words in the car years ago, after the mixer: *You come from nowhere.* They had virtually paralyzed him. He had not thought of those words for a very long time. His face flushed with heat.

"It's ridiculous, of course," Weisfeld went on. "These are small things they spend time worrying about. But you have to remember, it's possible."

"I'm an artist!" Claude protested.

"Yes, yes!" Weisfeld cried. "We know what that means. We know, but not everybody knows. Even some people who talk like —" He interrupted himself. "You remember when you used to play for Mrs. Fisk? For her little boy?"

Claude was stunned. Could Weisfeld read his mind?

"You remember Dewman Fisk," Weisfeld continued, raising his voice, "the famous ballet enthusiast and culture maven for the mayor? And the pretentious Mrs. Fisk, one of our best customers? You think they knew anything about it? About what it means to be an artist?"

Claude was doubly speechless — first the talk of the Fisks, and second the controlled anger in Weisfeld.

"They know practically nothing." He stroked his mustache as if to calm himself down. "Music is a decoration. A diversion to take their minds off their troubles. Maybe a hobby. To them, the artist is a high-class entertainer. They don't even know they don't know anything, those people. It can drive you crazy." He crushed the waxed paper from lunch into a ball and threw it in the trash. "So don't expect anything. Be careful with those kind of people."

16

OTTO LEVITS'S OFFICE was on Fifty-seventh Street, a few doors down from the Steinway building. It was small, its walls covered with signed photographs of musical artists of every description — Toscanini, Lily Pons, Geiseking, Ezio Pinza, Aaron Copland, Pablo Casals, Victor Borge, Fritz Kreisler, Fredericks.

"Did you get the check?" Otto asked.

"Yes. Thank you."

"Good." He moved some papers on his desk. "I thought it was time for a talk. You've done extremely well over the last few years, according to all reports. All kinds of bookings and everybody's been more than satisfied. They've usually wanted you back and I've had to explain about your special scheduling."

"Even the Swedish tenor? Svenvold?" Claude kept a straight face.

"Aiy yi-yi," Otto moaned. "A cuckoo. A complete crazy-head. He never did the tour, you know. Got lost for a couple of days, and when they found him he was trying to join the Salvation Army. The embassy took care of it. Shot him up and shipped him back to Stockholm."

"Well, he was something different. He wanted to sing with his clothes off, and said I should take my clothes off too and play naked."

"I know, I'm sorry, my apologies," Otto said quickly. "Ah, this business."

"A good singer, though."

Otto looked at him suspiciously for an instant, and then realized

Claude meant it. "Of course!" he said. "He was my client." He paused. "You handled it well."

"Hey. I just got up and left."

"Yes, but you did it nice. You were polite, he said, and respectful. He wrote me a note from the academy of laughter to apologize. He can't help himself sometimes."

"It's okay."

"And Fredericks sends his best. He called from Rome. We talked about this and that. Wants to know what you're doing."

"Playing and writing," Claude said. "Nothing's changed."

"Good. So now maybe we can pick up the pace a bit. Can you do an audition Thursday morning?"

"Sure. For what?"

"A short tour, but it could be important for you. Aldo Frescobaldi's permanent accompanist fell off his chair in a café in San Remo and broke his arm. Aldo needs somebody for three concerts — Philadelphia, New York, and Boston — coming up soon. It's an emergency."

After a moment of lightheadedness Claude crossed his legs and tried to appear casual. He had a dozen of Frescobaldi's RCA recordings and was aware of the man's reputation as one of the finest violinists in Europe. "I like that sound he gets. Deep, almost gritty sometimes, as if he's not afraid to let the violin sound like a violin."

"This could be good for you," Otto said, "but remember, he's listening to some other people. Plus he's sort of unpredictable."

"What do you mean?"

"Nothing like Svenvold. But he's a flamboyant character. Very dramatic. Given to grand gestures. An egomaniac, I suppose you could say, but nothing you can't handle. And the money will be very good. More than that, the word will get around."

"I'll do my best," Claude said. "Where and what time?"

"He'll come to you. Ten o'clock at the store."

On the appointed day Claude woke at five, ate a bowl of cornflakes in his room, and walked around the corner to let himself into the store before six. Weisfeld was still upstairs. Claude unlocked the register, neatened up the counters, swept the aisles, and unrolled the awning. When there was nothing left to do he went down to the studio and commenced his regular routine at the Bechstein. Very soon, he slipped out of time.

"Claude!" Weisfeld called from the door. "Come up, please."

As if startled from a complicated dream, Claude pulled his hands abruptly from the keys. Weisfeld seldom interrupted him, and so, fearing some mishap, he quickly climbed the stairs. As he emerged he heard the tinkle of the bell and saw an obese man, puffing and sweating, shirttail half out of his pants, pushing the door with his elbow. He had a violin case in one hand and a bulging briefcase in the other. The wooden floor seemed to bend under his weight as he approached the counter.

"I am Aldo Frescobaldi," he said.

"Good morning, maestro." Weisfeld cleared some space. "You can put your things here. I am Aaron Weisfeld, and this" — he extended his arm with a flourish — "is Claude Rawlings."

Claude understood why there were no photographs on the man's records. A veritable mountain of fat, his huge liquid neck as wide as his head. Even his eyes bulged, under black eyebrows so thick and wild they looked like exotic caterpillars. His hand covered Claude's like a pillow. He looked around. "Where do we play? I can't play here."

"Downstairs, maestro." Weisfeld came around the counter and reached for the briefcase. "May I help you with this?"

Frescobaldi descended, the stairs creaking ominously, carrying his violin. Claude took the briefcase and followed.

"If you need anything at all," Weisfeld said from above, "just let me know." He closed the door.

The big man went to the center of the room and turned slowly to survey it. "It is like the cell of a scholarly monk," he said. "Fredericks said you were a serious young man. Are you a monk? A monk of music?" He moved to the wall of bookcases. Over the years Claude had built up an impressive collection of scores — thirty or forty feet of shelves jammed with folios, in alphabetical order by composer — and more than a hundred books on theory, composition, orchestration, musical biographies, criticism, analysis, and various reference works. Frescobaldi tilted his large head to read the spines of the folios.

"No," Claude said, "but I try to keep things neat down here."

"Commendable." He extracted a book. "I myself am not a well-organized person. I thrive on chaos." He flipped through pages. Claude went to the piano. The big man came over and placed the open book on the music stand. "Scriabin."

Claude nodded, instantly nervous. Scriabin's music often made great demands, and he had not played the etudes in a long time.

"If you would start with the 'Mosquito,' please. Opus 42, number 3." Frescobaldi went and leaned against the wall, his hands clasped under his chin.

There was a long silence as Claude read through the bagatelle with his eye, listening to the music in his mind. It was a study in trills, and as soon as he had decided how to shape them, he raised his hands from his lap and played the piece through.

"Now opus 8, number 10, please," Frescobaldi directed calmly.

Claude flipped back until he found it. This one he remembered better, having used it to work on his thirds when he was young. It seemed Frescobaldi was starting out by testing his technique. Again Claude read the piece, listened to it mentally, and thought about it for several minutes before he played. It was difficult, but its mood was essentially playful, and as he finished he believed he had captured that.

"He was a great pianist," Frescobaldi said, "and he wrote for the piano. This is why I ask to hear it. Now something a bit longer. Opus 42, number 5 — affannato."

Claude studied the piece, slowing down for a close look at the fiery passages, speeding up for the melody which linked them. As he read it a second time, Frescobaldi came and stood by him. "I will turn pages for you."

"Thank you." Claude accepted the fact that there would be errors this time — the piece was simply too difficult to bring off without preparation — but he vowed to himself he would not be thrown by them. And so he plunged in, for three minutes on the edge, missing some notes but preserving the inner line of the piece.

"*Santo cielo!*" the big man said when the last notes died away. "What imagination, that man."

"I haven't played it for years," Claude said.

"Don't worry. When you play a wrong note at least you play it firmly. That's good." He opened his briefcase and spilled half the contents on top of the piano. He searched through the pile, selecting a couple of scores, and then dipped into the bag for a few more. Finally he handed Claude a folio with a bold red and black cover. Manuel de Falla. *Siete Canciones Populares Españolas*. "We will do the third. 'Asturania.' " He opened his violin case while Claude looked at the music.

From a technical point of view the piece was so simple it could have come from an early John Thompson lesson book. He noted the pedal markings and the double pianissimo. The melody had a brooding, melancholy quality, and Claude tried to get it in his bones while Frescobaldi checked his tuning by plucking his strings with his thumb. He flipped the violin into the soft folds of his neck and waved his bow.

"Begin."

Claude got to the second bar before the big man interrupted. "Good, good. The dynamics are very nice, but a little bit faster. Andante tranquillo. Keep it smooth when I enter on bar eight." He waved the bow in tempo.

Claude played with concentration, bringing out the melody in the bass softly and with expression, as marked. He felt the hair rise on the back of his neck as Frescobaldi released his first chain of quarter notes. The sound was soft but full, very full, with a kind of tangy, electrical quality, like warm honey and lemon, and terrifically alive, almost painfully alive. It seemed impossible that this rich, textured sound — soft, but filling the studio completely, seeming to gently press against the boundaries of its walls — had anything to do with the fat man with the small wooden box held between the twin orbs of his fist and his neck. As if in some magic trick or illusion, the sound transcended its means of production. Claude was so entranced he barely heard the piano until a Debussy-like half-tone movement of parallel fifths in his left hand brought him back. He listened to the mix as they played the simple refrain through to the double *ppp* morendo, and the end.

Claude looked up. "That's beautiful," he said. "I've never heard it before."

"Bittersweet," said Frescobaldi. "*Dio mio, che acustica!* It is like playing in the bathroom. In the shower!" He riffled the music on the piano, selecting several pieces. One after the other, with very little talk and few interruptions, they played Bartók's Romanian Folk Dance no. 3; Debussy's "The Girl with the Flaxen Hair"; numbers 3, 4, and 5 from Prokofiev's Five Melodies (op. 35). Stravinsky's incredibly tricky and exciting Tarantella from the *Suite Italienne,* and a dozen other assorted miniatures.

Claude had been unable to read Frescobaldi's mood. There was not a clue what judgments the big man was making about the piano, but Claude was reassured by the fact that Frescobaldi had seemed to be very involved in playing the violin, which suggested at least that Claude wasn't getting in his way. The man had appeared to play freely.

"Enough." Frescobaldi put down his instrument and dabbed at his huge brow with a handkerchief. "It is time to eat. Will you join me for lunch?"

"Thank you, sir."

"You have the afternoon free? No pressing appointments?"

"Correct," Claude said, flushing with pleasure.

"Good." He closed the violin case. "We go."

On the way out the big man said to Weisfeld, "My instrument will be safe down there?"

"Absolutely." Weisfeld saw the smile on Claude's face and managed a discreet wink. "I'll lock the door, even."

Claude gave a thumbs-up sign behind his back as he left.

The restaurant was only four blocks away, down the avenue, but Frescobaldi hailed a cab. Claude thought it was almost as much work for the man to get in and out of the cab as it would have been to walk. Somehow or other his shirttail had once again worked its way out of his pants, his tie was askew, and his handkerchief spilled from his pocket like a torn lining. He rolled through the front door of the restaurant as if coming in from a storm.

"Maestro!" A thin, balding man rushed forward. "To see you again so soon! What an honor!" He moved with Frescobaldi, who had not broken stride. The thin man waved his arms, signaling, as Frescobaldi nodded in response to the bows of the waiters as he made for the rear. "The same table, of course," the thin man said as he rushed ahead to pull it out from the banquette. There were perhaps a dozen patrons eating lunch, all of them watching as Frescobaldi collapsed with a sigh of anticipation.

"*Mamma, che fame,*" he murmured, oblivious of the attention. "Sit, sit," he urged Claude. Claude slipped into the narrow space opposite him. Waiters fussed over the table while Frescobaldi threw back his enormous head and studied the ceiling.

"*Vorrei una mozzarella in carrozza et una bruschetta,*" he said thoughtfully.

"*Sì, maestro,*" the thin man scribbled on his pad.

"*Vorrei delle fettuccine ai funghi e porcini.*"

"*Sì, maestro.*" More scribbling.

"*Stracotto di manzo al Sagrantino con contorno di spinaci.*" He lowered his head. "And the same for my friend, here."

"*Sì, maestro. Assolutamente.*"

"I leave the wine to you." He pulled at his tie and opened his collar. "I hope you're hungry," he said to Claude.

As the dishes arrived Frescobaldi fell to, giving the food his undivided attention. He did not talk, but occasionally looked up with a placid smile. Claude, who was full by the end of the pasta, watched with growing awe. The man ate slowly and steadily, putting away an enormous amount of food. When it became clear that Claude could manage no more than a taste of the meat, Frescobaldi looked concerned.

"No good?"

"It's delicious. I just can't eat this much at lunch."

Frescobaldi nodded, commiserating, and reached across for the plate. He cleaned it at a leisurely pace, sweeping up the gravy with small bits of bread.

They had been at the table for more than an hour. The big man ordered fruit, cheese, and grappa, folded his great hands before him and said, "Music, food, and women. These are the great pleasures, the lasting pleasures. You will learn this, my young monk."

"I would add books," Claude said, feeling somewhat self-conscious. "You know, good books."

"Of course! You are a reader. That is good."

"They don't let you down."

Frescobaldi's big face was capable of astonishingly quick changes of expression — all the more remarkable because when he played it might as well have been made of stone — and it now became somber. He seemed to be considering Claude's words. After a moment the fruit and cheese arrived and the solemnity vanished.

"You were very quick to understand the way I like to play."

"I've got your records," Claude said.

"Yes, but I never recorded those encores. Your time is very good — you play with the front edge of the beat, not just the back edge. You know how to lean, and you pick the right places to do it."

"Thank you."

"Don't thank me. About music I never say anything to be polite. I say what I think, good or bad. Life is too short."

"Okay."

They took another cab back to the music store. In the basement studio Frescobaldi went directly to the old couch against the wall and lay down, his huge belly as high as the backrest. "Call me in one hour," he said, spreading his handkerchief over his face.

Claude went back upstairs. Weisfeld was ringing up a sale. "He's taking a nap."

"Good," Weisfeld said. "So it's going well?"

"I think so. Yes, yes it is."

"I listened at the door a couple of times. It sounded good to me. The Stravinsky was terrific, by the way. Like you'd been playing it all your life."

"It moves so fast," Claude said. "Swoosh! A jet plane."

"I'd like to see that violin of his," Weisfeld said wistfully.

Claude was too excited to sit still, so he went outside, drifted up to Eighty-sixth Street to look at movie posters, walked around aimlessly, replaying the morning's music in his mind, feeling the emotions for a second time, reliving his few errors and trying to figure out why he'd made them. He came back early and walked twice around the block to eat up time.

Frescobaldi was awake when Claude descended. He handed over four folios. "I wanted to do the Franck, but it would take too much time. We will play these. Easily, without formality. Stop anytime you want to."

Claude read the titles. Sonatas op. 24 in F Major and op. 47 in A Major, nicknamed the *Spring* and the *Kreutzer,* by Beethoven; Debussy's Sonata for Violin and Piano in G Minor; and Prokofiev's Sonata no. 1 in F Minor, op. 80. He knew the first two well, was familiar with the third, but had never even heard a recording of the Prokofiev, which he instantly opened. At first glance it did not seem impossible.

"You would like some time to look them over?"

"Yes," Claude said, "if that's okay."

"I will go upstairs and make some phone calls."

Claude heard the creak of the stairs and the floor above as Frescobaldi crossed it. Without wasting a moment Claude went to one of the desks, pulled up a stool, and began to read. The Beethoven and the Debussy were clean, unmarked, but luckily the violin part of the Prokofiev was sprinkled with the big man's notes to himself, which helped Claude to get a handle on the piece. He put his elbow on the desk, his head in his palm, and concentrated, slowly turning pages.

"I can't," he said. He was lying on Obromowitz's bed, holding Obromowitz's old-fashioned telephone to his head. The sky was dark, turning from purple to black outside his window. "I have to work."

"Well then, I'll stay too," Lady said. "I'll beg off the dinner."

"Sugar pot, you don't understand. I wouldn't be able to see you. It's going to be night and day for me until we leave."

"Well, you have to eat," she said.

"When I eat I have a score in my hand. This is a tremendously lucky break for me. I can't blow it."

"You won't blow it," she said, as if it were completely impossible, which he found both irritating and reassuring.

"It's a lot of music. A *lot* of music. And there isn't much time. We're rehearsing at the store four hours a day."

"In your studio?"

"I have to analyze the scores, practice, get it all in my hands. Mr. Weisfeld has me on a schedule again, making me sleep eight hours, checking my food." He laughed. Despite Weisfeld's calm, methodical coaching, Claude knew how much pleasure the situation afforded him. The man fairly percolated with good cheer, which in turn gratified Claude at a fundamental level. It was rare, this ebullience. He seemed less pale, even.

"I might as well go, you're saying," she said.

"I'd be bad company. I wouldn't be able to help myself."

The line hummed for a moment. "God, I hate being with them all by myself. I hate this house and I hate that house. Maybe I'll just move out and go to graduate school."

"That's a thought," he said.

"I don't know what Mummy would do, though. You know what happened to Aunt Millie when Catherine eloped."

"Aunt Millie?" he said, rattled, stalling for time.

"Yes. Mildred Fisk. Aunt Millie."

"Mrs. Fisk?"

"What on earth is the matter with you?"

"Nothing," he said. "So what happened to her?"

"Three hours after they told her, she went blind, totally blind."

"Oh, come on."

"No kidding. It's called hysterical blindness. Nothing anatomically wrong, but she can't see."

"You mean she still . . ."

"Blind as a bat. They can't tell if she'll get better, but of course it's been years now."

"Jesus." He thought about it. "Do you think she could be faking? I mean, she always struck me as strange."

"There are tests, empirical tests," she said.

"How incredibly weird. I didn't know such a thing was possible. It's like something out of legend."

"My whole family is crazy, except for Grandpa." She made a clucking sound with her tongue. "Well, I guess I'll go. At least I've got my own car. Riding out with them is excruciating, I can tell you."

"I'll call you," he said. "You call me."

As tired as he was, he did not find it easy to go to sleep. Frescobaldi's voice spun in his head: "Phrase it like this, pull it out a little bit." Or: "*Ma, no no no!* It's the middle voice. Bring up the middle voice!" Or: "Wait for me. Wait for me there. Write in a retard if you have to." Or: "Again from fifty-nine. Again. Again. Again." Phrases of music rose and sank in his consciousness like the backs of whales breaching in some dark sea. He saw Mrs. Fisk, clothed in a toga like Catherine at the soirée but bent over, skinny arms stretched out before her, feeling her way through a forest of notes, stave lines, and accidentals. He saw Catherine, as a girl, in her velvet coat with the silver buttons, sitting on top of the treble clef, the heels of her patent-leather shoes hooked over a full-bar rest, glaring with an evil smile, tearing the petals from a daisy one by one.

After a long morning with the Prokofiev, Frescobaldi was about to put away his instrument when he happened to look down at some scores on the worktable. He bent over, reading, separating pages with his finger. "What's this?" he asked, picking up the loose sheets and bringing them to the piano.

"My song cycle," Claude said. "Just an experiment."

"It looks interesting. Let's try it." He put the music on the stand. "Your notation is very clear, at least. An old-fashioned hand."

"Mr. Weisfeld and I used to copy together. After a while people couldn't tell who was who."

"Very convenient. All right, give me the tempo."

The literary material was Blake — pairs of poems, one from *Songs of Innocence* followed by its counterpart in *Songs of Experience,* six in all. Frescobaldi said nothing after the first, or the second, so they played them straight through. Claude felt something close to rapture to hear his lines played so beautifully. He had not actually realized how much music was in them.

"Brother Rawlings!" Frescobaldi clapped him hard on the back, enough to move him an inch forward on the bench. "You surprise me! You delight me! These are very good. These did not come from the monastery."

"Thank you," Claude said, deeply pleased. "I don't know what you mean about the monastery."

"I mean it has blood! It has emotion! Sweetness, freshness, sadness. So much music today is mathematical. *Intellectual.*" This last with special scorn. "These little pieces are at least alive. You should prepare a violin transcription." He raised his violin to his neck. "Number three. I will show you."

They worked through the piece one small section at a time. Without disturbing the structure or the essential mood, Frescobaldi demonstrated opportunities for double stops, dramatic runs up to the bridge, broken chords based on an open G string, cleverly placed harmonics, and some supportive left-hand pizzicati. The result was to open up the sound and, without straining, to make the violin sound bigger, more elaborately playful, which worked well with Blake's image of a lamb. Claude made frantic notes, his hand almost trembling in his excitement.

"Work on them," Frescobaldi said. "Send them to me in Rome and I will look at them and respond."

"I will, I will. I can't thank you enough."

"No thanks, no thanks." He rapped Claude very lightly on the head with the top of his bow. "Music, also, is a brotherhood."

Spurred by this remark, and his general euphoria, Claude blurted out a question as they climbed the stairs. "Mr. Weisfeld would like to see your violin. Can you spare a couple of minutes? He repairs them, you know, sometimes."

"Of course," Frescobaldi said, edging himself through the door. "It's the least I can do. I mean to pay him for the studio time before we leave for Philadelphia."

"Oh, that won't be necessary," Claude said quickly.

"Necessary or not, I will do it." He advanced to the cash register and put his case on the glass. "Please forgive me, Mr. Weisfeld, I meant to show you this before." He unsnapped the clasps and whipped away the silk cloth.

"Claude," Weisfeld said, "go next door and get Bergman. Tell him to bring a large glass."

Claude obeyed, coming back with the old, stooped gentleman, wearing his spectacles with the small, black cylindrical magnifier clipped onto one lens, a large magnifying glass in his hand. After introductions, Weisfeld pulled out a square of green felt and spread it over the glass. He lifted the violin from its case, lowered it to the felt, and adjusted the gooseneck lamp for the best light. Soon both heads were bent to the gleaming instrument, Bergman's a little closer as he peered through his jeweler's glass, a handkerchief at his mouth so as not to breathe vapor on the varnish. They made hushed sounds and exclamations to each other.

"Maple."

"Maple neck."

Peering through the f-hole, Weisfeld said, "Willow blocks and linings."

"Look at that purfling! Beautiful!"

"Notice the archings." Weisfeld measured with a fine steel rule.

Bergman took the rule and measured the neck. "Thirteen," he said, and then measured to the bridge. "Nineteen point five."

They were like two surgeons examining the innards of a patient. Weisfeld looked up at Claude. "The varnish was general knowledge for a hundred years. Then around 1750 the secret was lost."

"Does the varnish matter?"

Weisfeld answered as Frescobaldi gave a chortle. "Oh yes, it matters very much. It affects the sound."

Holding the instrument by the scroll, Weisfeld gently turned it over.

"Beautiful flame."

"Lovely." Bergman agreed, raising his head.

"A Guarneri, maestro," said Weisfeld. "Of the later period?"

"It once belonged to Ysaÿe, so of course I had to have it."

All three men burst into laughter.

Claude missed the joke and looked from man to man. Only Frescobaldi met his eye. "Ysaÿe was the only virtuoso fatter than me," he said. "Much, much too fat, the poor man. I am a sylph by comparison."

Weisfeld lay the violin in its case.

"I have a Strad also," said Frescobaldi. "For Mozart."

"We are most grateful," said Weisfeld.

"Absolutely," Bergman added. "I've never seen one before. Only pictures. Now I'll be ready if someone wants to hock one."

"Hock?" asked Frescobaldi. "What is 'hock?' "

"Mr. Bergman owns a pawn shop," Claude explained.

"Aha, I see!" He nodded.

The three men laughed again.

After the fourth encore Frescobaldi stood in the wings wiping his face and neck with a towel, pausing every now and then to gauge the dynamics of the applause. "Are they still standing?"

From the peephole Claude said, "Most of them in the balcony. Most down front in the orchestra. The back is thinning out."

"All right. One last bow from the side of the stage. *Avanti!*"

Frescobaldi stepped into the light and the audience roared. Claude followed. He had learned by now that the big man bowed slowly and elaborately, like a Shakespearean actor, in such a way as to milk the crowd, and he timed his own simple movement accordingly. Their heads came up together. Claude led the way offstage.

"It is important to have a feel for the audience," Frescobaldi said. "You must time it so you can hear the applause all the way to the dressing room." He then moved off rather quickly.

Indeed, Claude could hear a faint echo as he approached his room, still gratified to see his name on the door. Elegant calligraphy on a cardboard insert. Once inside, he fell into an armchair. The management had provided a bowl of fruit and a bottle of champagne in an ice bucket, with four glasses. He stared at these without seeing them.

His body hummed with a comfortable and gradually waning tension, winding down like a gyroscope. Several things about the concert had surprised him. The piano had not been retuned despite his request from the afternoon, remaining slightly sharp in the treble. Frescobaldi had adapted smoothly and with apparent ease, but for Claude it was mildly irritating. Also Frescobaldi had been much more mobile and physical in performance than in rehearsal — dipping, bending, leaning backward, moving here and there for no apparent reason. The movements of his bowing arm had seemed almost flamboyant. For all that, his playing had been breathtaking — utterly clean and so filled with emotion, so exalted in its discoveries, the concert had the feel of a celebration of music itself. Early in the first Beethoven sonata it was as if both of them had somehow levitated an inch above the stage, held there by some indescribable force released by their communion. They had sustained this magic equipoise right through to the end, Claude fighting all the way to control his excitement. He was euphoric and humbled at the same time.

After several minutes of sitting in mindless bliss — his state not unlike the sky-blue sunlit drift of post-coitus — he re-entered the world with the decision to get out of his tails and into civilian clothes. He was standing in his underwear washing his face when Frescobaldi burst into the room, closing the door on a number of people behind him.

"There will be newspaper people in the green room," he said, opening the champagne. "I meant to talk to you about this on the train, but I forgot. I excoriate myself." In fact, the big man had slept through most of the trip. He had a remarkable ability to go to sleep in an instant, as if the handkerchief he dropped over his face contained ether. His snores were horrendous, the cloth puffing in and out. "The important thing is to say nothing important. They are not to be trusted, and few of them know anything about music. Just talk nice — nice audience, nice hall, nice concert, everything nice. Smile."

"Okay."

Frescobaldi poured two glasses of champagne, brought one over, and clinked a toast. "This has been good for me, playing with someone else. It was different. I found new things."

With the glass in his hand Claude was going to have to stand there in his underwear longer than he wanted to. Frescobaldi seemed not to notice his near-nakedness. "I have to go with the Italian consul to some special affair. I will see you at the hotel, either tonight or for breakfast, okay? You will be okeydokey? Eat a good dinner?"

"I'll be fine." Claude emptied his glass to be rid of it, so he could put on his pants.

Frescobaldi ate a couple of grapes. "Tell me," he said, "when we were waiting to go on, you seemed very relaxed. Like you were waiting for a bus. Don't you get a little . . ." He fluttered his hand over his heart and knocked his knees together. "A little scared? All those people? A little nervous?" He looked at Claude with genuine curiosity.

"Maybe the day before I'll be wound up," Claude said, slipping his arm into a sleeve. "But it's funny — before, maybe an hour before, I get completely calm. It's like everything drains out of me and I don't care about anything. I think it comes from Fredericks. Some kind of fatalism. He plays gin rummy before he goes on."

"He drinks?" Frescobaldi recoiled in astonishment. "He drinks before he plays?"

"No, no. It's a card game. A silly little card game."

"Ah!" He was relieved, and nodded.

"I'm not really aware of the people," Claude said.

"For me, those last few minutes — it is like hell." He poured and drank off another glass of champagne. "Black hell."

Claude stopped moving for a moment. "I couldn't tell," he said. "I didn't notice a thing."

"No one can tell." The big man tapped his head. "It is all in here." His eyes seemed to bulge under the thick brows. Then he shrugged. "It is the price I pay. Not so high, really. Now I go hear them tell me what a genius I am."

Claude finished dressing, packed up his tails, his music, and his good-luck piece in the overnight case, and went out into the corridor. He found the green room by following the noise.

Frescobaldi was signing programs, slapping backs, kissing hands, smiling, laughing, answering reporters, and moving almost imperceptibly toward the exit. Flashbulbs went off every few seconds. In his vitality and great bulk he seemed master of the situation, sweeping people up into his own enthusiasm, touching their hands or arms quickly, like a politician or a famous cleric. As they turned away some of them spotted Claude.

Claude signed programs, thanked people for their compliments, and made an effort to keep smiling.

"You're very kind," he said, and, "I'm glad you enjoyed it. I sure did," and, "Thank you so much."

"Is this your Philadelphia debut?" a reporter asked.

"Well, no, actually. But this is the first big . . . I mean, I've played in various places but not in this hall, not for such a large audience, in Philadelphia."

"How did you meet Frescobaldi?" Another reporter.

"Through my teacher."

"Was this a big break for you?"

"Yes, it was."

As the questions got more personal he excused himself and turned around, bumping into a tall, gangly young man who looked familiar.

"Hi! Remember me?" he asked, extending his hand.

"Of course," Claude lied, and shook hands. "I can't remember where, though. At the store?"

"Longmeadow. The Beethoven quintet. I'm Jerry Marx. The bassoon?"

"Oh, yes! Absolutely. How are you? What are you doing here?" Claude gushed, happy to have placed the man.

"I got my ticket weeks ago," Jerry said. "I never expected to see you up there. It took me a while to recognize you."

"Filling in," Claude said.

Jerry frowned. "No, I wouldn't call it that. It was extraordinary. I can't remember when I've heard —" He broke off and covered his mouth, looking down at the floor. Then he raised his head, speaking fast. "I have to go. I just wanted to tell you, I'm proud to have played with you. Years ago, maybe, and now you're . . . you're . . . Well, anyway, just keep on doing what you're doing."

Claude felt the man's emotion and didn't quite know what to do. "Good to see you," he said limply.

"Yes. Yes." Jerry left quickly.

Frescobaldi had made his escape and the room was emptying. Claude got his case and slipped out.

The dining room at the small, elegant hotel at which they were staying was closed — had just closed, the concierge was desolated to report — but food from the short menu could be ordered from the room, and was available at the bar, should monsieur prefer. Monsieur did.

It was dark. An elderly couple sat at the bar, but otherwise the place was empty. Claude sat down in a booth and ordered a roast beef sandwich and a glass of milk. After quite a while it arrived, a splendid presentation of sandwich, potato salad, cornichons, cherry tomatoes, parsley, and horseradish sauce. He ate slowly, savoring the flavors.

He pondered Frescobaldi's confession of stage fright. It seemed so entirely out of character, so unconnected to the rest of him. And yet the intensity with which he had said "Black hell"! Claude almost shivered at the recollection, and felt a wave of sympathy. At the same time he was proud Frescobaldi had told him. It was a mark of trust, one professional to another, and Claude would bet very few people knew about it. He resolved to tell no one. How strange people were, he thought, subject to all kinds of invisible forces, dealing with hidden devils and all the while keeping up appearances. He wondered if he was capable of that kind of bravery.

And there had been something spooky about the cadaverous image of Jerry, his head bobbing as he'd made his emotional speech. The bassoonist had treated him as a superior, as someone on a higher level altogether, and there was no doubting his sincerity. It was as if Jerry had been talking to a third person. All at once — between a cornichon and a tomato — a complex insight came to him, surprising him so much he stopped eating.

Claude had been working at music all his life, driven by the need to penetrate deeper and deeper into its mysteries and sustained by his ability to do so. His progress had been constant, reasonably steady, and tangible with regard to his instrument. The growth of his musical imagination was simply a fact, like the growth of his physical body, except that it promised to continue longer. In a certain sense he had taken all this for granted, assuming the same thing was happening to everybody who worked hard. But suppose it wasn't! Suppose people got stuck — developing to a certain point and then staying there. How long might he have stayed at his own personal wall without Fredericks telling him how to get to the other side? How many young musicians, having been told, were able to do it? Desire for growth did not ensure the fact of growth, he now admitted. It was more complicated. There were imponderables. So Jerry might be one of the unlucky ones, a good player — probably working in an orchestra, a passionate lover of music, but stuck — aware of the other side, yearning for it but unable to get there. Hence his emotion. Claude allowed himself to see himself through Jerry's eyes, and for a moment it scared him.

"There you are!" Frescobaldi entered with two young women in evening clothes. They swept into Claude's booth in a cloud of excited chatter. Introductions. They were both singers. Renata, who sat on Frescobaldi's side, from Turin, and Nancy, a delicate Eurasian beauty, from Fort Lauderdale, Florida, who slipped in next to Claude and immediately grasped his upper arm.

"It was beautiful," she said, her black eyes steady. "The allegro of the Debussy. Perfection!" She wore a peppery perfume.

"Coffee! Coffee!" Frescobaldi shouted to the bartender. "Black. Strong. A pot. Four cups."

"None for me," Claude said. "It's too late. Doesn't it keep you up?"

"Ha! That is exactly what it does. That is the whole point!"

Renata, pleasantly plump, blond, and glowing, gave a quick guffaw and kissed him on the cheek. "*Aldo, Aldo, cafone mio,*" she said tenderly.

"When was the last time we had coffee?" The big man pretended to search his memory. "Copenhagen?"

"Reykjavik," she said.

"Of course! There is nothing else to do in Reykjavik." He shook the booth as he leaned back in laughter.

"You look so young," Nancy said into Claude's ear. "Even younger than from the audience. Does it bother you when I say that?"

"I don't know yet," Claude said. "I'll have to think about it." Her small hand on the table seemed carved from ivory.

"Young is good," she said. "Young is very good."

The talk and laughter continued for an hour. Claude's spirits were high, and he contributed when he could, aware of Nancy's warmth beside him, feeling her hand on his knee as she emphasized a point, once squeezing his thigh while rolling her eyes. Her nearness dizzied him. The unearthly perfection of her skin seemed a challenge.

"*Perchè dio!*" Frescobaldi said. "He is closing the bar. Time to go upstairs."

Claude felt a frisson over his entire body at this news, because it was understood the women were coming too. Nancy even took his arm as they went to the elevator.

Jokes about how much space the big man took up in the small compartment. Nancy's thigh against Claude's. Giggles as the car rose slowly. Claude stared at Nancy's perfect ear — only inches from his mouth — and saw her pulse in the velvet softness below it. He imagined his hands in her blue-black hair, his fingers tracing her exquisite head. The gate pulled back with a crash and they stepped out into the corridor.

Frescobaldi had room 604 and Claude 605, directly opposite. They opened their doors simultaneously and Claude turned to receive a kiss on the cheek from Nancy, who then skipped into 604, following Renata, who was already throwing off her evening jacket. Frescobaldi, starting to close his door, looked up and saw the shock and disappointment on Claude's face.

"Ah!" Frescobaldi said, and bit his lower lip in chagrin. "Of course, you didn't know. My profoundest apologies. These are my habits, you see. When traveling. What a stupid I am. *Scusi.*" He closed the door.

The next morning, in the train, Claude and Frescobaldi sat beside each other in their first-class compartment, handing the Philadelphia newspapers back and forth. Frescobaldi read rapidly, snorting, muttering, sucking his teeth, treating the pages like so much wrapping paper, flinging them to Claude with impatience. "Blah blah blah blah."

The reviews were more than positive — they were laudatory. Claude was thrilled to see his name, thrilled to read the praise. "But these are great!" he said. "See here, 'A triumph for the Italian master . . . his angelic touch . . . a new standard for the Beethoven sonatas . . .' They go on and on about you."

"And you, too. 'Limpid lines . . . extraordinary supple tones . . .' Not that you don't deserve it."

"So what's wrong?" Claude asked.

"Nothing." Frescobaldi threw the paper aside. "These are very good reviews. These are what you call money reviews. But they don't say anything. I get tired of the gushing, always the same words that don't really say anything." He pointed his finger at Claude's nose. "Remember that when you get a bad review. Most of them don't know very much, and they are full of fakery."

Claude thought about it for a while.

"Understand it now, when they praise you," Frescobaldi said, popping a button on his shirt while shifting to a more comfortable position, "so you can keep a sense of proportion when they damn you. It is just words, just words, *caro*."

Claude looked at one of the reviews again, trying to read coldly. A number of adjectives seemed arbitrary, and there were more than a few strained metaphors, now that he searched for them.

"I see what you mean," he said. "But don't you think it's practically impossible to write about music directly? It doesn't lend itself to words. I mean, all you can do is skirt around it, sort of." He folded the paper. "I could write about the structure of the *Kreutzer,* technical stuff, but what could I say about what it means? I don't really think it *means* anything. I think it just *is*."

"*Eccolà*."

"When I think of the mood of it, the feel of it, what it reminds me of is a smell. The smell of the steam radiators at home in the fall when they'd first come on. When I was a kid. For a couple of hours there was this special smell. That's the *Kreutzer*. If I said that, first of all they wouldn't understand because you can't describe smells, and second they'd think I was crazy."

"Yes." Frescobaldi patted his hand. "Only another musician could understand. And not even all of them. Everybody takes everything so seriously these days."

"I'm serious," Claude said. "I mean it about smells."

"Of course. But to them it wouldn't sound serious. You know the story of Kreisler and Rachmaninoff playing the *Kreutzer*? At a big benefit?"

"No."

"They were very, very close friends. Kreisler lost his place in there where the violin goes pum, pum-pah pa-dum deedle deedle deedle. He forgot and began making it up. They'd played together so much Rachmaninoff knew how he would improvise, and instead of helping out he improvised a piano part to go along. You see! You are scandalized!"

"What happened?"

"Kreisler came over and whispered, 'Where am I? Where am I?' Rachmaninoff said, 'You're in Carnegie Hall.' "

They both laughed.

"He finally gave Kreisler a cue, of course, and they played right through."

"I can't believe it," Claude said.

"Nobody said a word." Frescobaldi folded his great hands on his chest. "I love those funny things that happen. How near chaos is! I have seen a conductor fall off the podium at the climax of *Tristan und Isolde.* Boom! Arms and legs flying in the air. I've seen a trombone slide sail into the viola section. In Austria once — Wagner again — a percussionist disappeared into his own kettle drum. It's wonderful! And nobody in the audience laughs but me!"

They accepted coffee from a white-jacketed porter.

"Kreisler was fun," Frescabaldi said in an expansive mood. "Not like that sourpuss Heifetz. For years Kreisler would play these little pieces — a Pugnani found in an old church, a Francoeur somebody discovered, a Padre Martini from an attic — and it turned out he wrote them all himself. Everybody was fooled, including the critics."

"But why would he do that? If they were good, wouldn't he want the credit?"

Frescobaldi shrugged. "Who knows? He was *méchant,* that one. I think he enjoyed fooling Heifetz and Zimbalist."

"It's amazing nobody caught on," Claude said.

"Not so amazing," Frescobaldi said. "Not really."

Waiting to go on, in the wings of Carnegie Hall, Claude leaned against the wall some distance behind Frescobaldi, alternately staring down at the tips of his own shoes and checking the violinist to see when he would go forward. Thus far Frescobaldi had stood motionless, like a great boulder, staring straight ahead. Claude sensed movement, behind and to his right. A stagehand creeping in the gloom to attend to some task. Claude waved him back. Finally Frescobaldi leaned forward on his toes, like a man going off a diving board, and propelled himself onstage. Claude followed into the growing applause.

Stage fright or no, it was always an especially charged moment. The dazzle of light over his shoulder, a whip of instantaneous brightness. The sense of exposure, as if walking into a giant x-ray machine. The sudden change of acoustics and the opening up of space, like being in the center of a rapidly expanding sphere. The blur of oval faces, pale in reflected light, two-dimensional paper masks rising in a low wave to the indistinctness of the back of the house. Dust motes glowing in the air over the stage. Utter darkness above.

The piano — its black strength so vast as to transcend its image — the piano waiting to enfold him. As he sits the x-rays disappear, canceled by a higher penumbra of power within which his body feels solid, warm, and lively to the business at hand. His mind is clear and already working. The music begins.

That afternoon he had met with Otto Levits when he tried the piano. (The stage at that time had not seemed a particularly remarkable place. Rather shabby, Claude had thought.) The piano was fine.

"Are you sure?" Levits asked. "I hear the one in Philly was not so good."

Surprised, because he couldn't remember telling anyone, Claude asked, "Where'd you hear that?"

"I know people. Relax, it wasn't in the papers. Aldo said you asked for a tuning and didn't get it."

"It wasn't a big deal," Claude said. "Anyway, this one is good. Better than good."

"Because all we have to do is go up the street and take you down to the basement. You can pick whatever you want."

"What basement?"

"Steinway. Up the street. Whatever you want, they'll bring it here, tune it, plenty of time for the concert. Free of charge."

"They do that?"

"Not for everybody. They already heard about you. They had someone in Philly. That's how I knew about the sharp treble. Aldo wasn't specific."

"Wow!"

"I told you word would get around."

"Yes, you did. You certainly did."

"Okay, we'll go with this one. The bench okay? Any adjustments?"

"I'm happy."

"Good. When my artists are happy, I'm happy." They climbed down from the stage. "Also, I'm glad to report something you already know. Aldo is happy. This is very important because it isn't always the case, sometimes, if you get my drift."

"He's been great to me," Claude said. "I like him."

In the office behind the box office they dealt with the matter of complimentary tickets. Most on Claude's short list had already been sent, but his mother, who hadn't wanted to come in the first place, relented if she could be assured a seat in the back row of the orchestra, next to an exit.

"This was easy," Levits said, handing him a pair. "The house is sold out. These people are delighted to sit in the tenth row instead of in back, so it's a trade. What is it with your mother? Is she claustrophobic?"

"No," Claude said. "I don't know. More like self-conscious. Shy."

"I see. Well, the seats are exactly what she asked for."

"Thanks."

Lady had not asked to visit his dressing room before the performance, which was just as well — there was barely enough room for Mr. Weisfeld, the only person he wanted around at this moment. Claude took off his street clothes while Weisfeld glanced at the newspaper.

"It looks like they really mean it about the el," he said. "Mrs. Keller already had an offer for her building."

"Is she going to sell? We've got all that stuff in there."

"Don't worry. *Never* is when she's going to sell."

Claude slipped the little wooden cross around his neck.

"What's that?" Weisfeld asked. "You're getting religious all of a sudden?"

"Just a good-luck piece. A maid gave it to me when I was a kid. I never figured out why." He touched it. "I wear it sometimes."

"You look good. Your muscles look good."

"I still do those exercises Franz showed me. The ones the maestro suggested. Plus I've added some. Every morning."

Weisfeld picked up Claude's dress shirt, gave it a couple of shakes, and held it up. Claude eased his arms into the sleeves. "How much time?"

"Plenty of time," Weisfeld said. "Bergman would sell, maybe. He talks about Florida. I've never understood the great appeal of Florida. So there's the beach, but what else?"

"I still can't quite believe this is happening."

"It's happening." Weisfeld now held his black jacket. He gave Claude a quick pat on the back as he put it on.

"I learned how to do this," Claude said, tying his bow tie. "No more clip-ons."

A sharp knock on the door, startling both of them. "Five minutes, Mr. Rawlings. Five minutes."

"I'll just sit here," Claude said, taking a folding chair. "I go sort of numb."

"Should I leave?"

"No, no." He reached out and touched Weisfeld's elbow. "It's like a nap or something, but I'm not sleeping. Wait with me."

Once again they seemed to levitate, picking up where they had left off in Philadelphia. For Claude, playing a particularly responsive and perfectly tuned piano, able, because of superior acoustics onstage, to hear Frescobaldi more clearly, picking up on the subtlest variations of timbre and texture, it seemed they had moved even closer, something he had not thought possible. It was not an effortless accord, however much it might have sounded so. Claude's concentration was so intense his shirt was soaked halfway through the *Spring* Sonata, while Frescobaldi's eyes seemed about to bug out of his head. But the power of the music in the abstract was especially strong, as if emanating from the very walls of the building. They were playing the music, minds, bodies, and souls stretched near to the limit, but it was also true that the music was playing them. A balancing act of excruciating fragility, but to Claude sweet beyond words, sweet beyond imagining.

During the encores Frescobaldi became exceptionally frisky. With the serious stuff out of the way — four beautiful sonatas in the bank, as it were — he let himself go with the flashy miniatures, showboating, adding some tricks and bravura effects just for the hell of it, out of high spirits.

He could hardly wait to get out of the wings for the last encore. "Let's do that thing of yours," he said abruptly.

"What?" Claude's mind began to spin.

"Those songs. Let's do number three."

"But we only played it once!" Had Frescobaldi suggested they ride out on the stage on bicycles, Claude could not have been more astonished. "It's too dangerous."

"Nonsense." The big man walked into the light.

Claude went instantly to the piano, stared down at the keys, and unconsciously covered his mouth with both hands.

"Ladies and gentlemen!" Frescobaldi shouted at the front of the stage. "For our last encore a charming little piece from a work in progress by my accompanist, Claude Rawlings." A large sweep of the arm and a short bow to Claude.

Applause.

Frescobaldi near him. "Remember the tempo?"

Claude nodded.

He played it almost without knowing what was happening. In Weisfeld's basement Frescobaldi had shown him some violin variations on the original melody, but now he left the melody almost entirely — swooping, skittering, looping around, throwing a spray of spiccato, flying staccato, and ricochet in all directions. He bowed near the bridge, he bowed over the fingerboard. He struck the strings with the stick. He made dozens of different sounds — from flute to banjo to something that actually sounded like the bleat of a lamb — all of it fitting together in a piece of musical architecture that dropped over the piano part as neatly as a cup on a saucer. Claude was astounded. It took him several moments to rise to the roar from the audience.

"For you, *caro,*" Frescobaldi said. "Forgive the liberties."

"It was incredible," Claude said. "Magic."

They took bows. They took many bows.

"This is real applause," Frescobaldi said in the wings. "They know when I say the last encore, I mean it."

Claude made his way to his dressing room, ambling almost, his jacket over his shoulder. He opened the door to see Weisfeld sitting on a folding chair, forearms on his knees, staring at the floor. Claude was about to say something, but then Weisfeld looked up, tears in his eyes.

"I was thinking back," Weisfeld said. He rose, averting his face. "Thinking back."

Claude dropped his jacket, took three steps forward, and embraced him, hugging hard.

"You played so beautifully," Weisfeld said. "It was splendid, splendid."

Holding him close, feeling Weisfeld's hands patting his back and then the back of his head, Claude said, "Aaron . . . Aaron." Breaking away, Weisfeld coughed into his fist and adopted a firmer tone. "I'm proud of you."

"And I'm proud of you," Claude said.

"So we're a couple of terrific guys."

"That's right."

"Toast of the town."

"Absolutely."

Weisfeld laughed. "Okay. I don't see a shower around here. Believe me, I'll be talking to the management." He pointed to the sink. "Wash the whole top of your body. Everything you can reach. You've been working hard and you are somewhat aromatic, if you don't mind my saying."

"Yes, sir."

Weisfeld went to the door. "Don't hurry," he said as he left, "they'll wait."

In the pandemonium of the green room Claude found Lady, her back against the wall, surveying the scene.

"Come with me," he said. "I'll get you some wine."

"God, it's loud in here." She wore a simple black silk dress, pearls, and pearl earrings. There was a natural flush of red on each of her high cheekbones.

Lady took a glass of white wine and Claude asked for ginger ale, drinking two of them straight down. "Did your parents come?"

"Mummy," Lady said, nodding to indicate Mrs. Powers across the room, in conversation with Anson Roeg. "Dear old Dad couldn't make it."

A stream of people came to shake Claude's hand, smile at Lady, and exchange a few words. The slender, graceful figure of Fredericks appeared. "Well done," he said, smiling. "Well done indeed. The Prokofiev was a particular treat." He turned to Lady. "So few pianists really *hear* Prokofiev."

Claude made the introductions, aware of Fredericks discreetly sizing her up, aware of his approval.

"Are you a musician, Miss Powers?"

"No, I'm afraid not." She gave a small laugh. "I don't think I quite *am* anything yet."

"On a quest, then," he said gently.

"Yes. That's it."

Claude had the feeling that something had transpired, but too quickly for him to catch.

Frescobaldi called from the center of the room. Time for photographs. The violinist kept talking to half a dozen people while the flashbulbs snapped. He held Claude against his broad hip, giving him a little shake now and then. "Smile," he whispered.

The crowd in front of them parted for a moment and Claude could see an open door, some people down a short corridor swaying back and forth. As his eyes adjusted from the dazzle, he could see Al standing in the crowd, waving his program to get Claude's attention.

"Sorry," Claude said, breaking away. He went straight through the door, ignoring the smattering of applause as he entered the corridor, and saw the look of relief on Al's face as he came to the velvet rope. Claude started to unhook it.

"She won't come back here." Al stayed Claude's hand. "She wants to go home, but I said it would hurt your feelings. Can you come out for just a second?"

"Didn't you get the passes?"

"Sure we did. But she ain't coming, Claude."

Claude was suddenly aware that everyone in the corridor was watching them, listening to their words, still as mice. He reached for the brass hook, but the usher beat him to it.

"That was mighty fine music," Al said as they went out into the orchestra. "I sure did enjoy it."

Emma was standing at the side of the front entrance. A few stragglers turned to look at Claude, one of them even stumbling on the steps to the lobby. Emma clapped her hands lightly as Claude approached.

"I heard everything, every note," she said. "It was terrific."

"Won't you come back and meet everybody?"

"Can't do it," she said. "Got to go home. Now, you know that fiddler upstaged you. Nice to see a big man that graceful, but he got to move around with that fancy stuff while you're stuck at the piano."

Claude smiled. "Nothing I can do about that."

"Your bows were good. Just like we did it in vaudeville." She reached for Al's arm. "We gotta go."

"All right, then," Al said. "Mighty fine music."

"Thanks for coming," Claude called as they descended to the sidewalk and disappeared.

The concert in Boston had gone well. Perhaps with not quite the same degree of verve as Philadelphia and New York, Claude thought, but the reviews had been no less enthusiastic. After a morning of interviews, including one for radio, Claude and Frescobaldi sat in the lounge at Logan airport, waiting for the violinist's flight to London to be called. A bottle of red wine (Mouton-Rothschild) stood on the table between them. It was the second. Frescobaldi, having been in a melancholy mood, had polished off the first almost singlehanded.

"That is a wonderful American expression," the big man said. "Being blue, having the blues. I get like that sometimes after a tour. Even a little one like this. Blue."

"It's a twelve-bar jazz form too. One, four, one five, four, one."

"The strength of simplicity." Frescobaldi looked out at the wide gray expanse, the airplanes moving, small figures making hand signals. "I love music, but sometimes I worry it is not enough."

"Not enough for what?" Claude asked.

"The violin is part of me. It grows out of my fingers." He wiggled his left hand. "I make music, and sometimes I think, oh, they give me tricks, they give me very hard tricks and I do them and everybody goes crazy. I love it when I do it, but when I get blue I worry." He drank some wine. "When I get very dark blue I think, well, it is just notes. Notes, lines, fancy patterns — like a game. A big game for grownups." He shook his head.

"You sure don't play that way," Claude said. "I can feel the inside of you when you play."

"That is nice, very nice."

"It's true!"

Frescobaldi rubbed his face. "Maybe I play too much the same things. They make you do it when you are famous. Years and years the same things, it gets harder." He looked up sharply. "Next time I will insist! I will insist! What can they do?"

"That sounds like a good idea." Claude spoke softly, aware of the oddness of the situation — himself appearing to give any advice at all to this great man — and yet deeply flattered by the intimacy.

"*Basta,*" Frescobaldi said, pulling at his collar. "You are good to come out here with me."

"My train doesn't leave for hours."

"*Dio mio,*" Frescobaldi murmured as a tall oriental girl walked by. "*Visto che casce.*"

"I can't thank you enough," Claude said. "I know you took a risk with me. You could have gotten anybody."

"Not so big," Frescobaldi said. "After the first day I knew we were sympathetic as players, with the music. So it was just were you strong enough for the pressure. Fredericks said yes, and he was right. Ah! They are calling my plane."

They walked to the gate, Frescobaldi carrying his violin case. When he reached into his breast pocket for his ticket another piece of paper fluttered to the floor. Claude picked it up and held it out.

"That is for you," Frescobaldi said. "I notated all that stuff I did with your little piece. Good tricks for you to remember when you write for strings. Don't forget to send me the others."

"Thank you, sir."

Frescobaldi shook his hand. "We will play again." Then he walked through the gate and was gone.

Claude got into New York at nine that night. He took a cab and asked the driver to drop him off at the corner of Eighty-fourth and Third. Walking up the street, he thought he saw a figure on the stoop of his building — a motionless shape under the streetlight. As he approached the shape became human, a woman, carved in stone, half her face in deep shadow. He was three steps away when the head turned.

"Lady!" he cried.

"There you are at last," she said, her eyes glassy.

"What's wrong?" He sat beside her — noticing as he put down his suitcase that she had one, too — and put his arm over her shoulders. "How long have you been here?"

"I don't know. A while." She didn't respond to his hug, but sat stiffly, looking at the sidewalk.

"Are you okay?" He felt a slight thrill of fear.

"Not really." She stood up abruptly. "We better go inside."

Mystified, he worked the locks and got her and the suitcases into the room. She went to the single armchair and sat down. He stood in the middle of the room trying, without success, to read her expression.

"What's happened?" Claude asked. "Something's happened."

"Can I stay here?"

"Can you — yes, of course. Of course you can. What is this?"

"As I walked out the door I vowed to myself I would never set foot in that house again. And I won't."

"Okay." He sat on the edge of the bed. "It sounds extreme, but okay. Are you going to tell me?"

"Mummy was trying to help. I really think she was. It was in the living room. She'd talked about the concert, and meeting everybody — especially that woman with the funny name, the writer — and he just drank his Scotch as always, but I could see his face was getting redder than usual. She said you'd played very well, and everybody thought so, even Muffy Peters, who only goes to those things because she's on some board or something."

"When was this? Tonight?"

She nodded. "Mummy always clips things out of the papers, you know. Stuff from the society page, or gardening tips, menus. Sometimes she reads them aloud. It's one of the rituals after dinner, when they're in the living room and she's at that little secretary and can't even see him. So she starts reading a review of the concert from the *New York Times,* picking out nice things about you, and I even tried to interrupt her because he was squirming around. When she started in on the *Herald Tribune* review he just exploded out of his chair and stormed out. He practically ran up the stairs and the dog started barking, and Mummy was all in a dither."

"Well, so what?" he said, exasperated. "I mean, so he storms out. It's his house."

"No it isn't, actually," she said. "But that wasn't it. He came down again."

At this point she stopped, her body taking on that odd stiffness again. She looked out the window.

Claude waited.

She sighed. "He had a file. Pretty thick." Again she paused. "You see, what he did was, he hired a firm of private investigators." She turned to look at him.

"What for?" he asked.

"To find out about you."

He had no reaction at first except one of surprise. "Me?" He gave an incredulous laugh. "Me?"

"We were both so stunned we just sat there and he read aloud, the way Mummy had from the papers. He skipped around and it didn't make a lot of sense until he got to the analysis part. 'Analysis and Conclusions.' "

A worm of nausea seemed to waken in his gut, to waken and slowly move through his body. He wanted to run from the room, run from the building before she could say another word, but he did not move.

"How he could do something so sneaky and shameful . . ." She shook her head, words failing.

"A report on me," he said, his voice neutral.

"Well, sort of. I assume they couldn't find anything bad about you or he would have read it. It was more background. Your mother — they use legal language, police language — cohabiting with a Negro male, Al Johnson, born 1911, that kind of thing."

"You knew that," he said.

"Yes, but I never told them, obviously."

"You didn't?"

"Al Johnson having fled the state of Georgia in 1934 to escape an indictment on a charge of assault and battery. Warrant no longer valid, statute of limitations." Her usual soft, throaty voice underwent a change as she quoted the language, becoming brittle with scorn, and Claude could suddenly hear both her father and her own disdain for her father. The information about Al did not particularly surprise him.

"Emma Rawlings," she went on, "under investigation by the House Un-American Activities Committee for Communist ties. Uncooperative. Known associate of Gerhardt Eisler. Something about an assault-and-battery charge against her too, dropped after three days served in jail."

"Jesus," he said, and then began to feel himself go numb — a contraction of his senses, the room growing dimmer, her voice more distant — as he sensed what was coming.

"Oh, Claude." She rose from the chair, came over, and knelt at his feet. "It said there was no record of your birth, or any marriage, or your father's identity."

"I see."

"And my father said —"

"Let's stop now." Claude touched his head reflexively. "I don't want to hear anymore right now."

"I feel so ashamed," she said, her forehead on his knees.

"Let's just wait for a while."

Nothing more was said, and eventually they went to bed, moving like sleepwalkers. Lady was exhausted and went to sleep as her head hit the pillow. Claude stared at the ceiling, heart pounding, inundated by a swirl of conflicting emotions throwing him this way and that like a leaf in the wind. He tried to calm himself by thinking how well he had done on the tour, but then the worm would move, the old worm of nausea that had been there forever, now reasserting itself. It was not that he thought the question of his possible illegitimacy was all-import-ant — he knew that many great men had been born out of wedlock — but rather a sense of shame that he didn't know the truth. He felt hemmed in by his ignorance. He experienced flashes of fear, even of terror, as the night spun on, that what he did not know about himself (the very state of not knowing) might overpower what he did know, that his identity might be stripped away in the process.

And down there with the worm was a strange desire to embrace the worst. The old man was stupid but he was right: Claude was an impostor, dishonest, shameful, his ignorance an elaborate device to give him the freedom to lie, to pretend he was like everyone else. He writhed in Obromowitz's bed until dawn, when he got up, dressed, and went out.

He ran the few blocks to the old apartment, made a tremendous racket going down the iron stairs, and pounded on the door with his fist. He waited. He kicked the door and pounded again. The very familiarity of his immediate surroundings — the chipped bricks, the drain under his feet, the heavy door only now touched by a stray ray of feeble sunlight, the damp, musky smell, the grime on every surface — all this for some reason infuriated him. He pounded until the door opened and there was Al, in shorts and a sleeveless undershirt, his face puffy with sleep. His jaw dropped in astonishment as Claude pushed past him.

"Where is she?"

Al looked at him for a moment and then called out. "Emma, it's Claude."

Claude watched the bedroom door until it slowly opened and Em-ma emerged, her large body wrapped in a plaid bathrobe. She did not look at Claude, but first moved to the kitchenette and got behind the counter. Her expression, when she raised her eyes, seemed a mixture of pain, sadness, and a kind of stoic resolve. He had the eerie feeling that she'd known he was coming.

They stood frozen in their places for some time. Claude's heavy breathing gradually subsided.

"No more bullshit, now," he said. "I want the truth."

She sat down on a stool and gazed over his head, silent as Buddha.

Al took a step forward. "How 'bout some coffee, Claude?"

"No." He stared at his mother. "You're going to tell me. I should have made you tell me a long time ago."

"Tell you what?" she said.

"Goddamn it! No more bullshit." He advanced to the counter and slammed down both his fists. She did not flinch, but stared straight ahead, rubbing her upper lip with her forefinger as if working out a puzzle.

"What's done is done," she said.

"Were you married? Or was it like" — he swept his arm to indicate the apartment — "this?"

"I was married."

"Then why . . . ," he began.

"I married Henry Rawlings in Toronto, Canada, two days before he shipped out."

"Canada!"

"He was Canadian."

"What . . . why . . ." In his surprise and confusion he stumbled over his words. "Why didn't you tell me this? Who was he? Did he have any family? Maybe there are people up there —"

She interrupted him. "I met him in show business. He had no family. It was very quick, and to tell you the truth I didn't know much about him. We were kids. The war was on."

Claude considered this, glancing at her, unwilling to believe he was getting the whole story. Something in her eyes revealed a deep stubbornness, an obduracy. "Well," he said, challenging her, "I can go to Toronto. I can find out who he was and what happened to him, since you don't seem to know or even care."

"That would be a waste of time," she said.

"I've got plenty of time."

She glanced at Al.

Claude jumped. "Leave him out of it! This has nothing to do with him." He turned to see Al, looking thoughtful, nodding quietly while fixing Emma with his eyes. Claude did not know how to interpret this gesture. He swung back to his mother. "There'll be military records."

"The thing is," Emma said, and paused, her hands coming together on the counter, "you've got the name, but I can't really say if he was your father or not." Again she glanced very swiftly at Al. "I don't know. My guess is, he wasn't."

After a moment of paralysis, his mind simply not working, he began a kind of mental free fall, turning and spinning without direction. He sank onto a stool and tried to collect himself.

"You mean . . . you mean . . . ," he said.

"I was a showgirl, Claude." There was the faintest catch in her voice. "I can't tell you who your father was."

For a long time the room was silent. Then Al moved forward, slipped behind Emma, giving her a pat on the shoulder as he passed, and began to make coffee. His back was to Claude.

"You knew about this?" Claude asked Al.

"Yeah. We got no secrets."

"Well good for you," Claude said bitterly. "You're a lucky man." He stared at his mother and saw a tear forming in her eye. He wanted to strike her. A ridiculous tear, he thought, a useless, mawkish, cheap tear. What he did was get up and leave without another word.

Claude and Lady holed up in Obromowitz's room for three days. Lady was serious about not going back to her parents' house, though she'd called her mother to tell her she was safe and well, and not to worry. Claude still thought she was being extreme — something made him uneasy, perhaps the abruptness of her decision — but he said nothing directly.

They talked all day. They talked having hamburgers at Prexy's. They talked in the delicatessen buying cornflakes. They talked late into the night, side by side in bed. They were young and preoccupied with the future, with the great open expanse of life that lay ahead of them. Claude was excited with his prospects in music. He wanted to play, but above all now, suddenly he saw it clearly, to compose. There was much work to be done. He confessed that he knew he might be fooling himself, that there was no way to know if he had the talent to write great music, but he was going to try.

Lady revealed a great deal of ambition, but in the abstract. She did not know what she would do, but whatever it was, it would be *real*. She expressed scorn for her mother's volunteer work, scorn for her father's make-believe work, and scorn for what she took to be a retreat from reality on the part of practically the whole upper class. She confessed that in many ways she had felt like a prisoner most of her life. What she would work *at* involved, in her mind, choosing among what seemed to her an almost infinite number of possibilities. She was quite sure she could do anything she set her mind to, but she was vexed by the fact that choosing one possibility precluded the others.

The decision to get married did not occur in a single moment, but rather emerged gradually. Once, when they had gone on an early morning walk near the Hollifield campus, a bank of heavy fog had swallowed them. They'd leaned on the top rail of a split-rail fence, both of them silent, entranced by the nacreous softness. Suddenly they'd heard hoofbeats, and then, so close they both fell back, there was the massive head and neck of a white horse looming over them, floating in the mist.

Lying in Obromowitz's bed with Lady's head on his shoulder, Claude said, "Well, it's good I'm going to be making more money now. We're going to need money."

"Money's no problem," she said sleepily.

"Your father and mother . . . ," he began.

"I have money of my own. Lots of it."

He thought this over for a minute. "That's good. As long as we have enough. There's no romance to being poor, I can tell you."

She shifted her head and he could feel the warmth of her breath on his nipple. "My great-grandfather left me a trust fund."

"I know about those. That's how I got the Bechstein," he said.

"Well, there's five million dollars in mine," she said with a yawn. "Can't touch the capital, though. Only the income."

They were married the following week in a civil ceremony at the Municipal Building. There were no guests.

PART THREE

17

FIVE YEARS LATER he awoke to the sound of Lady placing the breakfast tray beside him on the wide bed, on her side, which she had vacated as usual an hour or two earlier. Eggs, bacon, toast, tea, and the *New York Times*. He pulled himself up to lean against the headboard while she went over and sat on the window seat, looking out at the tiny garden. Slightly hung over, he rubbed his eyes. "What time is it?"

"Ten," she said. "Don't forget you've got the doctor's appointment at eleven-thirty."

"Right." He began to eat. Years ago, when they had first moved into the townhouse, she had brought him breakfast in bed to celebrate their first day of residence. For some reason she had continued the practice, always getting up before him no matter how late they retired. She never sent Esmeralda, the maid, but always brought it herself.

"What did you think of them?" she asked. The previous night they'd had a young poet and his mildly raucous wife to dinner. Everyone had drunk a good deal of wine except Lady.

"Very Harvard."

"He works awfully hard on his charm."

"Hmm." He sipped his tea.

"And he name-drops. I hate that."

"Well." Claude waved his hand. "He's clever anyway. And she was fun."

"Poor thing. He's half Jewish and her parents still give her a hard time."

"Fuck 'em," Claude said.

"Exactly." Lady had not seen her own parents since before her marriage. She occasionally talked to her mother on the telephone. Claude thought he'd seen her father getting into a distant cab on Lexington Avenue a year ago, but he hadn't been sure. It did not seem extraordinary to him that people could live within a mile of one another on the East Side of Manhattan and never bump into each other. In New York City it was possible — indeed, it required no particular effort — to live privately, to choose, if one was rich, precisely how much of the outside world one wanted to deal with. In the case of Lady and Claude, that was not very much.

For Lady the house was a protected oasis of domesticity, safety, and stasis. From it — especially in the first years — she had planned her careful forays outside. The committee to re-elect the junior senator. Assistant executive director of the Prison Commission. Assistant stage manager of a small off-Broadway production. She had worked in publishing, law, politics, and photography, always getting paid (no matter how little) and always leaving after a few months. These jobs were in the nature of experiments. A testing of the waters. After each she would repair to the house. Claude thought it slightly odd, whether she was working or during one of the increasingly long periods of not working, that she had never invited to the house anyone with whom she had been professionally involved. The house was off limits to the people she'd worked with, while at the same time open to those who had worked with Claude. He'd thought this might be an expression of extreme modesty on her part, but in truth he was so preoccupied with himself and his music, he didn't give the matter much attention.

Now, as he noticed her attire — the familiar modest dark green suit, white blouse, single strand of pearls — he realized it must be a school day. She taught art appreciation at Spence, her alma mater, twice a week. Her profile caught the gray light from the garden, and he was struck yet again by her beauty. A calmness, a mysterious repose that, paradoxically, he often felt the urge to disturb.

She got up from the window seat. "I'll be back at five," she said, and left the room.

He read the paper for a while, got out of bed, took a shower, and dressed. Gray flannel slacks, a pale yellow Brooks Brothers button-down shirt, and a cashmere sport jacket custom made by a tailor on Madison Avenue. As he brushed his hair a snippet of a melodic phrase popped to the front of his mind. Three notes and a passing tone, out of nowhere. He instantly recognized where the phrase wanted to go in the piano piece he was writing. Standing perfectly still, staring at the mirror but seeing nothing, he worked the phrase into the music in his mind, noting with a rush of pleasure how it connected to the other lines, how it solved certain problems, how it sparked the rhythm.

Recently he'd had a talk with Weisfeld about this phenomenon — the sensation of being a receiver, of the stuff arriving as if by cosmic special delivery. It was both tremendously exciting and slightly scary. "It's good, it's good," Weisfeld had said. "Practically everyone describes this. Who cares where it comes from? Let somebody else worry about that. And don't worry about controlling it. When it happens, it happens. Don't force it. Use it" — he held up a finger — "if it's good."

"It always seems good," Claude had said. "Better than anything I could think up myself."

"So?" Weisfeld had shrugged. "What can I tell you?"

Claude put down the hairbrush and went out into the hall, taking the stairs two at a time as he descended one flight and pushed open the door to the music room. He sat down at the Baldwin and went to work, knowing he had only half an hour but unable to resist.

In the event, he was late for the doctor.

"I'm sorry," he said as he sat down. "I got into something. I really should get a wristwatch."

Dr. Maxwell was a cheerful, roly-poly urologist of about fifty. He had seen Claude appear in concert several times, and confessed to a lifelong love of music, particularly opera. He was the leader of an amateur recorder quartet that he had formed with some of his medical colleagues. During his first examination of Claude's genitals he had abstractedly hummed an aria from *Tosca* while palpating a testicle. Now he sat down behind his desk, opened a file, and then stared off into the middle distance.

"It's too bad we don't have a history," he said.

Claude noticed Dr. Maxwell's uncharacteristically blank expression. "I never saw a doctor till I got to college, as I said." He waited, beginning to grow uneasy.

Dr. Maxwell tapped the file with the tips of his fingers. "Well, first of all, from the anatomical point of view everything is completely normal.

No blockages, no stray tubes or bad valves. Normal, normal. You're in remarkably good health generally, as well, so that's something to be thankful for."

"I get the feeling I'm about to hear something I'm not going to like," Claude said.

Dr. Maxwell nodded. "You are not producing live sperm cells, I'm sorry to say."

Claude stared into the man's steady gray eyes. "What does that mean? Why not?"

"It means there are no live sperm cells. None at all. Why? I'm not sure." He leaned forward and closed the file. "But that's the reason Lady hasn't gotten pregnant."

Claude's thoughts suddenly fragmented, skittering off in all directions, fading, slanting, or bouncing back on themselves. After a moment the spasm subsided and he realized he was still looking at the doctor. "Can we fix it? Is there some kind of treatment?"

Dr. Maxwell shook his head. "I can only guess at the cause. There are any number of viral agents — mumps, orchitis, undulant fever, for instance — and since we lack a medical history . . ." He shrugged and made a gesture in the air with his hands. "There are chemical agents, certain toxins. In fact, there are a lot of ways it could have happened. The best bet is an undiagnosed childhood illness from the right viral group. You might have had swollen testicles — there's no atrophy, by the way — or then again maybe not. Fever, chills, nausea almost certainly."

"You mean all this time I've . . ."

"I imagine so," Dr. Maxwell said. "I can't say with certainty, but it seems most probable. The trouble is, there's not much the sperm cells can tell us. Their only abnormality is the fact that they're not alive. Spermatogenesis itself is a process we don't understand very well."

Claude sat silently, staring at the closed file. He could see his own name on the tab. Part of his mind was trying to let the information in, and part was trying to keep it out. He felt a floating sensation, and simultaneously Dr. Maxwell seemed to be receding in space, like a trick shot in the movies. Claude watched the doctor's lips moving.

"Let me say again that in every other regard you are completely normal. The aspermia has no effect on your libido, your sexual life, desire, performance, and so on. You can and should consider yourself the same as other men, because that is the case — emotionally, anatomically you are the same. However, you cannot have children. You must reconcile yourself to that fact."

"Yes, I understand," Claude said.

"It can take getting used to, but my patients — I mean those in the same situation — have done well. Particularly those with a passionate interest in their work, like yourself. I suppose it helps them retain a sense of proportion. They tend not to dwell on things."

As the man went on talking, Claude gradually came back to himself. He barely heard what was said. Finally Dr. Maxwell walked him out to the door. At the last minute he grabbed Claude's elbow and caught his eye. "Mr. Rawlings," he said, "do not blame yourself for this." He waited for his words to sink in. "This is fate," he said, "as impersonal as the stars."

Claude found himself walking along the street without any clear idea of where he wanted to go. He wound up at the Ninety-first Street entrance to Central Park and proceeded to the reservoir, where he sat down on a bench and watched three pigeons scuttling at his feet.

That his body had betrayed him was a surprise, certainly, and yet there was something familiar in it, something that harked back to childhood and his anger at being thin and weak, his resentment at being trapped in his ridiculous skin. He had wanted nothing more than to transcend his body, to leave it behind through love and music. He had allowed himself to believe he was succeeding, but now, in an almost sinister fashion, hidden at a microscopic level, his old enemy again pulled him down. The gross, mute, stupid machine of his body was once again filling him with shame.

In years to come Claude's sterility would mean different things to him, rising and falling in importance according to where he found himself at various stages in his life, forcing him into tortuous philosophical speculations he might otherwise never have entertained, sometimes creating in him an almost unbearable sense of isolation, but sometimes, oddly enough, lending him a near-mystical appreciation of the value of life, of its unspeakable beauty. But for the moment, sitting on the park bench at the age of twenty-six, he was preoccupied with the practical.

Lady's announcement some months earlier that she had ceased using her diaphragm for the past year had stunned him. He could not understand why she'd kept it a secret, why he had not been included in the decision to have a child. He'd resented it more than he'd allowed himself to admit — not only for the fact itself, but because it tied in with other ways in which she kept him at a distance. For all her ambition she was a rather fearful person, he'd discovered, with a tendency to build elaborate defenses for herself before they were necessary. Silence, privacy, and occasionally secrecy were second nature to her. She could not share her sense of what was happening to her with him, could not reveal her sense of herself to him, and as a result he felt she didn't trust him.

It was confusing because he believed that she loved him, and if it was a guarded, somewhat timid love, it was nevertheless all that he knew, with nothing to compare it to. In every way that was possible for her she was supportive, generous, and as caring toward him as she might have been toward her own child. She made so few demands on him he felt almost lonely.

Educated by the movies, he had believed love would conquer all. It was not easy for him to give up that hope. But in their lovemaking she retained that distant air of an observer, of someone at a slight remove, never holding his lust against him but never understanding it either. He was, perforce, and without knowing it, a clumsy lover, utterly preoccupied with his own anxiety. The most common themes in his dreams of Lady were these: he would speak but have no voice; he would be in a position of great danger, but she could not discern the danger and hence remained calm and undisturbed; he would play the piano for her and she would try to change the music by turning the dial of the radio. In almost all his dreams she exhibited a kind of nonmalevolent obduracy against which any efforts of his own were futile. In his dreams he was a man beating his head against a brick wall, and knowing it.

He got up from the bench, the pigeons scattered, and he walked along the path. The fact that he could not have a child forced him now to think about why she had wanted one in the first place. To move deeper into life, perhaps. She had been unable to find any kind of work to which she could commit herself, and despite her silence he had glimpsed a certain amount of anguish and frustration. She might understandably consider motherhood as good work, something she could control and do well. (Had she not mothered him?) Nor would it be out of character for her to think of it as largely a private, feminine matter, particularly since the greater share of the responsibility would redound to her rather than him. Although Claude had not been privy to the steps she'd gone through on the way to her decision, he nevertheless recognized it as an act of courage. She had been driven very deep into herself, doubtless deeper than ever before, to come to such a point, to take what must surely seem to her the most profound risk of her life. And of course she'd done it alone.

Her hand flew to her mouth and her eyes widened when he told her. She reached back and grabbed the mantel of the fireplace.

"Some childhood illness, he thinks," Claude said from the couch. "I'm perfectly normal in every other respect."

"My God," she whispered. "Out of the blue like this. Is he sure?"

"Oh, yes. Quite sure." He looked down at the floor and shook his head. "I'm sorry."

She was beside him in an instant, her arm around him. "You poor thing. There's nothing to be sorry for. It isn't your fault."

"That's what he said."

"Of course he did."

"It feels . . . strange," he said. "I mean knowing. I've been this way half my life probably, but now I know, and I sort of wish I didn't." Even as she comforted him he felt a twinge of fear — another element added to keep them apart — and he got up to pace the carpet. She had passed her tests months ago.

"Do you want a drink?" she suggested. "I think we should have a drink."

"We can't pretend this doesn't change things," he said.

But she was out the door and on her way down to Esmeralda in the kitchen. He didn't know if she'd heard him. He didn't know if he wanted her to hear.

The matter was dropped. For some months there was quiet around the house, a feeling of marking time as they moved through their routines. Claude kept busy with his writing and his preparations for an upcoming chamber music recital. Lady puttered around, worked at her desk upstairs, and enrolled in some classes at the New School. When she gently introduced the idea of adoption one morning after bringing him his tray, he found himself nodding and agreeing that it might be something to look into. He felt he could hardly do otherwise. His hope was that it might be no more than a passing fancy, something she needed to cling to at the time and would release when she was strong enough.

But one afternoon he came home and found her having tea with her grandfather, Senator Barnes. The old man got up with a smile to shake hands.

"Good to see you, Claude. Lady tells me you're doing a concert up at Columbia next month."

"That's right. Schubert."

"Well, I'll have to try to make that. It would be a treat."

"I hope you can, sir."

Lady fussed nervously with the china and poured Claude a cup of tea, placing it on the table so that, when he sat, he faced both of them.

The senator was getting on in years, but with his clear, intelligent, penetrating eyes, his air of physical vitality, and his deep voice he still seemed larger than life to Claude. There was a vibrancy to the man's image, as if he were packed into himself, as if the specific gravity of his body were higher than that of ordinary men.

Lady glanced up as she passed Claude his cup. "We've been talking about adoption," she said.

Taken aback, Claude busied himself with his spoon. He was aware of the senator watching him. "Right," he said.

"Grandpa knows a lot, as it happens," she said.

"That's good," Claude said. "That's lucky."

"I helped Linda with the Heuval Foundation years ago," the senator said. "One thing led to another and I wound up involved with a smaller operation up in Larchmont. Very dedicated people, wonderful people. Just the right sort of organization."

"It's the kind of thing . . . ," Lady began. "I mean, the way it's set up, the risk is minimized."

"There is always risk," the senator said, looking at Claude. "I'm sure you both understand that." His voice was gentle.

There was silence as Esmeralda arrived with a plate of shortbread and small crustless cucumber sandwiches. She placed them on the table and left. No one touched them. As much as he admired the old man, Claude felt uneasy. The degree of seriousness in the discussion seemed premature, since he and Lady had not really talked about adoption at any length. It seemed that she was ahead of him, assuming he would somehow just come along, moved by the forward progress of events. She herself was nervous, slightly trembly, in this strategy, which he took as a warning to keep his misgivings to himself.

"But Lady," Senator Barnes said, "I want you to think about something."

She looked up at him.

"Let me speak as your grandfather now." He paused, and as a musician Claude could appreciate the timing. "You're thinking of starting a family, you two young people, and that is a noble enterprise. The future lies ahead of you, right you are, but I wonder if it's wise to fail to connect it to the past. I wonder if that's starting off on the firmest possible footing."

For one horrible instant Claude thought this was going to be yet another, albeit gentler, approach to the question of his own origins, but then he recognized that Lady was in fact the target.

"Do you mean . . . ," she started.

"I mean that this estrangement with your parents has gone on too long. Linda told me the whole story years ago. It was a shocking mess, of course, and Ted behaved badly. But I'm concerned that things might get set in stone here simply out of inertia." He gave her his full attention, watching her face closely, as if gauging precisely the right amount of pressure to apply. "Courage is called for now, it seems to me. Family is too important, Lady."

She said, almost under her breath, "If anyone needs a lecture on courage, it's him." Meaning her father.

The senator gave a little nod and sighed. "Well, perhaps he's learned something." He shifted his gaze to Claude. "Would it be intrusive of me to ask your thoughts on the matter?"

"Not at all," Claude said. "I've deferred to Lady, and I'll keep on doing that. At the same time, she knows I've always felt some doubts — I mean, this way everything just stays. Sort of frozen."

"I take your point," the old man said, tactfully leaving it at that.

Claude realized he wanted the senator's approval — as if it would work against the ill will of his in-laws — wanted to be included in the steady warmth that seemed a function of his strength. It was childish, surely, but in the presence of the senator he felt the quiet glow of decency he associated with the image of Spencer Tracy.

Lady stared into her teacup. She surprised both of them by suddenly saying "Shit" in a calm tone while tapping her toe on the floor.

"If it's your father you're after," the old man said, as if nothing had happened, "I can tell you it's your mother who hurts the most. She misses you."

"I talk to her."

"A telephone call every couple of months? Come now, Lady."

She sighed and leaned back.

"I wish you would consider Christmas this year."

"Oh, God," she groaned.

"If I can tell her you're thinking about it, I believe it would be a good start."

"Is it still the same?" she asked.

"Oh, yes. Eggnog at the Powerses', dinner at the Fisks'. Please do give it some thought, dear. It would mean a lot to me."

"Are you awake?" she whispered.

"Yes." It was three in the morning. He'd been watching the play of shadows on the ceiling cast by the streetlight through the branches of the tree outside.

"Me too," she said.

"Tell me about the place in Larchmont."

"He swings a lot of weight there. He can cut through the red tape. Otherwise it can take years and years, you know. A million forms, histories, interviews, and then you wait forever."

"What did you mean about risk?"

"They're very careful. It's a private organization so they can use their own procedures, and apparently they're very good at making a match."

"You mean the child and the people adopting?"

"It's only babies. The mother has the baby right there on the premises. She keeps it for four days — something about the health of the infant — and then gives it up. So you get a four-day-old baby."

"But what's this about a match?"

"Oh, you know. Background, religion, education — class, I suppose. The mother is supposed to be someone like me, similar to me. Grandpa says they're very sophisticated about that stuff."

"What about the father?"

"Oh, sure," she said quickly. "Somebody about your age who went to college, maybe even artistic."

He gave a short, bitter laugh. "Irony of ironies."

She rolled toward him and propped her head on her hand.

"I know," she said. "But with Grandpa handling it nobody's going to get into all that. It doesn't matter. It won't even come up. He guaranteed it."

"He's a thoughtful man," Claude said evenly.

"He's a sweetie, a real sweetie."

"And he wasn't a senator all those years for nothing."

"What do you mean?"

"He makes deals."

"Oh, it isn't really a deal. He'd do it even if I didn't see my parents."

"But you're going to see them, aren't you." It wasn't a question.

"I suppose so. It makes sense in a way. After all, they'd be the grandparents." She put her head back and looked up at the ceiling. "There's one scary thing, though, about the way they do it at Larchmont. We have to see her. Only for a minute, but the mother has to actually pass the baby over into my arms. We don't have to talk, but she has to give it to me herself."

"Jesus," he said.

"You can do that, can't you?"

"I guess. If we decide to go ahead."

They lay in silence for some time. Then she reached for his hand under the covers. "Please don't say no, Claude. Please, please." She squeezed his hand so tightly it hurt.

A week later she gave him some papers to sign, and he signed them.

Whenever Claude went to Juilliard he got lost. The layout of the place baffled him — halls stretching off in all directions, elevators that went up two floors, or three, or four, according to some mysterious plan, room numbers that made no sense — and always crowds of people rushing amid the muted cacophony of sounds from the practice rooms. It made him dizzy.

He went into the men's room and there was Fredericks standing at the urinal. Claude took the basin two over and said, "Good. I could probably never have found his office."

Fredericks shook himself delicately and zipped up. "It's right around the corner. He won't be back today."

"Does this place sometimes seem like a madhouse to you?"

"Ah, well." Fredericks smiled. "Students. They're like bees. They swarm. And everything is overcrowded."

They left the men's room and made their way to the small office, which was so filled with books and scores there was barely room for them to sit on either side of the desk. A portrait of Brahms hung on the wall.

"So," Fredericks said, "all goes well?"

"The orchestral suite I sent to Rochester got an honorable mention." He took a deep breath. "Three years now, and the best I've done is one third prize and some honorable mentions. It's depressing." He picked at the edge of the desk with a fingernail. "It's gotten to the point that I don't really want to send stuff out, but Otto says I should."

"Otto is right."

"But what's the point if I don't get to hear it?"

Fredericks swiveled in his chair to face the small window. "You know, when you were a kid I was struck by your patience. You had great patience studying piano."

"Did I? It didn't feel like that." Claude thought for a moment. "Of course, I always felt progress. I knew I was getting better bit by bit. Composing isn't like that. Every time I write something it's like going back to square one."

"Maybe that's not so bad. Maybe that's the way it has to be."

"Am I getting better?"

"What do you mean by better?"

"Now you sound like Weisfeld," Claude said.

"You've worked with progressively larger forms. Your string writing, in fact all your section writing, is getting more sophisticated. From the technical point of view, certainly you're getting better. How can you doubt it?"

Claude heard the impatience in Fredericks's voice and felt himself flush. He knew he should drop it, but something made him go on. "It's depressing," he said again.

"Maybe you need a change. Go work with Nadia Boulanger in Paris. That can be arranged, I think."

Claude shook his head. "My wife," he said limply. He did not mention the stories he'd heard about Madame Boulanger: her autocratic behavior, her dress codes, her need for constant flattery. He hadn't liked the sound of it. (Claude was unaware that he'd become more than a bit spoiled by his very comfortable life, the attentions of Weisfeld, Levits, and Fredericks, and his status as a "hot" young performer.) And New York seemed the center of the world. Had he not met Samuel Barber? Gian Carlo Menotti (at a party where, to Claude's intense embarrassment, the British poet Stephen Spender had made a pass at him)? Had he not been to dinner more than once at Leonard Bernstein's? Leaving seemed unthinkable. "It just seems to me I should be doing better."

"I wish you could hear the sound of your voice," Fredericks said.

Claude looked up, momentarily nonplused.

"Look," Fredericks said, "composing serious music is an act of faith. You can't *expect* anything, that's childish. Do it for its own sake, and if that's too hard, well then, don't do it." He put his hand out in the air, palms up. "Send the stuff out, but for God's sake don't sit around waiting for the phone to ring." He leaned back.

"I know, I know," Claude said.

"If you care so much about the competitions, you should be writing twelve-tone. Are you still so naive you expect justice? Look at Bartók. Of course he's a difficult man, but he makes barely enough to feed himself. Think about Béla when you feel like complaining." Aware that he might have gone too far — Claude's face was frozen in shock — Fredericks softened his tone. "I thought you were past this."

"Past what? It seems natural enough to me."

"Sure it's natural. It's also not very important. What you are looking for is authentication, Claude. But you're looking outside, to the system, and that's the wrong place to look. Bad music gets played every day and good music gets ignored. Everybody knows that. Forget about authentication. When it comes to writing music, all you can do is sign on for a way of life, and do the work. Do the work for its own sake."

Claude looked down at his hands. Fredericks was talking sense, but the brusqueness was unsettling.

"May I tell you something?" Fredericks asked. "As a friend? An older friend of long standing who cares about you?"

"Of course," Claude whispered.

"It's taking you a long time to grow up."

After a few moments Claude said, "I feel that sometimes."

"Have you ever thought why?"

"Oh, I don't know. Maybe I want to hold on to the wunderkind thing, just freeze everything. Some dumb part of me, self-image or something. Shit, I don't know." He got up, but there was no room to move, so he sat down again.

Fredericks nodded. "That could be part of it."

"I don't think about myself very much. At least not that way, psychoanalytically. I don't think about the past."

"Oh, psychoanalysis." Fredericks made a dismissive gesture. "All very well, I'm sure, but I'm thinking more along the lines of common sense, as somebody who's known you a long time. I may be completely wrong, of course." He fixed Claude with his eyes, waiting.

"Go ahead," Claude said finally.

"I'm struck by the fact that so much has been given to you."

Claude raised his eyebrows in surprise.

Fredericks started counting on his fingers. "First, the essential musical gift. God-given, if you will. I remember as a child how strange it felt in many ways, and I'm sure you felt the same." He folded a second finger. "Weisfeld, teaching you for twenty-five cents a week, for his own reasons." A third finger. "The maestro's generosity and his gift of the Bechstein." A fourth finger. "Leading into lessons with me, the most expensive piano teacher in the world, probably. And I forgot to mention Weisfeld giving you the basement studio." A fifth finger. "Your big break with Frescobaldi, which must have felt like sheer luck."

"My scholarships to two good schools," Claude said.

"The completely accidental but fortuitous fact that your college girlfriend, whom you subsequently marry, is a multimillionaire well able to subsidize your musical activities."

"I agree, I agree," Claude said. "Those things, and other things have been given to me. I am and always will be grateful."

"I know that, Claude. It's one of the most charming things about you. A lesser man would resent it."

"Good Lord, no."

"It's only human nature, but never mind, I know you don't. The point is, it may have affected you in other ways. Are you superstitious, for instance?"

"I don't think so," Claude said, and then suddenly remembered his lucky piece. It seemed such a small, isolated thing he didn't mention it. "You mean touching wood or walking under ladders? No, no."

"It would be understandable if you thought of the world in somewhat magical terms, considering that so much was given to you, as if by magic, if you see what I mean."

"Sure, but I don't think so. I mean, it's true I don't suppose I know myself particularly well, but I don't recognize that. I should ask Lady."

"You should understand that only so much can come in the form of gifts," Fredericks said. "Gifts can take you only so far. Eventually we are thrown back on ourselves. It's a cliché, but it's true."

Claude understood the implication. It made him uneasy to think about himself that way, and yet he felt some quiet stir of recognition deep down. There was even a distant flash of excitement as, for a split second, he sensed the vague possibility of transcending the circumstances of his life, of gaining a new kind of freedom. Was he strong enough? he wondered.

"Are you nervous?" Claude asked as the cab took them down Park Avenue.

Lady gave a little snort. "Not on your life." She'd dressed carefully, though. Brown suit, silk blouse, thin red scarf at her throat, silver snowflake pin on her lapel. She'd had her hair done the previous day, and although there were no major changes Claude wasn't quite used to it yet. "All this will be is a bore," she said.

When they pulled up in front of the house Claude paid twice the meter. "Merry Christmas," he said. He could see from the hack license that the driver's name was Horowitz.

"Thanks. Same to you."

The heavy iron door had been left ajar, and Lady surprised Claude by opening the inner one with a key. She led the way up the stairs, through the hall, and into the living room without hesitation. There were perhaps a dozen people standing around with punch glasses of eggnog, conversing in small groups. The first person to approach was Senator Barnes, smiling broadly. He gave Lady a kiss and shook Claude's hand.

"Splendid," the old man said. "Well done."

If Claude had been apprehensive about the possibility of an emotional scene of some sort, he had worried for nothing. Lady forged ahead, touched cheeks with her mother, nodded to her father, and said hello to a few people on her way to the punch bowl. There was no indication from anyone that anything the least bit out of the ordinary was going on. Once again Claude had the feeling that he had wandered into a smooth play in which all of the participants (except himself) were following to the letter the orders of some unseen director.

"Want some?" Lady asked.

"I don't know. Eggs."

"Have some wine, then," she said, motioning to the maid. "Got to have something. A glass of white wine for my husband, please, Maria." The maid nodded and left.

"Who are these people?" Claude asked.

"Some of their friends. A few moderately distant relatives. I have to mix, but why don't you sit down and let them come to you. Ha. Ha."

"Sure, but —" He was going to offer support.

"I know," she said, "but it'll be easier this way. Just the first go-round." She moved off to a small group by the French windows.

Claude thought he should at least present himself to Mrs. Powers. She was talking animatedly in a corner with an elderly gentleman, and as Claude approached he saw her eyes flit sideways and then back with incredible speed. She pretended to be surprised when he arrived.

"Hello," Claude said. "Merry Christmas." He did not offer to shake hands, since she held a punch glass.

"There you are, Claude," she said. "Judge Pearson. Claude Rawlings."

Nods. Smiles. The judge raised his glass just as Maria delivered white wine to Claude, who answered with a like gesture.

"We were just talking about that horrid man in Cuba," Mrs. Powers said. "It's such a shame."

"Yes, it is," Claude agreed. "I believe he's fooling the people. But then again, Batista was pretty horrid himself."

"Do you think so," said the judge with an edge of truculence.

"We used to have such nice times in Havana," said Mrs. Powers, "in the old days."

Claude held the judge's eye. "I was surprised to learn there were no public schools in Cuba."

"Catholic schools," said the judge.

"But no free schools," Claude insisted.

"Excuse me for a moment," Mrs. Powers said. "I must have a word with Maria." She broke away.

An exuberant, slightly flushed man in a bow tie touched the judge's elbow. "Freddie, I heard about the dwarf! I was next door defending Graff and Graff, but I couldn't get away."

Claude stood silently while the two men discussed a case the judge had recently heard involving a sexually deviant dwarf who had dressed as a child in order to infiltrate the children's sections of various movie theaters. Lowering their voices, watchful for the ladies, they traded off-color jokes.

"You'll have to tell Dewman," bow tie said. "He'll get a kick out of it."

"Dewman Fisk?" Claude asked.

Both men looked at him as if they'd forgotten he was there. "It was Dewman Fisk's law," the judge said. "He pushed it through when he was deputy mayor. Children's sections in the theaters." He turned back to the other man. Claude moved away and took a seat on a couch, holding his wine glass carefully. He could see Lady's back as she talked to her father, but could read nothing from either her posture or his expression.

After a while Senator Barnes joined him on the couch, sitting close. They watched the party for a few moments and then the senator spoke, not moving his head, looking out at the crowd with an amiable expression. "Whatever he says or does, ignore it. The handsome cowboy is a weak man, and like many weak men, he's a bully. You've got better things to do than play his game. And don't repeat this to my granddaughter, if you please." Then he got up and chased down Maria for an hors d'oeuvre.

Claude was both surprised and flattered that the old man would speak to him so directly. He felt recognized, trusted, and he was sorry he couldn't tell Lady about this new connection. He glanced at Ted Powers — talking to the judge now — and felt himself flush. There would never be any way to get through to the man, and the senator was telling him not even to bother to try. So be it, Claude thought, and despite everything he felt a twinge of regret.

When they left the house Lady turned toward Lexington Avenue, but Claude touched her arm and they went the other way, toward Third. It was a chilly gray day with small eddies of wind. The streets were quiet.

"Wasn't so bad," Claude said. "I felt like a piece of furniture most of the time, but that's okay. I'm glad we went."

"I suppose." Lady had a long stride, and they walked in the same rhythm. "Not a word, though. Not the slightest hint of any regret or responsibility from either one of them."

They turned the corner and started uptown. Third Avenue had a special smell — a combination of the elevated itself, with its wood, steel, and ozone, the flat odor of beer from the saloons (it seemed every fifth building had a bar), and the lingering scents of fruits and vegetables from the closed-up stands. More than any other street he knew, it smelled of life, as if the Irish, Germans, Italians, and Jews who lived in the upper floors of the low buildings, cooking for a hundred years, had impregnated the very cobblestones.

"Where are we going?" she asked.

"I thought we could say hello to Mr. Weisfeld."

At Eighty-first Street they found an open candy store and bought a *New York Times.*

"Did you know Dewman Fisk started the children's section in all the movies?" Claude said as they crossed the corner. "Christ, I used to hate having to sit there. You know, they'd catch me and march me over. Screaming kids, hard-ass matrons, plus it was always down front and to the side and your neck would ache."

"I didn't go much when I was a kid," Lady said. "Once in a while with my mother or the governess. *Fantasia, National Velvet,* that sort of thing."

"Abbott and Costello?"

"Oh, no. They were vulgar, supposedly."

Claude laughed. "Well, slapstick is supposed to be vulgar. That's the point."

"They let me see Chaplin."

"Yes, but Chaplin wasn't funny. At least he never made *me* laugh." He slapped the rolled-up newspaper against his palm. "I don't know what they're so afraid of. Your grandfather told me he wasn't allowed to read Dickens when he was a boy. Thackeray was okay, but Dickens was vulgar. Can you beat that? And I've heard really good musicians say the same thing about jazz. People who ought to know better." He shook his head.

"Snobbism," Lady said.

"I guess."

At the music store Claude peered through the window and then opened the door with his key. The silver bell tinkled in the empty room. He switched on the lights behind the cash register and gave the door to Weisfeld's rooms a couple of sharp raps.

"Maybe he's out," Lady said, peering into the harmonica case. "Look at this one! It's enormous. I didn't know they made them that big."

"He's never out. Almost never, anyway." He tried the door, which opened, and called up the stairs. "Aaron! It's me! Are you up there? Come down and say Merry Christmas. We brought you the paper."

Silence. Claude remained motionless, staring upward. For some reason he thought Weisfeld was there. He felt it.

"Why don't you go up? You say he takes naps, maybe he's taking a nap."

Claude closed the door. "No. I guess he's out." He did not want to explain that he'd never been upstairs, that it had simply been the unspoken rule for almost twenty years. He left the newspaper by the cash register.

They walked home, crossing Park Avenue at Ninetieth Street. They paused at the central island, where, because of a moderate elevation, they could see seven or eight blocks in either direction. The avenue was utterly still, free of traffic and pedestrians. It looked like a photograph from *Life* magazine.

"It's almost eerie," Lady said, her breath fogging the air.

At home, Lady went upstairs and Claude put Bartók on the record player and sat in an armchair with the score. It was *Music for Strings, Percussion, and Celesta.* Claude thought it the most important piece of ensemble music from the period just before the war, and he'd been studying it for more than a month, continuously discovering new things. After a couple of hours he went upstairs. Lady was taking a bath, but she'd laid out his clothes for the late afternoon gathering at the Fisks'. They were neatly arranged on the bed, the suit still in the dry cleaner's bag, the shoes side by side on the floor. She had even selected a tie, the one from Sulka she'd given him this morning.

They had planned to walk over to Fifth and down, but the temperature was dropping fast, and when Claude spied a cab coming their way with its dome light on, he flagged it down. He held the door for Lady and then got in beside her.

"Eighty-eighth and Fifth," he said, and caught his breath as he recognized the back of Al's head. "Hey, Al!" He was instantly nervous. This had never happened before.

Al turned and flashed a smile. "Hi, Claude. Merry Christmas, Mrs. Rawlings. Now ain't this a coincidence."

"Nice to see you again Al," Lady said. "Working today?"

"Oh, sure. Big tips on Christmas. Emma's out in the other cab. No stopping that woman." He engaged the gears. "You want the Park side or the street side?"

"The street, but it doesn't matter."

Al lowered the flag on the meter. "Just for show, folks," he said. "Emma's real happy with that color TV. It came day before yesterday and it works fine. I know she'd want me to thank you."

"Ah, well," Claude managed. "Good, that's good." He felt awkward, and was aware of Lady patting his knee and giving him a reassuring nod.

"We'll have to come over and see it sometime," she said.

"Why sure, anytime at all," Al said.

"Yes." Claude was remembering. Several months after his marriage he'd told Weisfeld about that terrible morning when he'd confronted his mother. "So if she doesn't know," Weisfeld had said, "she doesn't know. Too bad, although in the end what difference does it make, you are who you are. The one thing you can't do is leave that poor woman sitting in the basement thinking you've made some kind of a big-deal moral judgment. You know, about her love life back then when she was just a girl. That would be too cruel, Claude. Be a *mensch,* go over there." So he had gone, bringing Lady with him, and smoothed things over as best he could. Lady had been superb — tactful and generous in equal measure, helping everyone through without seeming to do anything. Now, as they approached the Fisk mansion, Claude felt guilty at how little he'd seen of them since.

"I hear you sometimes on WQXR," Al said. "It always gives me a kick when they say your name." He pulled up at the corner. "This okay?"

"This is fine," Claude said. "Lady, go ahead, would you please? I'll just be a minute."

Lady nodded and went into the mansion. Claude got in the front seat with Al. "How is she?"

"Fine, fine," Al said. "Staying even. Working hard."

"Good."

"There was a time there about a year ago . . ." Al readjusted his weight in the seat. "She read in the paper that Leo Szilard got cancer. He's a hero to her, you know, a big scientist but a rebel, all kinds of far-out ideas. So she calls the hospital to find out how he's doing, and somehow or other she's talking to the man himself. He picked up the phone by his bed and they get to talking."

"You're kidding."

"She'd call him every couple of days, and she was so excited about the whole thing I had to get watchful, you know, watching for the signs."

"What did they talk about?" Claude knew that Szilard had been one of the inventors of the atomic bomb.

"I didn't hear all that much. Like it was her thing. I don't know — he should try a vegetarian diet, how dolphins were just as smart as people, some book called *No More War,* different kinds of stuff. She got all whipped up about those calls, talking about them all the time like they were old friends, her and Leo." He smiled and shook his head. "I was worried for a while, but it turned out okay. She didn't go . . ." With his index finger he made an upward spiral in the air. "It was long distance too. To tell you the truth, I was relieved when the man died."

"Yes," Claude said.

"She was sad for about a week, and then she just forgot all about it. So it was okay."

They sat in silence for a while.

"I've been going uptown now and then," Claude said. "To the jazz clubs."

"All right." Al's eyes moved as he caught a woman hailing him from the next block. "Let's go together sometime." He prepared to pull from the curb. "Good to see you, Claude."

Claude got out and watched the cab move away. For some reason he had wanted to tell Al about the doctor's report, about the fact that he couldn't have children, but the moment was past. Now the cab turned east and was gone.

Lady had waited for him in the foyer. "We're in, we eat, and we're out," she said.

"That's fine with me," he said, accepting her direction.

The first thing he noticed was the lack of flowers. There was only a small Christmas tree in the corner of the living room. People were gathered in tight clusters around the room — the same crowd from the morning plus an equal number of others. A few children of various ages wandered about, on their best behavior, their voices low. Claude looked for Peter, but couldn't find him.

"There you are, Lady." Dewman Fisk lowered his long, basset-hound face to kiss her cheek. "And this must be young Claude. I've heard so much about you."

As he shook hands Claude realized the man did not remember him. "We met years ago, sir. No reason for you to remember it, though."

"Did we?" Fisk said easily. "Well, you must forgive me. So many artists over the years, I'm afraid as I get older . . ." His voice trailed off as his eyes picked up another entering guest. "Ah, there's poor old Henry. Excuse me." He moved away.

"I don't know why that man has always given me the creeps," Lady said.

"In what way?"

"Something oily. Something wet about him."

"Wet?"

"It's hard to explain." She surveyed the room. "My aunt must be in the library."

But she was not. Two boys of about ten sat on the floor under a tall window playing Parcheesi. Lady gave them a wave as she sat down on the couch in front of the fire. "I haven't the faintest idea who they are. Somebody's second cousins, I suppose."

Claude stood at the mantel.

Occasionally someone would enter the room, nod to them or say hello, and then go back to the living room. A maid brought them glasses of champagne and a tray of cheese biscuits.

"Who's winning?" Lady called over to the boys.

"I am," they said simultaneously, and fell into a fit of giggles.

A strikingly handsome woman with black hair and an olive complexion entered and came over to the fireplace. She wore a simple but elegantly cut black suit and no jewelry save for a bracelet of silver and jade.

"Excuse me," she said with the faintest trace of an accent. "I must see to the fire."

As she reached for the screen Claude bent over to pick a small log from the stack in the brass holder. "Here, let me," he said. When she'd opened the screen halfway he slipped the log onto the fire. Their eyes met as she closed the screen.

"*Hola,*" she said calmly. "It is you."

"Isidra?"

She nodded. "Now they call me Miss Sanchez. I am the housekeeper."

"Well, good. And the others? The driver — what was his name?"

"Oh, no. The others are all gone a long time ago. We have new people."

Claude glanced at Lady, who was watching the exchange with interest. "This is Isidra, I mean Miss Sanchez." The women nodded to each other.

"You are married?" Miss Sanchez surprised them with her boldness.

"Miss Sanchez gave me a little wooden cross a long time ago. I still have it, by the way," Claude said, turning back to her.

"That's good," she said with a slight smile. "Very good."

"No, I really do."

"It did the job, you could say."

"What . . . ," he began, then shifted. "I never understood why you gave it to me."

She nodded again to Lady and moved away a few steps. "I was very young. I saw the movies where you hold out the cross and the evil one shrinks and goes away. I was a silly girl, really." She turned and left the room.

After a moment Lady said, "What in heaven's name was that all about?"

Claude stared at the empty doorway. "I don't know."

"The evil one?"

He shook his head. "I haven't the faintest idea."

"Did she mean you?"

"No, I think she liked me. I know she did."

"How weird. That was a Chanel suit she was wearing, by the way. *Muy* expensive."

The day's light was beginning to fade as they went back into the living room. Four large round tables with formal settings had appeared as if by magic at the end of the room, just beneath the stage. At a sign from Dewman Fisk, Miss Sanchez went from group to group, alerting them that dinner was about to be served.

"I hope to Christ they didn't put us at separate tables," Lady said. "Ah, good. Here we are, across from each other."

As Miss Sanchez herded the two Parcheesi boys to the table, Claude leaned forward and asked softly, "Where are Mrs. Fisk and Peter?"

Miss Sanchez paused for a moment. "Mrs. Fisk prefers to eat upstairs. Because of her condition. They will be down for coffee."

Lady and Claude took their seats, joined by the children, Dr. and Mrs. Ogelvy from Cleveland, a middle-aged woman named Benedict from the governor's office, Lewis Jadot, an intense young man involved in set design, and an older couple whose names Claude failed to catch.

Lady's parents sat at the next table with Senator Barnes. Dewman Fisk was at table three, and Mrs. Pincloney, a famous, ancient, society grande dame, held court at table four. The low murmur of polite conversation accompanied the consommé.

Lady did her best to keep up a flow of talk, but it was heavy going. She asked one of the kids what he thought of the Beatles.

"They're neat. Ringo especially."

"I hate their hair," said the other kid.

"You're a musician, Mr. Rawlings," said Jadot. "What do you think?"

"Well, it's loud, but it's fun. They've broken out of the thirty-two-bar form for popular music, and that's interesting."

"I can't understand the words," said Mrs. Ogelvy. "I don't know what they're saying."

"Yes, it's hard," agreed Lady.

"Such a shame Dewman is no longer in government," Miss Benedict said out of nowhere. "We do so need people like him."

It was a great relief to Claude when dinner ended. He followed Lady to the sideboard for coffee and happened to glance up at the swinging door to the rear of the house when it was pushed open and Mrs. Fisk, her hand clasping the shoulder of a tall, emaciated young man, entered the room. She had apparently come down the back stairs. With a shock, and only because of the thick glasses, the lazy eyes, and the unhealthy whiteness of his skin, Claude recognized the young man as Peter. Lost in the folds of his suit, he was so thin, crooked, and dazed he looked like a dying man. (Which, in a sense, he was. Years later he was to leave home and go to the University of Chicago as a graduate student in history. In his small, luxurious off-campus apartment he would explode his brain with a German Luger pistol from his collection of World War II memorabilia. Claude would hear how he had lived alone, friendless, without a single telephone number in his new address book, how he had set a table for two, put some Wagner on the record player, sat down, and slipped the barrel of the gun into his mouth. His body was not to be discovered for some time, and the police were to have trouble establishing his identity, so empty was the apartment of any clues.) Claude watched Mrs. Fisk, her hand never leaving her son's shoulder, her eyes not visible behind black glasses, moving forward slowly, now and then stopping to respond to a guest's greeting, tilting her head, tautly smiling. Meanwhile Peter stood frozen, looking off in another direction.

"A tad spooky," Lady whispered, "wouldn't you say?"

Claude put down his coffee and approached Peter. It was hard to tell if the young man saw him coming.

"Hi, Peter." Claude tried to sound bright. "Remember me? It's Claude."

As he watched the pale face and the magnified eyes he was aware of a very quick movement as Mrs. Fisk turned her head toward him and stepped in beside her son. "Who?" she said. "Who's that?"

"Claude Rawlings, ma'am. It's nice to see you again."

"The piano player. You married my niece." Crisp.

"That's right." Claude saw now that Peter was looking at him. "How are you, Peter?"

"I gave up the violin. I became interested in chess."

"Really? We should play sometime."

"I haven't played in a long time." He spoke mechanically, without intonation. "Not since I won the Atlantic correspondence championship. I was thirteen, I think."

"Hey, that's great."

"Now I'm studying history at Columbia University."

"Peter was accepted early," Mrs. Fisk said, and gave the slightest pull. "Come along, dear."

"Goodbye," Peter said, and turned away.

"Okay," Claude said, and then surprised himself. "We should get together. Go to a movie sometime." Even to himself it sounded fatuous, hopelessly inadequate.

For the final event of the evening Dewman rounded up all the children, and a few young adults, to sing Christmas carols. Peter was not included.

"You'll do the honors on the piano?" Dewman asked. He did not wait for Claude's answer, but climbed up onto the stage and arranged the singers in two rows, the taller to the rear.

Claude went to the Steinway and saw a mimeographed sheet of paper on the music stand. Dewman handed out more sheets, full of enthusiasm. Words without music. Claude played an introductory series of chords so that everyone would at least start off in the same key.

"Jingle Bells." Dewman Fisk doing a spirited and unnecessary job of conducting, moving back and forth in front of the children.

"O Come, All Ye Faithful." Something odd in the contrast between the thin little voices and Dewman's long, sad face going through various contortions as if to lead them on to glory.

"It Came upon a Midnight Clear." His arms swinging out of tempo.

"Silent Night." His eyes welling with tears. Not from the music, Claude was sure, but from some private emotion within himself released by the ritual of the music. In a sense it was as if he were all alone on the stage, aware of the singers only peripherally, so caught up was he in the symbolism of the occasion, in some incredibly sappy, self-indulgent orgy of sentimentalism. Claude was alternately fascinated and sickened by the spectacle.

When it happened, it happened fast. Even though the procedures had been explained beforehand, time seemed to collapse from the moment the phone rang and they were instructed to come and pick up the baby the following day. Lady had been unable to sleep that night, Claude waking as she got in and out of bed. In the morning she kept up a line of nervous chatter and insisted on going over the directions to the home in Larchmont again and again.

Now, in the car going north on the parkway, she seemed calmer. Claude drove carefully, at an even speed, rarely changing lanes.

"It's happening," she said.

"That's right."

"Even when I was setting all that stuff up in the nursery — God, doesn't that sound odd, the *nursery* — even then it didn't seem real somehow. More like going through the motions. Propitiation or something."

"The baby will make it real."

"I don't want to name him for a week. I want to look at him for a solid week and then I'll know what his name is."

It was called Sevenoaks, a large nineteenth-century estate converted to its present use in the thirties. Coming around a curve in the country road, Claude caught sight of the main building — stone, three stories, slate roof — behind the iron fence and a scrim of bare trees. "There it is."

Lady looked, but said nothing.

Claude turned into the driveway. The instructions had been precise and detailed — exactly where to park, which entrance to use, exactly where to go once inside. They got out of the car and stood briefly in the cold air, gathering themselves.

It was silent inside. They followed the narrow oriental carpet to the third door on the left. Claude knocked gently and they entered.

Lady had spoken often of Mrs. Freeling, with whom she had had several interviews but whom Claude was meeting for the first time. He had created an image of a rosy, white-haired grandmotherly type, and was taken aback when Mrs. Freeling, a six-foot-tall redhead in her thirties with the body of a dancer and the high cheekbones of a fashion model, rose to greet them. He was aware that she did not take her intelligent gray eyes from him even as she greeted Lady and indicated they should sit down.

"I'm glad to meet you at last," she said.

"I want to thank you for your help," Claude said, slightly nervous. "Lady says you've been wonderful."

"That's nice to hear." She smiled and shifted her attention to Lady. "I expect you're nervous and a bit wound up, but don't worry. Everyone always is."

"I'm okay."

"Good. Now just a reminder. The mother and the baby are upstairs. We'll go up and go into the room. Conversation is not necessary, and in fact most of the time the handover is done in silence. But if she does say something to you, you should of course feel free to respond."

"Will anyone else be there?" Lady asked softly.

"No. Just the three of us, the mother, and the child. It's best to get it done as quickly as possible without seeming to rush. Do not reach for the baby. Allow the mother to give him to you, and once he's in your arms, turn and leave straightaway. We've found that's easiest on the mother, and we want to help her as much as possible."

"Of course." Lady's voice seemed to be getting smaller.

Mrs. Freeling's gray eyes moved once again to Claude.

"I understand," he said.

Mrs. Freeling picked up a telephone on her desk and dialed a single number. She closed her eyes when she spoke. "Are you ready for us, dear?" She listened for a moment. "All right. We'll be right there." She opened her eyes and hung up the phone. Moving fast now, she got up and led them out into the hall. They walked toward the center of the building.

"The west wing contains the kitchen and dining rooms downstairs, the dormitories upstairs," Mrs. Freeling explained. "Here in the east wing we have the offices, and the medical rooms above. We have an OR for emergencies. First-rate facilities, and I must say the senator helped us get them."

They entered the main hall and approached the grand staircase. The furnishings suggested a private mansion.

"Is it always this quiet?" Claude asked as they climbed.

"Only on days like this. Everyone stays in the west wing when there's a pickup. The whole place gets pretty quiet."

Claude reached out and gave Lady's hand a squeeze as they moved down the hall. She walked forward as if in a trance. Mrs. Freeling stopped at a door, rapped lightly on the top panel of frosted glass, turned the knob, and entered.

A white room. Hospital bed, big windows, a sink, and various shelves with medical supplies against one wall. The mother stood facing the opposite wall, standing quite near to it, her long brown hair hanging against her white shift, her left elbow visible, but not her face. She seemed very small to Claude.

"It's time, dear," Mrs. Freeling said gently.

Together they moved toward her.

Slowly, looking down into the face of her child, she turned around. Then she looked up, tears streaming from her eyes, which suddenly widened as she took a step back.

Claude heard Lady's sharp intake of breath, and saw her bend forward with her fist in her stomach as if she'd been punched.

"Joanna," Lady said, "Joanna."

Mrs. Freeling acted quickly, stepping between the two women, her back to the mother and child, her hands on Lady's elbows. "You know her?"

Lady nodded.

Mrs. Freeling looked at Claude. Behind her, Joanna turned to face the wall again. "Take her to the office, please. I'll be down as soon as I can."

Claude led Lady from the room. "Who is she?" he asked as they moved to the stairs.

"Oh, God." Lady quickened her step. "I taught her at Spence a couple of years ago. Joanna Moore. She was there for a semester. She's only a child."

When they got downstairs Lady broke away. "I have to get out of here. I'll be in the car." She ran down the hall and out the door, slamming it behind her.

Claude waited in the office for nearly half an hour. He was worried about Lady, and was considering whether to slip outside to check on her when Mrs. Freeling entered. On the way to her desk she gave a little skip and kicked a wastebasket so hard that it struck a bookshelf halfway up the wall with a tremendous crash. Papers floated in the air as Claude sprang to his feet.

"Oh, sit down," Mrs. Freeling said, jerking out her own chair. "It wasn't your fault."

"What the, I mean how . . . ," Claude began.

"This is what happens when we rush things, when we skip proce-dures." She held the sides of her head and stared down at her desk. "I should never have agreed to this."

"Does the fact that they know each other mean —"

"It means it's off," she interrupted. "Anonymity is absolutely basic. Think about it. Think about it for a minute."

He did. "Because of what could happen in the future," he said finally.

"I will never, never do this again," she said. "I'll resign if I have to."

Claude clasped his hands between his knees and avoided her eyes, feeling at a loss.

"You don't understand, do you," she said.

"It's gone wrong. It's very bad luck, and Lady ran out to the car, and to tell you the truth I'd like to just go out there for a moment."

"Yes, certainly, see to your wife. There's nothing more to talk about in any case. You can explain it to her."

Claude rose. "I'm terribly sorry," he said. "I can see how upset you are."

"That girl up there has had her baby for four days. And she was ready. Now it will be weeks. Weeks if we're lucky. I'm sure you can imagine how much harder that's going to make it for her."

He slowly nodded.

"Bad luck maybe," she said. "But there's no maybe about who's going to pay for it."

In the car Lady sat stiff as a statue as they drove back to the parkway. Claude started to explain, but she held up her hand.

"I know," she said, and began to weep.

"Shall I stop somewhere?"

"I just want to go home," she said.

18

CLAUDE had his hand on the doorknob before his mind registered the sign taped to the glass at the entrance of Weisfeld's Music Store: CLOSED. He was doubly confused. First, it was the middle of the afternoon on a cold Tuesday in February, a business day. Second, the sign, with a distinctive water stain in the lower right corner, was from the door to Bergman's pawn shop. Weisfeld's did not have such a sign. He got out his key and let himself in.

He'd come for a particular book on tympani from those that remained downstairs in the studio with the Bechstein, which he still played two or three times a month, but now he went to the counter and stood tapping his fingers on the glass. The lights were out, but even in the half gloom he could see that the store was in perfect order, everything in its place. He heard the distant sound of a jackhammer from Eighty-sixth, where they were tearing up part of the sidewalk. For some time he simply stood there. The last sale on the register had been one dollar and fifteen cents.

He went to the door in back, opened it, and looked up the stairs.

"Mr. Weisfeld?"

He cocked his head but heard nothing. He waited for several minutes and then put his foot on the first step.

"Mr. Weisfeld?"

He seemed not so much to climb the stairs as to very slowly float from step to step, his hand sliding along the thin banister affixed to the wall. Momentarily he had the sensation of being outside his body, watching himself. He moved up into wan daylight.

It was a surprisingly large room, almost empty of furniture. To his right an entire wall of books. In front of him two windows facing onto Third Avenue at the same level as the tracks of the elevated, a large desk before one window, a single overstuffed armchair before the other. To his left the north wall, upon which hung framed photographs of various shapes and sizes, forty or fifty of them covering that part of the wall best illuminated by the light from the windows. The odd emptiness of the room, the stillness, his own sense of illicitness, combined to create a feeling of unreality, as if he had entered a hallucination. Every angle, every shadow, every trick of the light, seemed charged with elusive meaning.

He crossed the bare wooden floor to the photographs, moving awkwardly because his body felt out of place here, like a loud noise in a cathedral. The photographs were old. A residential street in a foreign city, solid stone houses with granite second-floor balconies, carved pilasters around tall windows, recessed entries. A group of people in front of one particular house, posing for the camera. With a shock he recognized a young Weisfeld standing with a woman of about the same age, a five- or six-year-old girl in front of them, an older man with a large white mustache and two older women behind them.

The young woman sitting under a tree in a park, holding up an apple with an impish grin, offering it to the photographer. Dozens of pictures of her in various settings — riding a horse, holding a baby in her arms, mugging in full evening dress, kneading dough with one of the older women in a kitchen. Many photographs of the child. A shot of the old man on the steps of some large institutional building. Shots of the two older women, constantly together. Sidestepping along the wall, Claude began to understand that he was looking at three generations of a family somewhere in Europe, before the war.

He stepped back, taking in the whole display. Weisfeld's family. It was disorienting, like waking up in strange surroundings.

Now he faced the rear of the apartment. He moved into an empty hall, past a small kitchen, a bathroom, a sort of study, the door open, filled with books, musical scores, records, a large walnut radio-phonograph console, a drafting table, and an old, well-worn chaise longue. An impression of order, of meticulous neatness. He passed on to the last door, which was ajar, spilling a pale beam of yellow light, and paused before it.

"Mr. Weisfeld? It's me."

There was no answer. He placed his fingertips on the door and slowly pushed it open, his heart racing so fast he could hear his pulse in his ears.

Mr. Weisfeld lay fully clothed on a narrow bed, a book open on his chest, his thin hands illuminated by a reading lamp. As Claude moved closer he saw Weisfeld's pale face, eyes closed, the skin gleaming with sweat, mouth slightly open, and heard his shallow breathing. There was a wooden chair next to the bed, and Claude sat down just as he felt his knees go weak.

Weisfeld opened his eyes. They seemed unnaturally bright. "So here you are," he said.

"What's happening? You look sick, you look very sick. You look like you need a doctor."

"I am sick."

"My God," Claude whispered.

"The doctor has come and gone. One of many over a great many years. He left pills."

"What's wrong with you?"

"Did you see the pictures? In the front?"

"Yes, but —"

"That was my family. Father, mother, my aunt, my wife, and Freida, my little girl. We all lived together in Warsaw. It was a beautiful city then."

Claude started to speak, but Weisfeld cut him off by raising his hand. "Let me tell you the story." His hand fell back. "You're a man now. I can tell you the story. This is the right time." He paused, staring down at the book, which he removed from his chest. Claude saw him wince as he did this.

"Does it hurt? What hurts?"

"My father was a doctor. He also taught at the university. A distinguished man, a leader in the community — you see the way he stands in the pictures. Upright. Proud. Also very rich from his father, who owned mines. My wife had been one of his students. Freida was seven years old. My mother and her sister ran the house — both houses, although we had more servants in the country. Everything was wonderful, and I had never known anything else. I was spoiled, really, I have to say. A young artist all wrapped up in music and taking everything for granted." He raised his chin and looked off into space. When he spoke his voice was choppy, coordinated with his breathing. "So strange. It was so far-fetched, so impossible, there was a single tiny second just as I saw the blur, just before it happened, when I felt an urge toward something like laughter. I can't explain that." He reached up and rubbed his stubbled chin. "September first, 1939. There'd been an air raid in the morning. Nothing serious, just a few scattered bombs, nobody hurt. A symbolic gesture since they'd started the invasion, which we didn't know about. Just a show, but to be on the safe side we decided to go to the country house. We had a big car, a big, black Daimler as big as a tank, plenty of room for everybody. I drove, north along the river. Freida saw airplanes in the sky up ahead and I remember my father saying they were ours, they were Polish planes, so she shouldn't worry." Now he pushed himself up a little higher in the bed, wincing again, and reached for a glass of water on the bedside table. He drank slowly. A bead of sweat ran from his hair down over his temple. "We were on the outskirts of town when my father realized he'd forgotten his cigars. So I watched for a tobacconist and pulled over and ran across the street to get him some. I got the cigars and stepped out onto the sidewalk. A roar as two or three airplanes came from the south. I stepped off the sidewalk. I could see their faces through the windows of the Daimler. Freida was laughing at something. And then I saw the blur, like the faintest shadow line in the air to the roof of the car. You understand, it was not the shadow of the plane, it was the bomb itself. There was an explosion. It must have blown me all the way back, because I remember using the wall to get up. The Daimler was gone. There was a crater in the street." He turned his head to find Claude's eyes. "Now you see it. Now you don't."

Claude swallowed hard. Weisfeld's gaze seemed to paralyze him.

"You see what I mean?" Weisfeld said. "Impossible. A freak."

"What did you do?" Claude managed to find his voice.

"I don't know. I can't remember. But I can reconstruct what I must have done — not at that moment, but later. I must have walked home."

"You were in shock."

"No doubt. But I left the next day with a suitcase on the back of my bicycle. And those photographs were in the suitcase, so I must have put them there."

"My God . . ."

"I'm glad you came up here. You came up here all by yourself, so I don't have to feel guilty about it." He gave a wry smile.

"I should have come up here a long time ago." Claude pulled his chair closer to the bed. "Why didn't you tell me?"

"I didn't tell anybody." He thought for a moment. "Well, I told Bergman. He had worse. Believe me, two or three years later it was a lot worse. Him, I could tell."

"I don't understand," Claude said. "You could have told me."

"I know," Weisfeld said, but he did not explain further. "Ooof. I have to take a leak." In a series of careful procedures he sat up, shifted to the edge of the bed, and swung his legs over. "Could you get up for a second? I need the chair."

Claude sprang from the chair and started to reach out, ready to help.

"No, no. It's okay," Weisfeld said, grasping the back of the chair and pulling himself to his feet. "It takes a while, that's all." He moved slowly, one step at a time, pushing the chair in front of him for support.

"What is it? Do you know what's wrong with you?" Claude followed him into the hall.

"Yes. I know." He went into the bathroom and closed the door behind himself.

After some time Claude could hear him urinating, and heard as well a couple of short, tight gasps: "Ah. Ah." Claude put his hands against the wall and bowed his head, trying to think what he should do. Maybe Bergman was in his shop, maybe he . . .

The door opened and Weisfeld reached for the chair. "You can't win," he said. "Either it hurts because you can't take a leak, or it hurts because you can." He made his way back to the bed. As he lowered his head onto the pillow he closed his eyes. "Just give me a minute," he said, and instantly fell asleep.

Toward evening, when Weisfeld had again drifted off, Claude sat in the armchair in the front room, staring at the el. It was now closed, the entrances down at street level boarded up. "I knew I'd miss the trains," Weisfeld had said that afternoon. "Once in a while somebody would wave, you know, or a kid would give me the finger while I'm sitting at the desk. Ha!" Claude was wound up very tight, his fingers digging into the upholstery, his whole body gathered in tension as if about to receive some powerful, painful blow. He jumped as he heard the sound of someone coming up the stairs.

It was Bergman, carrying a cream soda and what appeared to be a container of soup. "Good," he said. "Very good. Is he awake?"

"I don't think so. He goes off every hour or so. How long has he been like this?"

"This bad? It started yesterday, maybe the night before."

"What's wrong with him?"

Bergman sat at the desk. "Tuberculosis."

Claude felt a kind of shifting or sliding inside his body, as if something hot had been released from the base of his throat. "How can that be? He doesn't cough! He hasn't coughed once!"

"It's not in his lungs. There are other kinds."

"What? What kinds?"

"His kidneys. His kidneys for a long time. It can hide there. But now Dr. Vogel says also maybe his heart."

"His heart?" Disbelief.

"I know, I know. You can have tuberculosis of the heart, it seems."

Claude looked out the window, seeing nothing. "We have to get him to a hospital."

"Sure." Bergman nodded. "That's a good idea. We should talk to him."

"I can't believe this," Claude said, his voice breaking.

"He thinks it goes back all the way to 1939, maybe. He got from Warsaw to the Baltic on a bicycle in the middle of the war. Some trip. Months. A miracle, you could say. In Sweden they thought he had typhus, but maybe that was it, and when he got better it went into hiding."

They heard a sound from the back. They got up simultaneously and went into the room. Weisfeld had propped himself into a sitting position.

"Soup, soup," he said, "wonderful soup. Soup of the evening . . ." He accepted the container and a spoon.

"Turtle it's not," said Bergman, placing the cream soda within reach on the table. "You seem in a good mood. Feeling better?"

"Claude has cheered me up." He took a taste.

"Claude thinks you should go to the hospital," Bergman said from the foot of the bed. Weisfeld frowned as Claude sat down beside him.

"Yes, right away," Claude said.

"So now it's unanimous," Bergman said. "Me, Dr. Vogel, and Claude. Everybody agrees."

"I understand, but no thanks."

"Aaron . . . ," Bergman began.

"Look!" Weisfeld pointed the spoon at his breastbone. "What am I pointing at?" He used the tone of a schoolteacher. "Me, right? My body, right?" He stared at Bergman. "Who gets to say what happens to this body? Me, that's who. Do I have to explain to anybody? No, I do not." He ate a little more soup and put the container aside. "Next case."

"Maybe they can help you," Claude said. "Maybe you'd be more comfortable."

"You think so?" Weisfeld said gently. "It's good to be optimistic. I appreciate it, but all the same I'm staying here."

Mr. Bergman sighed and shook his head.

Claude wanted to speak, but stopped himself with great effort.

"Somewhere," Weisfeld said, "Wittgenstein is talking about some people he disagrees with, some . . . philosophers he disagrees with. I can't remember where. He uses the phrase 'abject optimism.'" Weisfeld separated the words for emphasis. "It's an interesting idea." He paused and gave a very slow nod. "This is an idea Bergman and I are familiar with. Am I right, Ira? Bergman, and me, and people we knew."

"Shh," Bergman said softly. "Shh, now."

"Yes, you're right. My mind is wandering."

"Think of the boy."

"Absolutely." He looked at Claude and smiled. "Much better."

It took Claude a moment to realize they were talking about the Jews of Warsaw. The Jews of Europe, living and dead. He had an almost tangible sense of the unseen in Weisfeld, of the weight of the unspeakable past behind his dark eyes. No matter that Weisfeld had done his best to hide it all these years, Claude should have known, and now he felt shame for his self-absorption. There was a sense of everything collapsing down to the size of the room, as if they were drifting through space in a cube from one of Einstein's thought experiments, with no reference points except one another. For a moment those dark eyes seemed more than Claude could bear, but he held on and the moment passed.

When Bergman announced he was leaving, Claude followed him out to the front and down the stairs.

"I'm going to spend the night here," Claude said. "Upstairs."

Bergman thought about it, even glancing up at the ceiling as if he could see into Weisfeld's sickroom. "That's a good idea. It's getting . . . Someone should be with him. We can alternate nights, so I'll take tomorrow. What do you think? Vogel comes again tomorrow morning."

"Good. I want to talk to him."

"So we'll switch off, okay?"

"Yes," Claude said. "And maybe a nurse too. I'll talk to Dr. Vogel."

"Aaron can be very stubborn, you know. Very proud. So be careful with him. Something you think is no big deal can be important."

"Like a nurse, you mean?"

"Maybe. Who knows? It's important to him to get dressed in the morning even though he knows he isn't going anywhere, for instance. Little things."

"I'll be careful," Claude said.

"I was going to call you." Bergman patted Claude's arm. "He didn't want you to see him sick, but he wanted to see you, if you know what I mean. It's been like a little war."

Claude bowed his head and nodded.

Back upstairs, Weisfeld had drifted off. Claude sat in the chair beside the bed. Instinctively he picked up a book and opened it so as to appear to be reading. For a while he found his mind empty — thought and emotion temporarily suspended, even his body drained of tension. Eventually the words seemed to appear on the page as if out of invisible ink and he began to read. A biography of the Norwegian explorer Amundsen. Glaciers. White bears. White skies. White ice, white snow.

"Claude," Weisfeld said, "do me a favor before you go. My feet hurt and I'm too lazy to take off my shoes."

Claude got up. It was dark outside. He went to the end of the bed and unlaced Weisfeld's black shoes. "I'm going to sleep here tonight, in the other room, if that's all right with you."

"That's not necessary."

"I know it isn't. But I wouldn't be able to sleep at home. I'd be up all night worrying, so do me a favor." Gently, Claude eased one shoe off. The ankle was swollen. He removed the other shoe. There was a hole in the toe of Weisfeld's sock, and this ankle too was swollen, the skin blotchy.

"Such melodrama," Weisfeld said.

"It's just easier."

"Well, don't forget to call your wife."

Claude put the shoes on the floor by the side of the bed and sat down.

"How goes it in that department, by the way?"

Claude hesitated. It seemed wrong to talk about his own troubles, but then, perhaps because of what had happened inside himself when he had been pulled into those dark eyes, it seemed more wrong not to. "Not so good, I think." He told Weisfeld about his sterility, the bungled adoption effort, the sense of something hanging over them. When he'd finished Weisfeld didn't say anything for some time.

"This sadness," he finally suggested, "this sadness should go in your music. You understand? So it shouldn't get the upper hand."

"Oh, it's not so bad."

"You say that."

"I mean —"

"You don't take yourself seriously," Weisfeld said. "When there's trouble, you should take it seriously. What is it with you?"

"I'm sorry."

"And don't be sorry."

"The thing about sterility," Claude said, "it's important, of course it's important, but it doesn't seem pressing. It seems like something I'll be dealing with. With Lady, I don't know. It's almost like I'm her son or something. I know that sounds strange."

"No, it doesn't."

"It scares me. There's some kind of hollowness and I can't seem to do anything about it."

"Does she still want to adopt a child?"

"Oh, no," Claude said quickly. "All the stuff went to the Salvation Army the next day. She couldn't get it out fast enough."

"I see." He seemed to be tiring now, and Claude felt a pang of guilt.

"Things will work out," Claude said.

"Sure," Weisfeld said, and then added, "but take yourself seriously, and at all times be ready for anything." He took a breath. "This is ancient Jewish wisdom you're getting here, believe me."

"I understand. You've told me something like it before."

"I have?"

"Many times."

"Good. So listen." He closed his eyes. "Maybe this time you'll listen better. After all, a dying old man."

Claude watched the motionless face. "Are you dying, Aaron?"

"I think so." He went to sleep, eyelids flickering.

.   .   .

Claude slept little that night — episodes of dozing on the chaise longue punctuated by silent visits to the back room. Weisfeld was occasionally half awake, mumbling a few words, once giving a little wave with his right hand.

Just at dawn Claude went in to find him sitting on the edge of the bed, staring down at his shoes.

"What is it?" Claude asked. "What do you want?"

"I was thinking of that old suitcase. The one on the back of my bicycle. It's here somewhere. All beat up. Coming apart."

Claude moved forward and knelt before him. "You want me to find it? Should I get it?"

Weisfeld lifted his arm, wincing until his hand came to rest against the side of Claude's neck. He smiled, and then his eyes seemed to shift focus and he grabbed his lower lip in his teeth.

"Aaron —" Claude whispered.

"Something," he began, "something is . . ." And then his eyes went flat and he fell over onto his side.

Claude picked up Weisfeld's hand and held it between his own. That was how Dr. Vogel found them two hours later.

19

B IT BY BIT Claude began to close down. He wrote Otto Levits a card explaining that under the circumstances he felt it necessary to cancel all upcoming engagements, that as far as performing was concerned he should be considered on a leave of absence. Levits wrote back to say that he understood, but reminded Claude that in two months he was to record in the RCA sound studios. The time had been reserved and other people were counting on him. Levits had worked hard to put the deal together, and it was a significant engagement in terms of Claude's career. Claude did not respond.

Lady seemed to spend more and more time outside the house on unspecified pursuits. At dinner she was more than ordinarily quiet, and in general seemed to acknowledge Claude's loss by tactfully backing off, leaving him space, making no demands. Sometimes he was aware of her looking at him with concern, but as the weeks went by he sank gradually into a dull lassitude, a kind of torpor that blocked off his perception of much of his surroundings. The simplest actions became difficult. He might sit before the empty fireplace in the living room for half an hour thinking about whether to make himself a cup of tea. He could not read anything more demanding than newspapers or magazines. An entire morning might be spun around something as simple as taking a bath. He slept fourteen hours a day.

He was only minimally aware of what was on the television screen he watched much of the time. He did not answer the phone when it rang, nor did he open any of the growing pile of letters Lady had set aside for him on the hall table. When the letters began to spill off the table she got a basket.

He did not touch the piano or even enter the music room. He lost track of time. He drifted. Without music there was no time.

One night he awoke from a bad dream — a confused, surrealistic narrative of nameless dread — and was surprised to find his body in a state of sexual excitement. He saw that Lady was awake, lying, as she so often did, flat on her back with her arms crossed over her chest, staring at the window.

"You were talking in your sleep," she said.

"What did I say?"

"It didn't make any sense. I couldn't make it out."

"Bad dream."

"My shrink says maybe you should see somebody." For a year or so Lady had been seeing a psychotherapist once a week, apparently to discuss why, given her ambition and intelligence, she was having so much trouble committing herself to meaningful, challenging, long-term work. "She thinks you're having trouble adjusting," she said softly.

"I'm sure she's right," Claude said.

"What does it feel like?"

The question surprised him. He fumbled around in his head for a few moments. "It's hard to describe. Sort of like being wrapped in a cloud of nothing, drifting in nothing. I don't seem to care about anything. It's too much trouble even to think most of the time."

"Will it go away? Does it feel like it'll go away?"

"I haven't the faintest idea."

"Don't you think you should do *something*?"

"I feel like I didn't really know him. I knew part of him, part of him. I was just beginning to . . ." He didn't finish.

"He was a complicated man. You told me that once."

"Bergman told me he was the best young composer in Poland. Everyone said so. But all his stuff was left there. It was all lost. And after his family died he couldn't start again. I wasted so much time. I mean, I just went along with the way he was. I didn't . . . I never . . ." He found himself literally gnashing his teeth.

Gradually he calmed down. He turned onto his side and reached out for her hip, the warm softness of her skin just above the bone. They had not made love in a long time, but now he moved to her with some dim sense of the possibility of solace. As he kissed her shoulder, her hand found him and began to stroke, gently. He shifted his body up to prepare to enter her, but now he saw she was crying and felt her thigh roll in evasion.

"I can't," she cried, sounding almost like a child. "I can't, I can't. I'm sorry." Her hand was still on him.

"What's wrong?"

"Not inside me." She was pleading. "It's just something about they're all dead going in down there, it feels funny, it feels . . ." With tears in her eyes she continued stroking, started to slide down his body, and whimpered as he pulled away.

He began sleeping in the guest room, not emerging until late in the morning when he knew Lady would have left. He drank warm beer for breakfast and avoided the lower floors until Esmeralda had gone home. Then he would make himself a sandwich in the silent kitchen and wander through the house. Sometimes, without touching anything, he would look in the mail basket. Letters from Levits, a couple from the lawyer Larkin, something from Fredericks, even a note in his mother's hand, doubtless a letter of condolence. He knew that some of the letters might be important, as well as some of the phone calls he didn't answer, but it all seemed quite distant. Upstairs, with the door closed, he would drink beer, watch television, and go to sleep.

There was something recognizable about his isolation, about keeping caches of beer and peanuts near his bed, about staring out the window for hours on end, about the long, slow, aimless fantasies flowing through his head — plotless, surreal, and sometimes extraordinarily vivid. He became bemused by the textures and scents of his own body, or by very small details like the intricate weave of the pattern of the oriental rug, or shapes in the plaster above his bed. And then one day, as he sat on the floor idly building a house of playing cards, he remembered being locked in the basement apartment as a very young child, and how then, too, there had been no sense of the flowing of time but only an infinite present, a pervading, silent emptiness.

He wasn't keeping track, but it had in fact been twelve days since he'd laid eyes on her when she knocked on the door and came in. She entered hesitantly, but to him she arrived in a rush, a sudden, vivid presence bursting in upon him, alive to an almost painful degree. It was hard to look at her. She was perfectly familiar, and yet her exotic quickness added an element of strangeness, as if she'd come from outer space. Some part of his brain registered that she was normal and that it was he who had changed, but it didn't feel that way. She spoke softly, but it sounded loud.

"Claude, I'm taking a trip." She sat on the edge of the bed upon which he lay, and put her hand on his knee. "Tomorrow. Tomorrow morning."

"Where are you going?"

"Palm Beach."

"This time of year?"

"It's business."

"Oh."

"Well, just exploratory, really," she said. "Mimsi Dunne and I have been talking about opening a gallery, and there's a location we're going to look at."

"Mimsi . . ." He searched his mind.

"You know. From Locust Valley. The one whose husband died in the car accident."

"Oh, yes. Sure."

"We've done a lot of work on this." She paused. He could tell she was nervous. "Quite a lot."

"That's good."

"The thing is, if the location is right, we're going to move ahead. I might have to stay down there for a while."

"I see," he said, and pulled himself up to a sitting position. "I understand." He tried to gather his thoughts, aware now of danger, but it was like trying to swim in molasses.

"I'm worried about you," she said, looking down at her lap. "I think you're having some kind of a nervous breakdown."

"Oh, no. Really." He waved off the suggestion. "I'm all right, I'm just —" He was unable to find the word.

"It's been almost three months," she said. "I can't take it any-more. You've been off somewhere, and I know you haven't been aware of —" She stood up suddenly. "It isn't anybody's fault."

"No. Of course not." He was amazed to feel a tiny flash of anger, a small speck of emotion in the fog of his consciousness. She was bailing out. She'd talked it all over with her therapist, no doubt.

"You can't hide forever," she said. "There are things you have to do.

Maybe on your own you'll face them. This way it's like a rest home or something, and I'm the nurse. It's wrong, it isn't working, and I can't do it anyway." She paced to the window and back. "I'm sorry."

"You're right," he said. "I can't hide forever. She's right."

"I'll leave her number by the downstairs phone," she said, and stopped pacing. "Of course, it's understandable that you might not want to work with her, but she can refer you to someone. To the best, the very best. She knows the situation."

"Work," he mused. "That seems an odd thing to call it."

"Well, it isn't fun," she said.

He raised his head and looked at her for a long moment. "When you were — working — did you ever talk about why you're so afraid of my dead sperm?"

Her face froze in shock, turning chalk white. Her mouth moved but she was unable to speak. She turned and ran from the room.

When he came out of the guest room late the next morning, she had already gone. Downstairs the doctor's name and phone number had been left on the hall table. He held the slip of paper in his hand, wondering why Lady and her friends all seemed to have the same handwriting — the round, full, vertical letters, the periods that were actually tiny circles — and then crumpled it and threw it in the trash.

The next day he was sitting on the window seat in the living room, still in his bathrobe although it was past noon, when he was startled by a quiet cough from the hall. Esmeralda stood in the door frame, wearing a coat and carrying a small bag.

"I go now," she said.

"All right."

"The missus says I come one morning to clean. Monday is okay for me. Is okay?"

"Sure, that's fine." He realized she was eager to leave. "Esmeralda, did she fire you?"

"Fire? I don't know this word."

"Do you still have a job?"

"Oh, yes. The missus take care of me. I go work for her mother. My friend Louisa is there. Is good."

"I'm glad to hear it."

"Okay. Monday?"

"That's fine. You have your key."

She nodded and turned away. He heard her go down the stairs and out the door. He watched her walk quickly along the sidewalk. Just like that, he thought, admiring her practicality, her resolute stride.

He became aware that the doorbell was ringing. He thought that perhaps it had been ringing for some time. He lifted his head from the kitchen table. It was dark outside. He got up, walked through the hall, and opened the door. It took him a moment to recognize Larkin, who stood there with a thin briefcase.

"May I come in?" the lawyer asked.

"Oh, yes. I'm sorry." He stood aside.

"It's rather dark in here."

Claude turned on the light and Larkin looked at him. "You've lost weight. Is that a beard you're growing?"

"No —" Claude touched his chin. "I've just been . . . ah . . ."

"I need to talk to you."

"Yes."

"I've been trying to get ahold of you. Did you get my letters?" At that moment Larkin's eye fell on the basket of mail, and he realized he was standing on some more, which had collected on the floor in front of the slot. He stepped over to the side. "I see, I see."

"I've been preoccupied," Claude said.

"Perhaps we could go upstairs," Larkin suggested.

Claude led the way, flipping light switches as he passed them. They went into the living room. Larkin sat down on the couch and put the briefcase on the coffee table in front of him.

"I understand your wife is in Florida," he said.

Claude nodded.

"I got a letter from her attorney some time ago. A formal announcement of the commencement of a trial separation. I was sorry to hear it."

"You did?" Surprise seemed to rouse him. "Is that what she calls it? Why would she write you?"

"Well, she knows I handled some small matters for you in the past. I assume she thinks I'll be representing you if necessary in the future."

"If necessary," Claude repeated.

"The length of the separation can be an important element in any subsequent proceedings."

"You're talking about divorce."

"There was no mention of anything past —"

"Is that what's in the briefcase?" Claude asked. "Pull it out. I'll sign. If she wants a divorce, she can have a divorce. That's simple enough."

Mr. Larkin waited a moment, as he might have had a fire engine gone by on the street outside, siren blasting. "I can well understand that these are difficult times for you, Claude. But you must do your best to stay calm and reasonable."

Claude took a deep breath, shook his head, and sighed, "Ah, fuck it all, fuck it all."

"No," Larkin said. "Absolutely not."

Claude fell into an armchair and stared at the floor. He could hear the ticking of the grandfather clock in the hall.

"Don't sink," Larkin said.

"What do you mean?"

"Some people just sink."

Claude did not respond, but inside he knew what Larkin was talking about. He was surprised that Larkin had this knowledge. He would not have expected it of him.

"But that is not why I came." Larkin opened the briefcase. "I came because of Mr. Weisfeld."

Claude raised his head.

"Mr. Weisfeld has named you in his will, and I am the executor of that will."

"What?" Bewildered.

"He was admirably detailed in his instructions about the distribution of his estate. His books to the Jewish Historical Society, all his furniture, clothing, et cetera to charity. Some small bequests. But the bulk of his estate — that is to say, the building, which he owned outright, the business itself and everything in the store, and bank deposits amounting to thirty-six thousand four hundred and twenty-eight dollars — all of that he left to you."

It was as if Weisfeld had come back from the dead to stand in the room with them. The shock of his presence was so strong Claude felt an explosion inside himself, a great warm burst of Weisfeld's love magically blooming in his own breast, bathing him in redemption. He wept. He felt his soul being wiped away, simultaneously destroyed and remade, and he wept.

Larkin sat motionless until the final shudder had passed. "I'll leave you now, I can see myself out," he said. "I'm going to leave a copy of the will here for you, and I'd like to call your attention to the end of paragraph twenty-three."

"All right," Claude said, wiping his eyes.

"I want to see you tomorrow. Would eleven o'clock at my office be convenient?"

"Sure. Eleven."

"That's fine, then." Larkin got up and walked out into the hall. "Paragraph twenty-three," he called out as he started down the stairs.

After a while Claude leaned his head on the back of the chair and closed his eyes. He felt drained, but at the same time very aware of his body — of his feet, knees, hands, and elbows, of the low murmur of signals coming in from his chest, his face, and his scalp. He knew where his body ended and space began. It was a soothing sensation, and he fell into a half sleep.

The sound of a car horn outside brought him back, steady groups of triplets. He went to the window and saw a double-parked car, and then the figure of a woman behind the windshield of the car it had blocked in. She continued to blow her horn, pausing every now and then, peering out into the street, then releasing another series of triplets. Eventually a man arrived, making apologetic gestures, and drove the first car away.

Claude went to the coffee table and picked up the document. Paragraph twenty-three read as follows:

> As far as I know I have no living relations, but in the unlikely event that now or sometime in the future any individual should emerge claiming a blood tie, it should be understood that my wishes as expressed in this document transcend any such claims. The major beneficiary is Claude Rawlings, in support of his work, and because I think of him as my spiritual son. I could not have loved him more had I been his actual father.

Claude did not go upstairs. He stayed on the couch until dawn, with paragraph twenty-three on the coffee table within arm's reach. He read it many times during the night.

For the first time in a long time he awoke without trepidation. The clear blue sky, the steady sunlight spilling through the window, seemed to mirror his own calmness. The world was simply there. He felt a quiet wonder at its eternal otherness, at its uncaring peacefulness. He showered, shaved, and got dressed. He went down to the kitchen and made himself a full breakfast — bacon, a four-minute egg, English muffin, juice, and coffee — and ate with pleasure. There was a certain clarity to things. The taste of the blackberry jam, the sound of the water running in the sink as he cleaned up, the stiff texture of a fresh dishcloth. Sensation itself took up his attention, providing a rest from thought, from emotion.

As he walked downtown to Larkin's office he stopped keeping track of the street numbers and went five blocks too far and had to double back. From behind his desk Larkin at first made no mention of the previous night.

"You should understand that the actual transfer of the assets will take time. This is a simple estate, so I don't expect any delay, but the legal amenities must be observed. As executor I can and will release funds should you need them."

"No. That's okay. But can I go there?"

"The store? Of course. You can open for business if you want. The inventory, the paperwork has all been done. He was a remarkably orderly man, I must say, which made it easy."

"Yes. He was careful."

"The upstairs apartment might surprise you. He left specific instructions that it be emptied, cleaned, and repainted."

Claude considered this information. "Yes, I think I know why he did that. It was a kind of museum of his past, and he didn't want me to have to worry about it." He paused. "You know, in, what is it? almost twenty years, he never let me up there. He didn't know I would come there at the end, so if I hadn't, I wouldn't have seen it at all. What happened to his body?"

"He requested cremation and no ceremony. He paid in advance, by the way."

"His ashes?"

"No instructions."

"Have they been saved?"

"I don't know, but I can certainly find out."

"Thank you."

Larkin tapped his fingertips together and stared into the middle distance. "Also, you should know the Luris Corporation would like to buy the building. They have already approached me and I told them I'd get back."

"Who are they?"

"A very large real estate and development group. They are buying up the entire block front in order to build a high-rise apartment building. I believe their offer will be generous."

"I don't want to sell. In fact, I want to move in," Claude said.

"I see."

"What is it? You look worried."

"Just thinking," Larkin said. "Very powerful forces behind this Third Avenue rebuilding thing. The developers, the mayor, the borough president, construction unions, neighborhood civic groups, that sort of thing. They moved very fast down in the Forties and Fifties, and now the action is farther uptown. You can expect a good deal of pressure."

"Well, they can't *make* me sell it."

"No. Probably not."

Claude was surprised. "Why do you say —"

"Progress," Larkin said. "They talk about a grand boulevard to rival Madison, or even Fifth. *Everybody* is for it, all the newspapers, the chamber of commerce. The city government has been writing zoning practically to order. All structures built before 1901 can be condemned outright, for instance. An exceptionally powerful tool." He gave a wry smile. "They can't get you there, however. Your building went up in 1908."

"That's good."

"I advise you to give the matter some thought. With the government acting essentially in concert with the developers, and given what happened downtown, you can probably expect a fair degree of — what should I call it — harassment. Official harassment. It can get expensive dealing with it."

"Like what?"

"Building inspectors. Plumbing and wiring codes. Structural engineers, fire inspectors, that sort of thing. It's no joke. They used to take bribes, of course. Notorious corruption. But not with Third Avenue. Their job is to clear the way for demolition. So think about it. They've bought, or almost bought, every other building. You would be what has come to be called a holdout. A pejorative, in today's climate."

"I see. I guess I see," Claude said. "I'm grateful for your advice. And the advance warning."

"Just want you to know what you might be getting into. I hope you'll be dealing with all the mail that's piled up, by the way. It gives me the willies. There must be bills in there, things to be taken care of."

"I will. I promise."

"Feeling a bit better, I hope?"

Claude nodded. "Paragraph twenty-three woke me up, I think. I'll be all right now."

Coming around the corner onto Third Avenue, he was brought up short. The massive, dense, shadowy el was gone, the trolley tracks and cobblestones replaced by smooth asphalt, the sidewalks narrowed. Tall, futuristic aluminum streetlights soared upward and bent over the street like the antennae of some buried insect. And everywhere sunlight, a weirdly ominous brightness revealing the small, squat buildings lining the avenue. They looked like rotting teeth.

As he approached the music store he saw the large signs hung at the second-floor level of the adjoining buildings.

BUILDINGS
To be Demolished
New 16 Story Apartment
House will be erected.
J. B. Luris
148 West 57th St. PL7–6376

Moving to the edge of the sidewalk, he saw that the signs were displayed all the way to the end of the block. Except for Cunningham's Bar and Grill at the south corner, all the stores were closed — the butcher, the candy store, the fruit and vegetable store, the upholsterer, the television repair shop, even Bergman's pawn shop — windows boarded up. The entrance to Mrs. Keller's building, which had no street-level store, was open, but the developer's sign hung over the doorway. So Weisfeld had been wrong, she had sold.

He let himself into the music store, which looked different because of the flood of light inside it, and immediately went outside again to unfurl the awning. That made things somewhat more normal. He sat down on Weisfeld's stool behind the cash register and tried to absorb what he had seen. It seemed impossible that so much could have happened in so short a time. There was something unsettling, even scary, about the speed and the scale of the change. The essence of Third Avenue — the sights, sounds, and smells he had known all his life —

had simply disappeared from the face of the earth. What had appeared to be substantial was revealed as having been, in fact, an illusion.

The basement studio was exactly as he had left it. The score of Bartók's Concerto for Two Pianos, which he had been studying during the winter, lay open on the Bechstein. He glanced at his marks and notations with casual curiosity, as he might have had they been written by another person. The book on tympani was on his worktable. He couldn't remember now why he had wanted it, nor did he feel any need to remember.

He went upstairs into the apartment, which still smelled of paint, and wandered from room to room, making a mental list of the things he needed to get right away — a bed, a few chairs, a table, some lamps, simple stuff for the kitchen. He imagined an arrangement no less spartan than Weisfeld's.

Back outside, locking the door, he saw Bergman emerge from his shop. The guild sign of the three brass globes had been removed.

"I saw the awning," Bergman said. "I figured it was you."

"We should talk."

"The Automat? You got time?"

They walked up to Eighty-sixth Street.

"You know what it looks like to me?" Bergman waved to indicate the avenue. "Like a naked ninety-year-old woman. It hurts to look."

"They did it fast."

"Boom." Bergman clicked his fingers. "Like that. The only thing that slowed them down were the posts. The posts holding up the el. They went deep, bolted into big concrete pilings, but they figured out a way. Six-foot jackhammers, special torches, big cranes, different crews for each step. It was something to see."

In the Automat they drew coffee from the brass dolphin and took a table against the wall. Bergman stirred in sugar and blew across the top of his cup. He gave Claude a quick glance, as if loath to say the first word.

"I'm not making excuses," Claude said, "but something strange happened to me. Like hibernation. I just went into a cave for a while there."

Bergman nodded.

"I didn't know what to do," Claude said.

"Like what?"

"I don't know."

"Listen. The best thing — you were with him. That's what matters. Believe me, I knew the man."

"That's part of it," Claude said. "I didn't really know him. He told me what happened in the end, but all those years he didn't say a thing. I don't understand it."

"That's easy. He wanted you . . ." Bergman sought for the word. "*Separate*. He had to start his life all over again, and you were part of that. When you were just a kid he'd talk about you all the time, getting excited. When I first met him — in 'forty-two when he opened the store — the man was like a whadyacallit, those things in the movies, like a zombie. He never showed any emotion of any kind. You know what I mean? Just one foot in front of the other. Then you, a skinny little kid he's giving lessons to. He needed to keep you separate. You were new. This new good thing, and gradually he started acting like a halfway normal human being."

Claude stared down into his coffee, afraid to speak.

"You see," Bergman continued, "with you there was no guilt. You were separate."

"Guilt?"

Bergman sighed. "I know it's hard to understand. He felt guilty he wasn't in the car with them. He never said it, but I know it. It's crazy, but there it is."

At a level deeper than thought, deeper than logic, Claude instantly recognized the truth of Bergman's assertion. He knew it in his bones. "You're right," he said.

"Okay. Now you understand. You shouldn't worry."

"Jesus," Claude whispered, and shook his head.

Outside, walking back to the avenue, Bergman asked, "So, what'll you do, sell?"

"He thought Mrs. Keller would never sell."

"What could she do?" Bergman threw his hands in the air. "The city condemned the building right out from under her. At least she got a good price for the land."

"How about you?" Claude asked.

"No complaints. What I bought for six thousand I sold for seventy. I can retire in Florida, play mahjong with the widows."

"I don't think I'll sell," Claude said.

"Not even for that kind of money?"

"I'm going to live there for a while."

"You what?" Bergman was stunned. "But I thought you married a rich girl."

"Looks like that's over."

"Oh. I'm sorry to hear that." He moved closer so that their shoulders were touching as they walked, and inclined his head toward Claude, talking out of the side of his mouth. "Listen, I know everything's different these days, but don't be in a rush. Give it some time, maybe things will work out. You never know."

Claude smiled. "Aaron used to say, 'You never know till it's over — and then a lot of good it does you.' "

"Well, he knows now."

Claude stopped, his hand on Bergman's shoulder. "You believe that? You really believe that?"

"Absolutely." He held Claude's eye for a moment, and then they continued walking. "It's funny, me and Aaron. The fucking Nazis. We both lost our families, lost everything. He was high, and I was low, from the slums practically, but we had a lot in common. But what happened, it affected us differently. Sure I was a Jew, but I became a *serious* Jew. You know what I mean? It's what got me through. Aaron fell away. He lost God. Not just because of what happened to him, but the death camps, all the other stuff. I suppose I could've gone that way, but for some reason I didn't. Go figure."

It took two days to move in. From Al he got the name of a reliable man with a truck and a helper. He bought a bed from Mrs. Keller, a desk and chair from Mr. Bergman, and a few small pieces from other people on the block preparing to move out. He got some lamps from a furniture store a few blocks down the avenue at a going-out-of-business sale. Finally he drove over to the old house and took his clothing, his books, and his papers.

"Ain't you taking nothing else?" the older man asked. "This is fine stuff here."

"Nope. Everything stays."

"She kick you out, right?"

"Not exactly."

The old man shook his head. "Life is a bitch."

For the time being he kept the store closed and spent his time going over the stock and checking the books. In the evening he would either go out for supper or struggle in the small kitchen to make himself something. His helplessness irritated him, and he bought a copy of *Joy of Cooking* and read it cover to cover. It was a fascinating book, much more than a list of recipes, and in its explication of the basics assumed total ignorance on the part of the reader, which was in this case all too true. Claude found it oddly cheering, and read late into the night, feeling a mild echo of the excitement he had known as a child with the *Blue Book.* He learned to his amazement that hamburger meat would keep only a couple of days, while eggs were good for more than a week. He learned to beware of a high flame, how to make Wiener schnitzel, and the difference between a fast and a slow oven. The book was full of surprises, and seemed addressed directly to him.

One morning he awoke and knew, even before he opened his eyes, that he had to go down to the Bechstein. It was as if something had happened in his sleep, as if forces higher than himself had waged a debate while he was unconscious and the matter had been resolved.

In the basement he sat on the bench and stared down at the keys. In the past twenty years he had never gone more than three or four days without playing, and then only because of illness, travel, or some circumstance beyond his control. Now it had been many months, and he had no idea of what to expect. He was not afraid, but slightly bemused by the novelty of the situation. It felt at once familiar and exceedingly strange to face the keyboard, to reflexively adjust his posture, and to raise his hands. His hands wanted to play Bach, the little Fugue in G Minor.

The first three notes — the root, the fifth, and the minor third — seemed entirely magical. In their simplicity he heard the implication of the whole piece itself, and from that, from his awareness of the fugue, came an awareness of all-of-music, as if all-of-music were the overtones of any small part of music, as if all notes were contained in any single note. The perception was evanescent, but so powerful as to wipe away thoughts of himself. Music is here! Music has been here forever and always will be here! It was so much larger than life, so ineluctably strong, so potent an indicator of a kind of heaven on earth, that all else was swept before it. He saw this in a flash. In a nanosecond.

He took a random stack of music and placed it on the treble end of the piano — like the old days — and played one piece after another, moving them to the bass as he finished. He played all day, taking breaks every half hour as his hands stiffened up. He noticed a tightness in the muscles from his elbows to his wrists, and even a bit of lower-back pain in the afternoon. (He made a mental note to resume his exercise program.) His wrists were not as supple as they should have been, and his finger dexterity during fast passages left something to be desired, but he seemed not to have lost as much as he had expected.

After a pasta dinner upstairs ("And now we build the lasagna!" — *Joy of Cooking*), he called Otto Levits at home and apologized. He tried to describe what had happened to him, some kind of retreat, some kind of sleep.

"Okay," said Levits. "So now what's happening?"

"I played today. I'll need a month to get back in shape, but then I can work."

"In a month you can work! I'll get on this right away and send press releases to the musical capitals of the world. Maybe somebody will be nice and give you a job."

"Otto, I said I was sorry. I mean it. I couldn't help it."

"The *tsuris* I had on that record contract, you wouldn't believe. Five hundred phone calls with angry people. Actually, I got Feldman, so it all worked out. But how do I know you're not going to go to sleep again, or whatever it was? You can't do that in this business, you know what I'm saying?"

"I do, Otto. I truly understand." Claude took a deep breath. "It's over, Otto. I'm okay now. It won't happen again."

A long pause. "All right, all right. I believe you."

"Thank you."

"You're welcome."

"I didn't touch a piano. I didn't listen to records or the radio. I just got as far away from all of it as I could. But I can tell. A month for the hands. Maybe less. Probably less."

"Good. I'm glad to hear it."

"But this afternoon — I don't know how to explain it, it almost seemed worth it. I had a moment . . ."

"What? What are you saying?"

"When I began to play. I expected everything to be gradual, and yes, the technical part will be gradual, but the music, Otto, the music, all of it came back in a split second, in a rush, just pouring into me. It was indescribable."

"Okay," Levits said tentatively, drawing out the word.

"It really was."

"Ahh . . . ," he continued, still tentative, "during this period you wouldn't by any chance have been fooling around with that stuff they're all taking, that LSD stuff? I mean, this is me, Claude, this is Uncle Otto here on the other end, Uncle Otto you can tell anything, whatever it is, you know it's okay. What're you laughing?"

Claude straightened up and controlled himself. "I don't take drugs, Otto. And if I ever did, it certainly wouldn't be LSD, which is Nazi boots in the brain. Drugs scare the shit out of me, to tell the truth."

"Just asking. These days, I don't know, people seem to be going crazy. The hair, the clothes, this free love stuff. Kids saying the world started fifteen minutes ago. It's amazing what's going on. I got a cellist likes to play with her bazoombas showing, can you believe it?"

"Yes, I can."

"And she gets good jobs!" He gave a great sigh. "Well, what can you do."

Claude had indeed taken care of the mail, including a response to the Luris Corporation, in which he thanked them for their offer to meet for a discussion with regard to their possible interest in buying 1632 Third Avenue, but suggested that the meeting was unnecessary since the building was not for sale. He had thanked them again, and remained, et cetera. Nevertheless, he knew that the two men in blue suits who showed up one afternoon to tap incessantly on the windows of the shop were not there for violin strings. Claude unlocked the door and held it partially open, blocking the way with his body.

"We're closed," he said. "You can try Swann's over on Lexington and Seventy-third."

"Mr. Rawlings?" He was a young man, not much older than Claude, with a friendly smile on his square, rather handsome face. "Actually it was you we were hoping to get a word with. We're from Luris. My name is Tom Thorpe, and this is my associate, Ed Folsom."

"I did answer," Claude said. "I wrote last week."

"So you did," Tom's eyes crinkled slightly. "I hope we haven't caught you at a bad time. It'll only take a minute."

Claude opened the door. "I'm working on something downstairs," he said, automatically going over to Weisfeld's stool behind the cash register. Tom and Ed stood on the opposite side of the counter. Ed was middle-aged and heavyset, gazing about with dark, watery eyes.

"This is kind of you," Tom said. "I just thought it would be appropriate for me to introduce myself. Letters are so . . . impersonal. Person to person is the way to do business, as I'm sure you'll agree."

"Sure."

"Now, I read your letter. Very clear, and I thank you for it. Frankly, I came over to test the waters a little bit, you might say. See if we can find the tiniest bit of room to move around in, with an eye to working out some mutually beneficial arrangement."

"I understand, Mr. Thorpe, but —"

"Call me Tom. Please."

"I want to hold on to the place. It's meant a great deal to me for almost as long as I can remember."

"Oh, I see," Thorpe said, surprised. "I'm sorry, I had no idea. I thought you only recently, ah, I thought it was only some months ago that —"

"Mr. Weisfeld left me this place," Claude said. "He was my first piano teacher, and I worked here all through my childhood, as his assistant, sort of." Claude could see an emerging glint of impatience in Thorpe's eye and decided to speed things up. "I don't really own it, you see. It's more like it was left to me in trust."

"You are, however, or shortly will become, the legal owner, with every right to sell if you want to."

"Legally, yes."

Thorpe appeared to be pondering this.

"I thought," Claude said, "you could build around me. An inconvenience, but surely a minor one. I don't know much about these things. I hope it doesn't cause a problem."

"No, no," Thorpe said quickly. "Absolutely, we could build around. Certainly we could do that. It's just that from the architectural point of view — aesthetically speaking — there's a certain look we're after. The uninterrupted flow of the lines."

"Well, I'm sure it'll be a handsome building."

Thorpe seemed not to have heard him. Ed stood motionless behind Thorpe, his arms folded, leaning back against the huge mahogany display case, his dark eyes watching Claude.

"I do believe," Thorpe said, "in the light of your perfectly understandable emotional attachment to the place — we didn't know about that until today, which just goes to show you that face to face is the way to do business — in the light of that, I may well be able to prevail on the corporation to amend the original offer." He held Claude with an expectant smile.

"I'm sorry," Claude said. "I guess dealing with so many people, the different situations, you might think I was trying to jack the price.

People probably do that. I can imagine. But that isn't the case here. It isn't money. I'm holding it in trust, or at least that's the way I see it."

"Sure," Thorpe said. "The problem is, money comes into everything eventually. That's how the world works. Some things make you money, other things, well, other things can lose you money. Cost you money. There's an up side and a down side." He shook his head at this sad state of affairs.

Claude leaned forward and put his forearms on the counter. The other two men waited. "So my lawyer has advised me," he said finally, stressing each word.

"The thing is," Thorpe began, but his companion interrupted.

"Let's leave it there, Tom," Ed said, straightening up. "Mr. Rawlings has things to do. Thank you for your time, sir."

Thorpe's head swiveled in surprise.

"You're welcome." Claude nodded to Folsom. "Sorry I can't help you."

Claude showed them to the door, stepping back one step to watch them through the side panel of the window as they made their way down the sidewalk. Folsom walked directly to the corner, appearing to respond as Thorpe moved from one side of him to the other, talking animatedly. It was as if, trying one ear without success, he would scurry over to try the other.

A Cadillac limousine waited at the curb. Thorpe held the door for Folsom and followed him into the rear compartment. Then the car pulled away.

They all seemed to be Irish. Mr. Muldoon, a short, square man with crew-cut gray hair and green eyes set close to his nose. "I'm here to look at the wiring," he said, presenting his City of New York credentials.

"I'm just curious," Claude said. "What are you supposed to do if I say no."

"Whaddya mean? It's the city. You can't say no."

"So you go get a cop? Is that it?"

"Hey, give me a break here. They tell me to look at the wiring, here I am."

"Did they tell you what to find?"

"My tool chest is getting heavy. You going to let me in or what?"

Claude let him in.

Over the next week or so he let in Mr. Heaney, the fire inspector, Mr. Crawford to take a look at the plumbing, and a Mr. O'Dougherty, building inspector, who arrived with an assistant. Quite soon official letters started coming, which Claude forwarded to Mr. Larkin, who eventually telephoned.

"They have you over a barrel, I'm afraid."

"Can we appeal? Go to law?"

"Yes, certainly. But the expenses would be great and the outcome uncertain. We'd have to get bonded inspectors of our own to counter their assertions — and who knows, it's an old building, some of their assertions may be correct. The legal work would add up to a lot of hours, more if they made us jump through hoops, which we can reasonably assume they will."

"What do you advise?"

"If it was me, I'd sell."

"Yes," Claude said, "that's probably the rational thing to do." He paused. "I've thought about it, but for some reason I just can't bring myself to do it."

"In which case I see no alternative to compliance. If you comply, I don't see what they can do."

"What does that entail?" Claude asked, and then listened to the sound of rustling papers.

"Major items," Larkin said. "Rewire the whole building. Break through the rear wall on the first floor and install a fire door. Replace the furnace and boiler. There's some other observations about illegal pipe widths in the upstairs apartment, but that's about it."

"Can we use funds from the estate to do the work?"

"Yes we can. They will be more than sufficient."

"Let's do it, then."

"Okay. I'll get a letter off today that informs the city of our intent to comply. That will surprise them, I'm sure. We'll have to put the work out to bid. You want me to take care of that?"

"Please. And I appreciate your help."

"You'll be billed my usual rate. But this one is fun. I just hope nothing goes wrong."

In a matter of days, teams of Luris Corporation workmen erected a sort of open tunnel from around the corner on Eighty-third, all the way up the block, and around the corner on Eighty-fourth. Using pipe, plywood, and two-by-fours, a protective ceiling was mounted over the sidewalk. The structure did not stop for the music store, although access to the street was unimpeded. Claude was astonished at how quickly the work was done.

A week later his own workmen began arriving at seven A.M. every day, dispersing through the building to address their various tasks. Plaster dust filled the air as the old wiring was torn from the walls, and Claude was forced to pack up all the instruments without cases in sealed cardboard boxes. He covered the pianos with dropcloths, emptied the display windows, and piled up books, scores, supplies, sheet music, and parts into every enclosed or partially protected place he could find. Great crashing sounds emanated from the boiler room downstairs against the steady thump of boots from the men working on the pipes above. It was a daily scene of disorder and confusion, the workers in constant motion, dust everywhere, electric tools whining up to painful frequencies, wires tangling underfoot, equipment and building materials covering every surface.

Late one afternoon, after a week of chaos without any visible progress, Claude sat alone on a folding chair near the front door and regarded the mess. He was exhausted. It seemed to him that he had moved every object in the place a dozen times. He couldn't recognize the store, and he had a moment of doubt. Had he been wrong? Would the place ever look and feel the same? He got up and walked carefully to the rear, stepping over various hurdles, to examine the wall where the fire door was to be installed. It had already been stripped to the bare brick. He reached out to touch it, and then remembered the night he'd woken Weisfeld, who had come down disoriented in his nightgown. The bare brick was at the same spot Weisfeld had placed his hands. Claude interpreted this as more than a coincidence.

Larkin called the next morning.

"They've upped their bid fifteen percent. They say it's their last offer, only because their work schedule forces them to commit one way or another on the new building. What should I tell them?"

"I'd thank them, but no thanks. Sincere regrets that we weren't able to help." Claude had to shout over the sound of hammering.

"You know what surprises me the most?" Larkin said. "That they couldn't find some way to block our building permit."

"Maybe they ran up against an honest man."

Now the Luris trucks came early every morning and took all the space on the west side of the avenue. Waste chutes were constructed and demolition workers began gutting all the buildings simultaneously, starting at the top floors and working down, the whole length of the block. There were workmen everywhere, like ants crawling over some huge, ruined cake.

The last of Claude's crews to finish were the boiler men. Getting the new equipment off the truck and down the exterior shaft (as the Bechstein had come down) involved dismantling some of the Luris scaffolding, and a good deal of arguing, stalling, and consultation had to be gotten through before the job was accomplished.

After a second round of inspections by the city — conducted somewhat perfunctorily this time, Claude thought — the building was found to be in compliance. His next task was to complete the cleanup and replace all the stock. The original appearance of the store's interior was of course engraved in his mind, and he knew he could put everything back exactly where it had been. He started in the rear, by the new fire door. He also uncovered the Bechstein in the basement and began playing several hours a day.

One night, asleep in his bed upstairs, he woke up at the sound of a tremendous crash, so loud it might have been an explosion. He ran downstairs and found that a municipal garbage can had been thrown through the plate-glass display window, sending shards of glass half the length of the store. Rotten fruit, newspapers, a moldy bedroom slipper, and various kinds of trash spilled over onto the floor of the shop. Claude called the police and spent the rest of the night cleaning up. The next day he arranged for the open space to be covered with plywood. A week later the same thing happened to the other display window. With it also boarded up, it was very dark inside the store, and it became necessary to leave the lights on all day. Claude decided it might be wisest to wait before replacing the windows, and to put off the question of when to reopen. He consoled himself with the thought that now they had done everything they could possibly do short of firebombs, that he had only to wait them out. He believed they would not dare something as obvious as fire, and in that, at least, he was correct.

Working at the Bechstein, he became aware of a curious tension in the muscles of his arms and back, a kind of thickness in his body that kept the music from flowing as it should. He could control some of it by will, but could not entirely shake it. He called Fredericks in Paris, who prescribed long, hot baths, deep-breathing exercises, two-mile walks every day, sex every day (Claude let that one pass), and specific relaxation exercises for the hands, arms, and shoulders. Fredericks also said the problem was quite common and would no doubt go away even if Claude did nothing. The thing to avoid was becoming obsessive about it, which would only prolong it. "It will pass," Fredericks said. "Just work through it, and one fine day you'll wake up and it will be gone."

Claude had assumed that the demolition would begin at the end of the block. However, the tall crane with the wrecking ball parked directly in front of the music store. Claude ran out and began buttonholing workmen. Eventually one of the foremen told him the first building to go down would be the one next door, Mrs. Keller's. When Claude asked why, the man shrugged his shoulders. "That's the plan. Start in the middle and work out."

The next day Claude was unpacking books in the front of the store when a great, rippling crash jammed the air and the floor shook under his feet. A fine dust appeared as if by magic. Claude was squatting, and when, after a few moments, the next crash came it was so violent he lost his balance and fell backward. He got to his feet and wondered what, if anything, he should do.

The third shock was even more powerful, shaking the entire building. He happened to be looking at the E-flat silver bell over the door when it occurred. The bell rang faintly, and he was momentarily hypnotized by the sound. He focused entirely on the bell, and when it tinkled again at the next shock he found himself comparing its weak clarity with the deep, rumbling, chaotic sounds from next door. He stood motionless, closing his eyes and listening with total concentration, listening across the entire spectrum. Without thinking about it he began to time the blows of the wrecking ball, anticipating them.

And then something extraordinary happened. At the precise instant of the crash, followed a split second later by the bell, he hallucinated the full sound of an orchestra and a piano playing two chords in succession, the first chord dissonant and the second consonant. The hallucination was clear and precise, complete in every musical detail, which he instantly memorized. Then it was as if he had gone deaf to real sound. Although his eyes and the soles of his feet told him the demolition was continuing, he heard nothing. He held the memory of the two chords in his head and walked slowly to the rear of the store. He went down the stairs, got a pencil and paper, and sat at the Bechstein. It took half an hour to get the two chords out of his head and, fully scored, onto the paper. When this was done he sat for an hour looking at them, his mind working rapidly, spinning out every conceivable musical implication of the tension inherent in the chords. He glimpsed structure after structure, and as his excitement grew, so grew his ability to imagine ever more complex structures, until finally, trembling with exhilaration and terror, he forced himself to get up, walk around the studio, and calm down. He now had a great deal of work to do — an entire piece to write — and he knew he would have to pace himself. Otherwise the music would overwhelm him, suck him right out of existence like a great star swallowing a comet.

In the course of his studies Claude had learned a great deal about the concerto — from the baroque, through the classical and romantic, right up to Bartók's work before the war. He was aware of the ways in which the form had developed. As well, he knew of the double meaning of the word itself: to join together, to work in concert, but also, from the Latin, to fight, or to contend. The E-flat silver bell represented the solo instrument (piano) engaged in a battle for survival with the more powerful sounds of demolition representing the orchestra. This had come to him, he believed, in a moment of unconscious inspiration and had given rise to the aural hallucination, which he interpreted as a mysterious confirmation of the whole idea.

He pulled out the old blackboard and began sketching various ritornello-sonata structures using symbols, trying to decide on a rough blueprint. From his own library he got the score to Beethoven's fourth piano concerto and analyzed it, paying particular attention to the wild struggle going on in the second movement. He forced himself to leave the studio and pass through the escalating violence of the scene outside to go to the Juilliard library to look at Weber's Conzertstück, Liszt's two concertos, Copland's 1926 Piano Concerto, and even Schönberg's Piano Concerto of 1942. He drew schemata for each of them, took them home, and thought about them.

When he began to write the first movement he had several false starts. The first statement of the two magic chords was to occur in the second movement, and so he had to work backward to a certain extent, backward and forward at the same time. He was able to sustain the requisite concentration for stretches of two to three hours, at which point he would become slightly manic and begin to write too fast.

When this happened he would break for an hour, eat something, take a hot bath, read the paper, or work on the stock. Anything to stop chasing the music, anything to slow himself down. When he was calm he would go back to work. Very soon the days began to run together. The building continued to shake, the crashing and roaring, the jack-hammers, the air compressors, and the sound of the great trucks went on all day long, but he was too absorbed to notice. Often he would emerge from the studio in the middle of the night and be surprised by the silence.

In bed, he read Bartók scores until his eyes grew heavy and his mind drifted sideways. His dreams were surreal and filled with color. The wreckers woke him every morning.

He had a late supper at a bar and grill on Eighty-sixth Street. Corned beef sliced to order, cabbage, and a boiled potato from the steam table. When he ordered a beer it was green.

"What's this?"

"Saint Paddy's Day. The first one is on the house."

Then he noticed the decorations, green bunting, shamrocks cut from silver paper. It was a rowdy crowd at the bar, people standing two or three deep, knocking back shots, shouting and laughing, spilling beer on the floor. Many of them, he knew, had been drinking all day, having come back from Fifth Avenue and the parade, and would eventually stagger home to the tenements on the long, dark streets between Third and Second, Second and First. These were the diehards, workingmen in their twenties and thirties mostly, going for broke, and there was a dark edge to the general hysteria. He saw two bus drivers, still in uniform, each with a pint of half-and-half, drain their glasses in a race. The loser bought two shots of whiskey.

Alone at his table against the wall, Claude ate his food quickly, eager to be out of the din. He had a second beer and, just for the hell of it, a shot of Jameson. Aware of a comfortable warmth spreading from his belly, he moved carefully to the door.

"Sorry," he said. "Excuse me."

A dark-haired youth slipped on the wet floor and Claude caught his elbow in time to prevent his falling.

"Thanks, mate." He looked about sixteen years old.

Outside, the sidewalks were crowded with revelers, but they thinned out when he turned downtown on Third. After a block the avenue was empty of pedestrians, awash in the eerie brightness of the new streetlights which subtly changed the color of everything. Claude walked along, thinking of Fredericks's question about superstitiousness. He had answered it honestly enough, and he believed himself to be a rational man, but at the same time the magic chords had seemed to arrive from out of this world. The longer he worked on them, the more they seemed a message. It was uncanny how, wherever he was in the concerto, they seemed to contain the clues — sometimes faint and sometimes unmistakable — he needed to proceed. Like the golden pitcher of myth, they never emptied, never ran dry.

As he crossed the avenue at Eighty-fourth Street, he saw two men on the northwest corner with their arms linked, dancing a jig, dark scarves flying, their faces tinged green in the artificial light. They moved with precision, the heels of their heavy boots striking the sidewalk simultaneously, their thick bodies hunched as they danced in a circle, as if around some ancient, peat-fed fire.

As Claude stepped onto the curb they changed their direction and danced over to him. The taller of them reached out a curved arm, attempting to link with Claude and draw him into the dance. Instinctively, Claude pulled back.

"Sure now, you've got to dance," said the taller of the men, lunging to force his arm under Claude's.

"No, really," Claude began, but now the men were on either side of him, one holding his arm and the other reaching up to encircle his neck. They pushed him across the sidewalk toward the aluminum lamppost.

"What, what?" Claude managed to croak through the stranglehold.

"Everybody's got to dance," the tall one said, his whiskey breath hot on Claude's face. "Everybody's got to cooperate, don't you know." Suddenly he shot his elbow into Claude's stomach. Bent over, gasping, Claude felt his arm being wrapped around the lamppost. Another blow to his stomach and he fell to his knees. The shorter man held a foot-long length of pipe in front of Claude's face, showing it to him. The taller man held Claude's arm against the lamppost.

The pain was intense and the world began to get dark. He saw the greenish face and the brown teeth. "Next time, the hand." He blacked out.

Senator Barnes's limousine pulled up to the corner of Eighty-sixth and Park right on time. Claude opened the door with his good arm and got in.

"How long do you have to keep it on?" the old man asked.

"A month or so," Claude said.

The cast started at his left elbow and proceeded to the heel of his hand. There were holes for his fingers.

"Can you move them?"

"Yes." Claude demonstrated. "The doctor at Bellevue said I was lucky. A nondisplaced fracture of the distal radius, otherwise they would have to immobilize everything."

Senator Barnes leaned forward and slid open the glass panel to the driver's compartment. "One Forty-eight West Fifty-seventh, Henry." He slid the panel shut and fell back in his seat as the car moved forward. "Does it hurt?"

"Not now." He touched the cast. "In fact, I played this morning."

"You're kidding."

"A funny feeling with a locked wrist. It reminded me of one of my early teachers, Professor Menti, when I was a kid."

"Well, I'm glad you called me."

"I didn't know what else to do. I hope this doesn't make problems for you."

"It's a piece of cake," the senator said. "I'm glad to help. I felt very bad about what happened up at Larchmont."

"Nobody could have —" Claude began.

"Yes, yes, I know. What's terrible about things like that is the power that gets loose. I mean the destructive power. It's like the Greeks — some god acts on a whim and mortals pay the price. It was too much for her, the poor thing. Although I wish she'd shown a little more salt."

They rode on in silence. When they pulled up in front of the office building the senator glanced at his watch. Henry got out, walked around the front of the car, and opened Claude's door.

"This won't take long, Henry," the senator said, emerging.

"Yes, sir."

Upstairs, in the waiting room of the Luris Corporation, Tom Thorpe lunged up from his chair as Senator Barnes got out of the elevator. "Good afternoon, Senator. Mr. Folsom is —" His smile collapsed as Claude stepped forward. He looked from one face to the other, stunned into silence.

"Take us in," the senator said.

Thorpe moved down the hall, opened a door into a small office, ignored the secretary, tapped lightly on another door, opened it, and stepped aside. The senator entered, followed by Claude. Thorpe closed the door behind them without coming in.

Folsom sat behind a large desk, a skyline of the East Side revealed through the windows behind him. If he was surprised he did not show it, his dark, wet eyes slow and steady. He got up and extended his hand.

"Senator," he said, "this is an honor."

The senator did not take his hand. "Sit down," he said, as he did so himself. Claude took a chair. Folsom, his face still wooden, obeyed.

"I, ah, I'm wondering what —" Folsom began.

"Conversation is not necessary," the old man said. He glanced again at his watch and then removed two slips of paper from his breast pocket. He slipped the first one across the desk. "Call this number and tell them who you are. They're expecting you."

Folsom took the paper and held it with both hands, studying the single phone number as if it were a code to be deciphered. "Whose number is this?"

"The police commissioner," the senator said without expression. "Mr. Witte."

Folsom paused for a minute, reached for the phone, and dialed. As he waited his eyes went to Claude, flicked down to the cast, and then away. "This is Ed Folsom calling," he said. "Yes, I'll hold." He leaned back in his chair, looked at the ceiling, and gave a barely audible sigh. Then his head came forward. "Yes, this is Folsom." As he listened there was a slight compression of his lips. After perhaps thirty seconds he said, "Yes, I understand," and hung up. "Senator," he said, "there must be some kind of mix-up here. I can assure you I know nothing about —"

"Save it, save it." The old man slid the second piece of paper like a playing card. "The mayor is expecting your call."

Folsom licked his lips nervously and bent over the paper. Claude could see what would soon be a bald spot on the crown of his head. Folsom said, "I assure you this isn't —"

"Make the call."

Folsom did so. It took the mayor somewhat longer to say what he had to say than it had the police commissioner. Folsom replaced the receiver with care. His face was pale.

"Okay." The senator stood up and put both hands on Folsom's desk. "One broken window on that building, one chipped brick, one hot rivet on the roof and you're out of business. One broken fingernail on this young man and you're in jail. You had better pray for his health." He pushed himself up and turned away. Claude followed him out.

Halfway down the elevator the old man said, "I wonder where he got the name Luris? He owns the corporation — sixty percent of the stock, in any case. Big contributor to the Democratic Party." He gave a sudden, hearty belly laugh. "Lot of good it did him."

The cast on his left arm made a convenient paperweight as he scribbled away at the score, most often in the studio but sometimes upstairs at the desk in front of the window. As he got deeper into the piece he seemed to be able to concentrate longer, taking fewer and shorter breaks as the weeks went on. The fundamental line emerged, a kind of weaving in and out between the piano and orchestra, complementing one another and then opposing one another, which created a pattern linking all three movements. Writing the piano solos, he was guided by the fragile, spooky clarity of the bell. Certain sections were technically complex, but only as a development of fairly simple themes. With the orchestra, however, he went for dense textures, a lot of inner movement, tension, and occasionally violence. The two magic chords stood once in the second movement and once in the recapitulating third movement, like two mighty pylons upon which the entire structure was hung.

One day as he was coming back with a bag of groceries, his head full of music, one of the Luris foremen ran up the tunnel to catch him at the door.

"The glass is coming tomorrow," he said. "Is that okay? We can do it another day if you want."

"What glass? What are you talking about?"

"The windows." He gestured to the plywood sheets. "Didn't they tell you? Luris is giving you new display windows. Real thick plate. A lot better than the old ones."

"Are they really," Claude said. "Well, that's a nice gesture. Tomorrow will be fine."

"Okay. Right."

"I hope it won't be too messy. I've cleaned up I don't know how many times."

"Don't worry. We'll be using our best men. Old-timers, real craftsmen."

Toward the end he found himself writing so quickly it almost scared him. When all three movements were complete, he went back and worked bar by bar from the beginning, adding detail, editing, altering a bit of melody or the voicing of a chord. He did this time after time, a dozen or more times.

"Hey, don't you ever answer the phone?" It was Otto Levits. "I've been calling for days."

"I should get an extension down in the studio. I've been working."

"That's good, because I've got an engagement. The New Rochelle Friends of Music. You can do the Schubert program you did at Columbia. They specifically asked for it, so this is easy and it's good money."

"Otto, I can't."

"No, no, no," he exploded. "I didn't hear that! You never said that!"

"I've got a broken arm."

"This is a lie. Stay where you are, I'm getting a cab. I'm practically there already."

Half an hour later he came through the door. "What's going on around here? They're tearing down the whole block."

"Not quite. Not this building." Claude held up his cast. "That's how I got this."

"The cast is a ruse," Otto said. "I know all these neurotic tricks. I've been dealing with crazy artists my whole life."

"Sit," Claude said. "I'll get some coffee from across the street and tell you the whole story. You want a donut?"

"Plain. A plain donut."

When Claude returned they sat on either side of the counter and fussed with the food. "They don't have plain, so I got you a cinnamon."

"Fine. So?"

Claude began at the beginning and told him everything that had happened. Levits sipped his coffee and listened, his white eyebrows lifting as his eyes widened. As Claude described the visit to Folsom's office, Levits nodded, as if old truths were being confirmed.

"You should sue the bastard anyway," Otto said. "You're a pianist with a broken arm. One million dollars. I'd be glad to testify as an expert witness. Exaggerate a little, maybe."

"We can't prove anything," Claude said. "Anyway, I was lucky. A simple fracture. It'll be off soon. In fact, I've been playing with it on."

"I'll tell you what's lucky. It's lucky you knew Senator Barnes."

"That is true." Claude ate some donut and drank some coffee. "I would've had to sell otherwise. I see that now. A matter of time."

"I wonder who else they fucked over," Otto said. "People who didn't know anybody."

They ate in silence.

"Come downstairs," Claude said when they'd finished. "I want to show you something."

20

SHIRTS ON TOP, collars down. Free-lance musicians knew how to pack, he thought. He closed the suitcase, pleased that he'd managed to get everything into one bag, and went into the kitchen and made himself a cup of tea. He drank it in the front room, sitting on the corner of his desk, glancing out the window at the traffic on Third Avenue. It was a mild, sunny April day, just over a year since he'd moved in. One last time he ran over the checklist in his mind: passport, traveler's checks, address book, scores (in the suitcase), two Simenons to read on the plane, his lucky cross. He rinsed the cup in the kitchen, glanced in the bedroom and the study, and went downstairs. The suitcase bumped against the side of his leg.

Emma sat behind the cash register, making an entry in the ledger. Claude had been amazed at how quickly she'd learned the setup. It was as if she'd been a shopkeeper forever. Technical matters concerning the instruments were beyond her, but there Al had shown a flair. He was an excellent salesman, calm, patient, with never a hint of pressure.

Claude put down his suitcase. "I guess I'm off. Where's Al?"

"Downstairs moving stock."

It had become necessary to use part of the studio for storage. Business had increased dramatically since the old days under the el. Guitars of all varieties were particularly hot. But so were books, sheet music, and, for some reason, timbales. "Are you nervous?" she asked.

"Not yet. I won't be nervous till the day before."

"I meant the airplane," she said. "You couldn't get me to go up in one of those things for all the tea in China."

"It's a lot safer than driving a cab," he said. "Statistically."

"Well, I don't have to do that anymore either. I don't know why Al keeps doing a shift. We've got good people for both cars."

"He likes to move," Claude said. "Get out and around. See the sights."

"I suppose." She tapped her pencil on the counter. "Everything here will be fine. You shouldn't worry. We know how to do it."

"I have every confidence," he said, glancing at his watch. "I'd better get going. Say goodbye to Al for me."

"Will do. Break a leg."

He went out the door and jaywalked across the avenue to catch an uptown cab. As he stood on the sidewalk he looked back at the store. Wrapped on three sides by the soaring whiteness of the sixteen-story apartment building, freshly sandblasted, with newly painted trim and cornices, it looked almost quaint. It could be a tiny church, Claude thought, right there in the exact middle of the block. Even as he watched, two customers went in. He imagined the sound of the silver bell.

The cab dropped him off at the BOAC terminal, where he showed his ticket to an attendant and his bag was whisked away. He went inside, surprised to find so few people, bought a newspaper, browsed for a few moments in a tiny bookstore, and wound up at the BOAC desk.

"Good afternoon, sir." The man glanced at the tickets and returned them. "You can board now if you like. Gate twelve, right through there."

"Thanks. I guess I will. Is the flight crowded?"

A quick glance at his computer. "No, sir. I'd say about fifty percent capacity."

A British stewardess met him at the door to the plane. He felt a little thrill of pleasure at her accent. "Right, then," she said with a smile. "Through there to the first-class compartment. Seat 2A, by the window. They'll take care of you."

As indeed they did. A cheerful young woman named Edith fussed over him like a nurse. The seat next to him was apparently going to remain unoccupied, and she brought down a blanket, some pillows, and a pair of slippers. She leaned over him — a whiff of perfume — to adjust the window shade.

"There we are," she said, brushing her hair back over her ear. "What do you say to a glass of champagne while we're waiting?"

"That would be nice. Yes."

"Good," she said, as if he'd pleased her. "I think I can promise you quite a nice dinner tonight. They do lay it on up here. Five courses."

Later, as the plane took off, at the moment of lift, he had a definite feeling of transition, as if he were leaving a known chapter of his life behind him, back on the ground, to enter brand-new territory. It was exhilarating.

The drive into London surprised him. In the confusion he'd gotten a minicab instead of one of the traditional big black diesels he'd been looking forward to. He sat with his knees up and stared out the window. Bad roads and mile after mile of shabby residential housing. As they entered the city he began to notice the double-decker buses, strange advertising signs, and the general bustle of the sidewalks. He saw men with bowlers and umbrellas — although the sun was shining — striding along as they had in practically every British movie he'd ever seen. *Everything* was different — colors, textures, the light, the very air smelled different. It seemed like an alternate reality, but of course perfectly normal for everyone but him. A wonderful mixture of the exotic and the mundane.

"Here we are, guv."

Claude paid with the large notes he'd gotten at the airport, holding out his hand and suggesting the driver take a twenty percent tip.

The management of the London Symphony Orchestra had reserved a room for him at Brown's Hotel, a sprawling, slightly rundown establishment with a reputation for artistic clientele. The lobby was crowded with people speaking a half-dozen languages, and it took Claude a moment to find the reception desk. The clerk checked him in and a bellboy took him to his room.

Claude unpacked, took a long hot bath in the ancient oversized tub, and fell asleep naked on the bed. An hour later he was awakened by the telephone.

"Mr. Rawlings?"

"Yes."

"Ah, splendid. You've arrived, then. This is Albert Shanks from the LSO."

"Oh." He rubbed his eyes. "Hi."

"We thought if it's convenient you might want to drop over this afternoon. Of course, tomorrow will do if you'd like to rest. Just a chat, you see. Nothing that can't wait."

"No, I'd like that. How about two?"

"Twoish, then. I look forward to meeting you."

Claude spent the next couple of hours walking around the neighborhood, pleasantly bemused by the small scale of everything — the streets, alleys, and arcades laid out every which way, the buildings seeming to lean over the sidewalks. He came upon unexpected little squares, small parks, pubs, shops of every description, theaters, bookstores, all crammed together in the most cunning fashion. He lost any sense of direction, but wandered from one place to another quite happily, since every turn he took led, in a very short time, to some new and interesting nexus.

For lunch, standing up in an open corner shop, he had baked beans on toast and a cup of tea, listening to the language swirling about him — the accents, the speed, the slang. The streets were made for walking. When one of the traditional cabs came to a halt as he flagged it, he wondered how, big as it was, it could possibly negotiate the turns. Somehow it did, pedestrians skipping away with miraculous, insouciant agility.

The hall was a modern free-standing building on the banks of the Thames. Claude found this mildly disappointing. He had imagined something old and grand along the lines of Carnegie Hall. An attendant inside directed him to Albert Shanks's office, which turned out to be a modest-sized room with modern furnishings and a view of the river.

"So good of you to come," said Shanks, a long-haired young man, very pale, wearing black bell-bottom hip-huggers, a white turtleneck, a multicolored vest, and granny glasses. Claude was in a brown suit. Shanks got a large envelope from his desk and moved to the couch. "My congratulations, by the way," he said, sitting down and patting the couch in invitation. "The competition was intense, as I'm sure you can imagine."

"Thank you." Claude sat at the other end.

The phone rang but Shanks ignored it, and after four rings it stopped. "I can't give you the program because it's still at the printer. We're billing it An Evening of American Music. Trying to pull in the tourists, quite frankly. Our Mr. Dove will conduct the Ives, Copland will conduct *Billy the Kid,* intermission, and then you, with Mr. Dove again. It should be fun."

Claude gave a little laugh. "I hope so."

Shanks handed him the envelope. "Everything you need is here. The pass gives you ingress and free access to the building, including the practice pianos downstairs. We've also set up a rehearsal schedule which I hope doesn't conflict with anything."

"It won't. I'm not doing anything else."

"I'm sorry it wasn't possible to give you more time with the orchestra. We stretched it as far as we could, but you know how these things are."

"Sure," Claude said. "I hope Mr. Dove can go over the score with me, though. You know, just the two of us."

"I'm sure he's expecting that. His telephone number is in there. Now, how're your digs?"

"I'm sorry?"

"The hotel. Everything satisfactory?"

"Oh, absolutely. It's fine."

"You must take tea there. Charming. Try the Savoy Grille for dinner some night. Hard to get in, but worth it." He got up to shake hands. "Anything you need, just ring me up."

Claude fell into a comfortable routine, going over to the hall every morning to play in the basement, feeling fit, enjoying himself. Something strange had happened the previous year when the cast had come off. His left arm had felt light the first few days, practically insubstantial, and his freed wrist responded with a remarkable fluidity and suppleness, as if it had been packed in oil all that time. His right wrist followed like a dutiful student, and the arm and shoulder tightness that had plagued him disappeared completely. His fingers had never felt stronger nor more responsive to the images of the music in his mind. It was a joy to play.

Mr. Dove, a rather severe man in his fifties, formally dressed — the sartorial antithesis to Mr. Shanks — knocked politely on the practice room door one morning and came in with a score of the concerto. Claude had one of his own, and they sat at the nested Steinways and worked through the music for several hours. Dove was intelligent, scrupulous, and totally focused, possessing great powers of concentration. He did not chitchat or ask any irrelevant questions. He made good suggestions about matters of notation, tempo, and some of the score markings, explaining that "the British usually mark it this way." Claude was tired at the end of the session, but Dove still seemed fresh.

"We've gotten a lot done," he said. "Perhaps a short meeting next Monday? Same time?"

"I'm very grateful," said Claude.

"Not at all."

It became Claude's habit to take tea at Brown's every afternoon. Comfortable armchairs with handy side tables filled a long room off the main lobby. Waiters brought pots of strong tea and offered small crustless sandwiches — cucumber, cheese and tomato, watercress. A table of pastries was displayed under the tall windows. As the afternoon light softened, the room hummed with conversation, the clink of cups and saucers, and the rustle of newspapers. Scents of pipe tobacco mixed with the sharper, higher smell of Virginia cigarettes.

At first he didn't realize what he was seeing. A glimpse, through the people milling near the lobby, of a curved, black wing of hair below a pale jaw. It disappeared as a fat man interposed, and then Claude froze, cup in the air. Catherine walked into the room, her chin lifting as she scanned the crowd, looking for someone. Her darting eyes found Claude and stopped. A suggestion of a smile as she moved forward. He realized — and the thought seemed impossible, unreal — that she'd been looking for him.

"There you are," she said. "The man at the desk said you might be in here." She stood there in a simple dark green dress, buttoned to the neck, a tan raincoat over her arm. Thinner, but otherwise unchanged — enormous dark eyes, a faint flush under the cheekbones, the carved mouth that smiled full-out now at the effect of her entrance. "May I join you?"

Flustered, his mind racing, his body recovering from the shock, which had been as tangible as electricity — a frisson right up his spine — he got to his feet, knocking a saucer to the carpet as he did so. He tried to speak, but wound up nodding and indicating the chair next to his own.

She bent smoothly to retrieve the saucer. She had an air of composure, her movements suggesting certainty, an inner certainty he could sense but not name. He was almost overwhelmed by her proximity, by the power emanating from her small, narrow-shouldered frame.

A waiter had materialized out of thin air. "Will you be taking tea, Madam?"

"Yes. Thank you." She turned to Claude. "I read about it in the paper."

"Yes," Claude said.

"I called the offices and said I knew you."

"I thought you, I mean didn't you, aren't you in Australia?"

"I've been here for two years," she said. "I'm at London University."

"Ah . . ." His mind continued to race.

"I'm getting a doctorate," she said. "But what about you? How did all this happen?"

"Did you return my letter unopened, or did somebody else?"

A look of puzzlement. "What letter? What do you mean?"

"Nine years ago I wrote you a letter."

She frowned. "Nine years ago . . ."

"It was an invitation to my first major concert. The Mozart Double Piano Concerto, with Fredericks."

"I never saw it. You say it was returned?"

"Yes. It was right around the time you went away, the time you eloped."

Her hands were clasped between her knees. She looked down at them for a moment. "That explains it, then. Someone at the house sent it back. I'm sorry about that."

"It's okay," he said. "I just wanted to know. It's not important. But that concert was the beginning, in a way." As they sat drinking tea and eating sandwiches he told her of his career as a performer, Weisfeld's death, his estrangement from her cousin Lady, his attempts at writing music, which had culminated in the piano concerto which had won the London Symphony competition. She then told him of her discovery of medieval studies at the University of Melbourne in Australia, the birth of her daughter, Jennie, her breakup with her husband, and her immigration to England.

"You've never been back to America?" he asked.

"No. And I never will go back."

"But why?"

She shook her head. "Let's change the subject. Are you free tonight? Do you want to have dinner?"

"Why yes. Of course. I'd be delighted."

"Good." She rummaged in the pocket of her coat and wrote her address on the back of a British Museum call slip. "I have to run to pick up Jennie. Seven-thirty?" She stood, handed him the paper, and walked away.

He stayed in the armchair long after the tea things had been removed, his head back on the antimacassar. In some ways she was the same — her directness, bluntness almost, her quick intelligence, her odd tendency to go inward sometimes for a moment or two, staring at nothing, like someone in a brief cataleptic trance, and then come out of it and go on as if nothing had happened. ("He used to hate it," she would tell him later, speaking of her ex-husband. "I think it scared him. No, that's not quite it. He *resented* it. Whiteouts, he called them.") But she had lost the superior manner, the snobbishness, the habit of putting on airs like an actress playing a role. The disdain was gone, replaced by a kind of watchfulness. Her speech, however, had gone slightly British — idioms, traces of accent — and he found it unsettling. Not that she was affected, but more as a subtle expression of her eagerness to embrace the culture in which she found herself. ("Sometimes, in the shops, I can tell they don't know.") Most striking was her seriousness. Even when she laughed, it was somehow the laughter of a serious person. In this, oddly enough, she reminded him of Weisfeld, from whom in every other aspect she could not possibly have been more different. As the light failed he found himself hunched forward, head in his hands, staring at the carpet.

"Can I get you anything, sir?"

"What? No, thank you. I was just leaving."

A dark street. Row houses. The sidewalk was so narrow he almost struck the brick of the building when he opened the cab door. Number 84, gray plastic numerals tacked to the dark green wood. A small, narrow door, flush to the wall. He knocked, backing up a bit out of reflex and almost going over the curb. Down the block a drunk weaved in the middle of the street, bottle in hand, softly singing some strange modal melody. He paused under a lamppost, looked up into the weak cone of light, and then veered off into the darkness.

The door opened inward and Catherine stood with her back to the wall so he could pass. "Come in. Straight back."

It was a house built for midgets, cramped, low-ceilinged, everything too small. He passed two dark rooms on his right, ducked his head, went down a step, and entered a tiny kitchen. A girl of about six sat at the central table with a coloring book. She looked up — curly brown hair, green eyes, a dusting of freckles across her nose. "Hello," she said.

"This is Jennie," Catherine said behind him. "This is Mr. Rawlings."

"You called him Claude before," Jennie said, rolling her crayon in her fingers. "I'm going to Paris tomorrow," she announced to Claude.

"That's great. Do you speak French?"

"No, but my daddy'll be there, and he does."

"He has a place in the country," Catherine said. "She goes for a month every spring."

"We catch fish in the river," Jennie said, and went back to coloring.

He was startled to feel Catherine's soft touch on his elbow. She led him back to the front of the house, switching on the light in the first room. A desk, two chairs, a wooden rocking horse, and hundreds of books neatly arranged in stacked fruit crates against the wall. There was a dark, worn prayer rug and an electric fire. Cheap curtains on the window. A small, severe room, lit by a single bare bulb hanging from the center of the ceiling.

"We share the back room," she said.

He didn't know what to say. He went over and looked at the books. Many had markers — slips of paper with handwriting — spilling from their tops.

"All I do is work," she said. "Here and at the BM."

"What's the BM?"

"The British Museum. The reading room is my idea of heaven."

He turned quickly to see if she was being ironic. She was not. "Scholarly pursuits," he said.

"I'm a student. And I love the period."

"Do you know — well, I suppose you must — you know about your mother?"

"Yes. Would you like a drink? I have some cheap plonk, I think. I'll get it."

Plonk, he intuited, was wine. She returned with two glasses and a half bottle of red. She poured with a steady hand. They sat — she on the corner of the desk, he on a wooden chair — and she lifted her glass in a toast. "Here's to life," she said.

"Yes, indeed. Strange as it is."

She wore black slacks, a white blouse, and a gray cardigan sweater. "I've got some chicken."

He was torn. The intimate flat, the sense that he was a visitor at the physical center of her life, and that the circumstances, however mysterious, might reveal something, all suggested that he stay. Years ago he had been driven to distraction by her elusiveness, and would have thought this an opportunity to press, to flush her out at last. But now two things were happening to him: an urge to deny his younger, weaker self and the simultaneous perception that although everything about her situation had changed, reversed even, she was nevertheless still elusive, still wrapped in mystery. It was the sheer force of her personality, he thought, of her character, prevailing over any and all circumstances. His memories of her as the disdainful, precocious girl-child with a fondness for playing with fire, all those memories and others he had created to protect himself, all of it melted away in the face of her extraordinary self-possession. How was it that at twenty-six she was a full woman, with that still-point of womanly strength none of her contemporaries, in Claude's view, had been able to find? Or was it once again her beauty — even more striking now, a radiance to take one's breath away — affecting his perception of what might lie beneath it? Of her maddeningly secret soul?

"Let's go out," he said. "Is there someplace nearby? We can take Jennie."

"She's eaten." Catherine got off the desk and went into the kitchen. As she came back with the child, she bent over to kiss the top of her head. Jennie continued down the hall. Claude heard the sound of a door and the unmistakable tattoo of the girl running upstairs.

"She'll watch the telly with Mrs. Jenks upstairs."

"Mrs. Jenks?"

"Our landlady, poor old thing. All she has is this building and a tiny pension. She loves Jennie and Jennie loves her, so it works out."

"Is Jennie in school?"

"Oh, yes. The very best. He pays for it."

They walked the dark street, Catherine on the sidewalk and Claude in the gutter, took a few turns, and entered a small square. An Underground stop, a pub, a greengrocer's, a tobacconist, and a small Italian restaurant. There were seven or eight tables inside, only the two by the window occupied. Claude pointed at a double in the far corner and they sat down.

"This is a treat," she said, smiling, and opened a menu.

While she was studying it, Claude made a beckoning sign to the single waiter, a slight, sallow youth with bad teeth, and ordered a bottle of Bardolino. The menu was simple and the prices low. An entire meal cost no more than tea at the hotel. He gazed at her bent head, the hair so black it shone. "Mmm," she murmured, and then found another item. "Mmmm." He glanced at the menu but couldn't concentrate.

"Melon and proscuitto," she said as the waiter poured the wine. "Then directly on to the veal scaloppine with just a little pasta on the side."

"I'll have the same," Claude said.

They sat in silence for some moments. Claude felt almost dreamy watching her hands in the candlelight, glancing at her face — rose, milk, ebony, her eyelashes like thick brush strokes executed with oriental precision. She seemed entirely at ease, as if they were old friends.

"I hope you can come to the concert," he said.

"Of course I'll come. It's an honor. The world premiere, after all."

"I've never heard it. With an orchestra, I mean."

She thought about that. "You'll be rehearsing. Or have you already started?"

"Soon. Everything's been put back because of a change in Copland's schedule."

"That must be irritating."

"I don't mind." He tapped his glass. "I never get jumpy till the day before, so it doesn't matter."

"Do you know Copland?"

He shook his head. "But I think his music is wonderful. He's courageous."

"You mean the directness? Like *Appalachian Spring*?"

"Exactly. He's run against the trend." Claude was surprised and pleased at her observation. "You know his stuff."

"A little. The BBC. I listen at night sometimes, after Jennie's gone to bed."

"They talk about the folk themes, the jazz elements, but the thing is, when you really listen to it, it's very, very intelligent music, and full of emotion."

He went on for some time, talking about various modern composers, sometimes waving his knife and fork in the air. She ate steadily, cleaning her plates, even catching the last of the sauce with a bit of bread. "The trouble with me is," she said, wiping her hands, "I don't really know about anything much after 1500." She smiled with the faintest trace of slyness, as if to suggest a certain hidden pride in her deficiency.

"The Dark Ages," he said.

"That's usually a reference to *circa* 500 to 1000, but it's a misnomer. There was a lot going on in those monasteries."

"Not much music."

"Maybe not. Chants. I really know more about 1000 to 1500 — just up to the start of the Renaissance. It's a tremendously exciting period to study because so little work has been done. Practically fresh territory, you could say. Good for somebody young." She leaned forward in her enthusiasm. "I can actually make *finds*."

"You mean, what, manuscripts?"

"Well, that's always a remote possibility, but I meant more tracing influences across languages, across cultures, seeing things appear to sink forever and then show up unexpectedly someplace else, sometimes the last place you'd expect. It's like a hunt. Lots of hunts. I'm a huntress."

"Aha," he said, recognizing a flash of the old Catherine.

"I've published two papers. I'm good at it, and I love it."

He nodded. "You've found your work." After a moment he said, "I know it sounds old-fashioned, but I think it's incredibly important to have real work. You know? It doesn't matter what it is, just so it's something that tests you, so when you go forward you grow. A lot of people seem to go around in circles." He felt a twinge of guilt as he realized he was talking about Lady.

"Well," she said, looking down, "without work I don't know what would have become of me." She stated it as a simple fact, somehow conveying that further thought on the matter was irrelevant.

They walked back to the house at an easy pace, talking about London, the British tolerance of eccentricity, an actor named Terry-Thomas whose comedies they'd both enjoyed, and the craze for mod clothing. She made not a single reference to America, nor, following her lead, did he.

As they approached her door he felt himself shudder from the tension. He jammed his hands in his pockets. She took out her key and turned to him, watching his face for what seemed an eternity.

"I have to get up at the crack to take Jennie to the airport," she said.

"Yes, yes. Of course."

"But you need to call a cab." She opened the door. "Come in."

"That's okay. The main drag's over that way, right? There'll be a stand."

"There is one," she said. "Go left for a block."

"Good night, then." He backed up a step, and again his heel nearly went over the curb.

"It was lovely," she said. "Why don't you come tomorrow for tea."

"Okay. I will. Thanks."

The door closed.

The summer after his freshman year Claude had worked at the store while studying composition with Weisfeld.

"Take a good look at this," Weisfeld had said, handing him the score to Charles Ives's Symphony no. 2. "Tell me what you think." He had winked, something he rarely did.

Claude spent more than a week analyzing the five-movement piece, plunging deeper and deeper into the puzzle. When he thought he'd tracked everything down, he went back to Weisfeld. "It's very strange," Claude said. "The writing is beautiful, but what a weird way to go about it. The whole idea. I don't understand, really."

"How many did you find?" Weisfeld asked.

Claude opened the score. "Actually, I caught on before the ones he wants you to hear most clearly. 'Columbia, the Gem of the Ocean,' 'Turkey in the Straw,' 'Camptown Races,' 'America the Beautiful.' " He slowly flipped pages. "*Tristan*. The E Minor Fugue from *The Well-Tempered*. 'Bringing In the Sheaves.' Beethoven's Fifth. 'Massa's in de Cold, Cold Ground.' " He pointed with his index finger. " 'Joy to the World.' And this is Brahms. After a few days I began to think the whole thing may be quotes, all of it, some of it from hymns and stuff I don't know, or songs. You start getting into it and there are fragments everywhere, altered phrases, snatches. He does it so much you think, well, maybe he didn't write *any* of it, maybe the whole thing is made of quotes."

"It's a distinct possibility," Weisfeld said. "No one will ever know, of course."

"But why? I mean, you'd think he'd want to write some melodies himself. If he could do this — it's amazing, really — he could certainly write music of his own."

"I can't answer the why," Weisfeld said. "But the second part raises the question. Maybe it *is* music of his own. It feels like music to me. More than the sum of all the bits and pieces. I can feel *him,* if you get what I'm saying."

"Yes, I know. Me too." Claude thought about it for a while. "Maybe

. . . maybe he wanted to use the bits and pieces the way other people use notes. We all use notes, he used chunks. Maybe that was it."

"What about irony? Some people think — he was an odd man, they say — irony. Keeping his distance."

"I don't know," Claude said. "Yeah, maybe, but I don't know. It's really strange."

Now, in London, after a morning of playing in the practice room, Claude sat in the first row of the auditorium (built like a bowl, really) listening to Mr. Dove working with the orchestra on the lento fourth movement.

"Violas. That's a full eighth note. Why are you bouncing off it? It's a full eighth note. La dum, dum, dee dum. All right?"

It became apparent that Mr. Dove enjoyed an intimate and un-usually efficient relationship with the orchestra. They rapidly under-stood what he wanted. In many cases they recognized it when Claude couldn't, played it, and only then did Claude see — oh, that's what he meant. Over the years Claude had attended innumerable rehearsals, mostly with student orchestras, thrown-together ensembles, or re-gional orchestras around the United States. He was used to a certain amount of horseplay, good-natured (mostly) jibing, stalling, pleading, and argument. American orchestras sometimes seemed determined to show how democratic they were. This one was all business. The play-ers were highly disciplined. Claude knew they were a self-governing organization, but when it came to playing they seemed an extension of Mr. Dove's will. Or perhaps it was the reverse, perhaps *he* was an extension of *their* collective will. In any case, since they would be playing Claude's music, and since their sound was lush, balanced, and smooth, he was happy at what he saw and heard. They were very much *together*.

Mr. Dove called a fifteen-minute break and surprised Claude by coming over. He perched on the armrest of a nearby seat.

"It's a gorgeous sound," Claude said. "They're scarily good."

"What do you think Ives meant by the end?" Mr. Dove asked. "After the bugle call, that shocking last chord?"

"It's a puzzler," Claude said. "And it wasn't in the original score."

"He was just about your age."

"I guess the question is whether it's a synthesis, a kind of prophetic use of dissonance as the only way to put all the themes together and rise above them, or whether he's thumbing his nose at us."

"Precisely. One doesn't have to know, but it's interesting."

"I can see both sides. You know, he's so Brahmsy sometimes, so romantic it could be mockery. On the other hand, how could he catch that spirit so well if he didn't love it?" Claude shrugged helplessly. "I've never been able to figure him out."

"The younger players think it was prophecy," Mr. Dove said, nodding toward the stage. "The older players think he was cocking his snoot."

Claude laughed. "That figures."

He sat in the kitchen, at the same small table where yesterday Jennie had worked with her coloring book. Catherine was at the stove waiting for the kettle to boil.

"I was so lucky," Catherine said, speaking of her mentor. "For some reason we just hit it off right away at the very first meeting. She's tops in the period, by the way, and for a woman to achieve that in this country is not easy."

"How old is she?"

"Seventy. Part of it is passing on the torch. She got me in, she got me the scholarship, she did everything. I can never repay her."

The kettle whistled and she made a pot of tea. She opened the half-sized refrigerator for a pint bottle of milk. Claude could see a stick of butter, a cabbage, a small bottle of jam, and a single potato. Other than that, it was empty. He wondered if there was any connection between the extreme simplicity of her life and the monasteries she read about. Was she doing penance or was she simply poor? If she was poor, why was she poor?

"You people are rich," he said bluntly, wanting to demystify at least one enigma. "Why do you live this way?"

"This is the way students live."

"I know, but . . ."

"If you mean my mother and Dewman, I would never ask them. I take a small amount of child support from my ex, which is only fair. And as I said, he pays for the school because he wants a fancy school. Fine." Her eyes glinted with a flash of anger. "He doesn't like the way we live? Too bad. He shouldn't have moved his mistress into the next apartment."

"He what?" Claude was dumbfounded. To have a woman like this and . . . "Was he crazy?"

"No, no." She sighed and seemed to relax. "Silly, that's all. Shallow." She waved a hand to dispense with the subject.

"So what do you live on?" He regretted the question before it was out of his mouth, but she reacted as if it were of no importance.

"Three hundred a month from my father's estate."

"Lady had a five-million-dollar trust fund."

She smiled faintly. "From another side of the family."

"Oh, yes. Of course," he said, feeling stupid.

She poured him some tea, and he looked up to find she was suddenly weeping. She held herself erect, poured her own tea, and carried on as if nothing were happening. Almost immediately the tears stopped. She wiped her cheeks with a paper napkin.

He leaned forward. "I'm sorry," he said. "I shouldn't have brought up —"

"No, no," she said. "It's Jennie. It always happens." She stirred sugar into her tea. "A reflex."

The sight of her tears had both frightened him and prompted a great lurch in his chest, a wave of protectiveness urging him to some kind of action. Now he realized their cause had been hidden from him. She seemed to exist at different levels, all of them running simultaneously, some visible and some not. He wanted to press his head against hers, to put skull to skull and press until the bones melted and their brains flowed together. He wanted to look out from her eyes.

She had recovered herself completely and they sat in silence. He was aware that she was watching him. She got up abruptly and cleared the tea things. For a moment, the warm water running over her hands, she had one of her whiteouts, her body motionless, her soul out on some astral journey. Then she finished up.

He knew what was going to happen when she took his hand and led him out of the room. Something snapped inside him and waves of heat cascaded through his body. His vision closed down at the edges, so that her head and shoulders were all he saw. In the hall she put her arms around his neck and kissed him, a long, gentle, full kiss that obliterated all other sensation. When she moved her head back, breaking it off, she gave a long, voluptuous sigh as if she had been in pain, and now, instantly, it was gone. Her dark eyes were fully dilated, almost totally black, and seemed to look right through him.

In the front room she left the overhead light off, switched on the electric fire, and sank to the prayer rug. He stood for a moment in the gloom, his mind racing in a blur, his senses quickening to an impossible level. The carbon bars turned red. She raised her arm to urge him down and he sank to his knees and embraced her.

In the pale rose glow she removed his jacket as she slipped her tongue between his lips. She unbuttoned his shirt and pressed her cheek against his breastbone. Dizzy with the taste of her, the scent of her hair, the smooth warmth of her neck, he undressed her as she undressed him. They did it easily, their hands deft, as if they'd done it a thousand times before. Their open nakedness seemed miraculous, a gift from heaven stealing their breath away.

For three nights and two days they made love. The first time, on the rug, he had followed her lead, moving in the wake of her certitude, amazed at her strength, awed at the depth of her surrender to the forces driving them. He rapidly understood that for her — and very quickly for himself — what was happening was a way to get beyond the body (as, in music, Fredericks had taught him to go over the wall). Passion was a force to be fed, eagerly and gratefully fed like some hungry angel with them in the room possessed of the power to lift them out of themselves. Out of the body, out of the world to some deep blue otherness where their souls would join, in and with the blue. Sailing along together in the blue, the blue insupportable to a soul alone. Which cannot be known alone.

The second time, in the big bed in the back room, he was her equal. Deep, deep in his innermost self he felt dormant selves awake and move forward into completeness, as if he were a vessel only now realizing its destiny to be filled. He laughed and cried at the same time and she covered his face with kisses. Afterward, resting, his head beside hers, he suddenly heard the sound of a horse-drawn wagon going by on the street. The sound was receding and he realized he had been temporarily deaf. At that precise moment she said, "Listen, how the world comes back." And Claude was changed forever.

Late afternoon. They lay spooning under the sheets. The small dim room held them. Stacks of books. A dresser with a cracked mirror. Two stuffed bears of Jennie's.

"There isn't a line on your face," she said.

"There will be if you don't marry me."

She kissed the back of his neck. "I'm too old for you."

"What do you mean? We're almost the same age."

"I can see you when you're forty-five. Famous, good looking, confident, you'll have some fabulous girl on your arm. Twenty-five. Thirty, maybe." (This was in fact precisely what would happen.) Her tone was not playful, but neither was it sad. She was simply stating a fact.

"No, no," he sighed impatiently.

"Yes, yes," she said. "That's the way it works."

"Who says?"

"Christ!" She jumped up. "Tomorrow's Sunday. I have to run to the shop." She got out of bed and picked up her clothes from the floor — slacks and a sweater — her dark-nippled breasts swinging ever so slightly. He reached out and touched her thigh.

"I'll come with you."

"I've got you where I want you," she said. "Stay right there. It won't take a sec."

He drank in the sight of her. When she pulled the sweater over her head he lunged forward, caught her around the waist, and slipped the point of his tongue into her navel. She arched back, the sweater covering one breast now, and with both hands pulled his head in even tighter. "Ah, my hungry boy, my sweet boy," she whispered. "Do it."

"God in heaven," he said when she pulled away.

"Stay right there."

He heard her go out the door and the house was silent. Gradually his body calmed and he fell into a blissful half sleep, his mind drifting, taken up not so much by thought as by pure awareness. It was a new world, and he was overwhelmed by a sense of novelty, of a benevolence in the light, the air, the objects around him. He was alive in a new way, and the sensation was so beautiful he clung to consciousness. But then he slept.

Her presence woke him. She sat at the foot of the bed. "There's this woman I bump into in the shops. My age, four kids, simple hard-working housewife, something about her I like, although I hardly know her. We were on line at the checkout. 'My goodness,' she says, and she actually patted my hand. 'My goodness, but aren't we looking radiant. Don't we have roses in our cheeks.'" And then a smile of satisfaction appeared on Catherine's face, a sort of inward smile. "She gave me the quickest, most discreet little wink." She laughed and turned to Claude. "Isn't that wonderful?"

By Sunday night they had lost track of time and all but the most remote awareness of the outside world. Wrapped in a cocoon of love and trust, a trust so deep and yet paradoxically so natural, so elemental, Claude could not believe he had never experienced it before. The boundaries of thought seemed to blur, as had the boundaries of flesh, until they were as much one creature as two. They talked, they touched, they talked and their talk was unhurried. Most often it served no particular purpose except to give voice to their partly parallel, partly shared consciousness. Most often it was simply luxurious, but occasionally they questioned each other, or informed each other, filling in gaps as Jennie had filled her coloring book.

"I thought you were a terrible snob," he said. "Your disdain was lacerating. You broke my heart."

"Yes, I know," she said. "I was awful."

"Did you know I loved you?"

After a while she said, "I guess I thought you were in love with a picture you had of me. It was sweet."

"Well, I didn't know you thought it was sweet."

"It would have hurt you to know that. You would have felt patronized."

He gave a soft laugh. "I felt patronized anyway."

Or, together in the cramped bathroom as they took consecutive baths in the half-sized tub. "Do you remember that dance we went to at the River Club?" she asked, leaning against the sink, her arms folded in front of her. "God, it seems so far away. Lifetimes away."

"Of course I do," he said from the tub.

"Just before that, I began to think of you differently," she said. "All those silly boys, and you were in another category altogether. You had a certain . . . a certain *gravitas,* I guess is what I mean. You were naive, but somehow . . ." Her voice fell away. After a while she said, "And there was something about how *intent* you were to do well with the dancing. I could really feel it. It impressed me."

"You remember the ride in the limo afterwards?"

"Yes," she said. "I brushed you off."

"Why?"

"I got scared, I guess. I was starting to take you more seriously, and I couldn't let that happen."

He stood up, got out of the tub, and reached for a towel. She got it first and began drying him off, starting with the back of his neck. He bent his head.

"You were just a nice boy, you see," she said, rubbing his back. "And you thought I was just a girl."

"I don't understand."

She said nothing. She dried his entire body, slowly but not erotically. A loving task, as she might have dried her child, down on her knees on the bathroom floor. They went back to bed, under the quilt, pillows bunched up behind their heads. They lay in comfortable silence for a long time, so long that when she spoke it took him a moment to realize she was responding to his last remark. "I wasn't just a girl." She waited, then said, "I'd been sleeping with Dewman since I was thirteen years old."

He couldn't quite take it in. "What do you mean?"

"I'd been having sex with him."

"With Dewman Fisk?" He was incredulous, at a total loss.

"Oh, you know," she said quickly, "a powerful man, bringing all those famous people to the house." It was almost offhand.

As the implications dawned on him he remained motionless, staring at the ceiling. "Holy mackerel."

"I've never told anyone," she said.

He thought about it. "Not even your husband?"

"No."

He thought some more. "You mean he raped you? Why didn't you tell somebody?"

"He didn't rape me." Her voice was calm. "It wasn't like that."

More than anything — despite his confusion, his mind racing almost desperately — more than anything he wanted to avoid saying the wrong thing. They were in a zone of unreality, or so at least it felt to him as he struggled toward comprehension. For the first time since they'd knelt together on the prayer rug — which had been a couple of days ago but felt infinitely longer, outside of time altogether — he felt the presence of danger. What she was talking about was so alien, so utterly weird, that he might inadvertently, in his ignorance, do or say something to hurt her. Or *not* do something or *not* say something. He was locked.

"He started watching me when I was twelve," she said. "And then the next year it was games, and then, well . . ."

"But how . . . all those people in the house?"

"Never when my mother was there." She caught herself. "No, a few times when she was sick, I think. It wasn't continuous, you see. Sometimes months went by and I'd think maybe it was over."

"Did you want it to be over?"

"Oh, yes. Pretty quickly. But he knew just how to play it." She said this without any apparent bitterness. "By the time I was seventeen I couldn't stand it anymore. So I ran away with the first man who asked me."

"So people thought you'd just fallen in love and eloped."

"Except Dewman. He knew, I'm sure."

"And the son of a bitch got away with it." He shook his head. "Unbelievable."

Now little snatches of memory began playing in his head. Catherine coming down the stairs with Dewman right behind her the night of the dance. Lady's reluctance to talk about Catherine except for an occasional anecdote about school, and the observation that even as a young girl Catherine had been "hot" or "sexy" or "a vamp," and that it was "undignified." He remembered Peter's remark that she was always trying to be so "grown up." He remembered Catherine's no longer mysterious question about Dewman's response when receiving the laurel crown. Now he thought about the servant giving him the cross to ward off evil. "I think the maid knew," he said. "Or suspected, anyway."

"Why do you say that?"

"She seemed to be warning me of something. What was her name? Isidra. Could she have known?"

"I remember her." Catherine thought about it. "Maybe. We were never caught, but maybe. She certainly hated me. It doesn't matter now."

"Sure it does. She's still there. Only now she's the housekeeper and they call her Miss Sanchez. Your mother's out of it and Isidra runs the place. Lady said her clothes were very expensive, and I can tell you she doesn't look like a servant or act like a servant. Maybe he didn't get away with it altogether."

"It doesn't matter. I'll never see any of them again. I left it behind a long time ago." She turned on her side and put her hand on his shoulder. "I don't know why I told you."

A closed book for her. He understood that, and certainly he wasn't going to push. But another memory floated up and he could not stop himself. "The children's section!" he cried.

"What?"

"Did you know when he was deputy mayor he wrote the city law that mandates a children's section in every movie theater? You know, matinees and everything, so sex fiends wouldn't bother the children?"

"Don't be angry, Claude."

"Why not? He stole your childhood. You were living a double life before you were out of grammar school. You couldn't talk to your own mother, for God's sake. He put you in solitary. It's a fucking outrage!"

"Shh." She stroked his face. "Shh. Let's just lie here for a while."

"What a monstrous hypocrite."

"Shh. Hush now."

But hours later, when they made love, he felt it all falling away from him. As her soul welcomed him, his own was cleansed. As they ascended together into the blue beyond blue, all else was trivial. Life itself was trivial. They flew out of the world. Out of its present, and out of its past.

On Monday morning they went for a walk in a nearby park, which seemed to Claude not so much a park as a large chunk of unspoiled countryside. Rolling meadows, some mowed and some wild, great stands of trees, buttercups, even a brook. He was glad to walk. His body felt wonderful, glowing from within, loose, oiled, but his legs were not altogether dependable and he had a rehearsal to do in the afternoon. It was as if he were too light, too buoyant, and had to bring his body down a bit. After half an hour of wandering over the low hills, with Catherine beside him periodically holding his arm and pressing his side, he seemed to reach a perfect balance. They found an immense boulder, already warm from the sun, and sat with their backs against it.

"I feel like I've been asleep all my life," he said.

"Good morning, then."

"Sex is so powerful it's always blinded me. I've never really known what I was doing, in a way. You know, so eager, and maybe scared a bit, it seems like now."

"Well, there are an awful lot of women who don't particularly like sex, if the truth were known," she said. "Most women, I think."

"You're kidding." Although he was learning fast, he was not entirely free of his romantic miseducation from movies and books.

"For some it's a kind of social thing, no more important than that. Some see it as a sign that they're needed. A kind of reassurance. And then it can be an exercise in power over another person. None of these things means you have to like it."

"A tool, you mean."

"Sometimes. Sometimes just a gift to the man."

"Nobody talks about it like that."

"Of course not," she said. "But don't forget, there are women for whom it's just as important as it is to men."

"Forget!" he protested. "How could I ever possibly forget? Where we've been?"

"That's good." She smiled and gave him a soft kiss, surprising him. "Because it goes away, you know."

"Never."

"The passion does. It's too intense for us. It fades. Think of colors, colors gradually changing hue. It's like that."

"I don't want to think that."

"I know."

"It's like you're warning me."

She took his hand. "It's good I know these things. I'm not warning you. I'm not going to back off when the colors change."

"But you won't marry me."

"I'm not going to marry anyone. I have Jennie, my work, and my life. That's more than enough."

"Suppose your work took you to America? Some incredible job at Princeton or Harvard, say?"

"I wouldn't go."

She released his hand and they sat in silence for some time. Suddenly a large black dog ran out from behind the boulder and stood ten feet away, looking at them. Collarless, Claude thought, immediately thinking of his hands. The dog lowered its head.

"You," Catherine said firmly, "are a big, ugly, slobbering mess of a dog. We have nothing for you."

After a moment the dog pivoted on its rear legs and sprang away. They watched it cross the meadow, running full-out, its spine folding and unfolding like a hinge.

"The British worship animals, you know," she said. "It's ridiculous." She stood up and smoothed her skirt.

"Will you come to the rehearsal?" he asked.

"That'll be bits and pieces, won't it? I'd rather hear the whole thing in one go."

Claude entered the auditorium through a side door and paused. They were playing his music, the first tutti from the second movement, Mr.

Dove conducting from the piano. Claude stood with his back to the wall.

For the first few minutes he was too thrilled to think. The sound was there, alive in the air, and it made the hair stand up on the backs of his hands. He had heard it in his mind numberless times, an idealized version, but now it was real and what surprised him most was the grittiness, the textures. Rosiny strings, the wide, edgy sound of the brass, the ever so slightly fuzzy, plush depth of the woodwinds. Dove was not playing the full piano part, but only the cues and a reduction to the top and bottom lines. The orchestra dominated with its powerful, organic, almost funky sound. Claude bathed in it, simply drank it in through the pores of his skin, a huge, unconscious smile on his face. It worked on him like some euphoric drug, and it was quite a while before he could force himself to listen analytically.

Eventually the first violinist spotted him and pointed him out to Mr. Dove, who waved for silence. "There you are, sir," he called, glancing at his watch. "Well, we've done what we can by way of preparation." He got up from the piano. "Please join us."

Claude walked down the aisle, mounted the stage, and approached the nine-foot Bösendorfer grand.

"Anything you'd like to tell us before we begin?" Mr. Dove asked as he picked up his baton.

Claude faced the orchestra — so many people, old, young, a few women, a tall, thin black man in the contrabass section — and for a moment he was nervous. "It's an honor to be able to play with you people. I've got an awful lot of your records." A few smiles, a few nods of recognition. "About the music. Well, you'll hear it anyway, but I don't play the old way, louder going up, softer going down. Breathing, or whatever they call it. The dynamics should be as marked, so when we're playing a line together that's the way I'll be doing it. I guess that's it." He sat down at the piano. The score was in front of him. He looked up at Mr. Dove, who was turning pages at the podium.

"Right," said Dove. "First movement, second tutti. That figure. How do you want those sixteenths?"

Claude looked down at the keys, imagined the phrase in his mind, and played it with his right hand.

"Aha!" Dove leaned forward to address the players. "Distinct, but making a smooth curve. Right, then." He raised his arms. "Let's get it the first time."

They hopped around the concerto in this manner for almost an hour and then took a break. As the others got up, Claude remained at the piano and, very softly, played Art Tatum's version of "Tea for Two" just to stretch his fingers. One of the violinists, an older man with bags under his eyes, paused to watch. "Wonderful stuff," he said when Claude had finished. "Tatum was a master."

"Where can I go for jazz?" Claude asked.

"You mean clubs? There isn't much, I'm afraid. Ronnie Scott's in Soho. And one of our people works nights at the Castle, also in Soho. Let me get him, he'll know more." He moved away.

Mr. Dove came over with a couple of questions. "I take it you want a feeling of wildness in here, the free bars in B major, and D major scales for these horns?"

"Yes. Random sounds. A little pocket of chaos, like a building being demolished."

"Good. That's what we thought."

The older violinist returned with the black bass player, a man in his thirties with extremely long hands and a worried look on his face. Creases stood out on his forehead.

"This is Reggie Phillips. He knows all about it."

Claude stood up and shook the man's hand. "Hi. You play jazz at the Castle? I'd like to come."

"Just a trio. But Ronnie Scott's has a big band. Good musicians." He had a soft voice, barely above a whisper, and an accent that sounded Jamaican. "You'll have a good time at Ronnie Scott's."

Claude didn't know what to make of the man's manner. Reggie looked down at the floor, off to the side, his face averted, almost as if he were afraid.

"Well, thanks very much," Claude said.

Reggie started away, but then paused and said, "Your concerto is very good, very strong, and it has a freshness. Everybody is saying this." Then he walked off, threading his way through the folding chairs.

21

LORD LIGHTNING was a stocky, prematurely bald forty-eight-year-old jazz pianist whose café-au-lait complexion was the only obvious indicator of his Negro blood — one quarter, he had been told by his half-white mother before she died. His stage name had emerged because his right hand was thought to be faster than Oscar Peterson's, and because Light, as his fellow musicians called him, was, in fact, light-skinned, maintained a particularly dignified demeanor, dressed well (just short of dandyism), and had an almost obsessive interest in the royal family. He lived in a tastefully furnished Edwardian house in Hampstead (eight years to go on the mortgage, when they would throw the party to end all parties) with Reggie Phillips, bassist with the LSO, bassist with Lord Lightning's trio at the Castle jazz club, and companion of ten years. They sat in matching wing chairs in the front room, drinking tea.

"I think you're overreacting," Reggie said.

"The whole thing scares me to death." Light regarded the bone china service for a moment and reached for a lump of sugar. "We've got to be very, very careful."

"You don't know it's him. A single telegram, what was it, twenty-five years ago? Nothing since."

"That's the way she wanted it." Light sighed. "I was relieved at the time."

"Understandable." Reggie gave a soft laugh. "Considering."

"Don't be stupid about this, Reggie. It was more than that. The child never had to know, quite possibly. There was every chance it could grow up white, and in America that's . . ." He waved his hand and left the rest unspoken.

"Well, if it *is* him, he certainly wouldn't have any trouble passing."

Light made an impatient clucking sound with his tongue. "Passing is despicable. We thought we'd save him that, if it turned out to be possible. She was a remarkable woman."

"She was the *only* woman," Reggie said. "Unless you've lied to me."

"My dear, I do not lie about such matters, as you well know."

"Look, it's not my fault. What could I do?"

"The time is right, the name is right, and furthermore he's a musician. It's got to be him."

"We've been through this a dozen times," Reggie said. "I just want you to know it isn't my fault if he comes. He already knew about the club. I told him to go to Ronnie's, and he did, but now he's done that."

"What'd he think of the band?"

"He liked Tubby."

"Well, that shows good taste. How was he at yesterday's rehearsal?"

Reggie stared out the window. "Very serious. Intense. We played the whole concerto straight through for the first time. He seemed, he seemed . . ."

"What."

"He isn't a showy player, there's no theatrical stuff, but you could tell he was really out there, on another planet. A whole lot of energy coming from him, and the orchestra responded. He thanked us after, and he meant it."

"You like him," Light said simply.

"I don't even know him. He seems like a nice young man, he writes good music, and he plays beautifully. That's all I know."

"Is he . . . ?" Light let his voice fall off.

"No." Reggie understood instantly. "I think not."

Light nodded to himself. "Don't be insulted if I say I'm glad about that."

"Of course not," Reggie said. "I'm sure I'd feel the same."

"The dues — when you're young, that is — are simply too heavy." Light sighed. "When I think back . . ."

"I don't want you getting upset about this." Reggie placed his cup and saucer on the table. "He probably won't even show up, and if he does, you can handle it."

"I suppose," Light said. "But it's scary all the same. Who knows? He might take one look at me and know. He might feel it. Sense it."

"That's a lot of romantic nonsense," Reggie said impatiently, and stood up. "Start getting sentimental and *you'll* fuck it up."

"Where're you going?"

"I'm not going anywhere. I'll just put this stuff in the kitchen."

"No, wait. Sit down for a second," Light said. "Please."

"Christ," Reggie said, and sat back down.

"Tell me the truth, now. Don't just be nice."

"The truth about what?"

"About what I did. About what Emma and I did. You think it was right?"

Reggie shook his head. "What difference does it make? It was a hundred years ago."

"Reggie. Please." Light was a man who very rarely said please. He prided himself on his toughness, and Reggie, who had often counted on it, knew the toughness was real. Mental toughness, but also unambiguous physical courage. Four years ago they'd been accosted by three young thugs in an alley in Soho. Light had kicked one of them in the nuts, picked up the knife, stuck it in the boy's thigh, and watched the others run. "You picked the wrong poof this time, ladies!" he'd shouted, and then burst into laughter.

"How can I answer?" Reggie said. "I've never been to America. If I'd been born white in Jamaica, I would've tried to pass the other way."

"He's not passing. That's the whole point."

"I get that," Reggie said. "I see that. But the thing is, he'll never know. Suppose he turns out to be a great composer?"

"Yes. So?"

"He'll be a great *white* composer."

"Well, shit, he's more white than anything else. What was the word they used to . . . an octoroon! That's what he is. That's as far as they had a word. It's the edge. What would they say after that, a sixteentha-toon? The very faintest, slightest touch of the tar. Let's face it, he's white."

"You don't think he got the music from you?"

Light pondered the question. "It would be nice to think so," he said.

"But really, if you start getting too deep into that mystical blood stuff, it starts sounding like the Nazis. You know what I mean?"

"Well, man, *you* were the one who said it was important he was a musician," Reggie protested.

"I know, I know. This thing has got me going around in circles."

"I just hope he doesn't show," Reggie said. "I got you a seat in the back for the concert. You can see him, hear him, and then come on back here and everything's back to normal."

"That's what I'll do," Light said. "You're right."

When Claude got back to the hotel after the final rehearsal the concierge handed him two letters. He sat down on one of the lobby couches and opened them immediately. The first was on Cambridge University stationery.

Dear Claude,

Hello old friend. I'm up here doing physics with the famous Dr. Macintyre. Crusty old sod, but he's brilliant. We are about to unlock the mysteries of the universe, perhaps as early as Friday.

It was thrilling to see your name in the paper and to imagine what must have been happening to you all these years to lead to such brilliant success. World premiere with the London Symphony Orchestra! The Weisfeld Concerto. I remember him well. Will he be with you, I hope?

My teaching duties prevent me from getting down to London before the concert, but I will most certainly be there. A friend has gotten tickets. Do you think you could give my name to the powers that be so I can come backstage afterwards?

All best,
Ivan

Claude felt a rush of affection. His sense of Ivan was suddenly so strong the man might just as well have been sitting next to him. Physics, of course! Ivan would have changed, certainly, but Claude somehow knew they would be able to pick up their friendship as if they'd never been apart. Claude folded the letter carefully and slipped it into his breast pocket. It was a wonderful surprise, like some unexpected perfect gift, and he took it as an auspicious sign at exactly the right moment. He was strengthened by it, all the more since it had come out of the blue.

The second letter was in Lady's round hand. It had been forwarded from the offices of the orchestra.

Dear Claude,

Should I admit to you I cried when I signed the final papers? Silly, I guess, because we did the right thing, but there it is. Mourning the past. It's lucky the present is so interesting. We sold the gallery in a really sweet deal, and I'm thinking of getting a real estate license. It should be fun, there's so much action in this town.

We get the Sunday Times a day late but I did see the little squib in the music section. I'm so happy for you, really truly happy because I know how much music means to you.

Grandpa told me that my cousin Catherine is living in London now, going to school or something. Look her up in the phone book and tell her hello from me. She'll remember you, I bet. She never used to forget *anything,* or anybody, that girl.

Anyway, good luck on the opening, and lots of love,

Lady

He held the letter in his hand for some time after finishing it. The reference to Catherine had caused a brief moment of uncomfortableness, like a chill, but it passed very quickly as he considered the ironies of life. There was an innocent, childlike quality to the letter, and it seemed impossible to him that he had spent so many years with its author without sensing the sadness in her. The plucky sadness of someone who had missed the boat. A kind of bravely cheerful stoicism masking a private sadness. Marriage, to him or to anyone else, would never cure it. It was a much bigger boat she had missed, and now he felt a vague fear for her. He closed it off immediately. In the complicated equation of her life, he was no longer a factor. Against his guilt, he could only, quite sincerely, wish her well in his heart. The divorce papers, which he had yet to sign, could not carry as much finality as the letter he held in his hand. It was that brutally simple.

When Claude telephoned the Savoy Grille to book a table he was told, with excruciating politeness and profuse apologies, that the first available reservation was two weeks hence. On an impulse Claude called Albert Shanks and explained the situation. "I'd really like to take her someplace special." Shanks called back twenty minutes later. From his splendid office overlooking the Thames he had been able to arrange everything. "They always keep two tables for unexpected VIPs," Shanks explained. "*Bon appétit.*"

The degree of Catherine's excitement took him by surprise. She'd actually said "Oh, goody" and clapped her hands like a child. She'd taken a good deal of time deciding what to wear while Claude had watched her from the bed. He again reminded himself that she was no longer the girl who lived in the mansion on Fifth Avenue, who went to splendid parties, or to the Russian Tea Room in pearls and a velvet dress. She lived in a tiny flat, had an extremely limited social life within a small circle of academics, dressed like a student, and made things like split-pea soup for dinner, saying with satisfaction, "A bit of bread and butter and this will do us for two days." Yet she had retained a real enthusiasm for the high life, and the capacity to enjoy it in the most natural way, commanding instant respect from the Savoy's staff, for instance.

It had been a truly splendid meal. Caviar, and vodka so cold it had turned thick. A memorable lobster bisque. Dover sole with a delicate sauce, pencil-thin asparagus, wild rice, a lime sorbet, Stilton and fruit, champagne all the way through, and now coffee. They had been at table for almost two hours.

"Let's order the whole thing all over again," Catherine said. She had eaten slowly, savoring every morsel in a mild voluptuary trance. Claude had gotten more pleasure watching her than from eating his own meal.

"A meal to remember," he said.

"No rehearsal tomorrow?"

"Nothing now till the performance."

"You just wait?"

"Right." He drank some coffee. "I'll go in two or three hours early, play for a little while in the basement to loosen up, then just hang around."

"Waiting must be difficult."

"I'm lucky. Nervous in the morning, then it just smoothes out somehow."

"I was supposed to go to a couple of meetings, but I've canceled everything. You won't have time to be nervous."

He smiled. Never before had he felt such a continuous, pervasive sense of well-being, the sense of vast resources of strength within himself, more than enough to deal with any test. Staring into her impossibly beautiful eyes, he felt a rush of love and tenderness so deep he found himself grasping the edge of the table as if to locate himself.

"It isn't me," she said, reading his mind again. "It's really you."

"I'm in love," he said, "and it's you."

Finally they got up from the table, only vaguely aware now of the opulence surrounding them, and made their way out to the street. The night air was misty, creating a soft nimbus around the streetlights.

"Let's go hear some jazz," he said.

Lord Lightning sat behind the small desk in the storeroom–cum–green room–cum–office of the Castle going over the previous night's bar receipts when the door opened and his business partner — Evelyn Gladstone-Shinkfield, fourth Earl of Bumbridge, twenty-nine years old, skirt chaser, pink-skinned, blond-haired, otiose, clumsy, good-natured, rich, unemployed, and with no apparent interests other than girls and jazz — entered with his soft face knotted up in an expression of concern.

"Have you heard what happened to Miles Davis?" he asked.

"I have not," said Light.

"He was playing at Birdland and stepped outside for a breath of fresh air during his break. On the sidewalk, a policeman told him to move along, and when he tried to explain he was working there, the policeman hit him with his stick. Can you imagine?"

Light nodded. "Was he hurt?"

"Not seriously, but they did take him to hospital. A friend called from New York with the news. It's just unbelievable."

"An old story. No doubt Miles was reluctant to kowtow, and he paid the price."

"A barbaric city, I must say." Having told the story, Evelyn seemed relieved of a burden, and his face assumed its usual pleasant, dreamy look. "Lord and Lady Davidson are coming in late with a small party. I'll tell Andrew to try and keep table six for them."

"I'd rather you put them at eleven, if you don't mind."

"Really?" Evelyn's brows made two thin circumflex accents over his pale green, slightly bulbous eyes.

"They're adorable," Light said, "I love them madly, but they can get noisy, I'm afraid. Andrew should put extra bubbly in the cooler."

"I'll tell him," Evelyn said, and left.

Light continued to work on the receipts until Reggie entered. "He tell you about Miles?"

"The man is so frail," Light said, "it gives me the willies. He has that sickle-cell kind of body."

"Like those little nigger dolls, whatever they call them."

"Golliwogs," Light said. "And I've asked you not to use that word in my presence."

"I'm sorry. But sometimes it's the only word, sometimes."

"Try to work around it." Light glanced at his wristwatch. "Is Earl here? We're on in ten minutes."

"He's at the bar."

"How's the crowd?"

"Fine. Normal for a Thursday."

"Good."

Reggie left, closing the door behind him.

Lord Lightning pushed the papers to the side and stared at the Guinness calendar tacked to the door without seeing it. He had been trying to avoid thoughts of Claude Rawlings and his presence in London — his possible presence right here in his own club — but with limited success. He worried it like a sore tooth. Memories of Emma floated through his consciousness. Meeting her for the first time backstage at the Golden Theater in Toronto, where they were part of different acts. Her warm, earthy laughter at having been caught halfway through a costume change. The fullness of her breasts. The two of them sneaking into her hotel room a few nights later. The curtains billowing out from the single window, in the morning, before the rain. His astonishment at having made love to a woman. The equally stunning fact, when they met again on the vaudeville circuit months later, that she was pregnant. His confusion. Her calm acceptance of full responsibility. His tearful gratitude. Her comforting arms around him once more. Their strange time together in the basement apartment in New York City, a period in which he had floated, loving her dearly, but unable to make love to her. Finally, the soldier he'd picked up in the balcony of the Loew's Orpheum. His own enlistment in the military, and the lie that he'd been drafted. Now, sitting at the desk, he shook his head at the utter banality of it all, at his youth, his weakness, his fear. It had not seemed banal at the time, but it was hard to believe it had ever happened. It was like the memory of some B movie seen long, long ago. God in heaven, more than twenty-five years, he thought.

The idea of Claude Rawlings seemed to draw the marrow from his bones, to leave him hollow and fragile, all surface and pretense like some impostor trapped in a potentially revealing situation. And yet he was curious. A son. Flesh of his flesh. Soul of his soul. For a very long time he had blocked it out, lived his life like an amnesiac, but now it was upon him, as inexorable as the rain that had followed the conception in the gray light of a Canadian dawn. The cat was out of the bag, and it wasn't going to go back in. He planted his elbows on the desk, bent forward, and ran his hands over his bald head, slowly, again and again.

Claude had learned that the jazz scene in London was different than in New York. When they said "club," they meant exactly that, and it was necessary to buy a one-year membership to get in. So he was out ten pounds before he'd had a beer.

"Claude Rawlings?" Evelyn said, handing over the cards. (He'd had to take the door temporarily while Nigel was off helping Andrew restock champagne.) "Forgive my impudence, but are you the man on the program for An Evening of American Music?"

"That's right."

"How delightful. I hope you'll allow the Castle to offer a complimentary bottle of champers in honor of your first visit." He beamed, showing a lot of teeth.

Catherine sensed Claude's confusion. "That's extremely kind of you," she said. "We accept with pleasure."

Faintly, from behind the padded door, came the sounds of a trio playing "How High the Moon." As he and Catherine went through and into the smoky dimness, Claude noted with pleasure that the pianist was playing some interesting altered chords instead of the standard changes.

"More like a dungeon than a castle," Catherine said.

"The other club was in a basement too. It must be a tradition." All he could see of the pianist was the top of his bald head gleaming under the single rose klieg light. As he led Catherine along the brick wall to what Claude thought might be an acoustically well-placed table, there was a sudden awful screeching noise, sharp enough to wipe out the music for an instant. Claude looked over to see Reggie, who was playing while sitting on a tall stool, haul his big double bass back into its proper position. It had slipped, its sharp metal peg scratching across

the wooden floor, the chaotic sound magnified by electrical ampli-
fication. Reggie's eyes darted away from Claude. The pianist turned his
head to look at Reggie, his round, intelligent face showing surprise.
Then he looked down at the keys again.

Claude and Catherine sat at their table against the wall, and soon the
waiter brought champagne and glasses. It was a quiet club. The thirty
or so people sprinkled through the room had apparently come to
listen. Couples leaned into each other when they had something to say.
The waiter made no noise at all with the glasses, and carefully muffled
the pop of the cork under a number of white towels.

"I can see why they call him Lord Lightning," Claude said softly,
bending over the table and taking her hand.

"What do you mean?"

"The man is very fast. Art Tatum fast."

Catherine did not know who Art Tatum was, but she nodded anyway. She had not known what to expect, but was relieved the music
wasn't loud. Even the drummer played delicately, brushes flashing over
the traps and the cymbals in a silver blur.

Claude adjusted the angle of his chair, leaned his shoulder against
the wall, and listened to the music. The three men played together with
seemingly effortless intimacy, passing little figures and phrases back
and forth like a complicated game of catch without ever interrupting
the flow of whatever tune they were playing. Ellington, Monk, Horace
Silver, Tin Pan Alley, show tunes. Lord Lightning did not announce the
numbers. When a tune was over he would acknowledge the applause,
sometimes blowing a kiss, chat for a moment with Reggie or the
drummer, and then count off. Claude was impressed with the complexity of his improvisations. An eclectic player, he seemed able to draw
from many famous jazz pianists. He could do the Erroll Garner thing
— a metronomic left hand against a right hand drifting behind or
ahead of the time — without sounding like Erroll Garner. He could
play percussively in the manner of Horace Silver and then, going into a
bridge perhaps, start floating over the bar lines like Bill Evans (a
brilliant new player from Florida whom Claude had heard only twice).

"He's terrific," Claude said as the musicians broke and went backstage through a narrow door at the edge of the stand. "He'd do well in
America."

"Do you think he's American?" Catherine asked.

"I'd be surprised if he wasn't."

"He has an interesting face."

After a while Reggie came back out of the narrow door and approached their table. Once again he looked worried. Claude made the introductions. Reggie smiled quickly at Catherine and glanced at Claude. "Lord Lightning knows you're here. He'd invite you back, but the room is too small. Just a closet, really. He sends his apologies."

"Your solo on 'Blue Monk' was wonderful," Claude said. "How do you get the notes to sustain like that? They seem to go on forever."

"The instrument helps. Very old and very big. I got it in Germany. Thank you."

"Please have a glass of champagne with us. Lord Lightning, too, if he feels like coming out."

"We don't drink alcohol," Reggie said. "Neither one of us."

"Some coffee, then."

"He almost never comes out between sets."

Claude heard the resistance, but he felt so good, so exuberant and generous, he pressed a bit. It seemed a small thing. "I'd be grateful if you asked him. You never know."

Reggie fell into a mysterious paralysis, his long brown fingers touching the tablecloth, his eyes fixed on the brick wall. For some time he did not move. Claude looked at Catherine, who made a little face expressing puzzlement. Finally Reggie broke away.

Claude raised his eyebrows. "What was that? Did I say something wrong?"

"Strange," she said, her eyes following the bass player. "Some kind of protectiveness, maybe."

"Against what?"

"The public? Hey," she said with a smile, "you're the famous pianist. Aren't you supposed to know about things like that?"

"Frescobaldi used to look for girls in the audience. He used to find them, too."

"More power to Frescobaldi," she said.

And then Lord Lightning emerged, crossing in front of the bandstand. He raised his arm and clicked his fingers for the waiter, who was instantly at his side. Claude heard him order two coffees and two chairs. Reggie stepped out in front at the last moment. "Claude Rawlings," he said. "Lord Lightning."

Claude stood up to shake hands. He was aware of a certain intensity in the man's eyes, the almost uncomfortable sensation of being sized up. Claude introduced Catherine and the men all sat down. Chairs for the newcomers had arrived with magical speed.

"I had a white piano like that when I was a kid," Claude said. "But it wasn't a grand. It wasn't even a full-sized keyboard. Sixty-six keys."

"A nightclub piano," said Lord Lightning. "It probably had a mirror across."

"That's right!" Claude was delighted. "How did you know?"

"They all had mirrors," Reggie said. "They got it from the movies."

Lord Lightning heaved a great sigh for no apparent reason. He continued studying Claude until, as if suddenly reminded of his social duties, he turned to Catherine. "I hope you are enjoying the music, Miss Marsh, primitive as it is."

"Very much so. But Claude tells me jazz is anything but primitive."

"Does he, now." Lord Lightning seemed to relax a bit. "I must stop fishing for compliments. Reggie says I'm quite outrageous."

"It was a wonderful set," Claude said. "Compliments are in order."

"We damn near got turned around in 'Love for Sale,' " Reggie said to Lord Lightning.

"Earl is irrepressible," Light explained to Claude. "He gets carried away."

"I've heard Coltrane and Elvin Jones." Claude leaned forward with enthusiasm. "Where one of them *deliberately* turns it around and the other one doesn't follow. They'll play with that tension for ten minutes before resolving it. Whoever turned around comes back. It's terrific."

Lord Lightning smiled for the first time.

"What does that mean, 'turning it around'?" Catherine asked.

"Where the accent falls," Claude said. "It's usually two and four, but it can be one and three."

"People can get lost," Reggie said, "forget where the bar line is." Again he seemed to be talking to Lord Lightning.

"I've often wondered," Light said, "why, when the tempo is particularly fast, the *feeling* seems to drift toward one and three. A conundrum, if you will."

Catherine laughed, and when Claude looked over, explained. "Well, you know. Drum."

"I adore puns." Lord Lightning reached over and patted her hand. "Reggie hates them. It's good to have an ally." He turned his head to Claude. "Who is Weisfeld?"

The abruptness of the question startled him. "He . . . he was my teacher. No, more than that. My mentor, really. I started with him as a very young child." Lord Lightning waited, as if expecting more. "He died," Claude said.

"Ahh, that's a shame. I imagine he would have taken great pleasure seeing you up there with the LSO, playing your own concerto."

"We're five minutes over," Reggie said, pushing back his chair an inch or two.

"Reggie tells me you've been around to some of the clubs," Lord Lightning said, ignoring Reggie.

"Yes, but I can't understand why there isn't more jazz. This is a big city, after all. You only seem to have three or four clubs. There must be thirty or forty in New York."

"We would undoubtedly have more if we were allowed to book American players. The indigenous pool of talent is not large."

"But why can't you?"

"The unions. The government. Mr. Petrillo is still at the helm on your side, I believe."

"That's right." Claude was himself a member of local 802, although he knew nothing of its structure or policies. James C. Petrillo was a well-known leader, however, a sort of mini version of the coal miners' John L. Lewis.

"Aren't you an American?" Catherine asked.

"I was," Lord Lightning said. "But I stayed on after the war and became a British subject."

"That's what I'm doing," she said.

"Are you really? I did it in large part because I'm a colored man."

She nodded and looked down at the table. "I'm doing it for a fresh start."

At this point Reggie got up and went to the bandstand. He seemed to bristle with impatience.

"I still don't understand," Claude said. "I mean, *I'm* an American. *I'm* playing here and no one's objected."

"It only applies to jazz musicians. Classical players come and go all the time."

"But that's not fair," Claude protested. "That's not fair at all."

"It saddens me to say it," Lord Lightning said, "but there seems to be a good deal of evidence that Mr. Petrillo is reluctant to recognize jazz men as part of his constituency. Probably because so many jazz players are Negroes. He takes their dues, of course."

Claude shook his head. "I didn't know any of this. I'm certainly going to find out about it when I get back."

"We've made some progress with the concept of exchanges," Lord Lightning said. "Tubby Hayes is going to the Half Note in New York for two weeks and Zoot Sims is coming to Ronnie's. It's a start. The first important American player since before the war. People are ready to kill to get tickets. Do you play jazz at all, Mr. Rawlings?"

"Sure," Claude said. "I've always loved it."

"Perhaps you'd like to sit in."

Claude hesitated. For a long time now he had been concentrating on the concerto, living with it in his head, imagining the lines, hearing the chords while he shaved, walked down the street, or rode in a cab. He was steeped in this single piece of music, and for an instant he was afraid that playing something else would distract him. "I haven't played trio for quite a while," he said weakly.

"Oh, go ahead," Catherine urged. "It'll be fun."

"I don't know."

Lord Lightning looked from one to the other. "I tell you what. I'll call you up after a couple of tunes and we'll play something four hands. How about it?"

Claude felt his resistance ebbing. "What the hell," he said. "Why not? Okay. Thanks." His fear of distraction was probably irrational.

"Bravo," said Catherine, raising her glass.

They all drank, Lord Lightning's eyes seeming almost to blaze over his coffee cup into Claude's.

"That's nice of him," Catherine said after he'd gone.

"It's surprising. The last thing most jazz musicians want is somebody sitting in, somebody they don't know. But maybe it's different here."

As the music resumed more people came in. Eventually there were only a few empty tables. "I'll Remember April." "Green Dolphin Street." "Slow Boat to China." And then Lord Lightning was standing up, beckoning for Claude to join him. There was a buzz in the room as Claude stepped up onto the bandstand. Lord Lightning did not introduce him, but simply stood there smiling. "Top or bottom?"

"Top, I guess." Claude waited for the older man to sit back down on the bench, moving to his left, and then sat himself.

"What would you like to play?"

Claude had already decided. He felt the warmth of the man's body beside him, noticed for the first time that he was wearing a spicy cologne. " 'Honeysuckle Rose'?"

"Honey suck my nose," Lord Lightning said to Reggie and Earl, and he counted it off. Claude waited a full chorus, watching the chords, before he entered. He played with both hands, small intervals with his left and an accurate unison line with his right, following Lord Lightning's rubato phrasing. The tune having been stated twice, they began to improvise in alternate choruses, bebop lines with an eighth-note feel, each man picking up the tail of the structure made by the other. They played tag, executing more and more complicated figures and runs as if trying to top each other. Reggie and Earl accentuated the pulse with subtle bursts of syncopation. Claude laughed out loud at a seemingly impossible offbeat byzantine four-bar lick from Lord Lightning and tried his best to repeat it an octave above.

"Almost," said the older man.

Claude bore down and introduced his own baroque, searing, thirty-second-note knuckle buster. Lord Lightning tried to echo it.

"Close," said Claude.

The audience seemed to understand how much fun they were having. A few people were standing up, and there were even a few distinctly un-British shouts of encouragement. The two men at the piano were ascending the scale of virtuosity and swinging harder and harder at the same time. They were taking the tune apart. They were, as Claude would say later, "playing its ass off." Their hands never touched, each man leaving the shared area of an octave and a half above middle C as the other man entered. For all the ferocity of the playing, there was an underlying delicacy about space, almost like two animals in the wild.

They were playing without any preconceived plan, relying on traditional jazz conventions, breaking into "fours," for instance, at what felt like the appropriate moment. Four bars drum solo, four bars tutti, four bars bass solo, four bars tutti, and so on for two choruses. At which point something quite remarkable happened.

Claude and Lord Lightning were improvising contrapuntal lines, winding down to the final restatement of the bare melody with which they both knew they would end, when they spontaneously and simultaneously made a dramatic change in the harmonic structure of the first section of the tune. Claude would later wonder how they could possibly have done something so radical, entirely by feel, at the same moment. He thought Lord Lightning must have introduced a subtle variation of the voicings of his chords, which Claude had unconsciously picked up.

What happened was this: after having played the first four bars two beats G minor two beats C seventh, every bar since they'd sat down, they suddenly found themselves ascending by half tones every bar, creating an entirely new harmonic base upon which they improvised in brand-new scales. G minor C seventh, A-flat minor D-flat seventh, A minor D seventh, B-flat minor E-flat seventh, and then a quick little half-tone figure to come out exactly right on F dominant seventh. It was so exciting — the apparent escape from tonality like going off a diving board, the fresh and unexpected colors from the new scales, the return to the original key like the fit of a key into a lock — all this made the hair stand on the back of Claude's neck. They explored it for three more choruses, played it straight for one, and ended the tune. A great burst of applause, most of the audience on its feet.

"My goodness," said Lord Lightning.

"How did we do that?" Claude was mystified.

"Beats me. I've never played it that way."

"You haven't?"

Lord Lightning turned to Reggie, who was smiling for a change. "How'd you know we were going to do that?" Reggie had followed the shifts without hesitation.

"I don't know. I heard it."

"I've been playing that tune my whole life," Lord Lightning said, wiping his sweaty dome with a handkerchief. "My goodness." He looked out at the crowd and waved the handkerchief. "We have to give them at least one more, don't you think?"

"I'll tell you something," Claude said in the cab as they rode back to Catherine's flat. "I'm not sure I believe him."

"About what?" She was slightly surprised.

"About 'Honeysuckle Rose.' I mean, how could we both stumble upon those changes at the same time? He must have played it that way before."

"He certainly seemed like a happy man when you came back to the table. Like the cat that swallowed the canary."

"It was a lot of fun in any case," Claude said.

"And the Reggie puzzle is solved."

"What do you mean?"

"They're a couple. He practically came right out and told us. Reggie this and Reggie that."

Claude thought for a moment. "Yes. I bet you're right. I wonder why I didn't see it."

"I'm so glad we went," she said. "It was something to see you play, the way you throw yourself into it. It must feel marvelous."

"It does, it does. But tomorrow I have to get my head back into the concerto. That was a vacation."

"Something about that man," she mused. "I don't mean the music, I mean him. His intensity."

"I felt it too," he said. "Weight. Power. Something."

"He seemed awfully clever for a nightclub pianist."

"Hey!" he protested. "What kind of talk is that?"

She moved closer, taking his hand. "Sorry. Just thinking out loud."

22

Even before his eyes opened in the morning, awareness was upon him. He imagined the stage, the orchestra, himself at the piano. A brief flutter of anxiety, but then he woke fully and it was gone. Catherine was there beside him, giving a great yawn and stretching herself, arms out, fingers splayed.

"The sun is out," she said.

He kissed her shoulder. "So it is."

"Do you want a big breakfast?"

"Tea? Toast and jam?"

She got out of bed and began rummaging through the top drawer of the dresser.

"There's something special about the backs of your knees," he said.

"Is there?" she said without turning around. She reached behind herself and gave herself a little pat on the ass. "How about this?"

Instantly, he was aroused. She got dressed, came over, and pulled the blanket from the bed. "Aha!" she said, looking down. "What a devil he is. We'll have to take care of him later."

"I'm not allowed to have sex on the day of a performance."

For a split second she thought he was serious, and then they laughed together.

After breakfast she announced that she could no longer put off a thorough cleaning of the kitchen. "When a place is this small you can't let it get ahead of you." He went to the front room to spend two hours with the score. He was soon immersed in the music, going over aural memories from rehearsal, looking at his penciled-in notes, feeling the shapes his hands would take. Despite his vacation of the previous night everything was still there, readily accessible as he focused his concentration. He went through all three movements and closed the file. The best thing to do now, he knew from experience, was to put it out of his mind. He picked one of her books at random and opened it up. Facsimile pages of old manuscripts in a language he did not understand.

"Norse," she said, coming up behind him. "We should go out and get some sun."

They spent the morning walking, following any street wide enough to have a sunny side, going into a few shops but buying nothing except for a single rose Claude insisted she wear on the lapel of her jacket, ambling from square to square, watching the people, buying newspapers at a stand to look for mention of the concert, dawdling, talking, getting the giggles, half guiltily, at the sight of an obese woman trying to get on a bus with her arms full of packages. When they got hungry they bought some fish and chips and found a bench at the edge of a tiny park. The sun was full upon them and their fingers shone with grease.

"We can skip it if you want to skip it," he said gently, "but I don't understand about Dewman. You don't seem angry."

She ate for a while before answering. "Perhaps I am, somewhere, but I don't think about it. I haven't thought about it for a long time."

"It just seems —" he began.

"If there was seduction, I'm not sure I wasn't as guilty as him."

"But you were a child. He was a man in his forties and your stepfather. Surely he should have —"

Again she interrupted him. "A man." She gave a snort of derision. "So I thought. He was weak, insecure, and sentimental. *Sentimental.*" She looked directly at him. "He wasn't a sex fiend, he was a hopeless weakling. He'd burst into tears every Christmas when the children sang carols."

"Yes, but four years. Jesus."

"He was pathetic. That's what he used on me. He was good at that, very good with that stuff."

"I still think you should have blown the whistle on him."

"What for? It was my fault too." She wiped her hands on a bit of newspaper. "No. What I had to do was get out of there as fast as I could. Get out and never go back."

"Yes, but that was forced upon you."

"Life is complicated," she said with a little shrug.

Many times later in his life Claude would remember this conversation, and his respect for Catherine only grew over time (when, for example, he read of Dewman's death from cirrhosis in a glowing, lengthy *New York Times* obituary).

"Let me ask *you* something," she said. "Do you think — you and Lady — do you think your inability to have children entered in at all?"

"As a catalyst, maybe. We were just too young, I think. We didn't know what we were doing." Suddenly he stopped, looking up at the sky as a thought struck him. "It never occurred to me, but it could be part of the reason she married me was to get away from her family. She really loathed her father." He lowered his head and looked at her. "Like you eloping, but not as strong."

"Her father was a bully," Catherine said. "Maybe you're right. Of course everybody married young in those days."

They went back to her flat and made long love until the angle of the sun through the front window alerted him to the time.

"I should be going soon."

"I know."

"You'll come backstage afterward?"

"I will." She lay her head on his chest.

He went to the hotel to get his tuxedo. ("Tails are not necessary," Mr. Dove had said, to Claude's relief. "The LSO avoids excessive formality.") There were messages for him at the desk. A cable from Emma and Al wishing him good luck and informing him of the sale of a particularly old and valuable oboe, and of a woman who wanted to buy a harp, and did he know where they could get one. Requests for interviews from various newspapers and music magazines. An invitation to a reception at the American embassy, signed by the ambassador. A string of progressively more urgent requests for him to telephone Otto Levits. He glanced at his watch, figured the time difference, went to his room, and placed the call.

"Claude, Claude, where have you been? I've been going crazy here, so much is happening."

"I'm sorry. I've been busy."

"Busy? Busy with what? I call the hall, I call the hotel, I call Shanks, nobody knows anything. How am I supposed to do business here, I can't even talk to you?"

"You've got me now. What's up?"

"Everything is up. Two bookings for the concerto. Cleveland and Chicago, two more nibbling."

"The Chicago Symphony?" Claude felt a flush of pleasure. "Really?"

"Would I kid you? You're very hot all of a sudden. Van Cliburn, move over. Also, Frescobaldi is doing a six-city tour and he wants you, and only you. This is going to be very significant money, boychik, big bucks. But you've got to get back here fast. As fast as you can. Like tomorrow."

The line hummed. Claude felt a constriction in his chest, a breathlessness. Thoughts of Catherine flooded his mind.

"Hello," Otto said. "Am I talking to somebody?"

"Tomorrow is not possible," Claude said.

A pause. "Okay. Two days."

"I can't."

"What is it with you?" Otto exploded. "Are you nuts in some complicated way I haven't figured out yet? Chicago! Cleveland! Frescobaldi! Do you understand what I'm saying?"

"Yes. It's wonderful, Otto, it really is. It's just that . . ." He stopped, beginning to feel the sadness creep in.

Suddenly Otto was calmer. "All right. So there's something. Okay, let's talk it over. It's just that what?"

"Oh, God. It's too hard to explain. I can't put it into words."

"I see. You're telling me you've fallen in love with Aaron Copland."

Claude laughed despite himself, despite the pain — for that was what it was, a sharp stab of pain — brought on by the knowledge that he had no choice. "I haven't even met him yet. But Otto, there's something else. I'm going to need a little time."

There was a long, drawn-out sigh, and then silence.

"Otto?"

Claude heard the rustling of paper. "Four days. If you're not here in my office by Wednesday — which is the absolute limit — I'll have to give some serious thought to our association. There's too much pressure in this business already. I got ulcers, blood pressure, migraines. It's not just me, it's my family. I *know* what'll happen if you're not here by

Wednesday. The *hospital* is what will happen. You bring flowers it won't be enough. Am I getting through?"

"I will be there," Claude said.

"Wednesday?"

"I will be there Wednesday. I promise."

"Are you okay? Ready for tonight?"

"I'm ready. More than ready. I need tonight, and that's the truth. I need the music." He had realized this only a moment before he said it.

"Good, good," Otto said. "I'm sitting here in my office, but I'm with you. You know that. Call me tomorrow at home."

"Thanks, Otto."

"Play your heart out."

"One more thing. Could you call Al at the shop and tell him where to get a harp on consignment?"

"Easy. I even know who's trying to get rid of one. Madame Solange, plays cocktail hour at the Waldorf."

"Thanks again."

"Wednesday." He hung up.

Claude stared at the old-fashioned telephone. He thought of calling Catherine, but refrained. After a while he began to pace back and forth. He'd known he would have to leave eventually, of course, but he'd allowed himself to think it would happen at some indeterminate time in the future. Catherine's enjoyment of the dinner at the Savoy had given him the idea of a week in Paris together, which he had gone so far as to discuss with the concierge downstairs. Copenhagen after that, perhaps, to see Tivoli. None of that was possible now. Tuesday night he'd catch the last plane to New York. He knew what would happen after that. It would be a long time before he'd see London again, given what Otto had said. He felt great excitement at the musical prospects, but resentment at the timing. (He was to feel this again, many times, in varying degrees, during his long career as a performer and composer.) After circling the room a dozen times he stopped, told himself to calm down, and made himself take a long hot bath to relax his arms and shoulders. Halfway through he sang the Purcell very softly, feeling the weight of the words.

He walked to the concert hall with his tuxedo in a bag over his shoulder. It was a warm afternoon and the streets were filled with activity, but he paid little attention, concentrating on the rhythms of his body as he strode along, on the movement of his limbs and the smooth operation of his joints. He walked as if enclosed in a mild and invisible force field of self-preoccupation, and people somehow sensed it and drifted out of his way.

In his dressing room he inspected his tuxedo and hung it up. He laid out his shirt, cuff links, bow tie, and then contemplated the small wooden cross. His plan was to wear it tonight and then give it to Catherine. He suddenly wished that he had brought her, that she was with him now. He wondered how she would react at the news of his Tuesday flight. (She was to respond with characteristic stoicism. Not until the final moments, standing with her at the green door, the taxi waiting, was he to see her face register pain, and a concern, he saw with some surprise, for *him*, as her eyes filled with tears. "Take care" were her last words.)

He walked through the eerily quiet corridors and made his way to the Steinway in the basement. He sat down and began to play whatever came to mind. Bach for quite a while. Part of the Bartók Double Piano Concerto. Debussy's *Cathédrale Engloutie*. On a sudden impulse he delved into "Honeysuckle Rose," going over the new changes, seeing if there was any way to extend them. He played Chopin and finished up with Beethoven, the last section of the "Hammerklavier." His body felt marvelous, his arms, wrists, and hands working together as a fluid unit, his back without a hint of stiffness. He sat and enjoyed the silence, the cleansing silence, and then went upstairs.

His thought was to drop in on Albert Shanks to thank him for the table at the Savoy Grille. He knocked lightly and entered the office. Shanks was not there. A tall, thin man with gray hair stood with his hands behind his back staring out at the river, bending slightly at the waist.

"Sorry," Claude mumbled, and then froze when the man turned. It was Aaron Copland.

"Please come in," Copland said. "He'll be back soon. He went to get something."

"I just wanted, he did me a favor, I thought I'd . . ."

"I'm Aaron Copland," he said, coming forward.

"Claude Rawlings." They shook hands.

"Oh, I'm glad you came in. Have you got a minute?"

"Of course, sir. It's an honor to meet you."

"Let's sit, then."

He was lanky and seemed awkward, like some tall, slow-moving bird. They went to the couch.

"Are you at Claridges? The best hotel in the world, if you ask me."

"Brown's," Claude said.

"Oh yes, where the writers stay. I hope you're comfortable."

"Very. Although I haven't spent much time there. I've been staying with a friend."

"I was impressed by your concerto."

"You've seen it?"

"I've read it. Played the piano part. I was one of the judges." Suddenly he covered his mouth. "Oops. Wasn't supposed to say that. All very secret. But I don't suppose it matters that much now. Just don't tell anybody."

"I won't."

"It was strong, and fresh. I liked the way you drew from all directions. It was good to see that."

"Thank you, sir." Claude looked down to conceal the euphoric impact of this praise. "My teacher, Aaron Weisfeld —"

"There were many submissions, but an odd sameness to a lot of them, I thought. You know, school A, school B, and so on. Only two or three were really original." He paused. "You've played with Frescobaldi, I understand."

"My first big break."

"Good. Well, don't ever give up performing. We all need to make a living." He gave a wan smile. "I'm no conductor, for instance. Mr. Dove prepares the orchestra and I just put in an appearance. I perform. Luckily it's fun."

Claude was mildly shocked and his face showed it.

"There's very little money in composing, Mr. Rawlings. But we're not unique. Robert Frost once told me he'd never been able to support himself from his royalties alone. Can you imagine that? The most popular poet in the richest country in the world?"

"It's crazy," Claude said, and meant it.

"It's a nuisance. Money is a nuisance."

Albert Shanks came in, wearing a white Nehru suit and carrying some papers which he put on his desk. "So you've met," he said. "The last special reserve seats are now gone. A total sellout. The bloody Queen herself couldn't get in at this point." He rubbed his hands in satisfaction. "Bloody marvelous."

Copland gave Claude a quick, wry look.

The building was beginning to quicken now, as Claude strolled aimlessly from place to place. People moving purposefully in the backstage corridors, carrying instruments, clothing bags, or small suitcases. He saw a man with an open bottle of Guinness, another carrying a thin seat pad. Chairs and music stands were being set up onstage. The house lights went on and off mysteriously. As he paced the runway behind the back seats he glanced up through a glass wall to see people being turned away at the box office. He walked past the last-row aisle seat which was soon to be occupied by Lord Lightning, that seat being the rough equivalent of, and for the same purpose (quick exit) as, the one his mother had occupied in Carnegie Hall. (But he would not have the chance to appreciate the irony. The four people who knew the secret of his patrimony — Reggie Phillips, Lord Lightning, Emma, and Al, with whom Emma had discussed the wisdom of her withholding the truth, and the possible impact on Claude of her false story of promiscuity — these four would take the secret to their graves.) Claude walked around and around, listening to his body.

He stood in the wings for a few minutes during *Billy the Kid,* curious to see how Copland would conduct the gunfight sequence, a challenge for the tympani and a test of tempo for the conductor. Copland's baton technique was right out of the book, and he allowed himself very little body movement. Occasionally he would make a small one-legged hop for rhythmic emphasis, or jut out his elbow like a square dancer. Claude would not have picked *Billy the Kid* for this concert. It was ballet music, after all, and Claude was something of a stuffed shirt about such matters at the time. Pure symphony was his ideal. But the orchestra was playing beautifully, and the gunshot effects, when they came, were crisp and electrifying. Copland gave a nod of appreciation, and even smiled a bit as he moved on.

The music receding behind him, Claude went to his dressing room. He washed his hands, put on his tuxedo, and sat down. After a few minutes he lowered his chin and began deep breathing. He closed his eyes and silently counted each exhalation. When he reached twenty he visualized the descending escalator before him, so long it disappeared into the distant depths. In his mind he stepped on and began the effortless downward glide. Now he could see the first of the markers coming up on his right. The word ONE spelled out in green letters. Slowly he was carried past. He was moving down. TWO rose up, got larger, and vanished behind him. THREE. His breathing was now automatically deep and regular. He was aware of his relaxed body, and aware of the world around him. FOUR. He knew of the slow, steady, crystalline drip of the faucet into the washbasin, he knew of his breath, of the distant sound of an automobile horn, the closer murmur of conversation as a man and a woman passed by in the corridor, but he did not hear the sounds in the usual sense. They were small interruptions of a profound silence. It was the silence he heard.

A knock. "Five minutes, Mr. Rawlings."

Now he could see the end of the escalator and the brilliance of the green garden to which it carried him. A green of magic intensity. The green of Eden. He was enfolded.

"Two minutes, Mr. Rawlings."

After some moments he opened his eyes and got up. He walked to the door, turned the handle, and stepped out into the corridor. A young man of perhaps sixteen in a gray cloth jacket stood waiting. "Right, then, sir. If you'll just follow me."

The boy had long brown hair falling to his shoulders. Claude watched the gentle bounce of the hair as they moved through the halls to the wings at stage left.

"Good luck, sir." The boy left.

Claude saw the orchestra. Mr. Dove came up behind him. Together, they waited a moment. Then, briskly, Claude stepped forward into the light.

Author's Note

Body & Soul is to some extent a historical novel. Certainly the New York City described in its pages is long gone, replaced by another city of the same name. I've played fast and loose with dates, choosing to bend things a bit for the sake of structure. Chronology is preserved, I hope, but exact dates for various historical events — Eisler's escape on the *Batory,* the dismantling of the Third Avenue el, and so on — have been avoided.

Several years of reading about music and musicians cannot be adequately covered here, but certain books stand out in my memory: Hindemith's *Elementary Training for Musicians; The Great Pianists, The Virtuosi,* and other works of Harold C. Schonberg; Mr. Perle on twelvetone (although had I to choose between reading his books again and spending a week in a Siberian salt mine, it would not be an easy choice); and various writings of Leonard Bernstein.

My thanks to my colleagues at the Iowa Writers' Workshop for their support and help, especially Margot Livesey for her close reading of Part One, Jorie Graham for idiomatic Italian, Marilynne Robinson for liking Emma, Deb West for her careful work and her enthusiasm, and Connie Brothers for covering for me. Ned Rorem and Jim Holmes for good musical talk on Nantucket. Also the University of Iowa for encouraging the creative writers in its employ, no less than it does the scholars and scientific researchers, to do new work, and for giving us the time in which to do it.

I am deeply indebted to Peter Serkin, a man with extensive responsibilities to his public, his students, his art, and his young family, who nevertheless took the time to help me as an act of faith. He walked me through the Mozart Double Piano Concerto (which he had played as a boy with his father, Rudolf) at his piano in his studio. Over the years he made many invaluable suggestions, both large and small, which helped and encouraged me. All this despite the fact that we are not in total agreement about the twelve-tone system. Serkin is a champion of new music (which sometimes includes twelve-tone), an inspired interpreter of Arnold Schönberg among others, and a hard, courageous worker in the often difficult business of getting new music to larger audiences. He has not ceased in his attempts to educate me, and for that I am eternally grateful. The mistakes in *Body & Soul* are of course my own and in no way redound to him.

Candida Donadio for keeping the faith for more than thirty years. Sam Lawrence for taking the chance. My wife, Margaret, for more than I can say.

Special thanks to Camille Hykes and Larry Cooper, who helped me so much in the final stages. And also my thanks to the Guggenheim Foundation for their timely support.